THE REBEL

WILLIAM MORROW

An Imprint of HarperCollins*Publishers*

THE
REBEL

AN IMAGINED LIFE
OF JAMES DEAN

JACK DANN

THE REBEL. Copyright © 2004 by Jack Dann. All rights reserved. Printed in the United States of America. No part of this book may be used or reproduced in any manner whatsoever without written permission except in the case of brief quotations embodied in critical articles and reviews. For information address HarperCollins Publishers Inc., 10 East 53rd Street, New York, NY 10022.

HarperCollins books may be purchased for educational, business, or sales promotional use. For information please write: Special Markets Department, HarperCollins Publishers Inc., 10 East 53rd Street, New York, NY 10022.

FIRST EDITION

Designed by Jeffrey Pennington

Printed on acid-free paper

Library of Congress Cataloging-in-Publication Data

Dann, Jack.
    The rebel : an imagined life of James Dean / Jack Dann.—1st ed.
      p. cm.
    ISBN 0-380-97839-3
    1. Dean, James, 1931–1955—Fiction. 2. Motion picture actors and actresses—Fiction. 3. Traffic accident victims—Fiction.
4. Actors—Fiction. I. Title.

PS3554.A574R43 2004
823'.914—dc22   2003068880

04 05 06 07 08 JTC/QW 10 9 8 7 6 5 4 3 2 1

For Keith Ferrell

Could we ever forget Mr. Mullet . . .
or the savory delights of Dreamland?

CONTENTS

■

Acknowledgments   **xi**

Part One

1   Ting-a-Ling   **3**
2   Little Bastard   **15**
3   Second Chance   **25**
4   Rings Around the Moon   **27**
5   Overfreight   **38**
6   The Little Tit of Time   **54**
7   Somebody Up There Likes Me   **69**

Part Two

8   Improvisations   **87**
9   Looking into Heaven   **96**

10	Satnin	116
11	The Enemy Within	134
12	Twisting	152

Part Three

13	Bought and Sold	177
14	Twinkle, Twinkle, Little Star	182
15	Bug Fuck	198
16	Book of Secrets	211
17	Possession	218
18	Maya	231
19	Lions and Lambs	239
20	Cross-Eyed Boys	250

Part Four

21	Windows of the Sea	267
22	Methods and Martyrs	280
23	The Egg Trick	291
24	Sooner or Later	297
25	On Top of the World	307
26	Inversions	318
27	Lap of the Gods	338
28	The Politics of Experience	352
29	Bitch Luck Boogie-Woogie	367
30	Dancing in the Dark	377
31	Promised Land	386

The author would like to thank the following people for their support, aid, and inspiration:

Theresa Anns, Lou Aronica, Terry Bisson, Caren Bohrman, Lou Boxer, Paul Brandon, Norm and Paddy Broberg, Ginger Clark, Sean Cotcher, Lorne Dann, Ellen Datlow, Sue Drakeford, Tom Dupree, Harlan and Susan Ellison, Andrew Enstice, Dennis Etchison, Christine Farmer, Keith Ferrell, Lisa Gallagher, Scott Goldman, Merrilee Heifetz, Jennifer Hershey, Barrie Hitchon, Trina King (who deserves a commendation for research), Charles and Betty Anne Kochis, Deborah Layne, Mark and Lillian Levy, Patsy LoBrutto (who was there in L.A. on that perfect, golden afternoon), Barry N. Malzberg, David and Clair Marsh, Shona Martyn, John and Lesley McKay, Sean McMullen, Trish McMullen, Michael Morrison, Brian Murray, Maja Nikolic, Bill Nolan, Richard Parslow, Steve Paulsen, Randy Russell, Pamela Sargent, Al Sarrantonio, Peter Schneider, Stephanie Smith, Debbie Stier, Jonathan Strahan, Nick Stathopoulos, Norman Tilley, Liz Tomazic, Christine Valada, Melissa Warren, Len Wein, Phoebe Wise, Jack Womack, Kaye Wright, George Zebrowski, my U.S. editor, Jennifer Brehl, and my Australian publisher and editor, Linda Funnell, and especially my partner, Janeen . . . for love, constancy, and astonishing patience.

PART ONE

1955–1957

Some men see things as they are and say why. I dream things that never were, and say why not?

—ROBERT F, KENNEDY, QUOTING
GEORGE BERNARD SHAW

ONE

■

Ting-a-Ling

LOS ANGELES: SEPTEMBER 29, 1955

It was the same dream, the same ratcheting, shaking,

steaming, choo-chooing dream of being back on the ghost train with his mother. She is imprisoned in a lead casket in the baggage car, and he *knows* that she is alive and suffocating. But he can't reach her, even as he runs from one car of the *Silver Challenger Express* to another. The cars are huge and hollow and endless, and he is exhausted—James Dean, forever the nine-year-old orphan, on his way again, and again and again, to bury his mother in Marion, Indiana.

Mercifully, the whistle of the train rings—a telephone jolting him awake.

"Hello, Jimmy?" The voice hesitant, whispery, far away.

"Marilyn?"

"Well, who do you think it is, Pier Angeli?"

"You're a nasty bitch."

"And you're still in love with her, you poor dumb fuck, aren't you."

Fully awake now, he laughed mordantly. "Yeah, I guess I am."

"Jimmy?"

"Yeah?"

"I'm sorry. I love you."

"I love you, too. Are you in Connecticut with the Schwartzes or whatever the fuck their name is?" Jimmy felt around for cigarettes and matches, without success. He slept on a mattress on the floor of the second-floor alcove. Shadows seemed to float around him in the darkness like clouds.

Marilyn giggled, as if swallowing laughter, and said, "Anti-Semite. You mean the Greenes, and I'm not staying with them anymore, except to visit and do business. I'm living in New York now—like you told me to, remember? I'm at the Waldorf Towers. Pretty flashy, huh? But that's not where I am this very minute."

"Marilyn . . ."

"I'm right here in L.A., and I've got news and I want to see you." She sounded out of breath, but that was just another one of her signatures.

"I got a big race on Monday," Jimmy said, feeling hampered by the length of the phone cord and the darkness as he felt through the litter around his mattress. "It's in Salinas, near Monterey. You want to come and watch?"

"Maybe I do, maybe I don't."

"Shit, Marilyn. What time is it? I've got to get up at seven. And I've got to be awake enough so as not to crash into a goddamn wall. And—"

The phone was suddenly dead.

Marilyn Monroe was gone.

Jimmy should have known better. But it was—he got up and flicked on the light switch—two o'clock in the morning. Not late for Jimmy when he wasn't racing; he'd often hang out at this hour with Marty Wrightson, a studio electrician who claimed to be Jimmy's best friend. They'd go to Googie's or Schwab's on Sunset, which were the only places in L.A. open after midnight, or he'd drive around alone . . . or talk through the night to Marilyn, who would call whenever she felt the need.

The lights hurt Jimmy's eyes, and although he hadn't been drinking or doing any drugs, he felt hungover; and as he looked around his rented house, forgetting for the instant that he needed a cigarette, he remembered his dream—running through the clattering passenger cars of the *Silver Challenger*. "Momma," he whispered, then jerked his head to the side, as if embarrassed.

But eventually the light burned away the dream. He found the cigarettes in his bed, the pack of Chesterfields crumpled, the matches tucked inside the cellophane wrapper; and he sat on the edge of the alcove, his legs dangling, and smoked in the bright yellowish light. Below him was a large living room with a huge seven-foot-tall stone fireplace. He had bought a white bearskin rug for the hearth, and on the wall was an eagle, talons extended, wings outstretched, a bronzed predator caught in midflight. It belonged to Jimmy's landlord. He could almost touch his pride-and-joy James B. Lansing loudspeakers that just about reached the ceiling. Below . . . below him was the mess of his life: his bongos, scattered records and album covers, dirty dishes, dirty clothes, cameras and camera equipment, crumpled paper and old newspapers and books—a library on the floor. The walls were covered with bullfighting posters and a few of his own paintings, but pride of place was given to a bloodstained bullfighting cape that was cut into spokelike shadows by the bright wheel lamp that hung between the beams of the ceiling. Jimmy gazed at the cape and remembered when the Brooklyn-born matador Sidney Franklin had given it to him as a souvenir. That was in Tijuana. Rogers Brackett had introduced Jimmy to the matador, who was a friend of Ernest Hemingway. Brackett introduced him to everyone. All he ever wanted in return was Jimmy's cock.

But Brackett knew *everyone*.

Jimmy could still feel the dark presence of his recurrent nightmare. It blew through him like hot, fetid air, the hurricane of a fucked-up past, of memory. He had named it, thus making it tangible, absolutely real. *Black Mariah. Black Mariah. Black Mariah.*

Suddenly frightened, feeling small and vulnerable as his thoughts swam like neon fish in deep, dark water, he huddled up tightly on the landing. He wanted to cry. *Momma . . .*

He flicked his half-finished cigarette in a high arc across the room and wondered if it would start a fire. If it did, he would sit right where he was like a fucking Buddha and die without moving a muscle.

If it didn't, he would race on Monday.

The phone rang again. He picked up the receiver.

"Hi," Marilyn said. "You ready to go out with me?"

Jimmy laughed. "Why'd you hang up on me?"

"Because you were treating me bad. I've changed. The new me doesn't take shit from *anybody*, not even from the person I love more than—"

"More than who?"

"Anybody."

"More than Arthur Miller?" he teased.

She laughed. "Maybe a little, but you'd better see me now because who knows what could happen later."

"You're married, remember?" Jimmy said.

"But not for long, honey." There was a long pause, and then Marilyn said, "No, not for long." The sadness was palpable in her voice. "Well, you want me to hang up again, or what?"

"No."

"You going to see me then? Please, Jimmy, I don't want to be alone right now. I'll come over to you." Then, changing mood, "And who knows, we might both get lucky. Anyway, I'll show you my new car. It's a gift. And it's fabjous."

"From who?"

"I got it for doing a show with Art Linkletter. It's a Caddy DeVille convertible, and it's pink as your cute little ass. I love it." She giggled and blew into the phone. "I'll give you a ride, but you've got to make up your mind right now, or I'm hanging up. One . . . two . . ."

"Okay," Jimmy said. "I'm awake. But how the hell am I supposed to drive to Salinas tomorrow?"

"I'll bring you some pills."

"I can't drive stoned-out. You want to kill me?"

"No, Jimmy."

He knew she was laughing at him. "I'd show you the new Porsche, but it's at my mechanic's. I can pick you up with my station wagon. Where are you?"

"No, I want to drive," she said. "I'll be at your place in fifteen minutes. I've got something to tell you that you won't believe. You're still on Sunset Plaza, right?"

"No, Marilyn, I moved, remember? I'm in Sherman Oaks. 14611 Sutton Street. It's a log cabin, you have to—"

"I'll find it. Bye."

"I can't stay out long." But Jimmy was speaking to dead air.

ALTHOUGH HE COULDN'T BE SURE WHEN—OR IF—MARILYN WOULD arrive, Jimmy waited outside near the road for her. He wore jeans, a white T-shirt, scuffed black penny loafers, and the bright red jacket that Nick Ray had bought for him to wear in *Rebel Without a Cause.*

It was a cool night, with the promise that tomorrow would be a perfect day to drive his new flat-four 547 Porsche Spyder. He daydreamed about driving. There was nothing better than speed—the adrenaline surge that would open deep inside his chest, the pressure in his eyes as the liquid silver curve of the hood swallowed the road in one long-drawn gulp, and the beautiful, perfect, third-eye sense that he was about to rise, to lift right off the pavement, to go so fast that the car would shudder like a plane as it became airborne; and he'd rip a hole right through the sky.

Marilyn drove into the gravel driveway. The top of the pink Cadillac was down, although she had neglected to snap on the decorative leather boot. She smiled at him but looked tentative, as if frightened that he wouldn't recognize her or, worse yet, that he *would* recognize her and turn away. She didn't look like Marilyn Monroe. That was the guise that she turned on and off like a lightbulb. Jimmy understood all about that. They were both monsters that could turn into . . . themselves. And when they turned themselves on to each other, it was like driving fast, except it was in the eyes *and* the crotch. She wore tan slacks, a man's sweater that was several sizes too large for her, and a black kerchief tied around her head. If it were daytime, she'd be wearing sunglasses—all part of the uniform of a private person. She wouldn't be wearing makeup either.

"Well, it's certainly . . . pink," Jimmy said as he moved toward the driver's-side door. "You mind if I drive?"

"Yes I do. I'm driving." Marilyn leaned toward him for a kiss.

"But I have something to show you," Jimmy said. "Give you a kick like nothing else."

"You drive like a maniac, Jimmy. You scare me."

"You drive any differently?"

"I may be as crazy as you, but this is *my* car. If anyone's going to mess it up, it's going to be me. Now get in."

Jimmy put on his pout face and sat down beside her. She smelled strongly of perfume. Joy, her favorite.

"You want to come inside and see my house?" Jimmy asked.

"No, I want to drive." And with that she shifted the car into reverse and stomped on the accelerator. Tires spun in the gravel as the Caddy fishtailed backward into the street. Jimmy was thrown against the dashboard. Marilyn changed gears and laid rubber as she accelerated down the hill.

"You're high as a goddamn kite," Jimmy said. "You didn't even look to see if anything was coming, and you almost put my head through the windshield."

Marilyn giggled as she crossed over the double yellow line. "I love these wind-y roads, except it's so easy to get lost."

She raced around and down the mountain until she reached Mulholland Drive; then she turned onto the wide, straight road and accelerated until the car began to shake.

"Need to get your front end fixed," Jimmy said.

Marilyn laughed and slowed down to eighty. There were few cars on the drive. She untied her kerchief, and her blond hair, stiff from too many bleachings, was swept back by the wind.

"So what's your news?" Jimmy asked. "Word is that Fox is going to give you a hundred grand a picture."

"And I'm going to have director approval, too. Fox isn't going to stick it to me again, I'll tell you that."

"We should start a company to make films. I'm going to be the best director you ever saw. Nick Ray thinks so, and he's the best director I know."

"You think the sun sets in his ass," Marilyn said.

"Well, he hasn't done bad for me. *Rebel Without a Cause* is going to be a *big* hit."

"I hope so. I pray it'll be a smash."

"I should have insisted on doing my next picture with Nick," Jimmy said. "Man, I *hate* George Stevens. That bastard's got a God complex or something. He wouldn't even let me go to a race while I was working on his overblown abortion of a motion picture, and he wouldn't let me act, either. All the good bits of *Giant* are on the floor. What an asshole. He couldn't wipe Nick's ass."

"So we're back to Nick's ass, huh?"

"So it's true about the money?"

She raised her head, exaggeratedly sniffing the air, and said, "My partner Mr. Milton Greene, thank you, is negotiating everything. We'll see what happens."

"It *is* true . . . you bitch." Jimmy laughed and moved closer to her; she put her arm around him.

"My *corporation* will be paid, but I might take just a teeny bit for myself."

They laughed hysterically.

"And your corporation should buy you all the pink Cadillacs you can drive."

"I'll have a different one every time I go out."

"Are you going out much?"

"Constantly, and I have to drive back and forth from New York to the Greenes' in Connecticut. Do you think I would condescend to drive the same car every time I go to Connecticut? That would be like wearing the same dress to every party. No, sirree, I'll buy myself a *fleet* of new Cadillacs."

Jimmy ran his finger over her sweater and played with her breasts. Marilyn didn't seem to notice, although her nipples became erect. "I love these," he said.

"You could fool me. You're squeezing them like you're trying to make mud pies." Jimmy stopped touching her and stared ahead. His long brown hair, which was greasy and needed a wash, was tousled, and his eyes narrowed as they always did when he was concentrating. He pushed his thick-lensed glasses against the bridge of his nose; it was a nervous habit.

"Go ahead, you can make mud pies," Marilyn said.

"I never did that to Pier."

"You never squeezed her tits?"

"She didn't like it, maybe because they're tiny."

"So what did you do?"

"We just fucked."

"That's it?"

"Cuddled."

"You want to cuddle me?" Marilyn asked.

"Yeah, maybe, I don't know."

"I'll stop right here, we can do it right here. If we get caught, tell me *that* wouldn't make good copy."

"I want to talk for a little while," Jimmy said, sounding childlike. "And I want to drive."

"What do I get if I let you drive?"

"A cuddle and a ting-a-ling."

"A what?"

"You got to let me drive to find out."

"Okay. You drive." With that Marilyn slid onto Jimmy's lap and let go of the steering wheel. Jimmy grabbed it and pulled himself into the driver's seat.

"Jesus H. Christ!"

Marilyn giggled and let her hand rest on his crotch as he drove. She scolded him when he didn't get an erection.

"I can't do two things at once," he said.

"What if I do this?" and she slid across the leather seat so she could put her head on his lap. She bit him gently through the stiff denim of his jeans until he became hard. "Well, *that* seems to work," she said. She unzipped his fly, carefully worked his penis out of his shorts, and teased him with her tongue.

"You really do have a death wish, don't you," Jimmy said.

"If you say so. Do you want me to stop?"

"You probably should."

"Just think of it as a cuddle. My treat. I'm as good as any of those goddamn directors or producers you always used to complain about, aren't I?"

Jimmy laughed at that.

"Well?" Marilyn asked.

"Yes," Jimmy said.

"And do you want me to stop now?"

"No." He gave in to warm, wet bliss.

"Well, then you'd better say please or I'll stop."

"You're a bitch, Marilyn, do you know that?"

"Say please. I'm going to count to three. One . . . two . . ."

"Okay, please."

"Nope, too late," she said. She sat up and smiled at him.

"Too late, is it?" Jimmy said, stepping hard on the accelerator. "I guess it's time to teach you a lesson."

Marilyn giggled. "Better put that thing back in your pants first."

Jimmy grinned at her, adjusted himself, zipped up his fly, and said, "This ain't finished yet."

"Well, I would hope not. I expect to get some satisfaction for my persistence, and just remember you said please."

Jimmy turned off the headlights. "It's going to be *you* saying please very soon now."

"Turn the lights on, Jimmy. What are you trying to prove?"

"See those taillights up ahead? Must be a big Buick or maybe a Caddy like this one. Well, this is going to be like one Caddy kissing another. We'll just give his bumper a little kiss, a sweet little kiss, maybe something like your kissing my dick."

"What are you talking about?" Marilyn asked. "You really are as crazy as everybody says." But rather than fear, there was an edge of excitement in her voice. "Now turn the lights back on and let up on the gas. I'm telling you right now, if you mess up this car, I'll take a tire iron to that new porch of yours."

Jimmy laughed. "It's a Porsche, and you'd have to find it first." After a beat, he said, "Okay, now let's see what this pig can do." He put the Caddy into overdrive, and the red taillights ahead seemed to be rushing toward them. "The dumb bastard doesn't even know we're driving right up his ass."

"Goddammit, Jimmy, slow down!" Marilyn shouted, reaching for the steering wheel.

Jimmy knocked her hand away; his knuckles were white on the steering wheel. The speedometer read ninety. "You can scream, but don't touch."

Marilyn rolled up her window, as if that would protect her.

"No, roll it down," Jimmy said. "You got to be right there to hear it." The wind roared in his ears, a wonderful whistling whine, and Marilyn screamed as he drove her Cadillac into the ghostly white Lincoln Continental ahead. But it was indeed just a kiss, as bumper clanged against bumper—one bell-like note and a glimpse of a terrified woman wearing a chic red hat—and then Jimmy was pulling ahead of the Lincoln as the horn of an oncoming car blared and headlights rushed toward them. Jimmy veered back into the right hand lane just in time. Marilyn screamed again.

"Did you hear it?" Jimmy asked. "Ting-a-fucking-ling."

"Stop the car," Marilyn said.

"It didn't do no damage. It was just a kiss, sweet as a bell."

"Pull the car over right now, and put the lights on before somebody back-ends us or something."

"There's nobody else on the road."

"Jimmy!"

"Nobody else in the world." But he pulled over to the curb and turned off the engine. "Earth Angel" played softly on the radio, cicadas roared in the bushes, and the distant yet pervasive thrum of the road and city was felt rather than heard. The sky was black and smeary gray; here and there a star was visible through the clouds or smog.

"Did you hear the ting-a-ling?" Jimmy asked. His voice was low, childlike.

"Yes."

"I told you it would be a kick. You want to check the bumper?"

"No." Then, "I'm still shaking."

"Yeah, so am I."

"You could have killed us."

"Yeah, that's the idea, isn't it?"

"You could have killed that poor woman in the other car. She doesn't deserve that."

"How do you know what she deserves? Or who she might have just screwed over? What happens happens. You can't change it."

"So you couldn't help but drive into her car, right?"

"Yeah, in a way, I guess," Jimmy said. "Just like you couldn't help calling me up in the middle of the night and coming over to my house."

"Jimmy, hold me."

Which he did, and they made love awkwardly and passionately and quickly on the front seat while the radio played "Maybellene" and "Ain't That a Shame." When they were finished, Marilyn began to cry.

"That bad, huh?" Jimmy asked.

Marilyn smiled. "Yeah, Jimmy, you were terrible."

After a pause, Jimmy asked, "What's the matter, then?"

"I don't know. Oh, fuck it, yes, I do. It's Joe. He drives a Cadillac. A blue one."

"So?"

"So . . . being here, doing this . . . made me think about him a little."

"Have you seen him since you've been here?" Jimmy knew Joe DiMaggio and didn't like him. Marilyn's husband was so overcome with jealousy that he followed Marilyn around like a store detective; and Jimmy thought that he looked like a skinny, upchuck store detective with his big, narrow nose, greasy hair, and ill-fitting though expensive suits.

"No. I was going to call him, but I called you instead."

"He's a prick, Marilyn. How many times has he kicked the shit out of you?"

"It wasn't so bad, Jimmy. Maybe a slap, that'd be it. Not what you think. He'd just get crazy, and then he'd be beside himself with guilt, and he'd be crying and begging me to forgive him, and buying me every goddamn thing he could think of. I could've opened up a flower shop every time we had a fight."

"That's not what you used to tell me."

"Well, I was upset. I needed somebody to talk to . . . someone I could talk to."

"So you were bullshitting me all the while, right?"

She sighed and twisted herself away from him. "No, Jimmy, I wasn't bullshitting you. You just don't understand."

"What don't I understand?"

"That Joe loves me."

"I love you."

She giggled, combed her fingers through her hair, and turned back toward Jimmy. "You love to make mud pies."

"No, I mean it."

"I know you do, Jimmy. But you know what I mean; it's different with Joe. He loves me before himself. You and me . . . I don't know. No matter what we do, it's different somehow. Joe loves me more than his career."

"That's why he wants you to give up *your* career."

"I'm divorcing him, isn't that enough? But I just can't be cruel to him. I can't do that. And no matter what, I'll always love him."

"Aren't you worried he'll get shitfaced again with his pal Sinatra and break into your apartment like they tried to do last year? Christ, that was something. Did he go to court for that yet?"

"I don't know," Marilyn said.

"If you love Joe so much, what are you doing with Arthur Miller? Christ, he looks old enough to be your father."

"He's not old. He's only forty."

"I expect to be dead by then."

"You probably will be."

"So why are you getting rid of Joe, who loves you so much, and chasing this other guy?" Jimmy asked.

"What makes you think I'm chasing him?"

"You didn't tell me he loves you."

"Well, he does. He's crazy about me, and if he had his way, he'd have left his wife and kids for me, but I wouldn't let him do that. If you can believe it, I tried to talk him out of divorcing her. I don't want that on my conscience. But he says he can't live without me, and I love him."

"I can't believe that. But then I never understood your thing with Joe, either. Different strokes . . ."

"Joe and me tore each other apart. I couldn't be what he needs. But everything is different with Arthur. He's smart in a different way. He teaches me things I didn't even know I needed to know, and he's be-hind my career a hundred percent. With Joe, well, you know."

"Joe must know. The gossip's everywhere."

"I was going to tell him, so he wouldn't read it in the rags, but I just couldn't. I'm such a coward."

"You want to go back to my place?" Jimmy asked.

"Yes, but *I'll* drive." They switched places, and Marilyn turned the car around and sped back toward Sherman Oaks.

"So what's your news that you wanted to tell me?"

Marilyn turned onto Beverly Glen. It would be dawn soon, and she looked pale and worn and fragile in the dim, ambient streetlight. Her hair was frizzed by the wind. She stared ahead and drove slowly up the winding road, as if she wanted the ride to last as long as possible.

"Did you have a fight with Miller? Is that what this is all about?"

"No, it's about my life and not getting anything right."

"What would make it right?"

Marilyn laughed and said, "If I knew that I wouldn't be here. If Arthur makes the effort, maybe he'll get me. Or some secret somebody else you don't even know about."

"Why not me?"

"Because I'll always have you, Jimmy, just like you'll always have me."

Her timing was perfect. She drove into his driveway and kissed him good night.

"I thought you were coming in," Jimmy said.

"No, you go to your race."

"Where are you staying? I'll call you when I get back."

She gave him her generous lightbulb Marilyn smile and backed the car out of the driveway. "Maybe I'll call you."

TWO

■

Little Bastard

The phone rang.

Jimmy considered not answering it. He would often just let the phone ring, but he was worried that it might be Bill, who was going to be his pit man at the race, or Rolf Wütherich, his mechanic. Maybe something was wrong with the car.

He picked up the phone. "Yeah . . . ?"

"It's me, Jimmy. Marilyn."

"What are you doing up so early?"

"Do you still want me to go with you, to the race?"

"Yeah, sure," Jimmy said. "That'd be great. Are you at the hotel?"

"No."

"Are you okay?"

"No."

"Well, where are you? I've got to go over to the place I bought the car. It's in Hollywood. I'll pick you up in the station wagon, and we can talk on the way."

"It's better if I meet you there," Marilyn said. "What's the address?"

"It's twelve-nineteen North Vine. But we're not going to get much of a chance to talk with people all over the place."

"How many people you inviting? Your entire fan club?"

"You'll see," Jimmy said, grinning into the phone.

After a pause, Marilyn said, "I'll meet you there." She sounded nervous.

"It's Competition Motors. Pull into the rear. I'll be in the garage with my mechanic. I'm leaving now."

"Okay. Bye." She hung up.

But Jimmy was sure she wouldn't be meeting him at the dealership. It was just her way.

JIMMY WAS WRONG. WHEN HE PULLED HIS WHITE, WOOD-PANELED Ford station wagon into the rear of Competition Motors, he saw Marilyn's Cadillac parked in front of the garage. The front left fender was smashed in, and the bumper was dented. She'd done that since he'd last seen her a few hours ago.

He rushed into the garage to see a composed and vivacious Marilyn and a nervous schoolboy of a mechanic. As a teenager, Rolf Wütherich had been a Luftwaffe pilot in the last days of the Second World War; and he prided himself on being cool under pressure. But that obviously didn't extend to being in the presence of Marilyn Monroe. Jimmy knew her taste in men. She liked dark, swarthy types, and Rolf was perfect. He was built like Joe DiMaggio, strong and wiry; and he had black, wavy hair and a heavy beard that was always a shadow on his face.

Marilyn was switched on, but that was desperation—Jimmy knew it well.

"I see you decided to drive into the traffic instead of through it," he said.

"Ha-ha," Marilyn replied. She was leaning against the driver's side of the Porsche while Rolf had the hood up and was making adjustments to the engine—or pretending to. He nodded to Jimmy.

"What's wrong?" Jimmy asked him. "The timing?"

"It's always the timing with the engines. But don't worry, we have plenty of time."

"So I see," Jimmy said.

Rolf blushed and then seemed angry. "I'm supposed to have all the work done on all these"—he waved his arm toward five other aluminum-bodied Spyder 550s in the garage—"and work on your car, and spend the weekend away with you at the races. I could spend all day just working on your Spyder. Do you know how long it takes to assemble one of these engines? A hundred and twenty hours. And that's if you have an expert 547 mechanic, like me."

"So we won't have enough time?" Jimmy said.

"I told you, we have time," Rolf snapped, obviously flustered.

Jimmy grinned at Marilyn and motioned her to come away from Rolf and the car. "Okay, Rolf, I'm not trying to bug you."

"Well, it would be better if you weren't standing around and looking over my shoulder like you always do. I told you it will be ready, and it will." He didn't raise his head; it was as if he was hiding under the bonnet.

Marilyn grinned back at Jimmy, as if they were in collusion, and asked, "What's this business in the back?"

"What are you talking about?"

She stepped back to look at the words LITTLE BASTARD painted in script between the rear taillights. "That—the 'Little Bastard' business."

"That's its name, like naming a boat or something." Jimmy stared back at her, as if that was explanation enough, but Marilyn said, "Yeah . . . and?"

"Okay, it's an in-joke. Bill Hickman calls me Little Bastard because I call him Big Bastard. So it seemed natural to name the car Little Bastard."

"You're right, it fits," Marilyn said. Then she put her arms around him and whispered, "Jimmy, Jimmy, I need attention right this very minute. I feel like I'm going to shrivel up and die, which would save everybody a lot of trouble."

"Rolf, we'll be right back," Jimmy said.

Rolf nodded, still concentrating on the engine, but Jimmy had caught him peering up at Marilyn.

"Bye, Rolf," Marilyn said.

"Bye, er . . ."

"Call me Norma Jeane. That's what all my friends do."

Rolf nodded again, then turned back to the engine.

"I don't call you that," Jimmy said.

"Who said you were my friend?" Marilyn smiled at him, and Jimmy imagined she was radiating some sort of delicious heat. Once outside the garage, he pulled his arms around her and kissed her, tasted her.

"Gosh, what was that for?"

"Not being my friend," Jimmy said. Then, tentatively, "Would you rather I call you Norma Jeane?"

She laughed and said, "No. No matter how long we know each other, even when we're cute little old people, I want to be Marilyn to you. To Rolf, I'll just be Norma Jeane, no one special. To you, I want—"

"What?"

"I want to be everything, boys and girls all stacked together. I want . . . to be your hard-on." They both laughed like high school kids drunk on their own jokes. Although it was still early, Jimmy could feel the heat of the sun; it was going to be a hot, dry day. He looked at her car.

"How'd you make the fender bender?"

Marilyn's mood changed in an instant. "It's that scumbag Frank Sinatra. I swear he has no life of his own."

"What do you mean?"

"I was just going to ride around and think things through; but son of a bitch if I didn't see you-know-who in the rearview mirror. When I tried to lose him, I drove over the curb and took out a parking meter, and that's that."

"Well, you lost him," Jimmy said, looking around, distracted.

"That's why I didn't want to come to your house. In case I didn't lose him. That's all Joe needs to know, that I came to you. The poor bastard is messed up enough because of me, but I'm not his goddamn possession, Jimmy. Goddamn wops, goddamn all of them, every fucking one, even the pope." She started crying. Jimmy held her. "For all I know, goddamn Frankie is watching us right now. He's such a heel. He figures that if he can't fuck me, nobody can. But Joe, Joe's God according to Frank. He can fuck whoever he wants to. You, me, everybody." She started laughing again, although it was hard to tell if she was laughing or crying. There was an edge of hysteria in her voice. "Jimmy, I got to get away from here. I've got to get away from everybody, all of them but you."

"Okay. You don't have to do anything you don't want."

"Promise?"

"Promise."

"You want to go sit in my car?" she asked mischievously, suddenly changing mood, as if she'd just developed amnesia. "I'll show you my dent close up."

"What about Rolf?" Jimmy asked, smiling.

"Isn't he working hard on fixing your car? He could be at it for hours."

"Yeah, he could," Jimmy said as he watched a car drive into the lot. It was a battered Nash that looked like an overturned, rusty bathtub. Bill Hickman was at the wheel.

"Who's that?" Marilyn asked.

"Bill Hickman, the Big Bastard." Jimmy grinned. "I told you it would get crowded."

"Yeah, you told me."

Jimmy waved to Hickman, who was getting out of the car. He had a hard, weatherworn face; Jimmy had once told him he looked like a hit man for the mob. He started walking toward Jimmy and Marilyn, but Jimmy waved him off. "Rolf's inside the garage. I've got some . . . business to take care of here. Go on in, and I'll be with you guys in a few minutes."

"Okay, I know when to piss off," Hickman said, and turned around. He was wearing jeans and a white T-shirt—Jimmy's uniform.

"So what was that about?" Marilyn asked angrily.

"What?"

"So now I'm business, a few minutes' worth of business."

"Oh, shit, Marilyn. Two minutes ago you were going to kill yourself, and now you're mad because I didn't introduce you to Bill. I figured you didn't want to deal with anybody. You want to meet him? Come on. We'll go meet him."

Marilyn kissed Jimmy and said, "You're right, it's too crowded. Go back to the garage, and I'll be right there. I just need to get something from the car that I forgot."

Later, when Marilyn didn't appear, Jimmy went back outside to look for her.

But the Cadillac was long gone.

ROLF TUNED THE ENGINE FOR MOST OF THE MORNING, AND THEN they left for Salinas. Jimmy drove the Spyder with Rolf beside him— it had barely 150 miles on the odometer and needed to be broken in— and Bill Hickman and Sandy Roth, Jimmy's current photographer, followed in the Ford station wagon.

They drove down Cahuenga to the freeway, up Sepulveda to the Ridge Route and out of the city. They had sandwiches at a diner outside Newhall, and Jimmy and Sandy got speeding tickets in Kern County for going sixty-five miles an hour in a forty-five-mile zone. As Jimmy drove away from the handsome, clean-cut highway patrolman— who looked more like a movie star than he did—he shouted to Bill and Sandy that they'd all meet for dinner in Paso Robles, which was about 150 miles down Route 466. Jimmy continued driving north on Route 99. He got caught in traffic in Bakersfield, crept from red light to red light while everyone around him stared at the topless, bumperless, futuristic-looking—and obviously expensive—sports car inching along the palm-lined boulevard of Union Street, and then he accelerated to 130 miles an hour past the old air corps barracks and Minter Field, where he had raced twice in airport meets.

"You're going to blow the engine out and kill us both into the bargain!" Rolf shouted.

Jimmy smiled at Rolf's accent and let the needle drift back to seventy-five. "I just needed to see what it could do." He asked Rolf to light him another cigarette. Since the Spyder didn't have a lighter, the mechanic had to scrunch down into the leg well and cup a match against the wind.

"Thanks," Jimmy said. "What's the rev number? How's the oil temp?"

"How many times are you going to ask me? Everything is fine. When something's wrong, I'll tell you. Okay?"

"Okay."

They drove for a while in silence. Rolf squinted in the bright sunlight; he had forgotten his sunglasses. Jimmy wore clip-ons over his glasses. He reveled in the baking sun and the screaming of the wind as the car tore along the highway, its snub nose seeming to swallow the endless bit of road before it. Rolf's great head nodded forward as he fell asleep; then, jarred perhaps by dreams, he would jerk awake and look around, surprised. Jimmy was lost in the rhythm of the tires plashing evenly on the highway. He was serenely happy, as if he was going to drive right up the curve of the huge, blue, cloudless sky, and he thought of his mother calling him, calling his name, but her voice was hidden and disguised by the wind. So many familiar voices were buried in the howling around him . . . Marilyn's soft baby voice, his father's—stern yet squeaky—his own; and he listened. What was he saying? What was *his* secret voice calling him to do?

It was hot but not humid. The land was flat as a plate, and desolate. Skeins of dull gray barbed wire on the road shoulders caught and trapped the tumbleweed that skated across the dry fields. There were oil pumps on either side of the highway, black towers standing against the dead straw landscape and the blue-eye sky.

Rolf woke up and stared straight ahead.

"You okay?" Jimmy asked.

"Of course I'm okay. What else should I be?" Jimmy smiled and nodded. "I keep thinking about Marilyn," Rolf said. "Norma Jeane."

"Most everyone does."

"She's beautiful. Perfect." After a beat Rolf asked, "Are you in love with her?"

"Yes . . . and no. She's a friend. But she's too fast for you, Rolf."

"I'm pretty fast."

Jimmy laughed. "You couldn't catch her even if you were driving this. And neither could I."

"How is it with you and Pier?" Rolf asked.

"It isn't," Jimmy said. "She's married to Vic Damone, remember? She just had his kid. Perry Rocco Luigi Something Damone. Can you believe that?" Rolf didn't answer. Everyone knew that Jimmy was still seeing Pier. "My kid."

"What?"

"He's my kid. James Byron Dean, Jr. He sure as hell ain't Damone's."

"So what are you going to do?"

"Nothing I can do. She married him and gave the baby his name. She and him can eat pizza with her bitch of a mother until they weigh eight hundred pounds for all I care." Jimmy became sullen.

"I'm sorry," Rolf said. "It's none of my business anyway."

"That's right. But you're my friend, so *mi casa es su casa* and all that shit, right?"

"Right."

"What about you?"

"I see a few girls, but nothing. After they screw me around, I just go back to Madame Palm." He wiggled his fingers. "Less hassle."

"Amen." They both laughed.

Jimmy gripped the steering wheel tightly. There was a brown-and-yellow Chevy Bel Air sedan ahead that was barely moving. He pulled beside it to pass . . . and saw a Pontiac heading straight for him in the left-hand lane. There wasn't room to accelerate. The driver of the Chevy slowed down; Jimmy couldn't pull back behind it. He was trapped. The driver of the oncoming Pontiac veered off the road, which gave Jimmy just enough room to pass the Chevy. A shower of pebbles kicked up by the Pontiac's tires struck the Porsche and stung Jimmy and Rolf like wasps.

"Son of a bitch!" Jimmy shouted. Then he said, "Now tell me life ain't fucking wonderful. Fucking-A wonderful."

The highway shimmered in the heat, and mirages of what looked like black glass appeared and disappeared in the distance, like the cars they had almost collided with. Jimmy was going to win tomorrow. He daydreamed about what he would say when he received the trophy. He daydreamed that Pier would be there, with his baby—Pier and Dizzy Sheridan and Barbara Glenn and Claire Heller and Eartha Kitt and Arlene Sachs and Christine White and Ursula Andress, all the girls he loved, and, of course, Marilyn. Hell, he wouldn't even mind if Marty Wrightson showed up. And all the others—Rogers Brackett; his father, Winton; his uncle Marcus, his little cousin Markie; Aunt Ortense; George Stevens; "Gage" Kazan; Leonard Rosenman; Lew Bracker; Marty Landau; Nicco Romanos; Julie Harris; Elizabeth Taylor; and Nick Ray. He wanted everyone to be there, everyone he ever knew, the whole fucking world.

He wondered why Marilyn had driven off without a word. But that was Marilyn. You just can't depend on her. *Just like you can't depend on me,* he thought. The wind spun that thought away. *If only Mother could see me win . . .* The wind screamed in his ears like the whistle of a racing train.

Suddenly Rolf said, "Don't try to go too fast. You're supposed to be driving to get experience."

"That's what I was just doing."

Rolf smiled tightly. "That was you trying to kill everybody. But it's a big jump from the last Porsche you had to the Spyder. So try for second or third place tomorrow. Don't try to win. Just run the race and get to know the car. Okay?"

"Okay. You give me the pit signals. But I *will* win."

"You might, you might."

"Here," Jimmy said, as he pulled a ring off his index finger and gave it to Rolf.

"What's this for?"

"To prove we're friends. We are . . . friends, aren't we?"

"Of course we are, Jimmy, but you don't have to give me anything."

"I know, but I want to, all right?"

"I feel odd about this." Jimmy stared ahead and tried not to look hurt, although he could feel the heat coming to his cheeks. "Okay," Rolf said resignedly. "Thank you. You are my friend. You should know that." He had larger hands than Jimmy and could only fit the ring over his pinky. "But one other thing, Jimmy."

"Yeah?"

"Don't ever try what you did back there again when I'm in the car with you. There was a family in that Pontiac you drove off the road."

"Yeah, you're right, Rolf," Jimmy said softly in a little-boy voice as he slowed down to a crawl.

Although he didn't believe in God, he said a prayer in penance.

He'd gone fast enough for one day.

"THERE, YOU SEE, I'M NOT EVEN GOING THAT FAST," JIMMY SAID TO Rolf as he drove down Highway 466 into the grasslands of the Cholame valley. They had turned off Highway 33, and there were no other cars ahead. The distant hills north and south of the road burned yellow in the sun—they looked like great, golden ocean waves caught in mid-motion—and the white, almost phosphorescent guardrails seemed to flicker by like posts on a carousel. The sun was a glare. The sky was on fire. Jimmy adjusted his clip-on sunglasses, then held the wheel tightly with both hands.

"Everything is just fine," Rolf said. "Speed's fine."

"Oil temp okay?"

Rolf laughed. "Yes, Jimmy, for the thousandth time. Oil tempera-ture is fine. Everything's fine, except—"

"Except what?"

"You're burning too much on the downgrade. You've got to under-stand about this car. Just ease up a little. You'll get used to it."

"Christ, I'm crawlin' as it is," Jimmy said. "I'm doing sixty-five, for crying out loud." He saw a black speck way down the highway; it seemed to shimmer and blink in and out of sight in the heat haze swimming over the highway. Slowly, the speck grew larger. "This place reminds me a lot of Indiana, you know that? Except the sun never got this bright there. It's like goddamn CinemaScope." He pointed at a sign and said, "Cholame. Nothin' there but a post of-fice. It's a shed, man. A nothing place way out in nothing." He laughed at the idea of nothing being in nothing, and saw that Rolf was leaning out to see around the windshield. "What the fuck you doing?"

"That's a car up ahead, hard to see with the sun in your eyes. Slow down, you can get fooled on these highways."

"I am slowed down," Jimmy said, and he could see the car ap-proaching the intersection ahead where Highway 41 cut across 466. It was a two-tone, black-and-white Ford, and it was suddenly *right* in front of him. "What the hell is he doing?" Jimmy shouted above the wind. "Shit, you're right, the motherfucker is close."

The Ford approached the intersection and started making a left across 466 onto 41; there was no left-turn lane.

"He's *got* to see us. He'll stop. He's got to." Jimmy lifted his foot from the accelerator; he would only lose control by hitting the brakes hard. He veered to the right to give the other driver enough space for correction. It looked like the Ford was going to accelerate across the road, but the driver obviously panicked and hit the brakes. The car skidded thirty feet over the white median, taking up both lanes of the road. Jimmy tried swerving around it, but there was no place to go.

Everything shifted into slow motion. Everything became magnified.

Soft pillow pressure against his chest as the Spyder struck the black-and-white Ford Tudor sedan, tearing, grinding, the sound of a zipper being pulled down, magnified a thousand times, and the sedan ballooned into a black wall, or some impossibly crenellated black-and-white tower rising in front of him, rising and tearing and grinding, thunder and metal rain, and the other driver stared at Jimmy for but an instant; he had a look of cartoon surprise; he had widely set eyes and short blond hair and a clean-shaven face, an apple-pie boy; he was about the same age as Jimmy; numbness, shifting of weight, spinning, Jimmy floated through the air, weightless, beat, somersaulting, twisting, a glimpse of Rolf on the dirt of the roadside, beat, and the sky disappeared, everything turned candy-apple cherry red, glossy flat endless red, an eternity of glossy flatness turning into darkness, but Jimmy was afraid of the dark; he tore at it, pulled it away, and there, he could see himself, see his twisted left arm and broken leg; he had lost his shoe, *where is the shoe?* that was all that mattered; if he could think about his shoe, if he could visualize his shoe, if only he could find his shoe, he'd be all right; and he fell spun tumbled back home . . .

Back to his sweet, dead mother who calls him back . . . back into her dream . . .

THREE

■

Second Chance

Jimmy smells oil and gasoline and hears Rolf crying

"Jimmy, Jimmy, Jimmy!"over and over, and the voice is big and echoing, like God shouting through the clouds; and Jimmy realizes that he's looking up at the sky, which is cerulean blue, china blue like the scrolling on his Aunt Ortense's plates and teacups, and the clouds scud by above, probably pushed by the great hand of God; and God calls to Jimmy, only He sounds just like Rolf. Jimmy tries to move his head, but he can't. He can't move anything, but his pinky finger. God is allowing him to move that, and God-sky-Rolf calls to him again—"Jimmy, Jimmy, you okay? Jimmy, Jimmy?"— and Jimmy tries to talk back, but all he hears is his own "Ah," a puffing, an exhalation of breath, or maybe that's just the wind whistling through the brush; but then Rolf's voice changes, doesn't sound like God anymore, rises in register, becomes flat, and Jimmy recognizes that soft, sweet, high voice.

"Oh, Mother, why did you have to leave me?" Jimmy cries, just as he's done a hundred times before—every time he visited her grave in the Grant Memorial Park Cemetery in Marion, Indiana. The smells in the air change, subtly shift into Hoosier summer, childhood summer, and his mother says, "I never, never left you, Jimmy."

"Yes, you did," Jimmy says petulantly, or thinks he says . . . no, now he can hear his voice, the voice of a nine-year-old who has just lost his mother . . . again and again and again. "Yes, you did yes you did . . ."

"I've always been with you, in your dreams, in your mind, just like now, now wake up."

"I am awake," Jimmy says.

"Then get yourself up off that ground, you're going to catch a smacker of a cold, you are."

And Jimmy gets up. He can get up. He's not hurt, not in the least, although he's naked and hasn't yet grown his pubic or chest hair, but his mother doesn't notice. She's standing beside her grave right there in front of him. He can see her perfectly. She's real . . . really there. She looks exactly like she should—her brown, curly hair is thick and combed over her right eyebrow, she's wearing a shiny dress and her favorite necklace, which is made out of little gold hearts connected together, and she doesn't look skinny and shadow-eyed like she looked in the hospital; she's plump and healthy and pretty now, everything is back to normal, except for her eyes, which are different because as he walks toward her, a glow or a light like something phosphorous shines out of them, and it's like Jimmy can see his mother seeing him, bathing him in cool, phosphorescent love, and slowly, slowly, she lifts her arms heavenward to embrace him and protect him and save him. Her arms are cool . . . no, cold, icy, and Jimmy shudders, but he doesn't care, he's close to her now, so very close, touching, holding, caressing, and she whispers, "Jimmy, my darling sweet boy, you been resurrected up just like Jesus, and since Jesus has seen fit to give you a second chance, you need to do something wonderful and important with your life. You understand me?"

Jimmy nods and wonders what that could be. Suddenly his mother slips out of his arms, falling, dropping, sinking back into the earth like into quicksand. Jimmy calls to her, begging her to stay, and then, sobbing, falls onto her grave, which is pulsing and hot as a fever.

FOUR

■

Rings Around the Moon

When Jimmy opened his eyes, the air smelled of chlorine
as if just after a storm. The ceiling tiles floated like
clouds, and ghosts flickered around him and talked so
slowly that they sounded like old seventy-eight
records being played at thirty-three-rpm. Great groans
of explanation and inquiry. Movement, weather
changes, cloud-wet gloves touching, clasping, prod-
ding. His own voice sharp as a stiletto, and the whole
world was white and yellow—an undulating room in
the Paso Robles War Memorial Hospital.

The room heaved to the rhythm of his nausea and
the overwhelming, bone-crushing pain until one of
the flittering ghost nurses injected him with another

hot pulse of Demerol, then blessed no nothing, just flatness and folding and reaching into dreams and remembrance.

He tasted blood, swallowed blood, and tried to get up, but he
was in traction splints. He tried to talk, but his tongue was thick
and felt like it was getting larger, filling up his mouth and throat,
choking him; and his head was immobilized, as if held in a vise,
but he imagined he was all there, nothing missing. Just everything was in bits and pieces, James Dean all mixed up, frag-
mented, and as the Demerol took hold, washing cool and
delicious through him, he dreamed that he was a puzzle and that
he had to put himself back together. There, he found his torso, put
together broken ribs, the collarbone—broken, too—and fastened
a leg, mended the fractures, put a foot to the leg, and there, there
was an arm, and so it went, wrist to arm, and then fingers, fingers
wriggling, wriggling spider fingers, Spyder Porsche, driving, riding, crashing, and he remembered, remembered in still frames.
He was a movie, thin and transparent as celluloid, one frame at a
time, all the frames a life, which he was going to live, even now
as he fought for it, for life.

He heard a ringing. The phone? The *Silver Challenger* taking
him once again to his mother's funeral? It stopped, and he slipped
into the past, watched himself crash into the two-tone black-and-
white Ford. It was a tank, and his Porsche might as well have been
made out of Aunt Ortense's fine porcelain. He felt an instant of
sharp pain and then saw himself flying, falling, soaring again in
slow motion; and he saw everything close-up and magnified, a shuf-
fle of disconnected frames: the hood of the Porsche had sprung
open, the front tire had burst on the rim, and the entire left side was
mangled like a tin can that had been run over by a truck. Then a
siren, and two men jumped out of a Buick ambulance, both caught
in midair: one a hairy, bull-necked gorilla of a man, the other a
"skinny marink," as his mother would say; and one smelled bad,
and the other, the marink, smelled of cheap perfume, and they
lifted him into the ambulance, and Rolf was beside him, quiet as a
corpse; and there was jarring and pain, and then minutes tick-
tocking, pebbles from the road hitting the ambulance, and then
sleep, soft, pulsing cotton bliss, until the ambulance lurched, side-
swiped by a car swerving in front of it. The gorilla shouted. Jimmy
heard a woman's voice apologizing that it was all her fault, one
beat, two beats, all the way to twenty, then the siren roaring singing
cutting again, as the ambulance sped on. Jimmy tried to turn to
Rolf, but he couldn't move his head that far, and he tried to talk to

him, but Rolf didn't answer; and then the marink was feeling around Jimmy, putting his crabby hands into his pockets, riffling through his billfold; and Jimmy tried to say, "Get away from me, you douche bag," but God had silenced him for everything he'd done that was wrong, smote his blasphemous tongue right out, and all Jimmy could do was breathe hard and shiver, and as the marink robbed Jimmy, he whispered and sang to him, as if Jimmy was his long-lost buddy. "Hey, you should be thanking your lucky stars you ain't dead, Mr. What-ever-your-name-is, 'cause you is one lucky son of a bitch, you know that? I seen where you left your other shoe, right in between the clutch and the brake pedal, so now you're like 'my son John, one shoe off an' one shoe on,' you ever hear that song? Coulda been your foot still in there. Now if you was wearing a seat belt, you'd probably be one dead Indian. I don' believe in seat belts nohow, and whooeee, you certainly like to carry around some money." He shook Jimmy, and pain flooded through him like hot, blinding light. "Maybe you ain't so lucky, you ain't lookin' so tip-top . . ."

Jimmy slipped back into the clammy darkness, into the cold hands of death, and the ambulance wobbled and jiggled.

ANOTHER HOSPITAL ROOM.

This one in the more secure and up-to-date Santa Monica Hospital, where Jimmy "would get the best care from the best doctors in the world." It was larger and whiter and cleaner than the room in Paso Robles, but there were water stains on the modern acoustical-tile ceiling. A framed print of Van Gogh's *The Gleaners* hung on the bright white wall in front of his bed, and cards and arrangements of flowers were everywhere—on the windowsills, on every shelf and bureau. There were even a few huge bouquets on the floor. Cards and flowers covered a special table that had been placed near the door. The cards might be poetry, but the flowers were rainbows, hallucinated refractions of antiseptic, fluorescent white light.

The painkiller was wearing off; although Jimmy could locate the pain, it was far away. But in an hour it would be all over him again.

He asked for a drink of water.

Marty Wrightson leaned over him. He put a straw in Jimmy's mouth, and Jimmy drank greedily. After Jimmy pulled his head back, spilling water on his chest, he asked, "What are you doin' here?"

"Taking care of you." Wrightson was fair-haired, freckled, and fine-featured, except for a flattened nose. He was wearing a white shirt with a button-down collar, jeans rolled to make cuffs, and a threadbare sweater that Jimmy had given him.

"You got that pout face on," Jimmy said. His neck was braced, his face bandaged, and both legs were in traction. He could feel the dull ache of the catheter in his groin and the chill of a saline drip in his wrist. But he was enveloped in Demerol clouds, secure, protected. He was safely on the inside looking out.

"Can't help it. That's my face. I don't got another one."

"Too bad."

"Fuck you, Charlie."

Jimmy smiled, then closed his eyes. "How come you're here?"

"I just told you, Jimmy."

"Well, I wanna know."

"You asked me to stay, so I'm staying."

"What time is it?"

"About three in the morning."

"Don't you have a home?"

"Jimmy, you want me to go?"

Jimmy tried to move his head; he could just see the cot that was set against the wall. "No, man. I don't want to be alone. I get any calls?"

"Calls? You got thousands. I guess if you were going to practically kill yourself, you couldn't've picked a better time. *Rebel Without a Cause* is a big hit. And you're a big star."

Jimmy smiled.

Marty sat down on the side of the bed, felt for Jimmy's hand, and held it. Jimmy didn't pull away, as he usually did lately. "Anyone else in here?" Jimmy asked.

"No, don't worry."

"I don't worry," Jimmy said. "I don't give a shit." But that was a lie. Jimmy stared up at the ceiling. The water stain on the tile that was exactly over his tray table was shaped like a turtle. "How's Rolf doing?"

"Man, you did get a bang on the head," Marty said. "I told you, Jimmy . . ."

"Told me what?"

"He didn't make it."

Jimmy blinked.

"Jimmy?"

"Yeah?"

"You remember me telling you that?"

"Yeah," Jimmy said, "I remember." And he watched the turtle try to crawl across the ceiling.

THREE WEEKS LATER, AND EACH DAY AND NIGHT STILL CONTAINED two seasons: hot pain and cool Demerol bliss, but the worst was coming off the drug. Jimmy had become addicted, and his night nurse—a ruddy-faced fat woman who said her name was Mary Louise but allowed Jimmy to call her Lulu—withheld Jimmy's crystal injections of bliss until he screamed for a shot. Jimmy called her a cockteaser, and she would scold him and pat his bottom. Lulu also took care of what she called "the Marty Wrightson problem"; she would allow no more sleepovers, as she was sure that Marty was a pervert homosexual and a major dope dealer who would feed Jimmy something unthinkable from the streets—smack, or marijuana, or bennies, or who knows what. At 9:00 P.M. sharp Lulu would eject his agent, friends, studio executives, Warner publicists, the odd public servant, and celebrity well-wishers hoping to be seen, and Jimmy would be left alone with night sweats and nightmares.

But the days . . . Jimmy loved the October days when he could be magnanimous, witty, patient, childlike, vulnerable, irritable, social, brave, mature, and entirely himself. He was the new star. Doctors would examine him and tell him he was doing just fine. Friends would visit and comb his hair, read him poems from the *Complete Works of James Whitcomb Riley,* and rub his forehead with ice. Nurses would give him injections for pain (the day nurses didn't try to starve him of drugs), and he would fall into blissful sleep, only to be awakened again, snapped back into the autumnal world of his hospital room.

"There's a, a kid to see you?" Marty stood beside the bed. There was no one else in the room.

"You woke me up to tell me that?" Jimmy was dressed in black checked pajamas; his hair was washed and combed and lustrous; and although he wasn't wearing a neck brace, his right arm and shoulder were in a chalk-white cast that was covered with crayon drawings and get-well wishes. Ugly red scars cut across Jimmy's cheek and under his jaw.

"I thought you might want to talk to him," Marty said.

"Why?"

"Because you're always going on about his music. He says he's Elvis Presley, and he sure is a greaser and a half. He's got a black eye and looks like he hasn't bathed for a month. He's got a girl with him, a real plain country cookie."

Jimmy shrugged, closed his eyes, and said, "Bring him in."

"And what about his girlfriend?" Wrightson asked.

"You can bring in his whole goddamn family, I don't care."

THE PHONE RANG AS MARTY WRIGHTSON OPENED THE DOOR AND stepped back into Jimmy's hospital room. Behind him, looking lost and nervous and embarrassed, was a pimply-faced boy with slicked-back dirty-blond hair and an ugly-looking shiner under his left eye. The boy was holding hands with the red-haired girl Marty had described as a country cookie, and she certainly was that, Jimmy thought. She was right off the farm, and disheveled, not pretty but wholesome. Jimmy liked her immediately, whereas Elvis Presley looked like a wimpy asshole.

Jimmy laughed right at the boy, who was looking self-consciously at his shiny, pointy-toed boots; but Jimmy saw himself, saw the same vulnerability, weakness, and fear. The country cookie was a rag doll, but Elvis, black eye and pimples and silly-ass pink shirt and bolero jacket and all, was something more. Jimmy was going to play with him and find out what he was. Maybe the kid was into bullfighting—that would be a hoot. He didn't look at all like Jimmy had pictured him. He looked greasy and edgy, and it was as if Jimmy was peering at him under a microscope because he could see every blackhead and whitehead, every pore. This kid needed a bath; he smelled bad and his neck was dirty—either that or he had one of those diseases that makes the skin look patchy, as if he was piebald or something. Jimmy took great delight in that instant of microscopic examination. He smiled at Elvis and picked up the telephone.

"Yeah," he said. He'd discovered in the hospital that responding with "yeah" put people off, made them nervous, defensive, and respectful.

"Yeah, yourself, Jimmy. Guess where I am?"

He heard giggling and splashing and then a muffled sound. "Marilyn?"

"I'm in New York. Guess who I'm with—"

More laughter and splashing, and a male voice, an angry voice, Boston bean accent, and then the phone went dead.

"Hey, Marilyn, you there?"

Jimmy laughed and hung up the phone. Who the hell was she with? Arthur Miller would be too jealous to allow Marilyn to make such a phone call. Joe DiMaggio was out of the question. Sounded like she was at the beach, but it was too cold for that shit if she was in New York. You lie, Marilyn, he said to himself, laughing again, then looking around—everyone seemed bemused. "Marilyn Monroe," he said to Elvis Presley, just to get a reaction. "You know Marilyn Monroe?"

Elvis just shook his head, and damn if the boy wasn't shaking, just like Jimmy remembered himself doing when he was young and was forced to have his picture taken. He'd be all right until the photographer said "smile," and then Jimmy's neck would suddenly stiffen, like someone was holding his head, and he'd try pulling himself loose, which would only make it worse; and that caused the twitching; he remembered his mother saying just that, "Stop twitchin', Jimmy, you'd think someone was going to set your hair on fire," and he said "Momma" out loud. Must have been the Demerol, although he wasn't taking as much of that. Must have been that he'd been up all night, thinking about what his mother had told him in his vision, trying to figure out his new life. That had to be it.

Elvis shook his head and said No sir he didn't know Marilyn Monroe except for seeing her in her films. It didn't seem as if he'd heard Jimmy say "Momma."

"Hey you," he said to Elvis, "you're a guest here, so sit down right here in the place of honor." Seeing Elvis hesitate, he shifted his legs toward a chair and said, "And your friend can sit right next to you. I promise, nobody'll get hurt. How come you came to see me?"

Elvis looked like he was in physical pain. "Something I had to do, I guess." He spoke so low Jimmy could hardly hear him.

"Since he heard about your accident, he hasn't thought of anything else," Elvis's girlfriend said, speaking up when Elvis couldn't. "He just got it into his head that he had to see you, like it was something spiritual."

Jimmy laughed at that, and Elvis, blushing, seemed to shrink as he sat in the chair. He gave his girlfriend a smolderingly angry look, but that didn't last; he was too overcome with humiliation to concentrate on anything for very long. Jimmy looked at him hard. If you looked beyond the pimples and the grease-on-grease Vaseline brilliantine cornstarch hair, this boy was shockingly handsome. It was as if he was cut out of stone—a beautiful statue with a bad complexion. Something about him attracted Jimmy. "Is that right?" Jimmy asked.

"Yes, sir, I guess it is."

"Tell me why you really came here, Elvis."

"Don't really know, sir." Elvis spoke to the floor. Then he suddenly sat up and looked at Jimmy directly, and Jimmy felt his presence, strong and hot and wild and dangerous; and he wanted to get closer to him. "I seen your films and when you was on television," Elvis continued, "and I saw that—"

"What?" Jimmy asked.

"I saw that . . . you're what I'm gonna be. But that ain't right, 'cause I'm already what I'm gonna be." He shook his head in frustration, as if words couldn't describe what he was feeling; he needed paintings or drawings or diagrams or mathematics—or music. "Like we're both made of, uh . . ." He stopped there, midsentence. He'd given up. But he was still caught up in himself, and he wasn't the humble, shaking, pimply boy who had just walked into Jimmy's hospital room; he was lit, and even if he didn't have the words, he had the presence; and anyone could see that he knew it.

Jimmy watched him intently, feeling sucked in, fascinated; and he was sure that this was right now this very moment a case of what he called synchronization. He'd fought with Eartha Kitt over his theory that everything you were, everything you know could be compressed into one incandescent point of perfect focus—the perfect connection, perfection itself. Eartha argued that life couldn't be compressed down into a single thing—it was a symphony, not a single note. But Jimmy knew that was plainly wrong. Right now was a moment—or, who knows, maybe an hour or a day—of synchronization, and as Jimmy looked into this boy's eyes, it was hot connection and focus, and the boy's eyes seemed to be asking Jimmy questions, questions that Jimmy had never thought of before; it was as if Jimmy could see shadow-figure images in those sleepy brown eyes, but he couldn't decipher them. Elvis had clown eyes, Emmett Kelly eyes, controlled and sleepy and crazy dangerous at the same time.

"How'd you get that shiner?" he asked.

"Uh, got into a fight on the way here. Happens sometimes."

"Who won?" Jimmy asked.

"I guess I did. There were two of them and one of me, and I'm still standin'."

"You're sitting," Jimmy said, but Elvis didn't react; it didn't seem like he laughed a lot.

Jimmy leaned toward him and said, "Now, be honest with me, be honest as all the days and tell me your top secret."

"I don' know what you mean," Elvis said.

"Yeah, you do. What you know that nobody else knows."

"My momma knows my secrets," Elvis said seriously, without hesitation or embarrassment.

Jimmy laughed; he was laughing for Elvis, and he said, "Tell me the secret about you your momma knows."

"I dunno." Then after a beat he said, "I talk to her."

"Yeah?"

"But it's secret. Nobody else'd figure it out."

" 'Cause you got your own language, right?" Jimmy asked, thinking of his own mother, remembering their secret words and how they used to imagine things together and playact and make up places that were perfect; even now he could see Mildred, and for an instant, he felt her warm safety, her milky smell, the coarseness of her hair.

Elvis was taken aback. He kneaded the plastic armrests of his chair as if they were soft as dough. "How'd you know about that?"

" 'Cause I know." There was a belligerent silence between them, then Jimmy said, " 'Cause I had that with my mother, too."

"Elvis, tell me why you and Mom call each other Satnin." Elvis's girlfriend had interrupted Jimmy's moment of synchronization. There was an edge of anger in her voice, perhaps because she—like Marty— was being left out. Elvis looked down at his shoes again, as if he were suddenly caught out, embarrassed. Jimmy smiled at the red-haired girl, who said, "Well, he won't tell me, maybe he'll tell you."

"It's just lard," Elvis told Jimmy. "Comes in a can. Lizzie knows what it is."

"Do you?" Jimmy asked her.

Lizzie shrugged, and Jimmy could tell that whether something had happened on the way or right here right now, this boy wasn't going to be with this girl for very long. Jimmy could sense something sullen about her, but she fooled people with her sweetness, which was all cover. She was overfreight—that was another one of Jimmy's words, which meant baggage you couldn't carry any further. Most people got that way, and there was nothing you could do but keep away from them. But this Lizzie could hurt Elvis, or had hurt him. And now Elvis was sort of wrapped up in himself, protected from her, although he probably didn't even realize it. She was jabbing at him, Jimmy thought, but she fucked it up. He was already gone.

"Satnin," Elvis said to Jimmy, who nodded. He knew what it meant—everything soft and creamy and safe and comfortable, fat, fat was good, and he remembered how his mother's cancer made her smaller and smaller and skinnier and skinnier until she was nothing more than a skeleton, and then, when she was all dried out, when all the satnin was gone out of her and only the bones were left, she died and left him.

"Tell me *your* secret," Elvis demanded, and Jimmy told him about his vision of his mother and what she told him.

"You never talked about that before," Marty said to Jimmy, his

voice sounding angry and whiney at the same time. But he might as
well have been in another room; Jimmy didn't even hear him.

Elvis nodded and said, "I talk to my brother Jesse."

"Yeah?" Jimmy said.

"He's my twin. He died when we was born. I talked to him about you."

"Yeah?"

"An' he agreed I had to see you," Elvis continued. "My momma
says I got to live for Jesse, too. It's my responsibility."

"Your momma's a wise woman," Jimmy said, and it would be difficult to tell whether he was being serious or making fun of the boy.

Elvis nodded. "I also got a sign from God directly."

"What kind of sign was that?" The flicker of a smile.

"I saw rings around the moon," Elvis mumbled. "That's a true
sign."

"So did you get what you wanted?" Jimmy asked.

Elvis shrugged. "I dunno. I guess."

"You came all the way out here from, what, Georgia?"

"Memphis."

"From Memphis, and you dunno?"

"I guess I got somethin'," Elvis said.

"Do you believe in angels?" Jimmy asked Elvis.

"Yeah. I do."

"Well, this book is about angels and visions." Jimmy picked up a
small leather-bound volume of William Blake's *Songs of Innocence and
of Experience* from the bed table and gave it to him. "It's got pictures,
too; and the poet who wrote it saw visions of angels himself." After a
beat, he asked, "You ever see angels, Elvis?"

"No, but . . ."

"C'mon, tell me. But what?"

"Well, my momma showed me how if you close your eyes and relax
your mind in the right way, you can float into heaven."

"You done that?"

"Yeah, a little."

"And what'd you see?"

Elvis shrugged.

"Angels?"

"Maybe not yet," Elvis said. A smile whispered across his face.
"But sometimes I have nightmares."

"What kind of nightmares?" Jimmy asked.

Elvis looked at Jimmy, bemused, as if he was hesitant to answer,
then said, "I dream I'm about to fight somebody or about to be in a car
wreck, or that I'm breaking things, you know what I mean?"

"Why do you think you dream those things?"

" 'Cause I'm scared, know what I mean? Real scared."

"Scared of what?"

"I don't know." Then he stood up, looking suddenly frightened, as if for the last few minutes he'd been playacting, and now he was back to being himself. He started to leave the room.

"Hey, aren't you forgetting something?" Jimmy asked; Elvis's girl-friend sat in the chair and stared at her folded hands.

The phone rang. It was Pier.

Synchronization, Jimmy thought. Everything was going to be just absolutely perfect, fucking-A peachy-keen perfect. He put his hand over the mouthpiece and asked everyone to leave.

FIVE

■

Overfreight

Jimmy wasn't ready to leave the hospital—and shouldn't

have left it—but he was determined, and he told his
agent and his managers and the suits at Warners that
he was going to drop dead in this fucking sterile
white-and-aluminum hospital room, which smells
like strontium 90 and death, or something of that
order that stinks—Jimmy didn't know or care if
strontium 90 stank—and that he wanted to be alone
to recuperate and write in his diary (even though he
didn't keep a diary . . . but he thought he *might*), and
so—surrounded by his entourage like the Sun
King—he left his get-well-card-and-flower-filled
room on North Wing 4 of the Santa Monica Hospital.
He gave an interview from his wheelchair in front of

an emergency exit, where his car waited. Abbott and Costello, which is what he called his publicists, had arranged for a Cadillac limousine that would have made Elvis Presley swoon; they had also arranged for the press to know when Jimmy was being wheeled to a "secret" back exit. But Jimmy didn't give the reporters anything. He had a favorite reporter—Caroline Tuchman—and she wasn't there. When he wanted something known, he'd filter it through her.

He sat in the backseat with Marty Wrightson and his old friend and West Coast agent, Dick Clayton. The interior smelled of leather, cigarette smoke, aftershave, and sweat, and Jimmy was stoned. He opened his window, which blew Dick's thinning hair out of place, and grinned dopily at him, daring him to object.

Dick told him to close the fucking window.

Dick had introduced him to Jane Deacy, his New York agent, and had put in a good word with Elia Kazan when Jane told him that the director was thinking of casting Jimmy as a lead in *East of Eden* last year. Dick was a failed actor—Jimmy had once told him he had the lungs but not the talent. But he was a natural as an agent; and he gained Jimmy's undying loyalty during the filming of *Eden* when he used his connections to get him Pier Angeli's unlisted phone number. Pier's bitch of a mother had it changed to keep Jimmy away from her virginal pizza-pie Catholic daughter, and *nobody* else knew that number, not even Ted Ashton, Warners' publicity man.

"You know that Jane's coming in from New York to throw a party for you?" Dick asked.

"Yeah, I got the message," Jimmy said. "But it's bullshit. She should've been here to see me when I was in the hospital. If the situation was reversed, I would've been on a plane to New York to see her ugly ass."

"She phoned you every day. She's working her heart out for you, Jimmy, and she deserves better than that."

"You mean she deserves better than me."

"Read it as you will. Now close the window. You made your point." Jimmy pressed the electric switch in the hand rest, and the window whispered shut. "Are you sorry?" Dick asked.

"Yes, Dick, I'm very sorry."

Dick smiled and nodded, and Jimmy said, "Well, go on and tell me what Jane's really coming down for. This must be good 'cause *nothing* shuts you up."

"Contract's all set but the signing," Dick said triumphantly.

"With Warners?"

"Who else?"

"I hate those assholes. They threw me out of my house, remember, and I had to go live with you."

"That wasn't your house, Jimmy. That was your dressing room, for Christ's sake, and Jack Warner was worried about insurance liability."

"Bullshit."

"You were a squatter."

"A squatter who's making Jack Asshole Warner a lot of money."

"And you're going to make him even more."

"Oh yeah?"

"We negotiated a deal that'll give you almost a million bucks for doing ten movies over the next six years. And you can accept television offers and do a Broadway play a year, your choice."

"Big whoop," Jimmy said. "The money's not enough."

Dick laughed and looked at him in disbelief. "The money's terrific."

"Not as good as what Marilyn's making."

"Better."

"You lie, Dick. That's why you're an agent and I'm an actor." Dick didn't respond to that, and Jimmy glanced over at him to see whether he should apologize. "And what about *Somebody Up There Likes Me?*" Jimmy asked.

"That's on, if you're up to it. Starts shooting in February."

"And Pier—she's my costar?"

Dick smiled. "Yeah, she's still your costar."

"Well, fuck you, Charlie. I'm famous. Ask Marty over here."

Marty Wrightson looked out the window beside him. Jimmy was stoned, but he knew that Marty was playing his game of being the tormented soul, and Jimmy would have to deal with it later. *Hell no,* he told himself. *I'm sick. I need to be by myself,* and he felt the seat swaying and rolling beneath him; for a second, or maybe a moment—time would stretch on painkillers—he had the distinct sensation that he was riding a horse, riding in slow motion at a full gallop, jumping high and long over fences, then landing ever so slowly and the saddle pushing up against his crotch ever so gently, and Cisco the Kid was all sweat and muscle between his legs, and the wind was blowing right through him.

But there was no wind. The window was shut. Jimmy jolted back. "Is Cisco okay?" he asked.

"Your horse?" Dick asked, nudging Marty.

"Yeah," Jimmy said.

"He's fine," Marty said. He was still staring out the window at the houses that seemed to have been drilled right into cliffs and hills.

"Lew Bracker's taking good care of him. We can go visit when you're feeling better."

"He's in Santa Barbara?"

"Yeah," Marty said. "Nothing's changed. You've only been in the hospital for two months or so."

"Everything's changed," Jimmy said, laughing at himself. "And what about the Billy the Kid film? I really want to do that."

"Yeah, that's in train, too," Dick said. "You start shooting in April."

Jimmy began laughing uncontrollably.

"The film, Jimmy," Dick said. "Shooting the film. Man, maybe I should take whatever happy pills you're on."

"Marty, give him one of the Percodans. You got the bottle, right?"

"Yeah," Marty said, "I got it."

"Take away your pain, Dick," Jimmy said.

"No thanks." Then after a beat, "Jane and I had to do some fancy footwork to save your Billy the Kid picture."

"What do you mean?"

"Jack Warner wanted to cast your buddy Paul Newman for the lead."

"I never heard nothing about that," Jimmy said, coming alert.

"Warner didn't think you'd be ready because of the accident."

"Yeah, and . . . ?"

"We suggested he move the picture forward, and we made it part of the deal."

Jimmy nodded. "I want to see the final script. I want to play Billy the Kid straight, historical, like he really was—none of that Gene Autry shit. I'd rather have people hiss at me than yawn."

"There'll be more than enough time for all that, Jimmy," Dick said. "Just let Jane and me take care of everything. All you have to do is rest and get better."

"If there's anything to be taken care of, I'll do it myself."

"You know, Jimmy, you haven't even been awake long enough to be famous, and you're already acting like a royal prick." Jimmy smiled and nodded, as if Dick had just given him a compliment. "Keep it up and you'll end up back in Idaho."

"It's Indiana, thank you," Jimmy said. "And when is Jane coming in?"

"I'm picking her up at the airport on Wednesday, and we're meeting with Warner on Friday, and Friday night we're throwing you a big party at the Villa Capri—that's still your favorite hangout, isn't it?"

"Yeah," Jimmy said as he gazed out the window. They were driving up Beverly Glen. *Almost home. Please God, don't let any people be there waiting.* He gazed through the window at the impossibly luminescent grass and the silvery green leaves of the spiky trees clinging to the hills that rose along the road, as if Beverly Glen was a deep valley and the hills and steep lawns on either side were high, verdant cliffs, waves of green, long and undulating; and Jimmy imagined he was riding his horse Cisco again, riding beneath the green waves of a green ocean, everything sea green and burning emerald light. "But I won't be around for the party, or whatever business you and Mom are cooking up," he said. He always called Jane Deacy "Mom."

"Where are you going?" Dick asked. Marty had turned away from the window and was staring hard at Jimmy.

"New York."

"YOU LEFT THE HOSPITAL TOO EARLY," MARTY SAID AS HE RUBBED Jimmy down with alcohol. Jimmy gazed across the room. He was lying on his mattress, which smelled mildewed and stale, and looking down from his balcony bedroom at his living room. The pills had turned everything soft and deep, and he felt comfortable and sleepy and secure. It was late afternoon, and the sunlight seeped in through old, stained tan curtains. He stared at his bullfighting cape that was hanging on the wall like a sleeping animal that would at any moment come awake, unfurl its linen wings, bare its talons, and take flight. Jimmy imagined it circling the room, looking for food, and dropping down like an eagle to take Marty in its talons.

"Get me my cape," Jimmy said.

"Why?"

"I don't know why. I just want it. I'm cold."

"It's the alcohol. You just told me you were hot. This'll help break the fever."

Jimmy shivered. "Get me the goddamn cape."

Marty climbed down the balcony ladder and got Jimmy his cape. After he covered Jimmy with it, he said, "You should've let me throw the mattress down. You shouldn't've climbed up here."

Jimmy grinned at him, remembering that he almost fell off the ladder. But that was because of the pills. He was fine, other than that. The bandages were off, he could move his fingers, and after all that physical therapy in the hospital, he was the Charles goddamn Atlas of Sherman Oaks. But he was different now. The accident and the Demerol and his vision of his mother changed what happened in his head. And he looked different, too. The doctors said that they could repair the scars on his face with plastic surgery, but he wasn't having any of that. He liked them because they were on the right side of his face and looked like dueling scars—a long, almost closed-up *X* tattooed from his temple to his earlobe. X marks the spot. Jimmy's face was crooked; nobody had figured that out, but he had looked at himself in mirrors, memorized every feature. The *X* had evened out his face, disguised its crookedness, and it was a reminder—a note, written on his face—of what his mother had told him when she rose out of her grave.

Marty touched Jimmy's forehead. "You don't have a fever. But you felt hot before."

"I told you, I needed the cape. Lord, halleluiah, it's a miracle." Marty didn't respond. "That was a joke, Joyce."

"I just can't believe you talked to Elvis Presley about your mother."

"What? What the hell brought that on?"

"You never talked about her. It was always your big secret."

"I had this . . . vision."

"And so you tell *him*?"

"So?"

"What am I, chopped meat?"

"Yeah," Jimmy said.

"Well, I've had it. I'm going. You can take care of yourself. You told your dickhead agent you're going to take care of everything, so go to it."

"Don't let the door hit you in the ass when you leave," Jimmy said.

"You're an asshole, Jimmy."

"No, you're the asshole, for staying with me." That caught Marty, and he just nodded. "What do you want to know?" Jimmy asked.

"It's not about what I want to know."

"You wanted to be told first, right?"

"Yeah . . . right."

"Because?"

"You know why."

Marty was quiet, and Jimmy knew he was waiting, so he gave up some information about his mother and his vision, elaborated, lied, worked up all the bits into a coherent whole that he liked, that he'd invent and integrate into the myth he was creating of himself, for himself. He'd tell all this to Marilyn, and see how she would react. Where was she? She hadn't called for ages. He missed her, but it was Pier, Pier, Pier, *my God I'm going to see Pier, there is a God, there is a fucking God!* And as Marty rubbed his shoulders and talked to him, Jimmy dreamed of Pier, and Marty's voice would occasionally interrupt his daydreams, and Jimmy would listen to him, Marty his closest friend, Marty the poor, lost, lonely masochist, but he'd told him, he'd told Marty that he, Jimmy, was his own man, and if Marty couldn't accept that, then he could go and hang out with the rest of the overfreight.

Jimmy was in love with Pier. She was his one true love. His sister his twin his kindred spirit. She raged with delight. She was angry and playful, fragile, curious, childlike. She was . . . Jimmy.

And it was love at first sight. It didn't matter that she'd messed up and married asshole Frank Sinatra wannabe Vic Damone. The baby was his, Jimmy's, Jimmy and Pier's, and she knew that, she knew that every minute of every day, she knew that when she was screwing that greasy bastard of a husband of hers, she knew that when she was preparing his meals and washing his dishes, but she'd called, called, and everything changed.

"So are you feeling better?"

"Yeah."

"Jimmy, I—"

"Yeah?"

"You can't talk, can you?"

"Wait a second."

"Are they all gone? Even Marty?"

"Even Marty."

"This isn't going anywhere, I shouldn't've called, I—"

"I love you."

"That's what I wanted to say."

"I think about you all the time. When I hit that car, and I thought I just bought the farm, I was thinking about you, about—"

"Jimmy, I'm sorry, but I gotta go. But I want to let you know I'm going to be in New York. If you want, if you . . . I want to see you. To talk, and . . . I don't know."

"Sure, but—"

"Gotta go."

Click. Clickclickclick, and Jimmy felt Marty's hands moving down his back, pressing, kneading, his hands open over his buttocks, then pulling himself closer, tickling him, and Jimmy rolls onto his back as he dreams about Pier while Marty goes down on him and tells him he loves him, and Jimmy intones I love you I love you, and he visualizes the lobby of the Algonquin and imagines checking in at the desk, listening to John the bellman tell the same old joke, then up the elevator to his room to wait for Pier, and Marty is sloppy and sucking him hard, and Jimmy makes a list of what he has to do to get into that elevator, into that room, and he fast-forwards his fantasy, presses himself into Pier, and as he comes a telephone number appears like smoky sky-writing across a blue-screen sky.

Marilyn's.

HE MET WITH JACK WARNER AND HIS CATAMITE LAWYERS, SIGNED the six-year contract for ten motion pictures with all due ceremony, treated Mom with the respect she deserved, attended his party at the Villa Capri after all, schmoozed with Dick Clayton and the two dozen directors, producers, and reporters "you absolutely positively have to meet," talked happily with fellow racing driver Paul Newman, and got into an ugly argument with his old flame Ursula Andress, who crashed the party, went out for some air around ten o'clock, and didn't come back.

Took the red-eye to Idlewild Airport in the wastelands of Long Island, got off, jet-lagged, sleepy, stoned, cotton-mouthed, exhausted, all a dream—he'd ridden the *Silver Challenger* through the dark heavens, first class through the vaulting stars, dreaming yearning calculating working, dreaming of shadows, shirtsleeve buzz-cut shadows following him, grasping at him, then he was jolted into cold sweaty darkness by his own snoring, by the wheels touching tarmac, by a stewardess with a pimple on her chin and widely set green eyes. Then a cab to the city and now the entire gray autumn morning streamed into his cramped, rather seedy room. Dust poured through the overpainted window of his favorite hotel: the Algonquin. The Gonk. 59 West fucking Forty-fourth Street. Where Irving Berlin, George S. Kaufman, and Dorothy Parker hung out. The Algonquin Round Table a few floors below him. He could feel the thrum of the city, which was different from the beat of L.A. New York was concentrated energy. It was pure, it was the essence, it was home, New York was home, not the cold graveyard of Fairmount, Indiana, not the leafy hills of Sherman Oaks, California, or the phony baloneys in Beverly Hills, but dirty, noisy, polluted, beautiful, dick-hard, sky-high, slate-skied Manhattan.

He'd call down for room service. No, he'd go down and have breakfast in the dining room, and that Spanish guy—he forgot his name—would wait on him and call him Meester Den and make a fuss, just as he did when Jimmy was a down-and-out nobody and would come to the hotel for dinner with Rogers Brackett, and after dinner he and Rogers would hang out in the tiny Blue Bar with the writers and playwrights. Christ, even the bartender published with Little, Brown. It would be absolutely unimpeded fucking bliss.

"I made it," he whispered to his mother, to the dust, the light, the chipped enamel of the bathroom door, which was so close that he could almost touch it from the bed, and the telephone rang, as if the omniscient spirit of his mother had dialed his very number.

"Jimmy?" It was Pier's little-girl voice, the voice that fooled everyone into thinking she was almost prepubescent, a little girl, a fragile faun.

"Yeah, hi, where are you?"

"Home."

"What do you mean, home? You're in New York, right?"

"No, Jimmy. I didn't. Go." Baby breathing, the telltale shortness of breath, as if she'd just been spanked and had just gotten over crying and having a tantrum.

"Why?"

"I can't tell you that."

"Well, I sure as hell wish you'd said something before I got on a goddamn airplane for ten goddamn hours."

"Wasn't ten hours, Jimmy. But. I'm sorry, I tried, I did everything I could, it just didn't . . . it's just impossible."

"So that's what you're telling me? It's impossible?"

She stopped her ragged breathing and said, "I love you, Jimmy. I understood how much when I heard about your crash. Do you think I . . ." She let her voice trail off.

"You've thrown everything away once. Why not now?"

"You're being cruel."

"Just fucking honest."

"Do you still want to see me?"

"Why do you think I'm sitting here in this hotel room in New York?"

"You left me alone once to go to New York and do business, remember? But you weren't doing business. You were seeing your friends." Her voice started to rise. "So you can see your faggot friends."

"This isn't my fault, Pier. I came here only to be with you. I'm sorry for whatever I ever did to you. But everything is different now. So I'm right here. What do you want to do? Fish or cut bait."

She giggled. "What does that mean?"

Jimmy smiled in spite of himself. "It means when can you get on a goddamn plane and get over here?"

"Now."

"Today?"

"Yes."

"What is this, a test?"

"Yes. Do you still want me to come?"

"Yes. I'll see some friends in the meantime." Jimmy giggled, but Pier had already hung up.

JIMMY WAITED FOR HER FOR TWO DAYS.

He sat in his room and read dog-eared paperback copies of *Auntie Mame* and *The Power of Positive Thinking*, which he found in the night-table drawer along with a Gideon's Bible. He watched the news and *I Love Lucy, Ozzie and Harriet, Mr. Peepers,* and *My Little Margie.* He listened to the radio. He ordered room service. He finished his pills. He called Marilyn, but her maid or someone answered the phone and said that no she wasn't in and no she didn't know when she'd be back and wait a minute until I can find a piece of paper and I'll take your number what was your name again?

He went out.

Fuck Pier. Fuck Marilyn. Fuck everything.

He thought he might find Marilyn at the Actors Studio, which was an easy walk from the Algonquin. The school had moved from the Malin Studios on Broadway at West Forty-sixth to 432 West Forty-fourth Street. Jimmy hadn't been to the new location, but he figured classes would be at their usual times: eleven to two, Tuesdays and Fridays. He despised Lee Strasberg, the studio's director, who had humiliated him when he did his first solo presentation, a scene Jimmy had adapted from Barnaby Conrad's novel *Matador.* He'd used only three props: Sidney Franklin's bloodstained cape, a small white statue of the Virgin Mary, and a candle. Jimmy had followed the electric pulses of his sense memory, followed his nerves through the scene, found the pain and joy of the aging matador preparing for his final bullfight. Stood in the sunbleached coliseum of death and looked straight into the eye of the bull, the eye of the sun, the eye of the demon. He let his mother come to him and pull the tears out of his eyes, and when he was finished, he sat down exhausted on the stage to listen to "the Archbishop's" critique. Strasberg stared at Jimmy through his thick-framed black glasses. He stared without warmth, without expression. Strasberg was a slight man with thin white hair and a tight, squeezed face. He wore his knit shirt buttoned right up to the neck. "What were you trying to show us? What were you trying to do with that scene? No, I don't think we could even consider your performance as a scene. An exercise, perhaps." Dissecting his motivations, demeaning his craft, accusing. "You failed to create a sense of being in an authentic place. You're not doing the work. You're acting not being . . ."

And Jimmy flung the cape over his shoulder and walked out of the studio.

He felt everyone's hot stare.

He felt the humiliation now, all over again, as he walked down Forty-fourth Street, as he passed the Iroquois Hotel, where he'd lived on and off when he could scrape up the money. But he had the money now. He had the money, and he was as famous as any of the other Actors Studio actors, as famous as Brando or Monty Clift, whom he idolized. *Eat that, Strasberg.*

It was around noon, and the weather had turned bleak gray and bitter cold. The street was clogged with lunch-hour traffic. Horns blared, people hurried toward him and away from him. The damp air smelled of soot and burnt chestnuts. Jimmy pulled up the collar of his rather shabby brown canvas coat. He felt something hot on the back of his neck, and it came to him with the power of positive paranoia that someone was following him. He ducked inside a doorway and lit a cigarette. He looked around.

Pedestrians waited to cross Seventh Avenue. Everyone was in motion, hurrying, scratching, shifting, pushing, not because they had life-or-death engagements within the hour but because the city demanded motion. The wind didn't just blow; it snaked around, cutting at you from one direction then another, as if nothing was certain. Because nothing *was* certain here where skyscrapers grew like hard-ons, streets opened up, and steam poured through grates, the hot breath of dragons consuming commuters. The city was the pressure. No laid-back-hang-out-go-with-the-flow gang-bang bullshit here. This was real. Make it here, and Hollywood was butter on toast. Jimmy had made it. He was a little god in drag, hep to all the perturbations, vibrations, oscillations, contractions, and compression, especially compression, the pressure of the people walking past him, their auras pressing against him—the ancients were right about igneous rays coming out of everyone's eyes, as if we were all suns blasting one another with hot light, and Jimmy had felt that heat on his neck before, when someone was staring at him . . . thinking about him . . . dreaming about him.

Right now Jimmy was protected by the mass of stone around the doorway. But he *knew* that someone had been watching him. He inhaled smoke and sugar, tar and cement, then walked back out into the street and stood there like a buoy in the ocean of Forty-fourth Street. He imagined that fish in suits and coats and dresses and jeans were swimming toward him, swimming away from him, and he wished he had another Percodan to cool him out, take the edge off; but he'd run out of pills. Marilyn would have something; he was sure of that; and he felt certain she'd be at the Actors Studio. Strasberg and his claw of a wife would be exhibiting her. Look who we got, students, ain't we grand? She's an actress, now don't look at them tits.

Jimmy stood in the street and scowled at everyone passing by. Someone was hiding, watching from a distance. Watching him.

Something ugly and quick crawled down his backbone: fear. Panty-waist candy-ass, momma's-boy fear. Jimmy bowed to the invisible watcher and gave him the finger, then turned and hurried to the Actors Studio. It was a dirty white building that could have once been a church. He rushed up the stone stairs, passed the empty front desk and the bathroom doors designated ROMEO and JULIET, and quietly took a seat in the back row of the lounge, where Strasberg's class was in progress. He slumped down in his chair and pulled his collar up around his neck as if to hide from the others, but he was noticed immediately, and people glanced at him as one student whispered to another, "It's James Dean." He felt the dynamics of the room change. He was changing them by cowering in his coat and looking out from the dark into the world, by bathing it with his own igneous rays.

But Marilyn wasn't there.

Strasberg was in the front row gesticulating at two actors on the stage in front of him, like a Jewish priest blessing the congregation on Yom Kippur. He was wearing his old ratty woolen jacket and a shirt buttoned to the neck in straitjacket fashion—no yarmulke and prayer shawl for the grand rabbi of Method acting.

Jimmy wanted Marilyn, and she wasn't there, and he didn't want to explain his accident and answer all the bullshit questions every reporter had asked him, and he felt too lousy to go out for a beer and listen to the gossip, and somehow he was afraid, as he had been when he was walking and sensed someone following him. It was fear, he thought; that's what was following him because he was a chickenshit skinny-ass sissy, and he could hear his father's voice instead of Strasberg's—that voice might as well have been Strasberg's—the voice that had always called him a sissy; and Strasberg might as well have been his father; and Jimmy stood up and made for the door. He could feel everyone's gaze on the back of his neck as he left, all those eyes concentrating their Flash Gordon ray-gun heat on him, burning him, frying him. He wasn't in control, even when he felt he was the magnet, the focus; it was illusion, all maya, and just as he'd read in his Golden

Mentor paperback on the Aztecs, everything was fate and you couldn't escape it.

But he didn't have to wallow in it.

HE WALKED AND DAYDREAMED, AS HE USED TO DO WHEN HE FIRST came to New York—that was four years ago to the day, and Jimmy figured it was kismet again. He had lived in the Iroquois Hotel and was so scared of New York, of being made so small by the sheer towering, squeezing, claustrophobic mass of it all, that he spent $150 of the $200 that Reverend De Weerd had given him to get him started on his acting career. He spent it on movies. He saw three, sometimes four films a day, and that's what he did now. He saw *Marty*, Clouzot's *Les Diaboliques*, and just for the hell of it, Marilyn's *Seven Year Itch*. Then again for the hell of it, he went to Fifty-second Street and Lexington and stood on the same subway grate where Marilyn did her famous billowing-dress scene that got her into trouble with the ever-jealous Joe DiMaggio.

He didn't want to call any of his friends, didn't want to explain, didn't want their cold comfort, and he didn't want Pier. Fuck her absolutely. He wandered through the midtown streets as the false mist of dusk settled into evening.

At least no one was watching Jimmy—except Jimmy. No more pressure from the poisonous igneous rays of people's eyes. No more stalker. He/she/it had disappeared, dissipated like a fart into the dirty, smeary neon air.

His face a chilly mask, his hands thrust deep in his pockets, Jimmy daydreamed. He dreamed on his feet, and it was as if he was walking through fragments of movies, but these flickerings and fluorescences were just the accumulations of memory. Ghostly and disconnected, they were weighted with nostalgia, fear, and loneliness. Overfreight.

But Jimmy couldn't get rid of them.

He remembered riding in Pastor De Weerd's silver-gray Oldsmobile convertible, driving through the Indiana countryside in autumn when the trees were burning gold and red and orange and the cool, dry air smelled like apple cider, and the pastor was talking about adventure and music and how Fairmont was narrow and limited, that there was more to life than farming and small-town gossip—there was Tchaikovsky, there were poets and philosophy, there were bullfights in Mexico; there were good things and bad things—like serving as a chaplain in the infantry during World War II and seeing innocent people murdered, like coming home a war hero with a Purple Heart, a Sil-

ver Star, and a hole in his stomach as big as Jimmy's fist. "But the more
things you experience, Jimmy, the better off you will be," and the pastor stopped the car, and the wind was a hundred invisible streamers
brushing against Jimmy's face and bare arms and sliding ruffling tickling his scalp, and the pastor asked Jimmy if he wanted to put his hand
into the wound; and Jimmy didn't, but the pastor unbuttoned his shirt,
and Jimmy did it while the pastor told him how he had been shot, and
told him that he, Jimmy, should have no fear of death because it was
all a matter of control, of mind over matter, and Jimmy had a good
mind, a keen mind, and the pastor also told him that he was vile and
depraved and had to seek salvation, which Jimmy did, in the car that
paper-dry cock-sucking sinful day . . . but the world didn't collapse.

The pastor was still a hero.

Jimmy was still full of sin and guilt because after all, if he had been
pure, his mother wouldn't have died. So what difference did anything
make?

He daydreamed himself back to the Algonquin, and the doorman
said hello, and the lobby bar to his left was plush carpet and cocktails,
filled with the after-work and pretheater crowd, with editors, publishers, blue-haired old ladies, long-legged fashion workers, dowdy
tourists speaking to be heard across the Grand Canyon, and conservatively rich businessmen in pin-striped Brooks Brothers suits and
starched, cuffed white shirts, their sprayed and polished wives or mis-
tresses or secretaries sitting beside them like swans watching for food.

"Well, if it isn't Jimmy Dean." The voice was slightly slurred, but
he recognized it immediately. It was Rogers Brackett's voice, and right
now Jimmy would rather see anyone but Rogers.

"Hey, Rog," Jimmy said, turning toward him. He felt awkward and
embarrassed, as if he had just been caught out. The tension was palpable—Jimmy wishing to break free, Rogers looking hurt and defeated, which was his way of manipulating people into giving him what
he wanted.

"You want to have a drink?" Rogers asked. "Like old times?"

"Yeah, sure," Jimmy said.

"When you had your accident, I stopped over to see you. For old
times' sake. But your flackers wouldn't let me near you."

Jimmy looked down at the carpet and mumbled, "Yeah, they
weren't letting nobody in. I was too out of it to know what was going
on . . ."

Rogers smiled, looking uncomfortable as he led Jimmy to a small
table in front of the slowly ticking grandfather clock and insisted on or-
dering drinks from an attentive, liveried waiter. As they sat, Rogers nat-

tered on with wry puns and cutting observations until he had clogged his own throat, used up every atom of small talk and generosity and humor with "Jimmy, for old times' sake, pronounce *vichyssoise*."

Jimmy cracked a smile as he looked into the amber depths of his double Scotch and said, "Swishy-swashy."

Rogers laughed so loud that a blond woman wearing a low-cut black satin evening gown and a matching cookie-box hat turned in her chair and fixed him with a significant and haughty look, before turning back to her girlfriend, who was as squat and ugly as the cookie-box woman was long and beautiful. "But no vichyssoise swishy-swashy faggots for *you* anymore," Rogers said softly. He sighed and pushed his horn-rimmed glasses tight against the bridge of his nose with his forefinger. "I was just thinking about something you said."

"Something *I* said?"

Rogers smiled and said, "My tutelage wasn't wasted on you; you've developed quite a wit. Nasty, too."

"What are you driving at?"

"How did it go, let me think . . . ah, something like 'I didn't know it was the whore who paid. I thought it was the other way 'round.' "

Jimmy felt his ears burn. "It was an asshole thing to say. When you asked me for money, I—"

"Drop it. It's all blood under the bridge, Jimmy."

"Are things going better now?" Jimmy still felt the heat of humiliation burning in his face. He just wished there was a way to stand up and get the hell out of there; he could have done that last month, but he couldn't do it now. It was as if his mother's dead hands were pressing down on his shoulders, holding him in the cushioned, upholstered chair.

"A good advertising man will always find work. And thanks to the hospitality of my friends, I get by."

Jimmy shifted around in his chair and said, "Look, Rog, there's something I've been wanting to tell you, but I don't want you doing your usual asshole thing and laughing."

Rogers watched him. "I won't do my usual asshole thing. All that was just protective coloration. You hurt people, Jimmy. Sometimes I think you don't mean to—most of the time, but sometimes, sometimes you hurt people on purpose. Why?"

"I dunno. Sometimes it's like I'm watching somebody else being me. Mostly I . . . I dunno. But I'm going to change all that." Rogers raised his eyebrows, and Jimmy burst out laughing. A nervous habit.

"You said you're going to change all what?"

"How I treat people, friends."

"You mean like, what's your pet word? Overfreight? You're going to stop treating people like they were baggage, is that it?" Rogers looked suddenly angry, as if Jimmy had humiliated him yet again, and Jimmy could see his pain and wanted to assuage it, but obviously he was only making it worse.

"Yeah" was all Jimmy could say. He couldn't tell him about his vision, or that he had changed and was sorry. He couldn't tell him anything. Rogers sat there glaring at him, hating him, and Jimmy didn't know why. Perhaps he *thought* he knew. He had screwed Rogers over, humiliated him, and now this lovely, silly, funny, brilliant man didn't love him, didn't care about him, hated him. Not hate. Rogers was aloof now, distanced; he was in the middle of the queer circle and Jimmy was out. Jimmy had wanted to be out; and now he suddenly, desperately needed Rogers to be all right, to be in love with him, to care about him; and as Jimmy looked at Rogers's face, which was as crooked as his own, he sensed, for the first time, that he, Jimmy, had been bullshitting everybody—Marilyn, Marty, himself, especially himself.

He'd conned himself.

He'd become overfreight, and as if Rogers was reading Jimmy's mind, he said, "You're working up to telling me that you've changed, and that you're oh so sorry about what you did, that you want us to be pals and let's let bygones be bygones, right? That after your accident, you saw the light."

"Fuck you, Rog."

"Well, tell me I'm wrong, Jimmy. Look me straight in the eye and tell me."

Jimmy wouldn't look at Rogers. He mumbled, "I dunno, yeah, I guess you're right. Old Rogers Brackett, why he is *always* right."

"I can see through you like glass." Rogers put his fingers to his temples in an exaggerated gesture, as if he was a spiritualist medium. "You're itchy to slide around, aren't you, Jimmy? You're lonely and upset and ready for trouble. Tell me all about it. You can always talk to me. Did your girl ditch you?"

"I don't have a girl," Jimmy said.

"Tell you what," Rogers said, leaning forward. "I'll take you to a place in the Village where all kinds of shit's happening."

"What's that?"

But Rogers just closed his eyes, as if he could shut out the past and see into the future.

SIX

■

The Little Tit of Time

It was pouring slushy rain, and the humidity was thick

and uncomfortable. Jimmy and Rogers waited under the awning of the Algonquin while the doorman, a callow-looking young man, stood on West Forty-fourth Street and tried to flag down a taxi. The cookie-box woman was also waiting for a cab. She pulled her black diamond mink coat around herself and shivered.

"It's *cold*," she said to Jimmy. Jimmy nodded. "You know, you look really, really familiar. You look like someone in the movies. *East of Eden*. Cal Trask, *are* you Cal Trask?"

Jimmy glanced at Rogers and giggled.

"You are," she said. "Can I have your autograph?"

"This probably isn't the best time," Rogers said. "Weather is rather inclement, don't you think?"

"You're in the movies, aren't you?" she said to Jimmy, ignoring Rogers. "I'm sorry, I feel like such a fool, like a gawking teenager. Please tell me your name."

"It's James Dean," Rogers said, obviously enjoying this, as was Jimmy, though he hoped he wouldn't have to share a cab with her. She was beautiful in some fly-up-your-nose way: yellow-blond hair, pale powdered skin, startling baby-blue eyes; and a face that was all line and angle, as modeled and measured as her plucked brown eyebrows. The face of an aristocrat. It was the nose—she had a long, thin, aquiline nose, and her nostrils looked like they were always dilated, as if she were smelling everyone out. She was looking down her nose at Jimmy, who wondered what she would look like naked, what she would say when she came. Would she squeak or moan or probably be silent as the grave, an ice goddess?

Jimmy felt nauseated, but it passed. Too much liquor. It was Rogers's fault; he drank like a fish. Jimmy reminded himself that he was going to make things right with Rogers, but that didn't mean he had to sleep with him. No, that would just make things worse.

"*Rebel Without a Cause,* right?" Jimmy nodded. "That doorman's getting soaked out there," she said. "I feel terrible for him. He looks like he should be home with Mommy. Probably isn't old enough to vote. Never a cab in New York when you need it, huh. But if he manages to hail one, I'd be happy to share it with you . . . and your friend." She looked down her nose at Rogers, who winked at Jimmy.

Jimmy thought it was time to tell her that they were first in line, and it probably wouldn't be a good idea to share a cab since she was probably going uptown to Tudor City or somewhere, and they were going downtown, way down, but the new Jimmy didn't say anything. He could feel himself burning, as he did when he wanted to impress people, or when he was onstage or in front of a camera. Lights . . . on. Lightbulb, turn me on, but this furred-up woman in the silly satin hat was no Marilyn. She was bony and taller than he was, and Jimmy suddenly imagined himself fucking her in a satin-and-mink-lined coffin. He laughed.

"What's funny?" she asked.

"Nothing," Jimmy said, feeling guilty, as if he'd hurt Rogers all over again.

"You said you were going to the theater," Rogers said to the cookie-box woman.

"Yes. I got stood up."

"You didn't look like you were stood up," Jimmy said. "You were sitting there with your friend."

She laughed a bit too loudly. "I met her there."

"Sure you did," Jimmy said, smiling.

"Why . . . is it so hard to believe? Pretty girls get stood up, too, you know."

"What play were you going to see?" Rogers asked.

That stopped her for a beat, but she thought it over and said, "*Damn Yankees*. With Gwen Verdon. She's a wonderful actress. Do you know her?" But she didn't wait for an answer. "Where are you two going?"

"Yeah, where are we two going?" Jimmy asked Rogers.

"To the Village," Rogers said.

"I just love Greenwich Village, and the hipsters and the bebop and jive music and all that." She looked at Jimmy. "Are you going to a club?"

Rogers said, "Yes, but I don't think it's the kind of place—"

"I love to go slumming, and I'm sure I'd be safe with you." She looked at Jimmy, who laughed. "Well, can I? Please?"

Jimmy looked at Rogers, who shrugged and said, "Sure, we'll *all* go . . . slumming."

THE ZIGZAG CAFÉ WAS ON THE NORTHWEST CORNER OF BLEECKER and MacDougal streets, south of Washington Square, which looked like a Roman ruin, pale as moonlight in the roiling fog and pounding rain. Jimmy had heard of the Zigzag but had never been inside before. It was a bohemian insiders' bar, a place to be seen, providing you were cool enough to know who was seeing you. That alone was enough to have kept Jimmy out. The novelist Chandler Brossard had called it "Gargantua's mother's bra," whatever the hell that meant, but that's what Jimmy remembered. So here he was going out queer with Rogers and this blond broad who called herself Pamela and probably spent her life on a diet, who was obviously running around on her rich stockbroker doctor lawyer husband, who kept saying things in Latin such as *"Qui nescit dissimulare nescit vivere,"* probably just to impress Jimmy, which it surely did; but when he asked her where she'd learned all that, she'd look down her nose at him and arch her back so her tiny tits stood out like apples under her satin dress. Rogers chuckled because he understood what she meant, and translated for Jimmy: *He who does not know how to dissemble does not know how to live.*

So here he was with educated, smart-assed, apple-titted Pamela and

Rogers Brackett in this Thursday-night faggot pickup joint, but it wasn't
Thursday night, it was hipster night; and here he was without Pier, empty
and alone and raging in the marijuana-smoke-choked, hot-sweaty rum-
dumb gallery bar café where the junkies, anarchists, Stalinists, poets,
painters, visionaries, cynics, intellectuals, and queers hung out. There
were wannabe actors from Judith Malina and Julian Beck's Living Theater and the tender, sensitive shrinking violets from Paul Goodman's
therapy group. There was Jackson Pollock, and Larry Rivers, maybe;
and there was James Agee, and Frank O'Hara, maybe; and maybe John
Cage and Miles Davis and Gore Vidal, maybe, maybe, maybe; everyone
who was cool and gone and groovy and with-it *had* to be in there. The
place was mobbed with chicks in tight black sweaters and goateed hep-
cats drinking martinis, which were the specialty of the house because
they were cheap and strong as ethanol; and they were drinking the
strongest thickest blackest espresso coffee in New York and wearing
thirty-one-inch pegs and dark glasses and jeans and black turtlenecks.
But the café wasn't just noisy with music and poetry and hip existen-
tialist chatter, it was pandemonium, the pandemonium of a new age.

"You're going to love this," Rogers said to Jimmy. "You'll relate to
these drug fiends. They're all just like you, all 'oh spontaneous me'
people; and they worship you; they worship your tight little ass."

Pamela giggled and Jimmy said, "They don't even know me."

"Oh, yes they do," Rogers said as he waved to a burly, darkly handsome man wearing Levi's, shit-kicker boots, and a bright red-and-
white flannel lumberjack shirt. He had swarthy skin, high cheekbones,
wild blue eyes under heavy eyebrows, a full yet tight mouth, and thick,
coarse black hair cut short around his ears. He stood up and waved
them over to his table, which was in front of a makeshift dais. Behind
the dais was a scuffed and scratched black Steinway piano, a drum set,
and an exhibition of sculptures—four muslin-wrapped crates that had
been slathered with plaster of Paris; a gilt-framed photograph of the
bohemian poet Maxwell Bodenhiem hung crookedly on the smudged
white wall.

"That's who I want you to meet," Rogers said, leading the way.

"Who?"

"Guy by the name of Kerouac. Football player turned poet. Ever
heard of him?"

"Nope," Jimmy said, threading his way around tables; Pamela held
on to his arm possessively.

"So is this *him*?" Kerouac asked Rogers.

"Could be," Rogers said, smiling. "Jimmy Dean, this is Jack
Kerouac."

Kerouac reddened, as if now that he had said hello, he'd drawn a blank; but he recovered, shook Jimmy's hand, and called to a sleek-looking, dark-haired young man wearing horn-rimmed glasses, who was sitting at Kerouac's table with a platinum-blond woman. The woman wore a white strapless bathing suit, a gold ankle bracelet, and no shoes.

"Allen, I told you Roger wasn't a bullshit artist. Remember I told you about him and how he said he knew James Dean? Well, stand your sorry ass up and meet Roger Roger and James Dean." He tilted his head toward Jimmy and asked, "James Dean, right?" as if he still wasn't certain; and Jimmy smelled the sour stench of liquor on his breath . . . and something else, too, something nasty and decayed; it was obvious that Jack Kerouac, whoever he was, was fairly happily gingered up.

The dark-haired man of about thirty stood up and enthusiastically shook Jimmy's hand. He was dressed in a charcoal-gray suit, white shirt, and tie, and said his name was Allen Ginsberg. He bowed to Pamela and shook Rogers's, hand. "Blessings, Roger. Jack told me about you."

"It's Rogers."

"Ah," Ginsberg said. "Sorry."

"Hey, Roger Roger, come and sit down with us," Kerouac said, and he nodded to Jimmy, as if they shared some special secret. "This is my 'Good Blonde.' She drove us all out from Frisco, and that's not the first drive we've had, is it, baby?" He reached for her breasts and tweaked one.

"Ouch, you crazy beautiful bastard," she said. Her hair was platinum white and frizzy from too many bleachings.

Jack pulled chairs away from other tables; Ginsberg and the Good Blonde moved their chairs to make room for Jimmy, Pamela, and Rogers. A harried, goateed waiter rushed over to the table and took their orders: martinis all around.

"When's it all going to start?" the Good Blonde asked, glancing toward the stage.

"It's early," Kerouac said. "The band has only done one set."

"We should start," Ginsberg said to Kerouac, "or we'll lose the audience."

"Nah. After the next set. Trust me."

Ginsberg shrugged, and the band—which consisted of a piano player, a drummer, and a very tall, skinny saxophonist with a waxed red mustache and goatee—came back to the stage. Jack asked the Good Blonde if she wanted to crack an inhaler. She nodded, and he smashed a Smith, Kline and French over-the-counter inhaler on the table, carefully pulled out the three-quarter-inch strip of accordion paper, and dropped it into her martini. She quickly pulled it out and swallowed it whole. "Thanks," she said.

"Jimmy, I got another one, you want it?" Kerouac asked.

"What is it?" Jimmy asked.

"Bennie. Legal. Right off the drugstore shelf. Paper's soaked with Benzedrine. Good for you. Wake you up from the sleep of reason. Well?"

"Sure," Jimmy said, as Pamela pressed her knee against his leg to let him know she wanted some, too.

Jack smashed another inhaler cylinder on the table and worried out the accordion strip, dropped the Benzedrine strip into Jimmy's martini, and swirled it around with his finger. Pamela reached for the glass and downed the martini. Jimmy picked the strip out of the empty glass and swallowed it.

After the band had finished the set, Jack stepped onto the stage, waved his arms, and shouted for attention. "Hey, you bliazasting, stoned-out, jiving motherfuckers, are you ready for some goddamn poetry that will blow you away, tear the hair right off your asses, shrink your balls, and make you come in universal bodhisattva bliss?"

The crowd shouted back at him, and he seemed to love it. He stomped back and forth across the stage in his scuffed, heel-worn cowboy boots; and as he jived the audience into pandemonium, Jimmy imagined that the Benzedrine strip he had swallowed had somehow gotten caught in his lung. He was having trouble breathing, and he could feel it curled right up inside his chest like a worm gnawing at him from the inside, glowing hot, burning, and Jimmy started coughing, and remembered how one of his caps had come loose during the fight scene with Corey Allen in *Rebel,* and how it had caught in his lung, and the doctor had to stick long pliers down his throat to remove it. And now something was lodged in there again, only it was hot and electric and alive. He felt his throat constrict as the Benzedrine took effect, felt the heat in his chest, radiating through his arms and up, up, up, into his neck, face, head, boiling, broiling his brain; and he felt the engines inside himself surging, humming, thrumming, vibrating like locomotives on cold steel track; and he was thinking faster than he could remember, his thoughts were neon-blue lines skidding before his eyes, and he heard a rushing, heard the clapping and yelling of the crowd, felt Pamela's hand on his leg, her pale spidery fingers walking toward his crotch, and he was hot and erect, and he took her hand and put it on top of his iron-bar cold-metal cock while Kerouac called the skinny saxophonist onto the stage and said, "I'm just here to warm you all up, folks, before the real killer angel poetry starts blasting, but at least I come with music, so hit it, maestro"; and the saxophonist started playing, improvising on a melody that was as unformed, unfocused, and haunting as *Gymnopédies* by Erik Satie.

"Now, what I'm going to read you isn't poetry, it's a new thing I call pomery . . ." And he went on and on, sometimes making sense, mostly not, but it didn't matter to Jimmy because every word sounded holy; every word was perfectly shaped, round, and they floated away from Kerouac, accelerating, until they were like golden Ping-Pong balls bouncing against the walls and ceiling and floor, machine-gun *rat-tat-tat* bursts of Ping-Pong poetry words, and Pamela was rubbing his crotch and sniffing the smoggy air with her wide-nostriled nose, inhaling and exhaling Kerouac's used-up Ping-Pong words; and Jimmy felt good about the words and Pamela's hand and his cock, and bad about Rogers, who didn't care about him anymore, who—just like Pier—didn't love him; and as Jimmy came in his pants under Pamela's squeezing kneading bony bread-baking hands, Kerouac blew out a raft of Ping-Pong introductions for Ginsberg, who took the podium.

Clarity. Jimmy was absolutely, lucidly conscious, aware of every sneezing and wheezing, every shifting of hips, parting of lips, every whisper and "Oh, yeah."

Ginsberg began with hesitation. "I'm going to read a new poem. It's called 'Howl (for Carl Solomon).' Carl is my friend, he's God's criminal committing holy crimes. He once told me, and this is holy writ, divine illumination, that the thing about madness is that it entails no obligations." Ginsberg looked at the audience through Coke-bottle lenses. "He said there's no need to kill people in order to prove to them that you're insane. They know it already. So this is for you, Carl Solomon, for you holy, holy, holy, holy Solomon, and for holy beautiful Peter holy Orlovsky, holy holy Kerouac, holy Blonde, holy Pamela, holy Dean, holy, holy, holy."

Pamela giggled when Ginsberg spoke her name, and Jimmy could not help but grin at him, and then Ginsberg slipped into his poem, turning into a Yom Kippur priest, a cantor, he chanted as if he were singing scat to heavy, momentous chords; he swayed back and forth, shaking, and everyone around Jimmy was caught up with his words and rhythm. It was a revival meeting with Jack stomping around the room shouting and cheering: "Go, go, go. Yeah. Correct. Blow, fuckin' blow!" and the audience shocked by long saxophone lines of illegal dangerous words that smashed the black-tie boundaries—chanted images of homo-seraphic blow jobs and Caribbean love, and then Jack, dancing Jack kneeled before Jimmy like a dark, hungover archangel. Jimmy felt exhilarated, and it was because of Kerouac, who was like a puppy sniffing around him, wagging and dipping and swaying and trying to impress and ingratiate, and yet this poet was all ego and charisma, a dark, hard-on French-Canuk who was a fire fountain of life and exuberance; and Jimmy liked this doggy bearish man who wanted so much to be liked by Jimmy—he couldn't help himself.

"You know, Jimmy, I gotta ask you something, might as well be now. You like the title *On the Road*? It's my book, my best book, it's about being beat and free and on the road, and it's going to blow everybody right out the fuckin' door."

"Yeah, sounds okay to me," Jimmy said.

"I got other titles for it. Want to hear them?"

A woman at a nearby table told Jack to shut the fuck up; Kerouac gave her the finger.

"You really think this is a good time to talk about this?" Jimmy asked.

"Perfect time," Kerouac said. "You got to do everything now, right the fuck now, or it's gone forever, dead. You got to tell me which one you like best because this book's going to change the world, man." And he recited the titles, a poem of titles. "Well?" Kerouac asked. "Which one?"

"*Souls on the Road* ain't bad," Jimmy said.

"You like that better than *On the Road*?" Kerouac sounded suddenly angry.

"Dunno. Either one would be fine."

"But *which* one?" Kerouac pulled Jimmy's face close to his.

"Shit, man, I don't fucking know," Jimmy said, snapping away from Kerouac, thinking that he was going to have to fight him, maim him, kill him over the title of some book he hadn't even read and probably would never read. He looked into Kerouac's flower-blue eyes and wanted to pluck them out and put them in his own head, see through those eyes; and he put his arms around Kerouac, pulling him close, close enough to kiss and lick and smell, and said, "Leave it *On the Road*. Problem solved."

Kerouac, his face large as a planet, beamed at him. "You see? You see? You *are* God."

"Good for me," Jimmy said, and he felt transparently, brilliantly stoned. Everything was bubbling and vibrating; and if he wanted to, if he cared to look hard enough and closely enough, he could see into the atoms that made up this entire gone scene vibrating around like Ping-Pong balls. He could see into everyone, into Jack, Pamela, Allen, himself. He could see with the clarity of God, if he wanted to. And he looked over to see how Rogers was doing, to include him, to thank him, to let him know that he was enjoying all this hugely, *thank you Rogers thank you, everything's going to be different, I promise, I won't fuck you over, never ever again.*

But Rogers wasn't there.

Jimmy panicked. First his mother left him. Then Pier. Now Rogers. He knew he was thinking crazy; but he couldn't stop himself. "Where'd Rogers go?" Jimmy asked Jack.

"Dunno. Probably taking a piss. You see him go?" he asked the Good Blonde, who shook her head and told him to shut up and listen to Allen and stop trying to be the center of the goddamn universe.

"He left a minute ago," Pamela said to Jimmy. "I'm sure he'll be right back."

Good-bye, Rogers, Jimmy thought sadly. *I'll call you, I promise I will.* And he took a pink pill that Pamela gave him, but it didn't bring him up or pull him down; and then Ginsberg was done and everyone was standing and screaming and clapping and praying and dancing, and the air smelled like a fart and Jimmy had to get out, he couldn't breathe—it was that worm curling and uncurling inside his chest— and then Jimmy was out of the café, no transition, no getting up and pushing your way out of the crowd, just one minute stoned and sitting and the next minute stoned and standing, outside, in the fog swirling, cement glistening rainy night.

Standing stone sober in the sleeting rain, but only for a moment because Pamela, efficient as a doorman in her soaking wet mink, managed to hail a taxi. "My house or yours?" she asked mischievously, as she wriggled against him in the backseat.

"Go to the Algonquin," he told the cabdriver. "You know where that is?" The driver nodded and hunched forward. He looked to be in his sixties; he was a big man, overweight and sullen.

"You don't want to come to my place?" Pamela asked.

"Don't need your whatever walking in. I don't fancy hiding on a ledge in this weather."

"Who's my whatever?"

"Your husband . . . lover . . . sugar poppa."

"Go to hell, Jimmy." And she ordered the cabdriver to take her to East Fifty-seventh Street.

"Whatever," said the cabdriver.

Jimmy and Pamela fell over each other laughing.

"Come with me to the Algonquin," Jimmy said. "We'll work it out from there."

"Okay," she said, while Jimmy brushed her shoulders with the tips of his fingers. Then he slid his hands along the material of her evening gown, pulled her forward while he unzipped the back of her gown, and snagging the spaghetti straps with his thumbs, pulled them down her thin arms, exposing her breasts. Pamela watched him with her big, curious blue eyes, then leaned back into the seat. "Well?"

"Well, what?" Jimmy asked, looking at her tiny breasts. They were apples, indeed; and in the staccato flashing of headlights and streetlights, they looked white, stark white like flour, and her nipples were large and brown, like crepe.

"You just going to expose me to everyone on Seventh Avenue?"

Jimmy pushed against her nipple with his index finger, as if pushing a button, and said, "You're the whitest woman I've ever seen. Your skin's beautiful." He rested his head on her chest, playing doctor, listening to the fast *lub-dub* flutter of her heart, and then he licked her breasts, tasting salt and sourness—sweat and perfume—and he sucked on her nipples, which were erect. "You know that in the olden days the Aztec priests used to flay the skin off the people they sacrificed, and they'd have it tanned and turned into cloaks, which they'd wear."

"And you'd like to wear me, is that it?"

"Yeah," Jimmy said. "Something like that. I always wondered what it would feel like to have tits and be able to stick your fingers in . . . there." She jerked back a bit when Jimmy slid his finger under her panties and inside her.

"You two exhibitionists or what?" asked the cabdriver.

"You a voyeur, or what?" Pamela shouted back.

"Yeah, that too, but we're almost there, unless you want to get arrested."

"You want to get arrested?" Jimmy asked Pamela.

"Yeah." She unzipped Jimmy's pants.

"If it's your choice, would you suck somebody off or get sucked off?" Jimmy asked.

"What do you think?"

"Dunno." Jimmy continued rubbing her clitoris. She was all bone, he thought, a long beautiful blond skeleton with tits.

"You're a bullshit artist, Jimmy. Everybody wants to get pleasure, no matter how loudly they protest."

"No, that ain't true," Jimmy said, pulling his hand away from her. "Some people want to give, some want to take."

"And you and I are takers, is that it?"

"No. *You're* a taker." Jimmy grinned at her. "I'm a giver."

The cab stopped in front of the Algonquin, and the young doorman who had flagged a cab earlier for them opened the door and stood gawking at Pamela—cool, unperturbed Pamela, who blinked her big eyes at him and asked him with her precise Radcliffe diction if he would kindly zip her up. Disconcerted, the doorman blinked at her. He closed his umbrella, which was straining and being pitched this way and that by the gusting wind, and obligingly zipped up her dress.

Jimmy paid the cabdriver, who, unlike the doorman, was taking everything in stride and enjoying himself hugely.

Pamela did not seem inclined to move.

"Well?" asked Jimmy.

"Well, what?"

"Uh, Mr. Dean?" asked the doorman, recovering his composure. The rain came down in sheets, soaking him, but it didn't seem to occur to him to open up his umbrella.

"I'm going to my apartment, as I told you," Pamela said to Jimmy. "Would you care to be my escort?" She smiled at him. Perfect white teeth.

"Come on," Jimmy said. "We're already here. I'll buy you break-fast."

"And go down on me, right?"

"Right."

"Mr. Dean, I have a message for you," the doorman insisted nervously, as he talked past Pamela.

But it was too late because a very angry and wet Pier Angeli was standing right behind him. She told the doorman to get out of her way, in Italian. Then she threw herself into the cab, her knees hitting the edge of the backseat, her left elbow striking Pamela hard in the chest as she went for Jimmy. She would have scratched the flesh off his face, if he had not reflexively blocked her with his arms. She tore his shirt, broke her nails, and drew blood. She screamed at him in Italian, and then, seemingly, brought herself under control. She pulled herself out of the cab and focused on Pamela. *"Puttàna!"* she said, and spat at her.

Pamela wiped at her face, as if she had been sprayed with acid, and screamed, "Get the fuck away from me!" She threw herself backward into Jimmy's lap and kicked at Pier, catching her in the shoulder with a high heel. Pier slammed the door against Pamela and shouted, "Jimmy, *chi è quella puttàna?*" She laughed, then ran toward the sidewalk. Jimmy didn't understand but could guess what she said.

Pamela recovered and told the cabdriver, "Please get me the fuck out of here."

The cabdriver said, "Okay, lady, it looks like we're done here." He grinned at Jimmy and said, "You comin' or goin'?"

"Just get me the hell away from here," Pamela said, and she turned to Jimmy.

"I'll have to explain another time," he said to Pamela as he opened the door a crack and waited for a break in the traffic.

He had to reach Pier quickly and explain.

"Yeah, yeah, you bastard, you do that," Pamela said. "You can find me in the phone book. Just look up Pamela, Number One New York. Ta-ta."

Jimmy jumped out of the cab and chased after Pier, who was practically running down Forty-fourth Street. He caught up with her at Seventh Avenue, where she had to wait for the light to change. Her hair was plastered against her face. Her black skirt and white angora sweater seemed too large for her; they were wringing wet.

"Pier . . ."

"Bastardo," she mumbled, out of breath.

Jimmy took her by the arm, but she pulled away from him violently. The traffic light turned green, and she ran to the opposite curb, knocking down an elderly man walking a small mottled black-and-white Skye terrier.

"Oh, my God, I'm sorry," Pier said, as she helped the man up. "I'm so sorry . . ." His umbrella had been blown away into the street, and his dog was barking and snapping at her.

Wiping mud from his wet overcoat and straightening the brim of his hat, the man said, "You should slow down, miss. You're going to kill somebody running like that. Are you all right? Don't you have a coat? Now, there, there, stop crying."

Jimmy retrieved the man's umbrella. Mindful of the old man, Pier held on to his arm and turned away from Jimmy.

"I'm all right now, miss," the old man said. "Really, I am." He had a thin, tired-looking face, but his eyes were alive, intense. He took his umbrella from Jimmy. "Thank you, sir."

Jimmy nodded, then said, "Pier, we got to talk, and you can't stay out here in the cold and rain without a coat."

"That's what *I* told her."

"Go away," she said fiercely to Jimmy. "Go away."

"You heard the lady," the old man said, alert and wary. "I'll shout for a policeman if you try anything smart. I will—"

"Pier—"

"Everything is fine," Pier said to the old man. "Honest. And I'm so very sorry I knocked you down."

"Are you sure you'll be all right alone with *him*?"

"I'll be fine."

The old man looked sourly at Jimmy, shook his head, popped open his umbrella, and called to his dog, "Come on, Senator."

As soon as the old man left, Pier rushed off again.

Jimmy quick-stepped along beside her, begging and pleading and explaining until she slowed down to a walk, but he couldn't tell whether she had slowed down because of his exhortations or exhaustion. She was trembling, shivering in the cold and wet, and he draped his canvas coat over her shoulders. She pulled the coat around her and continued walking. She didn't respond to any of his questions, didn't acknowledge his presence. She was cold and dead to him, and he felt as if he would slip into blind panic; she was so close to him, right there breathing moving beside him, torturing him. He was going to lose her again. She was here and gone simultaneously. He'd fucked it up again, again, dammit . . . but it was her fault, her goddamn fault.

Jimmy felt a hot flush of anger, the worm glowing in his chest again. The drugs waking up . . . "I don't know what else I can say. I explained how everything happened." The grandfather clock in the lobby of the Algonquin ticking inside his head. Two ticks, three ticks, four ticks, five. "You said you'd be here two days ago, and you didn't come. You didn't call. You didn't answer your phone. What the hell was that, huh? What the goddamn hell was that? You just fuck me around and around, and I'm so stupid, I fall for it every goddamn time. Well, why don't you just go back to your—" Jimmy caught himself. She'd go right back to that wop bastard if he told her to. Then he giggled.

"What's so funny?" Pier asked, her voice broken, her breath short, as if she was a little girl who'd been crying so hard that now she couldn't catch her breath.

"Well, she talks."

"Fuck you, Jimmy Byron Dean, you son-of-a-bitch bastard. Leave me alone. Go away, you whore. You whore!"

"I was thinking about the old man you knocked down."

"You think that was *funny?*" she asked. "You are a terrible man, Jimmy. That's why I am finished with you."

"I was thinking about what he called his dog. Senator. Don't you think that's funny?"

"No. Go away, leave me alone."

"Where are you going?"

"Away from you."

"You're going to catch pneumonia."

"I don't care. I hope I do. I hope I die."

"Why didn't you call me?"

"I couldn't, I couldn't, I couldn't. My mother found out I was leaving. She called my husband and told him I was unfaithful. She beat me, and he beat me, and I'm not going back, not even for my baby, and you, you, you didn't lose any time before you found a slut to—"

"Pier, I explained. I was . . . I don't know." He lowered his voice. "You should have called."

"How could I call you when I was being beaten, answer me that?"

"Okay, but Pier, you've got to believe me, I've changed."

"No, you haven't. I gave up everything for you, and you . . . you . . ."

"I promise you . . ."

She shook her head, and Jimmy put his arm around her. "You have no right," she said, weeping.

"What can I do to make it better?"

After a moment she said, "Tell me something you haven't told anyone else before."

He turned her around, and as they walked back to the Algonquin, he told her about his vision.

"I'd bet my ass that everybody in Los Angeles knows that story by now," Pier said. "It's true, isn't it? Isn't it?"

"Maybe only everyone in Sherman Oaks." He grinned at her, but she wasn't having any of it.

"Tell me something that's not bullshit right now, or you'll never see me again."

"What I told you wasn't bullshit. It's important that you know about it."

"It's not enough," she said as they approached the Algonquin. The rain had stopped; the street was black glass reflecting silver.

"Well, what do you want me to do?"

"I want you to give up everything for me, like I gave up everything for you."

"Okay," Jimmy said.

"Okay, what?"

"Okay."

"Do you mean it?" Pier asked.

He looked at her, his head lowered, the bull glaring at the matador.

"Then you have to prove it."

"Can we go inside?" Jimmy asked. They stood under the hotel awning. "I'll buy you a drink."

"And a hamburger," Pier said. "But first you have to do what I say."

"Okay."

"Give me your address book."

"I don't have an address book."

"Liar!" she said, anger burning in her face. "Yes you do."

"I have . . . this." And he pulled out a small, dog-eared, cardboard-covered spiral notebook, which contained his thoughts, doodles, poems, addresses, and phone numbers. She snatched it out of his hand and started to tear the pages out. "What are you doing?" he shouted, grabbing for the notebook.

"It's the notebook or me," Pier said, looking small and fragile and determined in his canvas coat. "Which is it?"

"You're fucking crazy," Jimmy said, as she tore out all the pages and threw them into the wet street.

"Now give me your wallet. Give me your fucking wallet or get yourself another girl. You can call your bleach-blond *puttàna* back. I'm sure she'll fuck you for a quarter. Oh, my, Jimmy, did I tear up her address and throw it away? Oh, silly me." She was goading him on, and it would be only a matter of minutes, seconds before he slapped her, and then she would be gone, irretrievably out of his life. She would slip into the slippery mirror streets and disappear, only to reappear like Alice on the silver screen, ten feet high and looking down at Jimmy gloating . . . *you've lost me, you've lost me, you've lost me.*

Jimmy gave her his wallet—and she was crazy because she threw out every slip of paper, tore up his driver's license and registration, took out the ten- and twenty-dollar bills, and threw the wallet into the street.

Then she handed a twenty to a bum.

"Are you done now?" Jimmy asked. "Is there anything else you want?"

She nodded, grinning shyly. "Buy me a hamburger . . . and fuck my brains out."

Jimmy laughed and took her inside, into the lobby; but by then Pier was weeping uncontrollably, as if she had suddenly, unaccountably lost something precious.

SEVEN

■

Somebody Up There Likes Me

Los Angeles: March–April 1956

Back in L.A., in Sherman Oaks, but not for long . . . not
for long.

Jimmy had the money now—he was *hot*—and he
could live wherever he pleased; his plan was to move
right out of L.A., away from the scabrous glitz, away
from the pink palaces of Beverly Hills and the leafy elevated suburbs crammed with Jags and Lamborghinis
and pretty little cafés where everybody sits to be seen.
He wanted out of L.A., and out of New York, too. New
York, which had always been his spiritual home, the
place where he could ghost around freely, invisibly,
where his friends were *real*, even New York had become sour and grotty and leaden and claustrophobic.
A reflection of his own pain. He longed for his Aunt

Ortense and Uncle Marcus and their forty-acre farm in Fairmont, Indiana. He longed to play basketball with the guys on Sunday in the barn and smell ozone and hay in the leafy clean air before a storm. He wanted one of Aunt Ortense's meat loaf dinners. He wanted the high ceilings and vast spaces of childhood where everything was pure and bright and focused. He wanted his mother to sit beside him and read him stories and applaud when he pretended to be Mike Fink, boatman on the Mississippi, or Captain Stormalong, who used his magic sword to dig out the Panama Canal. *Playact with me, Momma. You say, "See the pretty waterfall," and I say, "Yes, I see it, I see it,"* and the thin, wavery ghost of Mildred stares through oceans of darkness and death and distance at him, and disappears as the world crashes around him, knocking, shattering, splintering.

"Stop it!" Jimmy shouted. He was lying on his mattress on the second-floor alcove of his house. The mattress was damp and smelled of his perspiration. Jimmy was dirty, greasy-haired, and cottonmouthed from pills and alcohol. "Go 'way!"

But the knocking became more insistent.

"You're going to break the goddamn door down!"

"Then open it, Jimmy, or I will break it, swear to God."

Jimmy recognized Marty Wrightson's voice.

"Go away, or I'll call the cops."

"I live here, too."

"Bull*shit* you do!" Jimmy shouted. "*I* live here. So fuck off and stop bothering me." He pulled his brown army blanket over himself, as if that would protect him, as if he could shrink the world into the damp smell of wool and sweat and cigarettes. But he didn't cover his face. He was claustrophobic and afraid of the dark, afraid of being buried.

More knocking. Shouting.

Jimmy climbed down the alcove ladder and unlocked the front door. It was a blindingly bright day, and he had to turn his head away from the light.

"Jesus, you're a total mess," Marty said as he stepped into the house. "I knew something bad was going to happen. I told you, didn't I? Well, didn't I?"

Jimmy just stared at Marty with his bull stare—head lowered, eyes gazing up at him.

Marty moved around the living room, picking up clothes and magazines and newspapers that were scattered everywhere. When Jimmy was stoned on prescription Percodan, he would throw sheets of newsprint from the balcony, one by one, and watch them drift and float like great flat birds. "There's major stuff you need to deal with. I don't care how fucked up you are, unless you want your career to go right down the tubes."

"Ah, so now you're my business manager," Jimmy said. He had always imagined himself walking the razor edge of a cliff, balancing perfectly, staying straight and pure and alive while others fell.

Marty stopped cleaning and faced him, as if he intuitively knew Jimmy was ready to listen. "Do you know how many times your agents have called you?"

"I don't give a shit."

"Well, you'd better start giving a shit," Marty said, "because Jack Warner's suing you and canceling your contract. And that's not the half of it."

Jimmy nodded and then said in a low voice, "I can't do *Somebody Up There Likes Me*. The deal was that I'd do *Somebody Up There Likes Me* when I was recovered. I ain't recovered."

"It's almost April," Marty said. "You were supposed to be *finished* with *Somebody Up There Likes Me* and starting the Billy the Kidd picture next month. You've hung everybody up."

"Yeah, poor Pier," Jimmy said.

"You insisted that you could work with her," Marty said. "You *demanded* that she get the part."

"Well, I can't work with her," Jimmy said, miserable. "I thought I could, but I can't."

"Because of this last thing with her in New York?"

"Yeah, because of that."

"She couldn't help what happened."

Jimmy came to attention. "How do you know if she could help anything or not?"

"Because she called me and told me," Marty said.

"What'd she tell you, that she loves her dago husband? Did Pier tell you that her scumbag mother and Dago Vic came right to my room at the Algonquin? I thought they were goddamn room service or something and answered the door naked." He chuckled. "That gave the old lady quite a fit. And they brought the baby. Can you believe that? They brought the fucking baby? I'm standing there with my balls hanging down, Pier's in the bed hiding under the covers like she's scared of the bogeyman, the baby's screaming . . ."

"She told me something about it," Marty said.

"And you know what I did? You know what I did when they begged Pier to go with them, and when Vic did his my-little-pussycat routine about the baby and how much he loved her? I didn't do shit. I just stood there like an asshole, naked. And do you know what he did?" Marty just looked at him, blinking. "He talked her into going with him, right there, with me standing right there. It was like I was frozen. I should have broken his head, I should have"—he paused, and Marty sat down beside him on the sofa. "That's not like me . . . not to do a goddamn thing, just to fucking stand there like a coward. And Pier left with them. I figured that if she could do that, then . . . she wasn't worth it, that's what I was thinking, and as soon as she left, I knew I'd blown it. I tried calling her, but I might just as well have tried to walk into the White House to see the goddamn president."

"All you have to do is make yourself available for your motion picture," Marty said. "You'll see her every day." He looked defeated, his shoulders rolled slightly forward, which belied the bitterness in his voice. Jimmy was *supposed* to be in love with him, at least a little bit.

"I *can't* do that. I can't face her now. Do you know what it took for me to try to call her? How much shit I had to swallow to just do that? And she couldn't be bothered to answer, to give me *something*. So I'm not giving her anything."

"You think you're hurting *her?*" Marty asked in disbelief. "She's going to be in the movie, no matter what."

"Good for her."

"And the movie is going into production next month."

"Good for it."

"And they're signing on Paul Newman to take your place."

Jimmy winced. It seemed that Paul dogged him everywhere. They had been fellow members of the Actors Studio; they looked enough alike that Elia Kazan wanted Newman to play his twin in *East of Eden*; they competed on the racetrack and in the studios. Paul was older. Jimmy was faster. But one stumble . . .

"Jimmy, you hearing me?" Marty asked.

"Yeah, I'm not deaf, dumb, and blind. Well, maybe I am. Did they sign with Paul yet?"

"Dunno. I'd have to ask your agent. You want me to call him?"

"Yeah, I guess."

ON THE SET OF *SOMEBODY UP THERE LIKES ME* JIMMY SWALLOWED his pride one last time and asked, "Why didn't you stay with me?"

Pier stood timidly before him, innocent in a white, lacy frock and little-girl makeup, and smiled. Her face was guileless and cruel. Perhaps she imagined that the cameras were still running.

Her gloating smile broke him out of his drug-laced depression; the memory burned angrily in his mind's eye, flickering yet constant, another loop of celluloid as real as the rushed, staccato-cut motion picture Robert Wise was directing.

Thank you, Pier.

JIMMY WAS DRUNK AND STONED, TO KEEP THE PAIN FROM THE ACcident at bay. "Yeah."

There was a sniffle at the other end of the phone line.

"Yeah?" Jimmy said impatiently.

"It's me, Marilyn." Almost a whisper, yet characteristically breathy.

"Well, big whoop," Jimmy said. "It's about time. Do you know how many times I've tried to call you? And how many times your cunt of a housekeeper, or assistant or whatever the hell she is, told me that you weren't there? Or *'Miss Monroe isn't taking calls'* in that sniveling up-your-nose voice of hers?"

"I'm sorry," she said, and then she started crying, wailing over the phone, taking deep wheezing breaths and choking, as though she was vomiting out emotional bile, and she started talking, running everything together, "I can't do it, I can't, I can't work like this. Oh, Jimmy, Jimmy, I can't do it . . . that stupid stupid bastard Don Murray, he says, he says I did the scene vulgarly, vulgar, he can't stand women, none of them can, they're afraid, the whole fucking stupid gang of them. Vulgar. Supposed to rip off my tail, this thing that sticks out of my—my costume in the back, and he needs to do it angrily, he needs to be mocking me, so I can react, instead he just lifts the tail away, and I didn't even know he did it, and I said, 'Rip it off, be rough with me so I can make it real and react,' but he's too afraid to act nasty because the audience might not approve, and, and the director, Joshua Logan, he sides with the others against me, you know what I mean?" She sounded out of breath. "I'm no trained actor, I can't pretend I'm doing something if I'm not. It's got to be real, I can't do it if it's not real, and he calls me vulgar because I told him that. They hate me, Jimmy. Jimmy, I can't do it anymore. They fucking hate me. Got to get out of here. Got to—" Then silence. Jimmy couldn't even hear her breathing into the phone.

"Marilyn? You there?"

After a beat, "Yes," and then she started again. "Jimmy, I can't fight them alone, I can't, I can't, I don't want this. I hate it. I want to— I can't fight it all by myself, and Arthur, he's not here, and I don't know about him, either. I don't know about anything or anybody. Even you. Good-bye, Jimmy. I shouldn't have called you, I, I—"

"Hold on," Jimmy said, sitting up on his mattress, his legs pulled against his chest as he felt around for a cigarette. "Don't hang up, I'm sorry I yelled at you. I miss you, that's all. I need you. Really. I do."

"I need you, too." A feathery voice. "You sound drunk. Or are you just sleepy?"

Jimmy laughed and said, "A little of both probably. What time is it?"

"I don't know. Not late. You're usually up all night."

"I've been going to bed early," Jimmy said. "You probably heard I'm working on the Rocky Graziano picture. With Pier, that hard-faced bitch. Everything's been so fucked up . . ."

"For me, too," Marilyn said. "Jimmy, you got to help me. I don't know who else to turn to."

"What about Arthur?"

"Poppa's in—"

"Poppa?"

"Sorry," Marilyn said, sniffling. "That's what I call him."

"Pretty weird."

"You want to listen or what? You're like all the rest, you can't stand women either, you can't listen to anyone but you, you—"

"Marilyn, I'm sorry. Calm down. I love you. I'm listening."

"Sorry."

"Go on."

"Arthur's in Reno."

"Nevada?"

"Yeah, he has to stay there six weeks and establish residency. For his divorce. That's why I can call you. Arthur's jealous of you. In some ways he's worse than Joe about everything."

"What do you mean?"

"Arthur doesn't want me to call you. He . . . wouldn't let me. He thinks it's bad for me, bad for our relationship."

"It's good for *our* relationship."

"You know what I mean," Marilyn said.

"Why should it be bad? Is he worried we're fucking?"

"Yeah, I guess." She giggled. "I'm worried we're not."

"Now you're starting to sound like your old self," Jimmy said. "But I can't believe that—"

"He thinks you make me too wild, and he says I'm too dependent on you."

"You're marrying Joe DiMaggio all over again."

"No, Arthur's different, Jimmy. He's . . ."

"What."

"He's smart, he shows me things, explains things, and he's a great writer."

"That doesn't mean you have to marry him."

"I know. I'm afraid of him, he's so full of anger sometimes, and then sometimes he's so gentle that I can't stand myself. But when he gets angry, he . . . you know, like Joe."

"You mean he hits you?" Jimmy asked.

Marilyn didn't answer, and Jimmy wondered if she was telling Arthur the same story about him. *"Jimmy hits me, Poppa. He gets so angry. But he can be so gentle that I can't stand myself."*

"I never hit you."

"You would never do that. Would you?"

"You think I would?"

"No." Then after a beat, "Jimmy?"

"Yeah?"

"You want to go out? I need you to hold me and talk to me and help me figure everything out." Jimmy lit another cigarette and had a coughing fit. He felt dizzy. "I can pick you up," Marilyn said.

"No, I'll pick you up. Where are you?"

"The Château Marmont. I'm living in the Jean Harlow suite."

"Big whoop."

Marilyn giggled, then sounded desperate. "Please don't make me wait. I can't stand waiting. I can't stand it here."

"I'll be right there."

"Promise?"

"Yes, just relax."

"Okay. And Jimmy?"

"Yeah?"

"I may not want to fool around because of Arthur. You know? Would that be okay?" That said in a small voice, whispery, hesitant.

"Fine. Whatever you want to do we'll do." And Jimmy felt suddenly relieved, almost happy, and the numbness of the pills receded to a tiny place in his chest. His head cleared, his headache dissolved, and he felt as if a cold, needle-sharp wind was passing through him, invigorating him, filling him with power, and he could feel the heat of the igneous ray-gun beams that poured out of his eyes into the darkness as he looked for his clothes and imagined Pier's dead shape beside him, under his sweaty blanket.

JIMMY PICKED MARILYN UP IN FRONT OF HER HOTEL IN *LITTLE BAStard II*, his new cloudy-day, silver-gray, flat-four Porsche Spyder.

Jimmy had cleaned and polished it with Blue Coral wax until it shined like Chinese lacquer; the convertible top was down, and the red leather boot cover was stretched tightly over it.

"Wasn't this car totaled in the accident?" Marilyn asked, looking surprised. She ran her hand over the smooth curve of the fender, studying it. "They really did a good job fixing it up, didn't they?"

"This isn't the same car, you dumbbell."

"Oh." She looked hard at Jimmy, said, "Don't you *ever* call me dumb," and then she smiled *Hello, Jimmy Dean, you're the most important person in the world and the only one I want to be with right now this very moment, and I love you, only you, you forever.*

She fumbled with the door. Jimmy leaned over and opened it for her, and then she was all over him, kissing pinching feeling him up, and, still out of breath, telling him that the whole world was fucked, completely fucked, but that was all right because they were going to drive right the hell out of it.

Showing off, he gunned the engine and drove straight for an attendant in a striped jacket, who jumped out of the way. Marilyn giggled. She wore a huge, floppy hat, a stained apricot-colored sweater that was several sizes too large for her, dark glasses, and no makeup. She was in disguise. Magic, she had once told him. She disappeared when she was in disguise. Nobody could see her, except those she made herself visible to. But a gust of wind caught her hat, and it sailed back toward the hotel. "Jimmy!" she cried.

Jimmy backed up, and the attendant picked up Marilyn's hat and handed it to her. "I'm going to file a report on that, sir," he said to Jimmy.

"Oh, it was my fault," Marilyn said. "I dropped something, and my friend leaned over to catch it, and, whoosh, the car went out of control. We could have *all* been killed, isn't that right, Jimmy?"

Jimmy nodded and said, "Sorry about that. I'll try not to hit you the next time," and once again Jimmy laid rubber. He drove down Sunset. The dashboard lights glowed like red neon, hazy in the humid night air, and Marilyn shouted for joy as she held her floppy hat to her head, but it was flapping like a trapped bird.

"Let it go!" Jimmy shouted, and she did; and Jimmy drove too fast, and Marilyn loved it.

"Jimmy, I need to talk." The city was soft lights, out of focus, the humidity occulting everything. "Take me to Santa Monica. I want to walk out on the pier. I want cotton candy. I want to ride the merry-go-round. I want to ride the pink horse." She squirmed against Jimmy, who took deep breaths, as if he had just this minute gotten over pneumonia and could breathe again. "Fuck me on the pink horse, Jimmy."

"I thought you told me you didn't want to fool around."

"I guess I just forgot for a second," she said, looking properly contrite.

"You and me, we should get married," Jimmy said. "Then we wouldn't be so fucked up."

She laughed, then stared at Jimmy, as if memorizing his face, as if this was going to be the last time she would ever see him. "No, Jimmy. Then we'd get all stuck, and you'd tell me you don't like this and you don't like that, and you'd fart in bed and leave the bathroom door open, like that."

"I do that already."

"No you *don't*." She paused. "Do you really want to marry me?"

"Yeah."

"No you *don't*."

They drove the rest of the way without speaking, without touching. Jimmy felt calm, at peace, lost in his own thoughts. The wind pulled Marilyn's overbleached hair loose and felt its way under her sweater, ballooning it a bit. She closed her eyes and leaned her head back.

Jimmy parked near the Santa Monica pier, and as they walked out along the boardwalk Marilyn said, "I'm starving."

"I'll buy you a hot dog."

"No, I'll buy you chili at Chasen's. That's what I want. The most expensive fucking chili in the world. And hot, I want it hot. I can afford it, I'm a president now." Jimmy giggled. "Well, I am. I'm president of Marilyn Monroe Productions. Beat that."

"Can't."

"You probably could. It don't mean shit. I can't do what I want, anyway.

"What do you want?" Jimmy asked.

"To act, to be an actor, without everybody being against me. *Bus Stop* is supposed to be *my* film. I'm the star. I should be able to have a say in everything, but you know what that little asshole Don Murray did? He went to the director and told him that he was walking unless I apologized to him. And Joshua Logan told me I had to do it, or the picture was going to fall apart. It's already falling apart. And nobody likes me, I hear them talking, I . . ."

"Go on," Jimmy said softly.

"I tried to apologize to Don."

"Why should you have to apologize to *him?* All you did is tell him you have a different take on the scene."

"I slapped him across the face with the tail of my costume after he pulled it off."

Jimmy laughed. "You didn't tell me you *hit* him."

"Don thought the tail should come off accidentally, which was all wrong. Completely wrong. There's supposed to be sexual tension between us. Heavy-duty. That's what makes it all work. I just did what the character would do. That's what I'm *supposed* to do." She shook her head and looked out at the ocean. Reflected light coruscated along its dark surface. The pier was crowded and noisy. "You should have seen the look on his face when I slapped him. Surprised the shit out of him, believe you me, and it was the first honest emotion he put into the whole motion picture."

"They kept it?"

Marilyn nodded. "He still doesn't get it. Nobody does. Maybe I'm all wrong . . . no, I'm not. I know that role. I *know* Cherie." And she suddenly became Cherie, the blowsy, second-rate torch singer from the Ozarks. She spoke the dialogue flawlessly, walked like a whore fancied up for the opera, became sad and funny and absolutely real, as real as Marilyn, and Jimmy could almost believe that she had done something to change the planes of her face.

"Every day I'm trying to *be* the character instead of 'indicating,' which is what everybody else thinks you're supposed to be doing," Marilyn continued, reverting back to her own character. "And everybody hates me 'cause I'm not being nice—the crew, the grips, the electricians, they all hate me now, but Jimmy, it takes every bit of concentration I've got to do it right, to get into the character."

"You just did it pretty good."

"You know what I mean," she said, frustration evident in her voice. "It's like I'm alone out there, and if I look at anybody else, like the crew, or anybody, then I get all flat and stale, and I lose everything." She turned to him. "Don't make a crack, Jimmy, I warn you."

They were at the end of the pier, and they walked back along the other side; the murmuring of so many voices sounded like the ocean, wave upon wave of white noise broken by *"Get away from there, you!"* *"Hey, wait for me!"* *"Cotton candy, get it here!"* *"Lenny, Lenny, don't you dare touch me."* *"Candice, haven't you eaten enough junk for one day?"* *"And then she—would you believe, she told her—"* The distant tintinnabulation of the merry-go-round, the creaking and shaking of the boardwalk, and the smells: salt air, ripe garbage, barbecued meat, taffy, buttered corn.

"And then when Poppa, uh, Arthur sneaks into town to see me, and then after he leaves, I . . . I can't get back to being Cherie. Everybody thinks I'm stupid because I forget my lines." She shook her head angrily. "It's not the lines. I know the lines. I just forget how to get back into Cherie."

"It's your company, your picture," Jimmy said. "You do whatever works for you. Fuck the director . . . and everybody else."

"No." Her eyes narrowed and she grinned at Jimmy. "I promised Arthur I wouldn't."

"Well, maybe he'll make an exception for me."

"Of course he would," Marilyn said, suddenly suffused with merriment. "You're not a director."

"Well, I'm going to be," he said earnestly.

MARILYN DIDN'T WANT A HOT DOG OR COTTON CANDY; NOR DID she want to ride on her pink horse. She really wanted to go to Chasen's in Beverly Hills.

"Everybody's going to be gossiping about us now," Marilyn said as they drove. "And you know what else?"

"What?" Jimmy asked.

"You know what they're going to think?"

"Who?"

"Everybody. They're going to think we just got done screwing."

"Why would they think that?"

"Because of the way I'm dressed. I never go out like this. It looks like we just got out of bed."

"Then why are we going?" Jimmy asked.

"To show this whole goddamn place that nobody owns me."

"Why would you care what anybody thinks?" Jimmy asked.

"I don't."

Jimmy laughed. "Well . . ."

"Just fuck off, Jimmy. It's because men are bastards."

Jimmy drove in silence. He sensed that Marilyn was just barely under control, that there was more she had to tell him.

"Jimmy?"

"Yeah."

"I don't mean you when I talk about all this shit."

"What about Arthur?" Jimmy asked, probing.

"I love him, but he's no different than Joe. And all those bastards on the set, that's work, they use everybody." Jimmy nodded. "But it's that prick . . ."

Jimmy waited, then asked, "Who?"

"Remember when I called you at the hospital?"

"No."

"I called and asked you to guess who I was with, but you were too busy being an asshole, so I hung up."

"Nice way to treat a sick person."

She didn't giggle. Maybe she didn't get it, Jimmy thought.

"Well, he's an important person, and he treated me like everybody else does. Except you."

"What'd he do?"

"The bastard stood me up, probably for some bimbo. Then he had his brother call me. To apologize. I told him to get fucked, too." Jimmy could barely hear her; the wind muted everything. He leaned closer. "You want to know who it was, Jimmy?"

"No."

Marilyn threw her arms around him. "I love you, Jimmy." After a beat she said, "Nobody's going to humiliate me ever again." She pulled away from Jimmy just as he slowed down on Beverly Boulevard. He stopped in front of Chasen's striped green awning. "Jimmy, did you mean it, about marrying me?" Marilyn asked.

"Yeah."

"No you didn't, but you know what? I'd rather marry you than Poppa. Or John Kennedy. Or—"

"Who?"

"They're all fuckers, Jimmy. Every single goddamn one of them. Let's get married."

"Now?" Jimmy asked, grinning mischievously at her.

"After we eat chili. I never get married on an empty stomach."

MARILYN LIED. SHE HAD NO INTENTION OF LOOKING SLOVENLY when she made her entrance with Jimmy. She ran her fingers through her hair, pulled her sweater down to reveal cleavage, which she augmented by rubbing rouge between her breasts; and she applied three different shades of color to her lips. As she entered the restaurant, she became herself—glowing, shining, radiating love and sexuality and need. She took up all the oxygen in the room, and Jimmy felt small and pimply and insecure.

"You, too," Marilyn said to him, and Jimmy laughed and turned it on.

The maitre d' led them to a small room reserved for special guests. The atmosphere was dark and smoky. The walls were covered with heavy wood paneling; the booths were red leather. The guests were here to see and be seen.

The waiter appeared to take their orders. He looked to be in his seventies. His thin white hair was greased back on his skull like a helmet; his face was square and jowly and ruined, yet you could tell that once he had probably been strikingly handsome. "Would you care for a drink, madam? May I suggest Pepe's specialty of the house, the Flame of Love cocktail?" He glanced at Jimmy.

Marilyn beamed at him and said, "Sure, I'll try anything. Jimmy, you want to try one?"

"Sure. What the hell."

"And I want your special chili," Marilyn continued. "I'm starved, please don't make me wait. Jimmy, what about you?"

The waiter turned to Jimmy and said, "May I suggest the hobo steak and fries, sir?"

"Okay," Jimmy said, "but I want the steak well done, nothing pink in the middle."

"Yessir." He scowled, then turned to Marilyn and asked, "And may I suggest the cheese toast as an appetizer?"

But Marilyn didn't seem to hear him. She looked past him, across the room, then stared down at her menu as if what she couldn't see couldn't hurt her, as if she could hide herself completely in the leather and parchment.

"Yeah, fine," Jimmy said, dismissing the waiter, who bowed and whispered away. Jimmy *knew* he was mocking him, but he was concerned with Marilyn. "You okay? What's the matter?" Then, after a beat, "Marilyn?"

She was trembling. She looked up at him. "I saw someone."

Jimmy turned in his seat, then turned back to Marilyn. "Who? I don't see anyone."

"That fat prick Budd Schaap. He's a private detective. He works for Joe, who is so goddamn jealous that he has to . . ."

"What?" Marilyn just shook her head. "Well, come on, we'll get out of here. I can lose the simple son of a bitch, or make him wish he never followed you. Then I'll buy you a grade-A Uncle Sam special hot dog. It won't be as good as Nathan's in Coney Island, but what the hell. Come on." Jimmy stood up, but Marilyn drew back from him. Feeling awkward, as if everyone in the room was watching him, he sat back down.

"I'm going to stay right here and eat my chili," she said, as though she had carefully considered one of life's important decisions. "Nobody's going to push me around. Not even"—she looked up and jerked backward—"oh . . ."

Jimmy turned around to see Joe DiMaggio and Frank Sinatra followed by a short, tubby man who somehow looked oddly familiar. They walked toward Marilyn and Jimmy as if they were raiding the restaurant.

"What the hell do you think you're doing?" DiMaggio shouted. "Just what kind of a wh— person are you?" He stopped himself from saying *whore,* but what he had started to say was unmistakable; it came out as a whooshing sigh. The room was suddenly dead quiet. No background hum and thrum of conversation. No coughing. No clatter of silverware.

"This is a free country," Marilyn said in a quavery voice, "and I can go anywhere I want. I can do anything I want, and nobody, nobody can stop me."

"No, you can't go around hurting people," DiMaggio said. His long face was tight with anger, and his cheeks and neck were red, as though he was simultaneously angry and embarrassed. He wore an expensive and conservatively cut brown suit, a white shirt with French cuffs, and a thin tie that seemed to be knotted too tightly. He was sleek and pressed and furious, and he stepped toward Marilyn. "Because I won't let you."

Jimmy stood up and glared at DiMaggio. *Come ahead, you wop bastard.*

"Are you going to humiliate me again?" Marilyn asked DiMaggio. DiMaggio stepped away from Jimmy and shook his great head. "Are you going to follow me home and kick in my door, like you did that poor old lady's?"

"That was a mistake," DiMaggio said.

"You should all be ashamed of yourselves," Marilyn said, glaring at Sinatra. Then she turned to the heavyset detective, who wore what looked like a newly pressed five-dollar suit; his brush cut only accentuated his broad, jowly face. "And *you* shouldn't be allowed to have a license."

"Son of a *bitch,*" Jimmy said, suddenly realizing where he had seen the detective before. "Hey, you," he said to Schaap. "You were following me in New York, weren't you? Weren't you!" He said to Marilyn, "I remember him."

"Well?" Marilyn asked DiMaggio.

DiMaggio was blushing and said, "He's . . . garbage. You can do better than *this*"—he glared at Jimmy, then turned back to Marilyn—"and that faggot playwright."

Marilyn stood up and said, "Come on, Jimmy, we're leaving," but Joe grabbed her.

"Please, we've got to talk. I'll explain."

"Let go of me!"

"I just want to talk to you for five minutes," DiMaggio pleaded. "I promise, that's all. Come outside with me, and I promise, I promise I'll make everything all right." He looked like he was in agony, beyond humiliation. "Please, honey . . ."

"Joe, you've got to stop all this," Marilyn said, sobbing. "You've got to stop hurting yourself. It's all over now."

"No, it's not, honey. I'm taking you home, everything's going to be fine, I promise."

Jimmy reached out to break DiMaggio's hold on Marilyn's arm. "You heard what the lady said. She's not going anywhere with you."

"Mind your own business, you sick little repulsive faggot."

"No, Jimmy!" Marilyn cried. "It's all right, don't—"

Jimmy swung at DiMaggio, and Sinatra stepped between them. Jimmy caught Sinatra square on the jaw. Sinatra fell backward, upsetting a table as people scrambled to get out of the way.

"Goddammit, Jimmy!" Marilyn shouted. "Goddamn you." She looked at Sinatra and DiMaggio, who had let go of her and stepped backward in surprise. "Goddamn all of you, every one of you, you're all the same!" And she ran out of the room. It was as if Jimmy had hit her instead of Sinatra. "You're all the same!"

PART TWO

1957–1962

EIGHT

■

Improvisations

"What are you looking at, Jimmy?" Gossip columnist

Hedda Hopper worried a pearl compact out of her little handbag and quickly swept the mirror around her face. Her powdered flesh was wrinkled and ruined, especially around her mouth and under her eyes, as if she were being punished for having seen and spoken too much. Her dyed red hair was pulled back into a neat coif, a platform for her flower garden of a hat. Yellow carnations and red tulips seemed to be growing right out of her head. "Well?" After a beat she said, "You've dragged me out to this"—she gazed at the counter where a group of young hopefuls were openly staring at her—"dive, instead of accepting my hospitality."

"You asked *me*, remember?" Jimmy said, his smile ameliorating his sharp tone. "I'm not comfortable in Beverly Hills." He leaned toward her, elbows resting on the table. "And would you really want me in your house? I might fart and stain your couch or something."

She chuckled. "You're such a shit, Jimmy."

"Yeah, you see, that's what I mean." Her laughter broke the tension he always felt with her. Hedda was a gorgon, perhaps the most powerful person in Hollywood. A bad word from her could ruin a career. Although Jimmy didn't like her, he had judiciously made her his confidante and let her peek and peer into his life. "Anyway," Jimmy continued, "Googie's is a good place for you to hang out. Look at all the wannabe actors staring at us. You could just pick one out at random and make his career."

"Why would I pick a he? I could pick that pretty little thing in the flowered dress there and make *her* career." Hedda smiled at a young woman sitting at the counter, who smiled back and blushed. "She's the only one who doesn't look like a bum who needs a haircut and a good hot bath."

"Then make her career."

"Maybe when I'm finished with yours. I think you owe me one for what I'm going to say about your acting in *Somebody Up There Likes Me. Somebody* must like you." She smiled smugly and glanced out the window. Jimmy knew she was checking on her car parked outside the diner; it was a huge black-and-blue Rolls-Royce designed to stop traffic and turn heads, which it did.

"You want to know why I was staring at you?" Jimmy asked.

"Why?"

"Because I was looking at the girl in your face."

"What?"

"The girl in your face. The one who was in all the silent films. The chorus girl. The heartbreaker. I've seen pictures of you. I think I'm in love."

She laughed nervously, loudly. "You won't find that girl in my face anymore. She left years ago and left this old lady who eats little boys like *you* for breakfast."

"I might like that."

"Watch yourself. Don't start any of your dirty-shirttail business with me. I still haven't forgotten the first time I saw you."

"Yeah, and I haven't forgotten what you wrote in that column of yours. You called me one of those dirty-shirttail actors from New York. You really seem to have a thing for dirty shirttails."

"I can easily write another article in that same tone."

"No, I apologize, huzzah, huzzah."

"That's better," she said. Another dirty shirttail came to the table to take their orders. Jimmy suggested the banana cream pie and coffee, which was what he was having.

"I just don't want to crawl around and be kissy-kissy," Jimmy said. "I don't want a good review for being a nice little fuck."

"Watch your mouth. At least give me a modicum of respect."

"I want it for being a good actor."

Hedda blew through her teeth and nodded.

"Well?"

"That's good," Hedda said. "Can I use it, or do you want it off the record? Remember, I told you I'd like to be your friend."

Jimmy nodded.

"Well, that still stands." After an uncomfortable pause, she said, "Anything you want to tell me?"

"I just won an Oscar for Best Actor in *Giant.*"

She laughed. "Yes, I seem to have noted that in one of my columns. But it's too bad you didn't have the common decency to accept it in person. Why on earth did you have Nick Ray accept for you?"

"Nick and I are forming our own production company, like Marilyn did."

Hedda nodded. "You mean Deanray?" She smiled gloatingly. "You'll read about it soon enough in my column." The waiter brought coffee and pie. She told him that she hadn't ordered pie but laid her fork on top of it protectively.

"So why bother interrogating me and playing these little mind games?" Jimmy asked.

"Because I wanted to see you. Because, God knows why, I care what happens to you. And I'm interested in how all this is going to affect your acting career."

"All what?"

"This business about directing with Nick Ray. Who ever heard of having two directors?"

"How do you think *Rebel Without a Cause* got made? Only thing was that I didn't get a director credit."

"And Nick Ray was just standing around admiring his fingernails."

"You know what I mean."

"I understand you're supposed to be doing a film about Billy the Kid for Fox, and Nick Ray is directing."

"Is that a trick question?" Jimmy asked.

She didn't give anything away, just stirred her coffee with a teaspoon and waited.

"I'll have a directing credit, but Nick needs it more than me, and this is off the record."

Hedda nodded, still stirring her coffee. "I've also heard a rumor that Paul Newman is doing the Billy the Kid film, and Gore Vidal is writing the script."

Jimmy felt pressure inside his chest, and his face was suddenly hot. Maybe something had fucked up the deal. That's what Hedda was telling him. He'd better talk to Nick again . . . and to Dick and Jane, his agents. "No, the deal's all set, just like I told you."

"And what's this about you and Nick also making a film for Warners about Jesse James with that greasy-haired crooner, Elvis Presley?"

"He's not exactly a crooner, and the deal isn't exactly set."

"Whatever—"

"I'm directing. That's what I really want to do. I want to be a great director."

"So you keep telling me."

"Don't you think I can do it?"

"Yes, I think you can," Hedda said. "But I don't think it's smart to compete against yourself."

"How will I be doing that?"

"You want to make a picture about Billy the Kid and another one about Jesse James both at the same time?"

"I'm directing the Jesse James picture," Jimmy said. "I'm not acting in it. Elvis is going to be the star. And the pictures won't be coming out at the same time. Anyway, everybody loves westerns."

"You *are* too acting in the Jesse James film."

"No, I'm not."

"Talk to Nick Ray again. If Buddy Adler's producing, he's going to insist that you play some kind of part. Mark my words. Not especially good for you to have a lesser role than that gyrating upstart. You'll build his career at the expense of your own."

"That's not going to happen."

"You need to have a heart-to-heart with Nick Ray. Don't let him lead you down the merry path."

"He wouldn't, and I wouldn't let him."

"And I'll bet you dollars to doughnuts that Adler brings his film out against your Warner picture."

"Wouldn't make sense."

"Not about sense. It's about ego and pride."

"Probably wouldn't matter anyway," Jimmy said.

Hedda watched him like an old cat. "Probably wouldn't."

Jimmy shook his head. "This *is* all off the record, right?"

"All off the record, Jimmy."

"I'll sure as hell talk to Nick."

Hedda nodded and ate the last of her banana cream pie. Without looking at Jimmy, she asked, "How's Marilyn?"

"As far as I know she's all right," Jimmy said.

"I heard a rumor that she overdosed on pills again. Did you hear about that?"

"No," Jimmy said, lying. "I thought she was happy with Arthur Miller."

"Well, I heard that she was calling for you all the while they were taking her to the hospital."

Jimmy *hadn't* heard that.

All he could do was stare down at the table and wonder why Marilyn had refused to take any of his calls. He imagined that the igneous rays streaming out of his eyes were burning two holes in the Formica tabletop.

NICK RAY INSISTED THAT THEY DRIVE ACROSS THE COUNTRY IN THE blue-and-gray Mercedes 300 SL he had bought with his bonus from *Rebel Without a Cause*. It was a gull-wing two-seater, noisy and uncomfortable, and tricky on fast curves. It was fast and sleek and beautiful, and as dangerous as any of the platinum-haired Parisian dancers Nick favored at the Lido. The interior smelled like a humidor because he had a secret passion for good Cubana cigars, and the cabin wasn't well ventilated.

"You've got to learn to appreciate a good cigar," Nick said authoritatively. He had curly gray hair, a lean, muscular body, and a long, handsome Norwegian face. Usually he spoke slowly and softly, as if every word and every subject had to be given equal weight, but since they had "escaped the lash of L.A.," as he put it, everything seemed to excite him and take his attention. He drove recklessly, relentlessly— the 2,996-cc straight six-cylinder engine whining loudly, the speedometer needle wriggling back and forth between ninety and ninety-five—and happily lost his cool. They won three thousand dollars at the Sands in Las Vegas, lost it at the Dunes, and then drove to Reno, the lucky town, the biggest little glitter town on earth, to win back twelve hundred of their three thousand. Gas money, and they drove all night, and blinked through the day, then drove again all night. They could afford to stay in any one of a thousand no-tell motels, or expensive hotel suites in any middling hay-brick town, but Nick craved the rattle and darkness and soul-mate smoky friendship of being on the road, and Jimmy understood; he loved it.

Driving was like dreaming, and the headlights were your eyes all lit up and pure. Jimmy ticked off the towns, as if he and Nick and the smooth breathing rattle groaning Mercedes coupe were one big clock chiming midnight. They ghosted through mountain and desert and prairie, all flattened out by the night, the heater breathing a blanket of hot engine breath over Jimmy and Nick, who were going to make a hundred motion pictures, drive away from their lives, dance in the desert, sleep with a thousand whores, discuss theater and jazz and life, get drunk and sober and share and dissect and understand their pasts. They were going to share a thousand more memories, drink a thousand more drinks, smoke a thousand cigars, and divine their future. And they were going to drive to Memphis, Tennessee, to meet Elvis Presley and talk his fat carny manager, Colonel Thomas A. Parker, into a deal.

"SO I'M DIRECTING *THE TRUE STORY OF JESSE JAMES*, RIGHT?" JIMMY asked.

"Christ, man, how many times are you going to ask me that?" Nick Ray hit the brakes hard and didn't clutch properly, which almost stalled the engine. He swore at the driver of a shiny red customized Nash who had cut in front of him. The driver gave him the finger and turned onto South Fourth Street.

They'd gotten lost in Memphis and found themselves on Beale Street, of all places, the blues heart of the South. It was six o'clock in the morning and pissing rain, but Beale was still alive with the night, with streetwalkers and pimps and winos, men wearing Panama hats and high-water pants too far up their waists, with black beauties in elegant satiny dresses rushing for shelter and cool-cat survivors still zipped up and slick and shiny, even now in the lumpy-clay morning light. The day workers with umbrellas looked tired and beaten: the barbers and bootblacks, the bellboys and chauffeurs and elevator operators, the maids and department-store clerks. But the cement shined with oiled rainbows, and Nick told Jimmy to open his window, such as it was, and listen to the music, for the street had a beat. Musicians were still jamming, unwilling to give up to the opaque gray onslaught of the day.

Nick parked the car. People gawked at it, hesitated, before rushing away. He snipped off the end off a cigar with a little plastic-slide box cutter, offered the cigar to Jimmy, who refused, then lit it and blew the smoke toward the window. "We got any of that Jack Daniels left?"

"Nope," Jimmy said, watching two men arguing in the street.

"I'm done, man, back on the wagon."

"What the hell are you talking about, Nick?"

"The booze. I'm done. Over." He smiled at Jimmy, then turned away.

The rain had stopped, and everything seemed slightly out of focus. Everyone and everything had been swallowed into the thin, gauzy morning haze.

"What about the cigars? You going to get rid of them now or what?" Jimmy asked.

"You mean cold turkey?"

"You said you were going on the wagon."

"Okay, there they go." Nick dropped his cigars into the wet street. "Happy? You owe me big."

"I don't owe you shit."

"Now tell me about Marilyn," Nick said.

"How many times are you going to ask me that? There's nothing to tell."

"You're in love with her, man, it's plain as your face."

"I'm still in love with . . . Pier," Jimmy said, almost in a whisper, reverently, as if he was disclosing his secret to a priest.

"Yeah? Maybe so, but you're running a game on yourself about Marilyn."

"What do you mean?"

"Just what I said. You're bullshitting yourself. You're in love with her."

"No, it's not the same. I don't get jealous of her. I don't have to be with her all the time. It's nothing like it was with Pier."

"Whatever you say, Jimmy." Nick started the engine. "Close the doors, we're going to Graceland. Elvis's new place. A mansion. Check the map. It's on the floor on your side." Nick picked through his wallet and read from the torn top of an envelope. "Three-seven-six-four South Bellevue Boulevard."

Jimmy found the map and peered into it; his eyes were bad, and not even his thick, black-framed glasses could resolve the small print. "He's got a mansion?"

"Elvis is hot, man, and being on the *Ed Sullivan Show* didn't hurt him," Nick said. "I've been trying to tell you. Christ, even starched-up, broom-up-his-ass Sullivan thinks he's 'thoroughly all right.' " Nick laughed at that. "Big money, that boy, and he's just beginning."

"Why don't we find a hotel and crash out for a few hours? Too early to go visiting."

"No, I want to get there. He'll be awake, he's a good hometown country boy, and they're all up at five."

"When are we supposed to be meeting him?" Jimmy asked.

"Tomorrow at noon for lunch with him and his family and the Colonel, but that doesn't matter. Trust me, Jimmy, better to follow your instincts and improvise; that's what we're going to have to do with the Colonel, improvise."

Nick drove through the morning rush-hour traffic, and Jimmy found station WDIA, which was playing "Hound Dog." "What the hell does he mean, 'crahkin' all the time'?"

"I think it's 'barkin' all the time,' " Nick said.

"That boy mumbles. Mumbled when he came to see me at the hospital."

Nick laughed. "And you don't, right?"

"No, I fucking don't."

"You're no help at all," Nick said, pulling over to the curb and taking the map from Jimmy. He nodded at it, as if the map could speak, then nosed back into the traffic. "We don't have a lot of time."

"What do you mean? We've got time. You figured it all out, or was that bullshit, too?"

"I figured everything out, but things change."

"Like what?"

Nick wasn't ready to answer that.

"You wanted to go on this trip, remember? I told you we'd be cutting it close, that I've got other projects scheduled. I haven't even called my agent to find out what was happening with that war picture, the one Brando was interested in doing, so it's between him and me, and since I've been up my own ass for the past few weeks, you *know* who'll get the part."

"He got it," Nick said. "It was a done deal."

"What do you mean?"

"Just what I said."

"How do you know Brando got it?" Jimmy asked, a hint of petulance in his voice; he was ready to give way to anger. Nick had done *something*; he was fucking with his head.

"I talked to Dick Clayton. He told me in confidence."

"Yeah, I'll bet he did."

"But he got you something better."

"What's that?" Jimmy asked.

"*Cat on a Hot Tin Roof,* from the Tennessee Williams play."

"Why is that something better?"

"Trust me, it is. Dick Brooks is directing, and he wrote the screenplay. He's very good."

"Well, I'm glad you think so. And I'm really glad that Dick thought enough to tell me about what he was planning."

"Couldn't talk to you, remember? We were traveling."

"Fuck you, man, just fuck you. You got no right to screw with my career. When did you talk to Dick, anyway?"

"Yesterday, when we crashed out at that bedbug motel. And a week ago before that."

"Why didn't you tell me before? Why did you do that behind my back?" Jimmy was talking softly now. Coldly. "Tell me right now or I'll rip the goddamn steering wheel off the column."

"I was protecting you."

"From what? You?"

"From the bullshit. I wanted you focused on *our* projects. We disappeared the world so we could get our psychology right. Hell, we worked out the knots for four motion pictures, didn't we? We plotted out the Mexican road-race picture. We decided what we're going to do with the story we're buying from the teacher in Arizona . . . man, that's the perfect vehicle for you. We worked out how we're going to do the Jesse James picture as a ballad and leave the Billy the Kid picture like you wanted it. Now we've got more than plans; we've got substance."

"You are so full of shit," Jimmy said. "So why is it that the world gets disappeared for me, but you get to make phone calls?"

"You could have called your agent any time you wanted to, Jimmy."

"The deal was that we wouldn't make any phone calls, remember? That was *your* rule."

"I guess it was. I apologize."

"So why are you telling me all this shit now?"

"Because the vacation's over, man. Shift in focus."

"Yeah? Why?"

"Because I also spoke to the Colonel, and he told me that Elvis got his induction notice for the army."

"So we're screwed."

"No, we just have to push things up a little," Nick said, "which is what we're doing." After a beat he asked, "Am I forgiven?"

"No."

"You should show respect to your elders."

"Well, you got one thing right: you're old."

"Well, am I forgiven?"

Nick waited for Jimmy to start laughing.

NINE

■

Looking into Heaven

The eighteen-room Georgian mansion was slightly pink in
the rain-greasy morning light; the Tishomingo lime-
stone façade glistened, and the Corinthian columns of
the portico were the color of the mist. The house was
wreathed with ancient oaks and surrounded by thir-
teen acres of lush, rolling meadows. Everything was
painted, smeared, limned with transparent light. It had
the flat immanence of a dream, and Jimmy wondered
if he was indeed dreaming it all up.

Seven A.M. and the high filigreed gate was closed
to the dozens of hard-core fans who slouched against
the wrought-iron gates, crouched on their haunches in
the wet, puddled driveway, and stood like dime-store
Indians staring at the house, waiting for a revelation or

a visitation from the god within. The ghostly children turned and stared when Jimmy and Nick pulled up in the mud-streaked, gull-winged Merc.

"You really think this is a good idea?" Jimmy asked.

"Come on," Nick said, giving a push, and the doors sighed open.

"I'll wait in the car."

"Come on, it's not raining."

"You really think I want Elvis's fans crawling all over me?"

"Oh, my, aren't we infatuated with ourselves."

The fans watched Nick as he rang the bell, and they turned to Jimmy, finally recognizing him. Teenage girls rushed toward the car; Jimmy pulled the doors down, awkwardly maneuvered himself into the driver's seat, and started the engine.

"Hey, who are you?" Tapping on the windshield. Smeary hand-prints. Girls in tight blouses and jeans, girls in skirts, girls showing him cleavage, girls in sneakers and knee socks, teased hair and pony-tails, all teasing, all children, milky adolescents, pimply, vivacious, heart-shaped mouths willing, eyes wide, blinking, all because he was a lightbulb, a ten-foot-tall image on the tatty screens of village theaters and three-month drive-ins; and there were the boys, Elvis look-alikes with hair slicked back into D.A.'s, but without scars, without *james-deans*—that was what *Life* magazine called the self-inflicted scars.

"Are you really James Dean?"

"You *are!*"

"Hey, everybody, look! It's James Dean! Look, he has the scars and everything!" And a tall, gangly boy standing beside Nick Ray asked him if that was true, is that really James Dean? and who are you, man? and, man, James Dean was really cool in *Rebel*. But when Elvis himself came out of the house and walked over to the gate with two boys in their late teens or perhaps early twenties, everyone rushed toward him. Elvis's fans pushed and pressed against the wrought-iron rails as if they could somehow slip through them or push them down flat upon the grass. One of the boys flanking Elvis was burly, with a helmet of coarse, greasy black hair, which he'd styled into an elephant-trunk wave; the other boy was clean-cut, freckled, with a shock of curly red hair. They were both dressed in black, their shirts buttoned to the neck, their engineer boots cleated and scuffed. But Elvis, and no one else, was the lightbulb here. Elvis smiled at Nick and told him to come in. Then he waved to Jimmy and distracted the crowd by signing auto-graphs and talking to them as if they were his long-lost relatives while the other boys opened the gates.

Nick stepped into the yard, and the boys, who barred anyone else from slipping through, motioned Jimmy to drive in. Jimmy parked in the circular driveway beside a white Cadillac and two Lincolns; one of the Lincolns, a wine-colored Premiere with a white top, had smashed windows, torn trim, and names and numbers scrawled all over the body and windshield with lipstick. Even the whitewall tires were covered with names and numbers.

Elvis stepped over to Jimmy and said, "Yeah, we're going to have that fixed." He shrugged, gazing at the graffitoed Lincoln. "Happens all the time." From Elvis's stance, feet apart, hands in his pockets, and the way he gazed at the car with his head down, one would think that he was mirroring Jimmy, as if, right now, he was acting, and had James Dean down pat. Jimmy noticed that he looked different. His nose was different. His face was smooth, the pockmarks lathed away. He was also dressed smartly in a red cashmere sweater, black pants that were only slightly pegged, and maroon penny loafers. But he still had a strong, musty odor.

Elvis looked nervously at the ground, then raised his head to Jimmy, giving him back Jimmy's own bullfighter stare. "You look like you seen a ghost, man. Do I have a booger on my face or something?"

Jimmy smiled at Elvis, radiating him, examining him, but Elvis looked him right in the eye, and Elvis's eyes seemed to reflect Jimmy's questions back at him, mocking him; and Jimmy felt a surge of adrenaline and anger, and he shook his head. "No, you ain't got a booger on your face. It just looks . . ."

Elvis blushed and looked down at the ground again. "Yeah, I had all that fixed. When I was a kid, I had pimples real bad, you know, the kind that don't come to a head, they just get hard and look ugly. I used to cut them with a razor and squeeze—" He laughed and said, "I'm sorry, you ain't interested in talking about pimples. I'm just so happy to see you that . . . that I don't know what I'm saying, I—I— I, see, there I go again. Man, I ain't stuttered since I don't know when." He laughed, as did the two boys standing near Elvis and Jimmy.

"You still stutter, Elvis," said the red-haired boy, who upon closer inspection looked older than Elvis. He was muscular and had the kind of jovial, baby-fat face that would be the same when he was thirty. "You just get so excited you don't realize it. Like every time you meet a new broad."

The boys laughed and Elvis cut them dead. "Watch your mouth. This is James Dean." He spoke in a soft drawl, and he still looked at Jimmy tentatively, as if he wasn't sure of himself, as if he would suddenly, hopelessly, revert to being the dirty, pimply, and frightened urchin that visited Jimmy in the hospital.

"What do you mean, you got everything fixed?" Jimmy asked, ignoring the others.

"I had my nose fixed up and my face scraped in the hospital. I have this doctor, and he can make you look like anybody you want. I mean it. I could have told him to make me look just like you, Mr. Dean, and he could've done it."

"Mr. Dean?" Jimmy laughed. "You're a big star now, man. We're equals. You can call me Jimmy."

Elvis blushed and nodded. "I got my teeth fixed up, too, and so did these guys, they went with me. And, uh, Jimmy and Mr. Ray, this here is Lips"—he introduced the burly, dark-haired boy—"and this is Baby." The red-haired boy shook Nick and Jimmy's hands and grinned, showing off perfectly even, whitened teeth.

"You guys have quite the names," Nick said.

"Yeah, they all got their own history to them, too," Elvis said. "Lips got his name way back when we were all living together in the projects 'cause his middle name is Lipton." Elvis separated the name into "Lip-ton."

"That's right, Mr. Dean," Lips said, bowing. "Thomas Lipton Ditmar at your service."

"And you're quite the baby," Jimmy said to Elvis's smiling red-haired friend.

"That's what everybody says, but don't let my handsome face fool you, actor boy. I'm the meanest goddamn motherfucker you ever did see." That said in a honey drawl. Again, he smiled affably at Jimmy; it was a likable smile—a dental hygienist's dream—and a likable face. Only the eyes were a bit narrowed.

"You use the Lord's name in vain again, Baby, and your ass is out of here," Elvis said. "I mean it, you slip one more time, and you're gone. You got that? You got it?" Elvis leaned toward Baby as he talked. "I got family in this house, and that's the only thing I asked of you, and you, too." He turned to Lips, as if both boys had committed the same unforgivable offense.

Baby and Lips nodded. "Sorry, boss."

"Elvis, you come back in this house right now!" shouted Elvis's mother, Gladys. She stood in a housedress in the mansion's large front doorway. "You're going to catch your death of cold standing out there in all that rain, and what's going on out there anyway? Who's there with you? Are you all right?" Jimmy could hear the anxiety in her voice.

"No, Momma, everything's better than fine," Elvis said. "You just go on back into the house. I'll be right in, I promise. I got a surprise for you."

She stared at Nick and Jimmy and the sports car. "You come back inside right now, Elvis."

"Don't worry, Momma. It's not raining, but I'm coming right in. Now go on in, or *you'll* be getting a death of cold." She made a face like a scolded child and went back into the house.

"I'm sorry about that, Mr. Dean," Elvis said, "but Momma worries herself sick over me. You can't imagine. When I come back home from a tour, she's a nervous wreck. You'd think I was risking my life every night."

"You are," Baby said. Then to Jimmy, "You ever see the crowds at his concerts?"

"No, can't say that I have." Jimmy was prepared to stare Baby down for that "actor boy" crack, but now Baby was dancing around him, just trying to please.

"Well, if it wasn't for the police holding them back," Baby continued, "they'd tear Elvis apart, pull out all his hair, rip off his clothes, gouge out—"

"Okay, Baby," Elvis said. "They get the picture. Enough."

Baby grinned, and Jimmy said, "I told Nick we were coming here too early. Now we've got you into trouble."

"No, no, Momma will be excited to meet you and Mr. Ray."

"Is the Colonel here?" Nick asked, stepping into the circle.

"Yes, sir," Elvis said. "He's always a day early when he's gonna do business. He told me that's the way he works."

"So he's here, at the house?"

"Yes, sir, he's stayin' right here with us. Him being here keeps these boys in order, I can tell you that." He smiled at Baby and Lips, who, as if on cue, took out plastic water pistols and started shooting at him. The fans outside shouted and egged them on.

Elvis jumped away, laughing. "Mind you, if the Colonel saw you acting like that in front of these people, he'd have your ass."

"Which one?" Lips asked. "His or mine?"

"All of our asses." Elvis looked shyly at Jimmy, as if embarrassed. He was polite to Nick, but it was obvious that he was in awe of Jimmy. "We'd better go on in, or Momma will have a cow."

Elvis waved good-bye to the fans and promised to come back out later and sign some more autographs. As they walked to the house, he told Jimmy, "Ain't no way that the Colonel will let me sign anything unless it's one of his pictures of me. But I don't pay him much mind about that. The fans is everything. Where would I be without them?" He looked at Jimmy, as if he could provide the answer.

Jimmy just shrugged and felt a twinge of jealousy. *I wonder when*

I'll be able to afford a house like this. He shook his head, as if in response to Elvis's question. *But this ain't Los Angeles. You can probably buy anything cheap in Memphis, Tennessee.* Suddenly he felt vulnerable, and angry again. *But who cares about a house? I don't. Momma's gone. Momma . . . And what the fuck am I doing here, anyway?*

Buying myself a greasy-haired, ducktail actor, that's what.

Jimmy had seen *Love Me Tender,* which hadn't impressed anyone; it was B-grade all the way. But Nick had managed to get hold of Elvis's talent test from Paramount, and that was something else. Elvis had performed a scene from a motion picture Hal Wallis had in production: *The Rainmaker,* and Elvis, though raw and awkward, certainly had the juice. He could act, and the camera loved every greasy angle of him. He was natural on screen, deep and three-dimensional and beautiful. Wallis had told Nick that he felt the same thrill when he first saw Errol Flynn on the screen. Elvis had the same power, virility, and sexual drive.

Fuck Wallis, Jimmy thought, and fuck Nick, too, for bringing him here, for taking him out of his life for the past three weeks, for trying to make him his own. To own him. Nick was just like everybody else. Dangerous, prying, using. Overfreight.

Suddenly Jimmy found himself bereft and standing in front of Elvis's mother. She had been waiting for Elvis in the entrance hall, under the flickering ceiling lights that simulated stars blinking through hand-painted clouds. It was a strange, surreal effect, and for an instant Jimmy imagined that bits of her were missing, or gauzy; but her face seemed lit, as if all the pinpoint lights were directed at that fleshy, thick, sallow-lidded face, a face that gravity and pain and sadness had weighted down, distorting her mouth and cutting deep lines from her pug nose down down and around to that pouting, clenching, frowning full mouth: testaments to her war with everything sinful and bad and dangerous in the world.

She was part ghost, and the rest was flesh, perhaps warm and cozy and satiny to the touch, or perhaps cold, cold dead fish flesh, like in his dream when his mother rose from the grave to embrace him after his automobile accident; and he wanted to put his arms around this heavy, sour-smelling woman, who was nothing like his own blessed mother, who was nothing to him; and it was crazy, he thought, fucking, flipping crazy; and he remembered what Elvis had told him when he'd come to him in his hospital room, when he'd quaked in fear and told Jimmy his secrets.

Jimmy nodded to her and, as if thinking out loud, mumbled, "Satnin." Gladys looked at him quizzically.

"And this," Elvis said, "is James Dean, Momma. The one I been telling you about. And this is Mr. Ray, he directed *Rebel Without a Cause,* you remember me telling you about that." Elvis leaned over to her and nuzzled her cheek with his own and said something in a soft, baby voice, then stood straight and said, "I apologize for the way the house looks. We ain't got anything in yet, except this." He pointed to the array of ceiling lights that flickered like stars. I dunno why this got done first, but when I was in Hollywood, Mr. Dean, I saw something like this in the Grauman's Chinese Theatre, and I loved it, so I thought I'd bring it right here for Momma. And we got some furniture, too, but not much yet." Jimmy couldn't imagine what else Elvis intended to cram into the palatial rooms; from what he could see from the entrance hall, every room was already filled with bric-a-brac and velvet furniture.

"Elvis, why don't you show your friends around, and I'll see about gettin' breakfast for everybody," Gladys said.

"Momma, we got a cook to do that so you don't have to work."

"You just go on and show Mr. Ray around," Gladys said, "and I'm going to speak to Mr. Dean here for a minute." Elvis seemed confounded by that. "Go on," Gladys said. "I ain't going to say nothing bad to this boy that you got to worry about."

Elvis seemed to consider that, then shrugged and said, "Okay, Momma. Come on, Mr. Ray, I'll show you around. Mr. Parker should be around somewhere. He's up early, earlier than us, usually, but I ain't seen him yet this morning." Feet stepping through soft carpet, Elvis and Nick and Baby and Lips disappeared into the velvet rooms. Jimmy heard Elvis explaining, "Now, there's two things about this house, one is that it had to have the most beautiful bedroom in Memphis for Momma, and the other is a real soda fountain with an ice cream thing, which is that, over there, and outside in the back—I'll show you—we got a pool and . . ."

"My boy told you things when he went to see you, didn't he?" Gladys said to Jimmy. Jimmy nodded, but he didn't look at Gladys. It was as if she was sacred, like Elvis thought she was. "And you know things about Elvis, I saw that, and you're close to your own mother, I see that, too. That's right, ain't it?"

"Everybody's close with their mothers," Jimmy said.

"Ain't always so, is it?" After a beat she said, "Elvis said you got a special way with your mother."

Jimmy looked at her now. "What do you mean?"

"Talking. Elvis told me you and your mother got a special way of talking, too."

"My mother's dead."

"I know, and I'm sorry for you."

Jimmy shrugged. "I was nine years old when it happened."

"Satnin. You know about things. I know you do. I can see that, and so could Elvis, even before he met you, that's because Elvis is special. People come through him, you know what I mean?" Jimmy shook his head. "You know about the comin'-through? It's part of our church, sometimes people are . . . sort of like . . . there are people God chooses, like my Elvis, who can show God to people. God told me when I had my own comin'-through that Elvis was coming, that he was coming to *me* and that he was special, and that he was going to perform wonders, that's what God revealed to me, and when God told me, I fainted right on the floor in the church. Fainted right there and then, and the pastor had to take me into another room 'cause I didn't want to wake up. It was like I was looking into heaven, that's just what it was, and I saw things." She nodded and said, "I saw things," and she looked hard at Jimmy, as if he held the secret to her son. "Elvis told you he's a twin, too, didn't he? He don't tell that to no strangers, but he don't think of you that way. He thinks you're . . ."

"What?" Jimmy wanted to know that.

"Like him. He told me about how you had a vision, that was the first thing he told me when he came back from seeing you . . . that and how it was over with him and Lizzie." She shook her head. "Sweet girl, but not for my Elvis. You met her, she was with him." Gladys paused, as if considering. "You see, Elvis ain't just living for himself, he's living for Jesse, his brother who died. Stillborn." She smiled at Jimmy and looked distant. "Elvis calls him his original bodyguard. Elvis took over his soul, his spirit, that's what my Vernon thinks. That's my husband. You'll meet him, too. You know, when Elvis was born, there was two glass bottles sitting on a shelf in the room, and as soon as I started having my babies, one of them glasses fell right off the shelf and crashed. All by itself. You go ahead and ask my husband about that. He'll tell you."

She drew closer to Jimmy, just as she did with her Elvis, her eyes sad and watery, her mouth drawn down at the corners, and said, "Take care of my Elvis, Mr. Dean. He trusts you . . . and so do I. And watch out for the Colonel. He's helped Elvis and got us all this—although I wished he hadn't; I'd be happier living alongside my sister in Tupelo like we used to—but the Colonel, he's out for his own gain. You watch, he'll be showin' himself soon enough. He's up to something, else he would have been all over you, big as life." And she leaned toward Jimmy and kissed him, her smell starchy, her dyed curly black hair scratchy against his face, and she whispered, "You watch over him, he's a very nervous young man. You talk back to him real soft, and he'll come around." Then, as if catching herself, she stepped away from Jimmy and said, "Now I'd better see to breakfast. You come with me. They'll all be in the kitchen soon enough, you don't need to worry about that." She laughed, and Jimmy followed her into the large white kitchen, where a tall, skinny woman was fussing over a twelve-burner stove. Sitting alone at the kitchen table and drinking coffee was a rumpled-looking, overweight, and balding man.

"Good morning, Gladys," he said brightly.

Gladys said hello and then started arguing with the maid.

The man looked at Jimmy and smiled broadly. "Well, I know who *you* are, son, and I'm pleased to make your acquaintance. Elvis talks a blue streak about you. He thinks the sun shines right up your pants." He took a dainty sip of his coffee and laughed. "And there, all along, I was thinking it was shining up *my* pants. We haven't been properly introduced. I'm the Colonel. Everybody just sort of figures I know everyone."

"I'm sorry, Colonel," Gladys said without turning to look at him. Then to the cook, who wore a starched, white uniform: "I'm going to cook Elvis's breakfast, Carrie." She broke Carrie's name into two words. Cah. Ree.

"No, you ain't, ma'am. Elvis said you wasn't to be cooking anything. That's my job. You wanna get me fired, is that it?"

"Yes," Gladys said. "And how you cooking them eggs? You know Elvis likes them hard, or he won't eat them."

The Colonel motioned Jimmy to sit down with him, but when Jimmy began pulling out the chair at the end of the table, Gladys said, "No, not there, Mr. Dean." She spoke gently, explaining: "That's Elvis's place. He's fussy about that, and I give him his own special knife and fork that nobody else uses. Why don't you sit down right there next to the Colonel?"

Jimmy did as he was told, although he wasn't entirely comfortable being so close to the fat man. The two men inspected each other, and Jimmy would have bet that the Colonel and Gladys were related. The Colonel had double chins, a large but tight smile, and the same round face. Although at first he seemed like a good old boy, there was something ripe and feminine about him. Instinctively, Jimmy didn't like him and remembered what Gladys had said. "You a colonel in the army or what?" Jimmy asked.

The Colonel was unfazed by the question and continued to smile. "I was in the Sixty-fourth Regiment during the war, son. I was stationed at Fort Shafter in Hawaii, and I was in charge of antiaircraft guns for Pearl Harbor." He leaned against Jimmy, as Gladys had done, and said, "But it was Governor Jimmy Davis of Louisiana, Jimmy Davis himself, who invested me with the rank of colonel." He told Carrie that he was ready for his eggs sunny side up and that his coffee was colder than a witch's tit.

"You just watch your language, Colonel," Gladys said, as she put down a special place setting at the head of the table for Elvis.

"Sorry, Gladys."

"Bacon and eggs okay for you?" Gladys asked Jimmy, who nodded and thanked her.

"Where *are* those boys?" Gladys asked, and she called out for Elvis, who was already on his way because he appeared with Nick, Baby, and Lips a few seconds later. Nick and the boys had been roughhousing, pushing and shoving one another; but as soon as Elvis saw the Colonel, his demeanor changed completely. He nodded and sat down in his chair, as if the Colonel had castigated him without a word.

Nick said hello to the Colonel, who nodded imperiously to him. The good-old-boy smile was gone. Jimmy figured this was the real Colonel—mean and gritty and no-nonsense. *He's playing good cop with me and bad cop with Nick,* Jimmy thought, feeling a sense of foreboding. He glanced at Gladys, who had been watching him. She nodded, as if to say, I *told* you so.

Carrie slid a plate piled high with overcooked bacon saddled with two eggs in front of Elvis. Then she brought a large plate of buttered toast. "And now here's your eggs, Colonel. Three of 'em. And you got the same thing," she said to Jimmy, giving him his eggs, then a napkin and silverware. "Toast is there for all of you. Now, what will everybody else be havin'?"

Elvis elbowed into his food. "Where's your father?" Gladys asked, sitting down beside him, as if to protect him from the Colonel.

"He's out in the back, checking out the chicken coops."

"You mean he's taking down my hog pen," Gladys said, giving the Colonel a nasty look. "The Colonel don't believe it's proper for us to have our own hogs," she said to Jimmy. "Because of the movies or something." She made a face.

"Momma, leave it alone."

She gave Carrie—who had her back to her—a dirty look and said to Jimmy, "I'd give the world to have things as they was back in Tupelo. I want to live where I can raise my own chickens and do my *own* cookin'."

"Momma, you got chickens, and ducks, and peacocks, and everything else, but you shouldn't have to cook no more."

"There's nothin' for me to do here but look out the windows."

"That ain't true, Momma."

"What, then?"

"Well, you take care of me and Daddy."

She shook her head, and Elvis leaned toward her.

The Colonel wiped his plate with a piece of toast. Then he pushed the plate away and said to Nick, "We weren't supposed to meet until tomorrow."

"Yes, I know," Nick said, "but Jimmy and I have been driving cross-country. We went to my hometown in Wisconsin and Jimmy's hometown in Illinois. Sort of a trip down memory lane, and we just got into Memphis a bit early. So instead of going straight to a hotel and sleeping it off"—Nick laughed at himself—"we figured we'd take a look-see and say hello." He nodded at Gladys. "We really didn't figure anyone would be up."

"Too much booze and too little sleep," Jimmy said, trying to be helpful; but the Colonel didn't seem to hear him. He was focused on Nick. "You know about our arrangement? It's really very simple. Elvis takes care of the singin' and I take care of the business." He looked at Elvis. "Ain't that true, son?"

"Yes, sir, I guess it is, Mr. Parker." Elvis had finished his food and nervously drummed his fingers on the table.

"Sure as shit it is," the Colonel said, turning back to Nick. "And I got to tell you, I don't take kindly to anyone interfering with my boy."

"Just what are you getting at?" Jimmy asked.

But the Colonel didn't even acknowledge him. He kept his attention on Nick. "You ain't going to get nowhere by trying to go through Elvis to get around me. We're a team, like I told you."

"We didn't intend on going around you, as you say," Nick said.

"And we don't need this shit, either," Jimmy said, and he stood up. "Elvis, good seeing you again. Too bad about the movie, hey?"

"Cool out," Nick said to Jimmy, then to the Colonel: "We can talk business like gentlemen or go our separate ways. That would be a shame, though, because together, we could really do something for Elvis."

"Ah, yes, for Elvis," the Colonel said, smiling. "Well, maybe I just jumped the gun. I saw you doing exactly what I would have done, getting here early and insinuating yourself around my boy here, and I don't like that kind of shit much, no sirree."

Carrie put more toast on the table and served the others their bacon and eggs. Gladys wouldn't eat; she just sipped her coffee and looked worriedly at Elvis.

"You better sit down, Jim," the Colonel said. "You're going to disturb everybody's breakfast standing over us like that. Come on, sit down, boy, and I'll tell you a funny story."

Elvis looked up at Jimmy and said, "Please, Mr. Dean, sit down and have some more coffee, or maybe more bacon, or anything you want. It'd be awfully important to me if you could stay. And to Mr. Parker, too." Elvis looked at the Colonel like a dutiful son getting permission from his father, then leaned forward and patted Jimmy's hand. Gladys nodded to Jimmy, and he sat down, as if his own mother had just spoken to him.

The Colonel spoke to Jimmy now—the old circus carnie salesman hawker obviously realizing that Nick wasn't the sole decision maker. "You boys know about Jayne Mansfield. You probably know her, hey?" The Colonel winked, as if he was mimicking W. C. Fields or Wallace Beery. Nick and Jimmy exchanged glances. "Well, Jaynie wanted Elvis to sing a song for her movie *The Girl Can't Help It*. You know that film, Nick?" Nick just listened. "Well, I told her that it was fine, if she wanted Elvis to sing a song because that's what he does, and our fee would be . . . how much was it, Elvis, do you remember?"

Elvis started tapping his fingers on the table again and shook his head.

"I guess I'll have to remember, huh. It was fifty thousand dollars, which was a fair price when you consider that Elvis's first album is selling seventy-five thousand copies a day and is the best-selling album RCA ever had. Right, Elvis?"

"I guess so, sir."

"And 'Hound Dog,' that sold a million copies in eighteen days. Ain't that right?" Elvis just stared down at the table. At least he had stopped drumming his fingers.

"Elvis sets records with every song he records," the Colonel said, and laughed. "Sets records. RCA would be nothin' without Elvis, that's for sure. If we walked away from them, they'd be nothin', nothin' at all. Anyway, Jayne Mansfield, she figures I'm too expensive, so she goes to talk with Elvis himself. What'd you think of her?"

Elvis shrugged. "She's a nice woman." Then he looked back down at the table.

What the hell hold did the Colonel have over this boy? Jimmy asked himself. He shifted his chair away from the Colonel and closer to Elvis, which seemed to make Elvis even more nervous, as he began tapping his fingers on the table again.

"What she say to you?" the Colonel drilled Elvis.

"Nothin' much," Elvis said. "Just what you said, that she wanted me to sing something for her picture, which would've been fine, I guess, if it was all right."

"That's right, Elvis. That's exactly right." The Colonel spoke to Jimmy now. "She called me and said that everything was fine and dandy, that she'd talked with Elvis and he was fine about doing a song, so I didn't have to worry. And you know what I told her? I told her I wasn't worried at all, and I was pleased that she and Elvis had worked everything out. But the price was still fifty thousand dollars, all the same." The Colonel chuckled and said that it was pretty near time for his first cigar of the morning.

"Did Elvis do the song?" Jimmy asked.

"Didn't quite work out. Seems that Miss Mansfield's got her own money problems, poor thing. But that was all right with me and Elvis because we do things according to plan and don't need Elvis playin' behind her movie, do we, son?"

"No, sir," Elvis said softly.

Just then a thin, placid-looking, gray-haired man walked into the kitchen. Gladys nodded to him and said, "Mr. Dean and Mr., uh . . ."

"Nick Ray," Nick said helpfully.

"Yes, and Mr. Ray, this is my husband, Vernon." Vernon nodded but didn't offer to shake hands.

"Me and Vernon was outside doing some work," the Colonel said. "Vernon, you take my seat and have your breakfast."

"No, I ate," Vernon said, looking like the ghost at the table.

"Well, we're supposed to be having some sort of a meeting tomorrow, ain't that right, Nick?" He didn't wait for a response. "But no time like the present, I always say. That okay with you boys?"

"That's fine," Nick said. The Colonel looked at Jimmy, who nodded. "You look like you're worried about me," he said to Jimmy.

"Why should I be worried?"

"Don't know. Maybe 'cause I'm older and wiser." He slapped Nick lightly on the shoulder and laughed.

"Yeah, I guess that must be it," Jimmy said.

"Well, then, let's discuss this motion-picture offer of yours and get it over with. I can have my cigar, and so can Nick. If I remember correctly, you smoke the odd cigar, don't you, Nick? And the rest of you, you can finish your breakfast in peace. Vernon, you mind if we use the game room to talk? That'll be private for us." Vernon shrugged and took the Colonel's seat.

"Who you got to be private from?" Gladys asked. "You can talk right here. Nobody's going to bother you."

But Elvis was already at the door, following the Colonel.

Jimmy glanced at Gladys, whose face was tight, chagrined, and then at Vernon, who didn't seem to care about much of anything at all. It was obvious who was in control in this house.

ELVIS WOULDN'T SIT DOWN, BUT LEANED AGAINST THE POOL TABLE and tapped his fingers constantly on the polished wood-rail trim; his right leg pumped up and down, beating out a rhythm to some pounding blood music only he could hear.

"Son, you sure you don't want to sit down here with us?" the Colonel asked.

"No, sir," Elvis said.

Nick and the Colonel were sitting on a velour couch; Jimmy sat opposite them in a black leather chair. "Cigars, gentlemen?" asked the Colonel as he pulled two Havana cigars out of his shirt pocket. Nick accepted. Jimmy gave Nick a dirty look, but he just shrugged.

"Elvis, you want one of these? I got more in my room, only take me a minute."

"No, sir," Elvis said again, averting his eyes from the Colonel.

The Colonel's got to have something on him, Jimmy thought, sensing the boy's humiliation, which was palpable as a bad smell.

"I got these," Elvis said, opening the cellophane wrapper of a package of Hav-a-Tampa cigarillos.

Taking deep pulls, the Colonel lit his corona-sized cigar, then offered his lighter to Nick. "So what's this about a movie?"

"Just as we discussed," Nick said. "It's a great vehicle for Elvis. This is going to be a serious motion picture. Jimmy and I have put together a team of the best people in the business." He kept looking up at Elvis, including him. "We've hired Walter Newman. He did *Man with the Golden Arm*. He's a terrific writer, and Jimmy's also brought a writer on board, guy by the name of Jack Kerouac. We've got an entirely new take on Jesse James. We're going to do it entirely as a ballad; it's going to be the myth of Jesse James, bigger than life, in CinemaScope, bigger than *Giant*." He looked at Jimmy and smiled. "No offense."

I should be doing the talking, Jimmy thought. How the hell has Nick gotten away with pitching films? He shrugged reflexively and noticed Elvis watching him, studying him.

"My boy just did a cowboy movie," the Colonel said.

"We saw it," Nick said. "We also saw his test for Paramount." Nick looked up at Elvis. "The test was terrific. You've got real talent, Elvis, but you didn't get enough of a chance to try it on in *Love Me Tender*."

The Colonel chuckled. "Well, my poor boy over here who didn't get a chance to try on his talent, he somehow managed pretty good. *Love Me Tender* outperformed *Bus Stop* and *The Seven Year Itch,* and did as well as your picture, Jim."

"Marilyn Monroe will play Zee," Nick said.

"Who the hell's Zee?"

"That would be Jesse James's girlfriend," Nick said.

"And you're going to get Marilyn Monroe to do that?" asked the Colonel.

"We've already talked to her."

"Talk is cheap."

"We'll guarantee it," Nick said.

"No, we *won't,*" Jimmy said reflexively. What the hell was Nick up to? He hadn't said anything about Marilyn, except that he wanted to cast her. Then he said, "Fuck this, anyway. If Marilyn told Nick she'd do it, she'll do it. Ain't no guarantees."

The Colonel seemed to love that. "Well, I'd expect you'd expect us to sign *something* on the dotted line." He guffawed. "Or were you maybe just thinking of doing this friendly-like, nothing in writing, that it?"

"Look," Jimmy said, glancing at Nick and playing along. "Nick shouldn't've said anything. Marilyn would be a bonus."

"No, my boy would be the bonus."

"Okay," Nick said.

"Do you want to do this film or not?" Jimmy asked Elvis.

"Ain't about what Elvis wants to do," said the Colonel. "Sorry, Elvis," he said in a soft voice. "You just sit back and relax." Then the Colonel said to Jimmy, "It's what I want him to do, which is always what's best for his career."

"And what do you think that would be?" Nick asked.

"Wait until you see the kind of numbers *Loving You* does, and his next picture, *Jailhouse Rock.* All you're telling me is that you got an artsy-fartsy picture and want Elvis to be the star so you can sell it."

"We want Elvis because we see talent," Nick said, leaning forward, straining.

"Well, all my boy's talent is there to make money for him and his family." The Colonel put out his cigar, and its bitter smell permeated the room. "So what's your offer, remembering now that our contract with Paramount allows us to make only one outside picture this year."

"We can offer—"

"Why don't you hold on to that thought for a minute, 'cause I got to piss like a racehorse. All that good coffee does it to me every time."

After the Colonel left the room, there was an awkward silence.

Jimmy got up and stood in front of Elvis, as if this was to be a private conversation that Nick somehow wouldn't hear. "Elvis, what's the deal here? That man talks about you like you're meat. When he's here, you look at your feet. I don't mean to—"

"Maybe you should let that go, Jimmy," Nick said.

So what if we don't get Elvis? Jimmy thought. They could get Paul Newman in a flash. Or he could play the goddamn role himself. James Dean: Billy the Kid and Jesse James all tied up in one. Look out. "Why do you let him do that? You could ride over him like a train if you wanted to."

Elvis didn't move, didn't look up. He was trapped, whether it was by Jimmy or the Colonel.

"Elvis, man, I'm sorry, but stop drumming your fingers. It's driving us all crazy, except probably the Colonel, who'd like it if we were all being driven crazy."

Elvis grinned and put his hands in his pockets, as if only that could stop them from tapping and drumming and crawling about like blond spiders. "I got an idea how to handle me better than anyone else has as far as keeping me in line," he said in a slow drawl, as if thinking things through. "Mr. Parker, he's more or less like a daddy to me, even though I got my own daddy. But Mr. Parker don't meddle in my affairs. Ain't nobody—nobody—can tell me to do this or do that, except me. Mr. Parker knows all about business, and I don't. I wouldn't have all that I got if it wasn't for him." Elvis looked up at Jimmy with his sleepy eyes, as though he could think his unresolved thoughts right into Jimmy's head. "Mr. Parker never butts into my record sessions," Elvis continued. "He leaves me to do what I know how to do, and I don't butt into business because that's what he knows how to do."

"That's exactly right," the Colonel said, walking into the room; he had obviously been eavesdropping. He sat down beside Nick but spoke to Jimmy. "I just thought that before we start, you should understand the lay of the land, and I figured that Elvis would probably tell you himself. You see, Elvis, I got the seventh sense, too, ain't that right? I keep telling you. You make sure you tell your momma that. Vernon already knows." He smiled at Nick and said, "Now, you were going to make us an offer."

"Yes," Nick said, "but before we do that, we should discuss time."

"What do you mean?" asked the Colonel.

"Well, Jimmy and I are a bit worried about Elvis receiving his induction notice."

The Colonel smiled and nodded. "Do you think I'd waste our time if I didn't think Elvis was going to be available? That's all taken care of, isn't it, Elvis?"

"I guess so, sir."

"What do you mean, taken care of?" Nick asked.

"Oh, the boy's going in, all right. And he's not asking for any dispensation, no sirree. He's going to do his tour and serve his country like a man. That's the way he wants it." The Colonel looked to Elvis, who nodded without conviction. "But the government's being very understanding, and they've agreed not to take the boy until he's fulfilled all his obligations. Now, what we've got to decide is whether making this movie should be one of his obligations or not."

"And you can guarantee that he'll be available?" Nick asked.

"Just like you can guarantee Marilyn Monroe. Now, as you were saying about your offer?"

"Elvis, the way we work is that you and Colonel Parker will get to see the script," Jimmy said before Nick and the Colonel could talk money, "and if you want to have input, that's what we're looking for. Nothing's set in stone. Nick and I work out a lot of it as we go, and you'd be involved in that."

"We don't care about the script right now," the Colonel said.

"What do you care about?" Jimmy asked insolently.

The Colonel chuckled. "Well, first off would come Elvis here, then, I suppose, my dear wife."

"You don't even want to see the script?" Jimmy asked, looking at Elvis, willing him to defy the Colonel.

"I don't, but Elvis here might. There's only one thing in a script that interests me."

"Yeah?"

"How many songs it's got." Jimmy shook his head, and the Colonel leaned back, put his arm on the upholstered crest of the couch, and patted Nick, as if they were the best of friends. "If we don't start talkin' turkey, I might just go for a stroll in the meadows. Mighty beautiful country, don't you agree?"

"We could pay a hundred thousand," Nick said, leaning forward, "and that's pushing it to the limit. There, no bullshit, no back and forth, a price that's more than fair."

The Colonel patted Nick again. "Well, Nick, that's just fine for me. Now how about my boy?"

"That's our budget," Nick said.

"You haven't done your homework proper," the Colonel said. "I expected you'd have heard some sort of gossip about the deal I cut for Elvis with Mr. Hal Wallis and Twentieth Century-Fox. Now, maybe I got my head up my ass, but it seems to me that you two boys are doing this film for Fox." He made a clucking noise with his tongue. "So, since we're talkin' about asses and all, why don't you just shit or get off the pot. What are you going to do for my boy over here?"

"That's the deal," Jimmy said. "Take it or leave it." He glanced at Elvis, who was looking so hard at the Colonel he should have been burning the back of his fat red neck.

"We might be able to work something out with points," Nick said.

"Deal would be fifty percent of net profits, and Elvis gets publishing rights to the songs," the Colonel said.

"This isn't a musical," Jimmy said.

"You mean to tell me, son, that after *Love Me Tender* grossed four point five million dollars, you're going to argue with me about the music? You know what they wanted to call that picture before we came in with the song 'Love Me Tender'? They wanted to call it *The Reno Brothers*. The song was a number-one hit."

"Then we should share a percent of the song rights."

"You will, but not publishing rights. *The Reno Brothers* was always going to be a second-class picture, unless they did something like get Brando or my boy—or somebody like you, Jim—to give it pizzazz. Elvis is what that picture's all about, nothing else. Now, I can be a fair man. You offered a hundred, and I said that's fine, if it was only for me." He patted Nick on the shoulder again. "But we'd all agree that Elvis is worth two of me any day of the week—I'm the poor relation here—so we'd come down to three hundred, and only because I know Elvis wants to work with Jimmy here. That right, Elvis?"

Elvis ignored him. He looked angry, or perhaps it was just anxiety.

"No way we can go three hundred thousand dollars," Jimmy said. "No fucking way." I'm *not making that kind of money*, he thought. *Maybe I need an asshole like the Colonel for an agent, too.*

The Colonel made a clucking sound again. "Your momma wouldn't tolerate that language, nohow, would she?" he said to Elvis.

"Maybe we could go up to one twenty-five," Nick said, "but the budget just isn't there, and there's no way we could go fifty percent net."

"Then we ain't got a deal," the Colonel said, and he stood up. "Now, I expect you folks will be staying around for lunch or something. I got to take Elvis here out for some business, so good luck. Elvis, I'll meet you out by the cars in ten minutes."

"Okay, one-fifty," Nick said. "We can't do better than that. That's stretching it, and we'll have to find ways to cut in other areas."

"You do that," said the Colonel, "but one-fifty ain't the number."

"Well, I'm done," Nick said to Jimmy. He stood up, pressing out the wrinkles in his slacks.

"Yes, you are indeed," the Colonel said, and walked out the door, slamming it behind him.

"Well, that's that," Jimmy said to Elvis.

"No, it ain't," Elvis said, and he ran to the door, opened it, and called the Colonel. "Mr. Parker, would you come back here, sir?"

"Come on, Elvis, we're done here!" shouted the Colonel.

"No, we ain't," said Elvis. "Now, please, sir, come back in here for a minute."

Enraged, the Colonel stepped back into the room. "Now, Elvis," he said in a forced soft, soothing voice, "we agreed that you sing the songs and act and all, and I decide the deals, ain't that right?"

"Yes, sir, that's right, but—"

"But what, son? Ain't no buts, or everything we worked so hard for goes right down the tubes."

"I always go along with you, sir, but"—Elvis stepped away from the Colonel as he talked—"I got an idea."

"Son, this ain't the place for that. You want to talk, we can talk all morning together. All day, if you want."

"You see, sir, I want to act, I mean really act, like Mr. Dean here, and like Mr. Brando and Richard Widmark and Rod Steiger. I want to learn to act like them, like a serious actor, because I know that I can do something with it, Mr. Parker, just like I knew I could sing, and it's the most important thing in the world to me, more important even than singing. And I want to do like Mr. Dean did with Mr. Ray and have something to do with everything, with what the characters say and the script and how everybody feels and all."

"We'll find exactly the right films for you, Elvis, never you worry about that. The big film companies are coming to you, son. You ain't going to have any problems in that department, believe you me."

"No, Mr. Parker, I want to be in *this* film."

The Colonel looked stunned, like a deer caught in the headlights of a very slow car. It was obvious that Elvis had never spoken up to the Colonel before. "Elvis, that ain't going to happen." He turned to Nick and Jimmy and shouted, "It *ain't* going to happen! Now, don't you fuck with my boy no more."

"What kind of language is that?" Jimmy asked, and the Colonel started to go for him.

"Go ahead, fat man, take your shot."

"Jimmy, shut your mouth," Nick said. Then to the Colonel: "I apologize for Jimmy. He's still young. You know how it is. Look, maybe we can cut something here or there. Maybe we can raise the points."

"I wouldn't even talk to you for less than two hundred and fifty," the Colonel said. "And Elvis is the star." He turned to Jimmy and said, "And you take a part in the picture, too, Jim. You play opposite Elvis, but my boy is Jesse James and you're a supporting actor."

"That's not going to happen," Nick said.

"Why not?" asked Jimmy. "Hell, I could play Jethro Bailey, the preacher."

"You don't have to do nothing like that," Elvis said, drawling softly and staring at the floor. He was shaking, with either determination or fear. "I want to do this film, Mr. Parker. If Mr. Ray says he don't have more than a hundred and fifty, I think we should take that and maybe you could work something out with everything else."

The Colonel patted Elvis on the shoulder and said, "Okay, if you really want to do this." He looked at Nick and said, "I'll come down to two hundred. That's final."

"We just can't do it," Nick said.

"Do something with the points then," Elvis said. He had stopped shaking and stood slouching just like Jimmy, mirroring him, as if he could only do this if he could *be* Jimmy.

The Colonel looked surprised, but he smiled. "Elvis, you been into a six-pack or something this morning?"

"No, sir. But this is personal to me, like music. I want you to fix this, sir."

"Ain't nothing to fix. You want to give everything away."

Elvis shook his head. "I want you to fix it fair, Mr. Parker."

"Okay," the Colonel said. "Nick, the boy wants to do your film. I ain't going to argue. You say you can't do more than a hundred and fifty. Okay, if that's what Elvis wants. And fifty percent of net profit, like we agreed."

"I'm sorry, Colonel—" Nick began, but Elvis interrupted him.

"Mr. Parker, I think twenty-five percent would be just fine, don't you?"

"Okay, boys, twenty-five it is." And without looking at Nick or Jimmy or Elvis, he left the room.

Elvis followed.

TEN

■

Satnin

Connecticut in a rented Range Rover. The air dry as
paper, the sky blue and cloud-fluffed and unpolluted,
hills leafy green, charged with black and purple, the
road twisting, turning, meandering without resort to ruler
or compass through God's country, USA. On a perfect
day like this, fate and history and all the secrets of life
could be delicately etched into the airy blue heavens.

Jimmy, however, felt leaden in this weightless, un-
freighted world.

He glanced upward, reading the death notices up
there in the big, baby-blue sky.

Son of a bitch bastard.

Cisco the Kid—his horse—had died on the same
day that Buddy Holly, the Big Bopper *hellooooo baby,*

and Ritchie Valens were killed in a plane crash. Frank Lloyd Wright died a week ago—and that threw Nick Ray into deep mourning because Nick had studied with the architect. The cigar-chewing Cuban premier, Fidel Castro, was speaking in New York, the Dalai Lama had just disappeared from Tibet, and Paul Newman, costarring with Geraldine Page, finally had a hit in the Broadway show *Sweet Bird of Youth*. Jimmy loved Geraldine. He had worked with her in Billy Rose's abortion of a play, *The Immoralist*, and she had been his only friend, his only solace, on the set.

That show had opened in February 1954—a lifetime ago.

Now Jimmy was rich and famous, as famous as his protégé Elvis Presley, and everything was going well, or so everyone told him—Mom Deacy and Dick Clayton were over the moon, as Mom put it. They had worked out a much better deal for him at Warners, and he had beaten Marlon Brando for the role of a blond Nazi officer in the adaptation of Irwin Shaw's *The Young Lions*. The days spent hanging out with Rocky Graziano and the hard workouts with Mushy Callahan and boxing champion Tony Zale had paid off. *Somebody Up There Likes Me* was a hit. Bigger than *Giant*, or Elvis's *Love Me Tender*, for that matter. The reporters compared him to Brando. *The New York Times*, ever sour, wrote: "Mr. Dean plays the role of Graziano well, making the pug and Marlon Brando almost indistinguishable."

He was the star, not Pier.

Hedda Hopper was right about Buddy Adler bringing *The True Story of Jesse James* out against *The Left-Handed Gun;* both films did come out at the same time, but they also did big box office. It was rumored that Jimmy would get an Oscar for Best Supporting Actor (as Frank James) in *The True Story of Jesse James*. Hedda called him a genius.

Nothing for Elvis.

But that son of a bitch could certainly sell a motion picture—maybe it was worth all the bullshit dealing with the Colonel to get Elvis on board. Left-Handed Gun *was a blockbuster, and except for the title song,* "Young Dreams," *Elvis didn't even sing. And we proved he could act.*

Who was it that called him "the next Dean"?

And who was it that said that Elvis paid for my new mansion in Beverly Hills?

Fuckers.

THE EIGHTEENTH-CENTURY FARMHOUSE, WHICH MARILYN CALLED AN old saltbox with a kitchen extension, was situated on almost four hundred acres of woods, hills, fields, and pastures. Standing behind the glass doors of her living room—as if she could see out but no one could see in—she watched Jimmy drive up the driveway. She slid open the glass doors, which opened onto a large veranda, and ran out to meet him. Two dogs ran ahead of her: a mournful basset hound called Hugo, and Cindy, a mongrel spaniel she had taken in. Cindy barked and jumped at Jimmy as he opened the door.

"Get down, Cindy!" Marilyn shouted, laughing. "She won't hurt you. She only bites me." A grin, and then, "I didn't know who it could be," she said, hugging and kissing him before he could even climb out of the Range Rover. Marilyn was wearing jeans that were torn out at the pockets and a black corduroy work shirt that was worn and too large for her; it probably belonged to her husband, Arthur Miller.

"Who'd you expect?" Jimmy asked, petting both dogs, allowing them to get his scent, lick his hands and his face. He glanced around. A pond that was near the house caught his attention; the late-afternoon sunlight gave the surface of the water an odd quality—it looked like it was lit from below, glowing. He felt a sudden, unexpected yearning for his mother and remembered his dream of her rising from her grave. He had failed her. But the water—it was the color of his dream.

His thoughts drifted to Gladys, Elvis's mother. *Satnin.* Everything soft, safe, secure.

"Jimmy?"

"Yeah?"

"Pay attention to *me*. I've missed you. I need you. Get your stuff, and I'll show you around."

He followed her into the house.

"You know, it's dangerous being on a farm," Marilyn said breathlessly. "Being alone here. Anybody can just drive up . . . and kill you. You should see some of the people around here." She turned to him, flashing her private, childlike smile, the one never seen in photos or at parties, and said, "These country people, they look just like *you*." She led Jimmy through the living room into a large, beam-ceilinged bedroom, and before he could even put down his duffel bag, she threw her arms around his neck and kissed him.

"Wait a minute," Jimmy said, laughing. "What's all this?"

"What's all what?"

Jimmy sat down on the bed and shook his head. "You know how long it's been since we talked or anything?"

Marilyn sat down next to him, reached over to the night table, and closed a hinged, gilded frame that contained portrait photographs of her and Arthur. "You playing hard to get?" She giggled.

Jimmy could see that something had changed; she was, somehow, more in control of herself. "I think we should talk," he said.

"About what?"

"You know about what," Jimmy said. "Why you wouldn't take my phone calls after your overdose. I kept getting your maid, who acts like she's dumb as a door." Jimmy shook his head, as if surprised that he wasn't angry. But the Demerol, which he more than occasionally took for the pain that still lingered from the accident, smoothed out his anger. "It's been almost a year, for Christ's sake."

"Longer," Marilyn said, watching him, as if she were worried.

"Yeah, well?"

"I called *you*, remember?"

"Took you long enough," Jimmy said. "I blamed it on your husband's jealousy, that you didn't call. But if you wanted to call me, you'd have called. Right?"

Marilyn glanced at him, nodded, and then leaned down to pet the basset hound, which was wagging its tail so hard its entire rear was in motion. "Hugo follows me around everywhere. He wants you to pet him."

Jimmy patted the dog's satiny head, knowing exactly where to scratch it, and said, "I never even knew you had this place."

"I don't. It's not mine; it's Arthur's. Oh, I helped him decorate it and renovate it, and he bought it with my money."

"It figures."

"This was supposed to be the place where we were going to live until we died . . . that's what Arthur promised me, anyway." She looked at the night table, at the closed picture frame, and said, "He usually works here at the farm, and I stay in the apartment in Manhattan."

"When you're not trying to kill yourself."

That caught her. She stiffened and said, "That's a mean thing to say, Jimmy. That's as mean as what all the others would say." But there was no quaver in her voice, no shine of tears in her eyes; nor did she sound angry. "I don't like it here. I prefer the city."

"Then why are you here?" Jimmy asked. He already loved this place. It reminded him just a little of his aunt and uncle's farm in Illinois— childhood and security, plowing and harrowing, dogs and cats, cows and barns, and rope swings and puppets and gravy on mashed potatoes and drawing and cloud-magic dreaming.

"Because Arthur's off somewhere, working on that script with John Huston, the script he's writing for me." She sighed. "That's another story."

"Yeah?"

"Yeah. Arthur said it was going to be his valentine to me. The most personal gift anyone could give. He said his script would enhance me

as a performer. That's what he told me, and with a straight face, too."
She laughed, but it was almost a yelp of pain. "His *gift* cost my company two hundred and fifty thousand dollars." She laughed softly. "My company. That's about in the same state as his gift." After a beat, she continued, "And do you know what the movie's going to be about? Well, you can get it from the title—*The Misfits.*"

"Everybody knows about it, Marilyn. Hell, everybody we know is supposed to be in the goddamn thing—Gable, Monty Clift, Eli Wallach, and you told me you were crazy about Huston as a director." She nodded. "Everybody's in it but *me.*"

"Yeah, I think that was the idea," Marilyn said. "But I wouldn't want you in it, anyway."

"Fuck you very much."

"Because it would spoil things."

"Well, I wouldn't want to spoil things for you," Jimmy said sarcastically.

"For *us.* Arthur is bound and determined to poison everything. He doesn't know it—he doesn't see it—but that's what he does; and I don't want you fucked up with all that. He hates you, and I won't let anything hurt us."

"There ain't no us," Jimmy said. "If there was an us, you'd've called me."

"I did call you," she said in almost a whisper.

"After a year."

"It was because I didn't want to spoil it."

"Marilyn, you're not making any sense."

"Spoil what we have."

"Spoil what?" Jimmy asked. "We don't have *anything.* Hiding out from me for a year didn't exactly help our relationship."

"It shouldn't have done anything to our relationship. You should just . . . know, that's all. You shouldn't need me to tell you why I was keeping away from you."

"Well, I don't. So tell me."

"Because I didn't want everything else to spoil it," she said, insistent. "Because you're my best friend. Because you're the only one I trust."

Jimmy sighed and shook his head, and reached over to pet the dog. *It's no fucking use. She's determined not to make any sense.*

Marilyn pulled her shirt over her head and slid her pants off. She wasn't wearing a bra, and she never wore underwear. She lay back on the bed, blond and white and naked, and her eyes glistened now with tears.

"What the hell are you doing?"

"Jimmy, fuck me," she said in her whispery voice. "Just fuck me. We don't have to do anything else."

"It doesn't work like that."

"Touch me, then. Don't be like all the others."

"Like who?"

"Like everybody but you and me. Like everybody."

"You're just going to lay there?" Jimmy asked.

"Until you do something."

"I am doing something. I'm petting the dog."

"Well, pet me."

"I'm shy in front of animals." Jimmy grinned.

She struggled not to but burst out laughing. "Well?" She rested her weight on her elbow and told Hugo to "cop a walk. Go on. Go on." The dog padded out of the room. "Well?"

"I can't just *do* it," Jimmy said.

Marilyn shifted closer to him. Her breasts jiggled, and Jimmy, almost absentmindedly, prodded at her nipple. She giggled. "You're still a baby."

"Yeah."

"And you still want to be in every movie anybody makes."

"So?"

Marilyn shifted onto her back, and Jimmy put his hand between her legs. Marilyn moaned, as if he had just bought her an ice cream, and reached over to touch him; and then she was on her side and he was beside her on her inside her, her freckled back against his chest, her dry halo of hair in his face. Now he was holding her blond rose breasts, slowly slowly working himself in and out of her, quietly, gently, reflexively, it was if they were both alone but together; now kissing the nape of her neck, smelling her—autumnal, sweaty-clean, a hint of Joy perfume and alcohol, sweet and cloying—and now coming quietly together, breath deepening but not quickening, not the sandpaper razor rattle of passion, this was warm water molasses cleansing, sliding, ether floating, spinning, turning, pumping, everything deliciously wet focused toward sleep-jolting, heavy-sinking completion.

"I tried to pull out," Jimmy said afterward.

"I didn't want you to." Marilyn put her hand on his thigh behind her. "Don't take it out yet. There's something I have to tell you, and I want you inside me just a little longer, just in case."

"Just in case of what?"

"I want everything inside me," Marilyn said. "All the juice."

Jimmy chuckled. "I can't make heads or tails out of you sometimes."

"I'll give you head later, and you're just about in my tail right now, so I think you've got the best of both worlds, don't you?"

Jimmy, no longer erect, squeezed out of her.

"Oh, you promised."

"Sorry, just happened. I'll get a towel."

"No, stay here." Marilyn sat up beside him. She plumped up the pillows and leaned back, then touched his face, resting her hand on his almost hairless chest. "You want to know why I didn't call you?"

"That would be nice."

"Remember when I took all those pills?" Marilyn wouldn't look at him. She gazed at the door, which was open, and Cindy came into the room, stood near the doorway, and looked hopeful. Ignoring her, Marilyn said, "I was pregnant."

"Are you sure?"

She nodded. "I know I was pregnant. I missed periods and . . ."

"Yeah?"

"And I had a bad bleed, and I know that's when I lost it."

"That still doesn't—"

But Marilyn didn't let him finish. "The baby . . . I know it was yours. That's why I wanted you, that's why I wanted to see you."

"But you wouldn't see me," Jimmy said.

"I wanted to see you, and then . . . and then I couldn't face you. I'm sorry, Jimmy."

Jimmy held her, and she let go, crying and wailing.

"How did you know it was mine?"

"I just knew. It couldn't have been Arthur's. He hasn't touched me. It could have been . . ." She shook her head. "I knew it was yours, and I wanted it more than anything, more than everything." She had stopped sobbing, and now she motioned to the dog, which ran to the bed, as if it understood her thoughts and signals better than Jimmy. She patted the sheet, and Cindy jumped onto the mattress and settled down beside her.

"You were going to say it could have been somebody else's. Who's that?"

"Would it make you jealous if it was somebody else?"

Jimmy shrugged. "No, I guess not." He laughed. "I guess that's why we're not married or anything."

Marilyn leaned toward him, caressing him, touching his still-sticky penis, making him hard again.

"That's a good trick."

"Isn't it, though?" After a beat, she said, "Would you marry me?"

"We had this discussion before, remember? Anyway, you're already married."

"Not for long . . . not for long."

"That bad?"

"No, not that bad. Just nothing. Arthur's become a . . . a scientist." She laughed. "Yeah, that's it. He looks at me like I'm somebody to study, like a bug. It's all for his work, and he hasn't done shit in I don't know how long. Now it's the screenplay. He thinks he can get back where he was by climbing on my back. Like everybody." She looked hard at Jimmy and said, "I know I'm not being fair to him. He doesn't mean to be a cold bastard. He just is. You should have seen what he wrote about me in his diary when we were in London. After that . . ." She shrugged. "I don't feel much of anything for him." She stared toward the doorway, musing, as if perhaps Arthur Miller might storm in at any moment. "How can that be?"

"I don't know."

"He wrote that he thought I was some kind of angel and then discovered he was wrong. That I'm a bitch."

"So what? He was just writing in his diary. People say all sorts of dumb shit in diaries."

"No, he meant it. He wants to use me and get out, but I'm getting out first."

"Are you divorcing him?"

"I don't know. I don't know what I'm doing. I just know that I wanted to see you and make you feel better about . . . everything."

"Thanks. Now tell me who the other guy is."

"Which other guy?"

"The one who could have knocked you up."

"Don't talk like that, Jimmy. It was *your* baby."

"And if it was, what would you have done?"

"Given it everything."

"Would you have told Arthur?"

"If you wanted me to I would have."

"And just now?" Jimmy asked. "What was that about?"

"I don't know what you mean."

"You wanting me to come inside you."

"You know what that was about," she said in almost a whisper.

"And if you get pregnant?"

"That will be wonderful. I'll be happy."

"So what then? You going to divorce Arthur and marry me?"

"Would you want that?"

"I don't know." And Jimmy and Marilyn started laughing; they couldn't stop, and the dog jumped off the bed in fear. When they were finished, and Marilyn was left with the hiccups, Jimmy asked again, "Who's the other guy?"

"I really think you're jealous, Jimmy . . . no, you're never that way, that's why I can tell you everything. It's Jack Kennedy."

"You told me you met him. I figured you screwed him."

"I did more than that."

"Yeah?"

"I fell in love with him."

"Then why are you trying to get me to knock you up?"

She stopped touching him and said, "You and I, that's got nothing to do with anybody else."

"I don't think he's going to be so hot for you if you're pregnant."

Marilyn smiled wistfully. "Maybe it will make him hotter, more ardent. Isn't that a wonderful word, Jimmy? *Ardent*."

"Would probably scare the shit out of him."

"Does it scare the shit out of you?"

"What? Him?"

"No, me being pregnant."

Jimmy shrugged. "No, but like you said, it's different with us."

"He *is* in love with me," Marilyn insisted.

"If you say so."

"He's going to marry me, Jimmy, you just watch and see. He promised me. He's going to seek an annulment from Jackie—"

"*Seek* an annulment?"

She looked suddenly embarrassed. "That's what he said. And he's also . . ." She gazed dreamily toward the doorway again, as if any second now John F. Kennedy would walk in, and he'd be as big as life and stronger than Charles Atlas.

"And what?"

"And he's going to be the president of the United States."

Jimmy laughed. "You think so, hey?"

"He will. He told me he's definitely going to run, although it's going to be really tricky, getting the nomination, what with Stevenson and Humphrey and Symington and Johnson and every other goddamn Democrat all in the running."

"You really are getting into this."

"Oh, there's more, but I can't tell you that here."

"Why not?"

She laughed. "Because I'll tell you later when we go for a walk, okay?" Jimmy shrugged. "I'm keeping a diary," Marilyn said. "I need to remember everything Jack and Bobby tell me."

"Bobby?"

"Jack's brother. He runs everything for him. He's kind of a sour-puss, but sweet, too."

Jimmy was going to tell her that these guys were just going to use her, but she looked so hopeful he couldn't bring himself to say anything.

"You're thinking bad thoughts, Jimmy Dean," Marilyn said, scolding.

"I'm not thinking anything."

"Jack makes me happy, and he's exciting. It's all exciting. What else have I got? The apartment in New York? Arthur staring at me like I'm a bug?"

"You've got work," Jimmy said.

She snorted at that. "It always turns out bad, for me, anyway. Did you see *Some Like It Hot*? Don't. It's fucked, completely fucked. Jimmy, I want to do serious work. I discussed doing a picture with Marlon and Marty Landau. It was called *Some Came Running*, or something like that. But like with everything, nothing came of it. Just like nothing came of that picture you and Nick wanted me to do. My agents at MCA can't do shit for me."

"You've got your own company. You can do whatever you want."

"Yeah, right. As long as I play the dumb blonde."

"The movie Arthur's writing for you won't be like that," Jimmy said, trying to soothe her.

"It's humiliating. It's his way of making me look dumb in what everyone will think is a serious movie."

"Then don't do it."

"It's too late. I'll just do it and get out."

"It's your company, Marilyn. You don't have to do anything you don't want to."

"I've got obligations to Fox, and the company isn't mine anymore. Arthur got rid of Milton Greene and put his friends on the board. They're all shits."

"Then start a company with me. Like we used to talk about. Look, I got to tell you about—"

But Marilyn was caressing him again, smiling up at him, forgetting about business and grief, and they would talk outside later and walk in the woods, and she knew exactly how to touch him, and she wanted to tell him secrets, but not now, there, the dog's out of the room, right there you see I know right where to touch you where it feels perfect, and she squeezed him and sucked him and took him in, and he made bread with her flesh, reciprocated with smooth touchings and yearning and now ardor, he was her word *ardent,* all for her, tasting her, eating her, licking her, breathing her perfumes, entering in out in out, forgetting, forgetting, forgetting. *Pier . . .*

MARILYN HAD PUT ON WEIGHT, AND HER SKIN WAS PERFECT—RADIant and unblemished. She had become the quintessential Jewish wife, sleek and zaftig and high-breasted, a blond kitchen goddess redolent with fertile promise—the queen bride of the Sabbath in jeans and work shirt.

She made omelets for lunch.

Eggs Parmentier, she called them, giggling at her pretentiousness. The eggs were gooey rich, peppery, and mixed with last night's roasted potatoes: a home-fry omelet. She gave him buttered toast and strong Colombian coffee stiffened with cognac; and they ate, laughed, got drunk, slept it off, and took a late-afternoon walk in the woods. The dogs ran ahead, free, disappearing into the green shadowy twilight of copse and soil, of boles split by lightning, of mulch and oak and pine, all the sweet, decaying, earthy smells . . . there, the scent of squirrel, creatures scurrying fluttering in the trees, in the branches reaching up to heaven—dog heaven, rich with rot and texture and the dolorous songs and screeing screaming of birds nesting and warning one another above.

"I like it in here," Marilyn said, almost in a whisper. "It's like a church, don't you think?"

Jimmy nodded; actually, he would have preferred to wander through the fields, explore open country. Woods always made him feel claustrophobic; they smelled of rot and death. "So tell me more about your lover."

"You're my lover," Marilyn said.

"You know who I mean."

Marilyn giggled. She wasn't hungover; neither was he, for that matter. They'd slept enough, and the Demerol had smoothed out the booze. Jimmy felt tired but rested, as if he'd gotten too much sleep. Leaves rustled around him; everything whispered, as if trying to tell him something. "You *are* jealous," Marilyn said.

"So humor me."

"I feel sorry for him."

"So do I," Jimmy said playfully.

Instead of batting him or pretending she was angry, she squeezed his hand and said, "He's not in love with Jacqueline Bouvier—that doesn't even sound like a real name, does it?"

"Does yours?"

"Yes, it most certainly does. Haven't you ever heard of the Monroe Doctrine? There are thousands, millions of Monroes. They're all over the place." She giggled. Jimmy grinned, and she continued, now serious. "Their families made them get married."

"Is that what he told you?"

"No, but I know," Marilyn said. "Now stop fooling around. I'm serious. You asked me about Jack, and I'm telling you. You want me to ask *you* questions?"

"No. Truce. I give up. Go on."

"I feel sorry for them, locked into that kind of a marriage, not being in love with each other. It was Jack's father's fault. He set it all up, you know, like royalty marrying royalty. It's not fair for her, either. Anyway, Jack's going to get an annulment."

Jimmy just walked along with her. They came to the edge of the woods, and he was relieved to be out, to be back in the sun, which was low, soon to be lost in a darkening red haze behind the mountains.

Marilyn called to the dogs, then said, "I hate it when you do that."

"Do what?"

"Not say anything. It always means that when you do, it will be something bad. Well?"

"I think you should be careful."

"That's what you always say."

"I was right about Arthur, wasn't I?"

"He's really a very good man. He helped me a lot, taught me things I wouldn't know now. I don't regret being with him, even though it's . . ."

"What?"

"Over." She continued. "But it's going to be different with Jack. It's not as if I don't know him, or love at first sight, or anything like that. I've known him for years."

"I don't believe you."

"Almost five years, Jimmy. You see, you don't know everything about me like you think."

"I guess I don't."

"And I've told Jack all about you."

"Oh, great. Thanks. Just what I need."

"And I want you to meet him. He thought maybe at the Cal-Neva Lodge, you know, the place where Frank always hangs out."

"You mean Old Glass Jaw?" Jimmy asked.

"You shouldn't call him that. It's not nice."

"I thought you hated his guts for following you around all the time."

"Frank's not so bad once you get to know him, and he's a friend of Jack's. Anyway, a woman's allowed to change her mind if she wants."

"I really don't think he'd be thrilled to see me."

"No, he's over all that. He figures you didn't mean to punch him, and I think he respects you for it. Men are all entirely crazy, you know that, don't you?"

"Known if for years," Jimmy said. "Why does Kennedy want to meet me?"

"Because you're part of my life."

"So's your maid. Does he want to meet her, too?"

"Forget it, Jimmy. Let's go back to the house. It'll be dark soon anyway."

"Why does he want to meet me?"

"Because . . . I told him you'd help with his campaign. You know, give it profile."

Jimmy laughed. "Where did you get that word?"

"Just forget it, Jimmy, okay?"

"Anything else he'd like, while you're at it?"

"Yes. Your singer Elvis Presley could help him, too."

"Christ, so that's it. Marilyn, he's just using you. He's never going to marry you."

"You can think whatever you want. It's a free country."

"How can he marry you? That would be the end of his political career."

"No, it wouldn't. We wouldn't get married until after he's president. Then it won't matter."

"It sure as hell would if he wants to run for a second term."

"Marrying me would *give* him his second term. Everyone would love it." She paused, as if savoring the thought. "Jimmy, he loves me, he really does. You've just got to believe me."

"I believe you, if that's what you want. But you know it's absolutely bug-fuck crazy, don't you? *You're* absolutely bug-fuck crazy."

"I haven't told anyone else about this, and I didn't even feel right about talking about it in the house."

"Why?"

She shrugged. "Bobby told me to be careful, that there are ears everywhere." After calling to the dogs again, she asked, "What do I have to do to convince you?"

"Of what? That someone's hiding in the closet listening to us and watching us fucking?"

"No, that I'm not bullshitting you about Jack. He really does want to meet you, and everything I told you is true. In fact, you were discussed at an important meeting in Chicago."

"Oh, great."

"I was there, at the Ambassador East, with Frank and Jack and Bobby and Mayor Daley." She giggled. "He looks like a pig, squinty little eyes, but Bobby tells me he's really powerful. And Sam Giancana was there, too."

"Who?"

"Sam Giancana. He owns the Cal-Neva with Frank. I told you about him. Johnny Roselli works for him."

"You mean to tell me your senator is hanging out with Mafia guys?" Jimmy asked, bewildered. "That's really fucked, you know that? You should stay away from them. I don't know what you see in Giancana. Talk about squinty little eyes."

"You judge people too harshly," Marilyn said. "Before you know them. You never even met Sam."

"Yes, I did. You introduced me to him, remember?"

"That was in a restaurant. What'd you say? Hello?"

"What did you expect me to say? 'Go on any hits lately?' "

"Okay, let's not talk about it," Marilyn said. "I'm sorry I brought it up." After a beat she asked, "Where the hell did those dogs go? Maybe they got lost. Maybe they're hurt. They always come when I call them." She looked desperate. "I don't know what I'd do if anything happened to them."

"I'm sure they're fine," Jimmy said.

"No, something's wrong, I know it. Everything's wrong. I'm sorry, I'm sorry I told you stuff about Jack. He told me to be careful, he warned me, but Arthur's right, I'm stupid, I'm too trusting, I'm—"

"Marilyn, stop it. The dogs are okay."

"No, they're not. If they're okay, where are they?" She shouted to them again. "Cindy! Hugo!"

No response.

Marilyn and Jimmy walked along the edge of the woods back to the house. It was Jimmy's favorite time of the day, the blue time just as the sun was setting; the quality of the air was different, the light long like soft neon, the background color of Jimmy's dreams and nightmares; and he thought again of Elvis's mother, Gladys, and the hillbilly word that Elvis's brat of a girlfriend had brought up at the hospital: *satnin*. This was *satnin* time. The world was getting tucked up for the night, safe and tick-tock cozy, and Marilyn looked like a ghost, white and beautiful and perfect—and frightened.

The dogs barked and ran to meet her—they had been waiting in front of the veranda steps.

MARILYN WAS STARING AT JIMMY.

The fire in the living room crackled and wheezed and whistled as the flue hungrily drew up the smoke. Cicadas roared outside, as constant and loud as the surf in Malibu, and the windows were as dark as black glass.

"I want you to hold me," Marilyn said.

"Too hot."

"Then we can sit away from the fire . . . or go into the bedroom." Marilyn got up and took some pills, then refilled his glass.

"What'd you just take?" Jimmy asked.

"A Nembutal. Just to relax."

"I thought you *were* relaxed," Jimmy said.

"I am. Just for the buzz. You know. You want one?"

"Yeah, what the hell."

She gave Jimmy a Nembutal, and he swallowed it with a gulp of Drambuie.

"Okay, you've had your pill. You ready to go to bed?"

"Jesus Christ, Marilyn—"

"Just to cuddle. I'm too tired to fuck. I just want to be held."

"Why?"

"Why?" Marilyn repeated. "Because . . . because I'm scared."

"Of what?"

"Of what's going to happen. Of who's going to get hurt."

"And who's that?"

"I don't know. Maybe Arthur . . . maybe you."

"*Me?* Why me?"

"I don't know. I don't know how you feel about me."

"Yes you do. What are you fishing for?"

Marilyn looked into the fire. "Nothing, Jimmy. If that's what you think, then we have nothing more to say to each other."

"Isn't that a line from a film?"

"Probably." She giggled. "But I mean it."

"You think you're going to hurt me because of the Kennedy business?"

"I don't know. You already think I'm trying to use you."

Jimmy started to speak, but Marilyn interrupted him. "And you're probably right. I'm awful, but I guess that's one of the reasons why I wanted to see you. To ask you to help Jack. Do you hate me?"

"Yeah," Jimmy said matter-of-factly.

"Well, fuck off, then."

"You asked."

"You should know better."

"How?"

"You should know I wanted to see you because . . ."

"Because why?"

"Because I love you."

"Obviously you don't love me as much as you do Kennedy," Jimmy said.

"Now who's fishing?"

"Do you?"

"I love you more."

"And that's why you think you can use me?"

She looked away from the fire and grinned at him. "Well, will you do it?"

"What?"

"Help Jack."

"What do you want me to do?" Jimmy asked.

"Do you know Peter Lawford, Jack's brother-in-law? He's a friend of Frank's."

"Sinatra?"

"Yeah. Peter has all the plans. All of Frank's friends, the whole Rat Pack, are going to help. You know, raise money, help with the image, do special concerts and rallies. You need that in politics."

Jimmy laughed. "You do, huh?"

"Yes, Mr. Big Shot, you do."

"And how do you know?"

"Because I've been studying and listening to what everybody says. Jack's friends may think I'm wallpaper, but Jack and Bobby don't. They talk to me and tell me things." She sounded sleepy. "Like about the problems in Illinois, which is why they need the machine there to bring in the votes, because that's the way it works there, and it's different everywhere." She paused. Then, raising her voice, insistent, "I've been learning, Jimmy. My friend Lester—he's the editor of *The New York Times*—he's teaching me things, and so are Bobby and Jack. I'm *not* stupid. This isn't rocket science."

"I never said or thought you were stupid."

"You fucking well implied it."

"Well, I didn't mean to."

"I'm not stupid about politics either," Marilyn said. "I think about it all the time. Christ, I've had to, being married to Arthur with all his problems with that goddamn Un-American Activities Committee." She had slid out of her Nembutal stupor. "I'm savvy about this shit. You think because I care about Jack Kennedy that I'm blind to everything that's going on. Well, I'm not. You know who'd be a good president? Stevenson. You know why he'll never make it? I'll bet you money, Jimmy, he doesn't make it. You know why? Because he can't talk to people, only to professors. And Justice William Douglas would make a fantastic president, but he's been divorced, so he couldn't make it. And Rockefeller—"

"Okay, okay, I believe you," Jimmy said, smiling. "You win. I give in."

"Good. Then let's go to bed." Marilyn told the dogs to stay and Jimmy followed her into the bedroom. "Are you going to help me?" she asked.

"With what?"

"Jack." She smoothed the sheets, undressed, and got into bed. "Well?"

"Yeah, I'll do anything for you."

She grinned at him, her eyes wide and glazed, and patted the bed.

Jimmy took his clothes off and slid under the covers beside her. He was in no shape to make love; the Demerol dulled him, protected him, centered him. But Marilyn really did just want to be cuddled; it would be good to sleep and dream everything bad away. He could stay with Marilyn forever, right here where it was safe from Nick and Mom Deacy and fans and himself. He started to drift off to sleep.

"Jimmy?"

"Yeah?"

"I'm sorry about Elvis. I heard about his mom dying and how distraught he was. If you can help Jack, it doesn't matter if we can't get Elvis."

"Jesus, Marilyn, you're like a dog with a bone." She reached over and grabbed him, hard. "Watch the balls, and you know what I meant." But he was getting excited in spite of himself. "I'm going to see Elvis in a couple of weeks."

"Yeah?" Marilyn caressed him, and he slipped in and out of dreams; everything was warm, fire warm, and yet cool, finger sliding, nail-edge cool.

"Nick and I are going to try to get Elvis to take a part in a picture we're doing with Jack Kerouac, the writer I was telling you about."

"The *On the Road* thing?" Marilyn asked.

"Yeah," Jimmy said, impressed. "I talked to Elvis's manager, and he didn't say no and wave his goddamn cigar in my face, which is a good sign. I think he's getting a little nervous that Elvis has been away in the army too long, I don't know. So maybe I can ask Elvis about helping you out, but the real problem is the Colonel. He's probably as right-wing as Hitler."

"You get Elvis. I'll get the Colonel."

"You don't even know him."

Marilyn smiled. "Don't have to." And with that she was sound asleep, her hand on Jimmy's lap.

ELEVEN

■

The Enemy Within

"Yeah?"

"Is this James Dean?"

"Who wants to know?"

There was a pause on the telephone line, then the caller continued in a Boston-bean accent. "This is Bob Kennedy."

"Yeah?" Jimmy said, surprised. He sat up in his bed and looked out onto Forty-fourth Street. Snow had turned to sludge, and the unusually clear sunny day seemed only to emphasize the dirty grittiness of the city.

"Marilyn suggested to my brother that I give you a call."

"She did, huh? Okay, what can I do for you?"

"Well, I have a business proposition I'd like to discuss with you. I think—I hope—you'll find it interesting."

Jimmy waited for Bobby Kennedy to continue. He fumbled nervously on the bed table for a cigarette and a hotel matchbook.

"Well?" asked Kennedy, obviously not willing to continue.

"What kind of proposition?"

"Look, I'm not really comfortable using the phone for initial discussions. It always fucks everything up."

Jimmy smiled, somehow surprised that the attorney general of the United States would say *fuck*.

"Would you care to have dinner together, and I'll lay everything out for you?"

"Sure," Jimmy said, exhaling two columns of smoke through his nose. "Where do you want to meet? I'm at the Algonquin." He laughed at himself, a nervous laugh. "Well, obviously, you already know that since you just called. The restaurant here isn't bad. They do a reasonable steak, and the waiters have been here longer than the hotel. They'll mispronounce your name, but at least they're consistent."

The attorney general didn't chuckle; it was obvious that he was uncomfortable and focused on getting this done. "Ah, I'm in Washington. I was thinking we could meet at my home in Virginia. It's pretty informal. We've got horses, if you like to ride, and I can guarantee that my wife, Ethel, makes the best clam chowder you'll ever eat. And the steak will be better than anything the Algonquin will serve."

"Don't you think Virginia is a bit far for me to go for dinner? Last I looked, I was in New York."

"You're leaving for the Coast tomorrow night, am I right?" the attorney general asked.

"Yeah."

"And you're booked to leave on Pan Am Flight five-sixteen out of Idlewild at five-fifteen."

"How'd you know that?"

"Not exactly rocket science. I can have a car pick you up at the hotel and take you to the airport. I'll have a plane waiting for you."

"I've already got tickets for L.A."

"No trouble. I'll get it all fixed. You'll stay the night with us, and then we'll get you to L.A."

"I'm not sure," Jimmy said.

"Well?"

Jimmy knew he was making a faux pas. *He's the goddamn attorney general.* "I'm sorry," he said. "You're just sort of catching me by surprise here. I don't know much—or care much—about politics, so if that's what it's about—"

"The president and I certainly appreciate all the help you've given us during the campaign. But I guarantee this isn't about politics. At least not in the sense that you mean."

"You sure you want me at your home?" Jimmy asked, immediately regretting the words. He felt his face grow hot with embarrassment. *What the hell kind of a question is that to ask, you asshole?*

The attorney general laughed and said, "Look, we're not very formal at Hickory Hill. I promise you won't be uncomfortable. I can have you picked up at one-thirty tomorrow. Will that give you enough time to take care of whatever you have to do?"

"More than enough," Jimmy said.

"Great. See you tomorrow night."

Kennedy hung up without a good-bye, and Jimmy felt an embarrassing, anxious jubilation. *He's only a goddamn politician. But what does he want with me?*

Jimmy would visit Marilyn tomorrow and find out.

THANK GOD FOR JOE. THANK GOD FOR JIMMY. THANK GOD I COULD *reach Joe at his home in St. Petersburg Beach. Thank God that Joe could reach Jimmy. Thank God Jimmy was in New York. Thank God for God.* Marilyn giggled at herself. She was thinking in poetry.

She sat by the west windows in a large, comfortable sunroom; reproductions of impressionist paintings hung on the pale, yellow walls, and the couches and cushioned high-backed chairs were worn and inviting. Marilyn wore white slacks and a powder-blue sweater. Whitey Snyder had done her hair. Ralph Roberts had been over to give her a massage and would be back later. She had gained some weight and was feeling more herself because she was in a regular hospital now, the Columbia-Presbyterian Medical Center, which was where she should have been in the first place. She should never have been put in that rubber room at the Payne-Whitney Psychiatric Clinic.

She thought of her *ex*-psychiatrist, Dr. Kris, who had tricked her— *You belong in that rubber room, not me, cunt*—and then picked up her gold Parker pen and started writing a letter to Dr. Greenson, her psychiatrist in Los Angeles. Her Jesus, that's what she called him. She giggled at the thought of starting it with "Dear Jesus," but she wasn't going to be fey. This was going to be a serious letter. She was going to tell Dr. Greenson what *really* happened to her at the hospital.

Again she giggled. *Thank God for God.* And started writing . . .

"Hey—" The voice sounded familiar and gentle, calling her, as if out of a dream. "Hey, you, blond girl."

Joe? No, it wasn't Joe. She looked up. "Jimmy, hi."

"You writing a letter?"

"No, I'm composing the Gettysburg Address." Marilyn giggled and focused herself on Jimmy, who was wearing jeans, boots, and a pullover sweater under an expensive bomber jacket. The jacket was brown, glossy, and new, the collar fur-lined. Jimmy's face was still flushed from the cold. "You look good enough to eat."

"I don't think they allow the patients to do that in the hospital."

"They probably do in this one," Marilyn said. "You want to go back to my room?"

Jimmy shrugged. "You like it out here better, don't you?"

"Nurses and orderlies have big ears."

Jimmy nodded and Marilyn said, "You've got something on your mind. What is it?"

"I came over to say good-bye. I'm flying back to L.A."

"Today?" Marilyn looked small, frightened, and disappointed. Jimmy nodded again. Marilyn stared at the table where she had been writing, then picked up her diary, stationery, and pen. "When are you leaving?"

"In a couple of hours."

They walked down a high-ceilinged hallway. To their left were windows. Below, swirling snow, a few trees, and a picnic table in a desolate square, and a parking lot enclosed by cold gray buildings.

"I'm moving back to L.A.," Marilyn pronounced, surprised and pleased to have just made the decision. "You know, there was a time when all I could think of was this far, faraway place called New York. It seemed so exciting to me, and I wanted the life—you know, studying at the Actors Studio with Lee, being part of the whole cool, hip, groovy scene." She shook her head and laughed. "I wanted to be a New York girl, *the* New York girl in beautiful clothes, admired by everyone. How stupid was *that?* What did it get me but a divorce, bad memories, and failures? So much for all that. So much for Mrs. Arthur Miller. So much for Marilyn Monroe Productions. So much for my dogs and walks in the woods. What I need, Jimmy, is in L.A.—you, Dr. Greenson, film work, my own place, and the sun. No more snow and forever gray, cold days . . . like this." She scowled.

Jimmy followed her into her room. The rich, cloying scent of flowers was strong; Joe DiMaggio must have sent another truckload of roses and lilies and tulips. Books were scattered over the unmade hospital bed. The bed table and a small desk were covered with papers, magazines, scripts, trays, and plastic cups.

"Sorry about the room," Marilyn said, "but I don't like letting the cleaners—or for that matter even the nurses—in. They're all so nosy, you wouldn't believe it."

"I was here yesterday, remember?" Jimmy said gently.

Marilyn pushed the papers aside and got into bed; she patted a space for Jimmy. "Yeah. Of course I remember. Sit here with me. I want you to hold me before you go."

"What if Joe comes in?"

"He just left a while ago. He's okay about us."

"Joe's not okay about anything," Jimmy said.

"He's changed his attitude about you since you and he rescued me."

"Yeah," Jimmy said sarcastically.

"Yeah." Marilyn giggled. "You and Joe must have torn the hospital apart. I still don't know how you got me out. What did you do, threaten Dr. Kris?"

"No, we didn't threaten her. We just explained that if she didn't help us get you out of there, we'd tear off all her clothes, tie her up, and throw her out the window."

Marilyn pulled her knees to her chest in delight and laughed. "No, you didn't."

"Okay, maybe I lied about tearing off her clothes; but after we talked to her, she was more than willing to help us get you out of there."

"Remember when we were in the cab, after you and Joe busted me out?"

"You mean when *you* threatened the doctor?"

"I didn't want Dr. Kris in the car with us."

"You didn't want to go to another hospital, either, but that was the deal. She's still your doctor."

"Not anymore."

"Christ, I almost felt sorry for her," Jimmy said.

"She's a cunt," Marilyn said, as if simply stating fact.

"She kept saying she did a terrible thing, and there you were screaming your lungs out at her, calling her every name in the book."

"She deserved it."

"She probably thought she was doing the right thing for you," Jimmy said.

"Bullshit. If you think that was the right thing—to lock me up in a rubber room—then you can—"

"Marilyn, cool out," Jimmy said. "It's me, Jimmy, remember?"

She reached for him and started crying, "I'm sorry, Jimmy. You and Joe saved me, and I'm acting as bad as Dr. Kris." Jimmy stroked her hair. "I'm never going to see her again. Dr. Greenson would never do that to me." After a beat, she asked, "Jimmy?"

"Yeah?"

"Do you love me?"

"You know I do."

"Enough to marry me?"

"Yeah, I guess."

They both started laughing.

"Jimmy?"

"Yeah?"

"Do you think I should marry Joe again? He really loves me."

"I don't think you should marry anybody."

"Even you?"

"Maybe me."

"I got a call from Jack about you," Marilyn said.

"Yeah, I wanted to talk to you about that," Jimmy said, relieved that Marilyn had brought it up. "I got a call from his brother. He wants me to meet him in Virginia about some sort of project, but he wouldn't tell me what it was."

Marilyn shrugged. "That's typical Bobby."

"What do you mean?"

"He's like that. Everything's a big secret with Bobby. Jack calls him 'the Policeman.' "

"So what's it all about?"

"I don't know," Marilyn said dreamily. She looked at him and said, "I'm so tired, Jimmy."

"But Bob said that *you* suggested he call me."

"I don't remember that."

"The president must have told you *something*."

"No . . ."

"Marilyn," Jimmy said, frustrated. "Come *on*."

"I don't think you should do it," Marilyn said, her voice muffled, and then her breathing changed, became deeper.

"Marilyn?"

"I love you, Jimmy, don't leave me . . ."

JIMMY TOOK A SHUTTLE TO WASHINGTON NATIONAL AIRPORT, and was met by a limousine that took him to Hickory Hill, Robert F. Kennedy's home in McLean, Virginia. The driver, a young flirtatious Justice Department secretary called Betsy, parked the limousine in the circular driveway of the antebellum mansion, and the twilight quiet was suddenly broken by dogs barking and children screaming.

Four huge dogs, the largest a black Newfoundland, barked and snarled and jumped at the car, their claws scratching against the windows. The children, who seemed to range from around five to ten years old, were also jumping. They shouted for Betsy to come out and play with them. "You promised!" The youngest was barefoot and dressed in a little white nightgown. She stamped her feet in the snow-patched grass and cried, pleading for attention.

"I'm not going out there," Jimmy said, reflexively leaning away from the barking, snapping dogs.

"We got something to show you!" one of the children squealed.

"What's big and green and's in the dining room?" shouted another.

Betsy laughed and said to Jimmy, "Don't worry, the dogs won't hurt you. Neither will the children—probably."

Then another voice shouted at the dogs: "Brumus, Meegan, get away from that car!" Then at the children: "Mary Courtney, get yourself inside the house and get some clothes on. Kathleen Hartington Kennedy, you're the oldest, it's your responsibility, now you take your sister inside. All of you, inside right this very minute."

"No, Mom! You promised we could stay up and meet the guest."

Jimmy got out of the car to meet Ethel Kennedy, who smiled at him and shook his hand heartily. She was dressed in a heavy white cardigan and a wool skirt. Petite, rather plain-looking, and in her early thirties, she seemed to radiate energy. She was a tomboy grown up. She had widely set blue eyes, an impish grin, and short, light-brown hair. "It's a pleasure to have you at our home, Mr. Dean. I've seen all your movies."

He liked her immediately. "Call me Jimmy," he said.

"Don't worry about your luggage," Ethel said. "Betsy will get one of the servants to take your bags up to your room."

"I've only got the one—"

"Leave it," Betsy said. "It'll all get taken care of."

"We've got chickens, and they're green," said Mary, the barefoot five-year-old who had circled around them; although obviously freezing, she had no intention of being left out.

"Yeah," Jimmy said, laughing. "Well, *I* like green eggs and ham."

"You *do?*" she asked, impressed.

"Of course, doesn't everybody?"

"But you can't eat my chicken, can he, Mommy?"

Ethel just shook her head.

"Come on, everybody, up to the house," Betsy said.

But Mary rushed over to Jimmy, who swept her up in his arms. "You're going to turn into an iceberg—a *green* iceberg," he told her.

"I don't care. Can I stay with you?"

Jimmy looked to Ethel, who laughed and said, "She can be a pest. You sure you don't mind?"

"Not at all."

"Bobby should be home soon," Ethel said. "He's sometimes late on a Friday, but he told me it was important, so he'd be home right along."

Jimmy considered asking her if she knew why he wanted to talk to him but thought better of it. For the moment, this fine, chilly, perfect moment, he was happy. He could see an old stone barn and stables. To his left, the neatly cut lawn declined to a tennis court and swimming pool. There was room here, acres and acres of woods and fields and lawns, and the air smelled like autumn leaves with a faint sniff of ozone, as if a storm had blown away all the pollution, all the miasmas of New York and Los Angeles and Washington, D.C. This wasn't Illinois, which was brown and yellow, but it was home; he felt that with every step, with the wriggly worm Mary in his arms, and the dogs snapping, and the rabbits and cats and horses and who knew what other animals just out of sight. Instead of buying that monstrosity of a Georgian mansion in L.A., he should have gotten out, bought in the country, where he could breathe. He could buy something like this. He wasn't a Kennedy, but he sure as hell could afford it. He caught a faint scent of manure. Indeed, they had horses, and he felt a pang over the loss of his own horse, Cisco.

The house was elegant and messy and completely lived-in; it also smelled of cat piss. The rooms had high ceilings and large crystal chandeliers, and the woodwork was painted white. The large rooms were brightly and festively lit, and Jimmy was somehow reminded of Christmas; but the dining room was dim, a single blade of smoky twilight cutting in through a gap in the drawn curtains. It wasn't a large room, and the heavy curtains and Gillow dining table made it look even smaller. Claustrophobic rather than cozy. There was a huge green centerpiece on the table.

Jimmy put Mary down. The child complained, then wandered away.

"Can we show him now?" asked one of the boys, who looked about seven.

"No, David Anthony, we can't. Now go wash your entire big mouth out with soap." The children howled at that, and Ethel told Jimmy it was a private joke.

"My mother always told me it was impolite not to include the guest," Jimmy said, chiding her.

"Well, if you're a good boy, Mr. Dean, maybe we'll just do that—later."

Jimmy grinned and said, "Jimmy. Remember?"

"Okay, Jimmy," Ethel repeated, and she squeezed his arm, reassuring him. "Bobby told me you wanted a steak, so the cook's going to grill you one special. I promised Bobby and the children fried chicken, so—"

"You don't have to cook anything special for me. I'll be happy with whatever's on the table."

"Well, then you'll just have to have both," Ethel said. "And clam chowder. He said you wanted clam chowder."

"Really, I'm happy with anything."

"Do you even like clam chowder?"

Jimmy laughed. "I never gave it much thought, to tell you the truth. When I talked to your husband, he told me you make the best clam chowder."

Ethel laughed. "It's like the fried chicken. He told his brother that I make the best fried chicken in the world. You'd think after all these years he'd figure out that I can't boil water. His sister Eunice makes the best fried chicken in the world. All I did was get the recipe from her and give it to my cook. Now my cook makes the best fried chicken in the world." She laughed and winked conspiratorially. "Well, maybe you shouldn't tell Bobby. Let him keep believing against all odds that I really *can* boil water."

She led Jimmy into the library and asked him if he wanted a drink.

Suddenly there was a commotion.

"Look, mister, look, look at this!" shouted Mary. Betsy and the other children were all around her, chasing a green chicken that was flapping its wings, skittering around the room, slipping on the polished floorboards, and making terrified screeching noises. Then it disappeared into the darkened dining room.

"See, I *told* you," Mary said to Jimmy.

Joseph trapped the chicken under a side table and caught it.

"Mary, I *told* you to leave that chicken alone!" Ethel screamed. "Now you've spoiled everything." Mary started wailing and ran over to Jimmy, as if for protection. Then Ethel snapped at Betsy. "Get these children taken care of. It's all *your* fault. Can't you do anything right? My husband should fire you."

"I'm sorry, Mrs. Kennedy."

"Then see to the children. *Now*." Betsy rushed the children out of the room.

"Not a brain in her head," Ethel said. "Bobby tells me she graduated Phi Beta something, but she's dumb as a door, anyway. Thinks women should have the same rights as men, and she can't even hide a chicken." Ethel grinned at Jimmy.

"It was . . . green," Jimmy said.

"Well, forget you saw it. It's a surprise. Now sit down and relax, if you can after that, and I'll fix you a drink." She shook her head and said, "I'm not being a very good hostess. I'm sorry, did you want to go to your room and freshen up? It's up the stairs, third bedroom on the left."

Jimmy smiled. "No, ma'am. I'm fresh enough."

"Good for you," she said, grinning. "Now, do you drink—or just smoke pot?"

"Well, normally I just smoke pot, but since this is a special occasion, I'll take a drink."

"Martini?"

"Fine," he said, giggling and settling into the scuffed leather sofa, while she mixed the drinks. Then there was another commotion, children shouting and laughing. Robert F. Kennedy was home. When he walked into the room, Ethel kissed him, gave him a martini, and handed another to Jimmy, who stood up to greet the attorney general.

"Okay, kids, stop jumping or Daddy will spill his drink."

"But you promised you'd pick me up!" Mary said.

Bobby put his drink down on a sideboard and picked her up. "I'm really glad you could make it," he said to Jimmy, shaking his hand. "Sit down, please. Did you eat with the kids?" he asked Ethel.

"No, they're eating with us. This is a special occasion, remember?"

Bobby smiled and nodded. "Ah. Then we'll talk later," he said to Jimmy.

Jimmy nodded. He was more focused and less relaxed. Bobby was after something, and Jimmy wasn't going to let his guard down; although here, in his house with Bobby's family, he couldn't help but feel a certain kinship with this wiry, nervous-looking man. Perhaps it was because they both had the habit of lowering their heads and staring out at people, as they did with each other now. Bobby picked up on it immediately. "You know," he said to Ethel, "remember what that asshole reporter wrote in that Atlanta paper—"

"Your language."

"—about how I look through my eyebrows like a coon peering out of a henhouse?"

Ethel laughed. "That one really caught you, didn't it?"

"What's a coon, Daddy?" asked Mary.

"It's an animal, honey," Bobby said. Then to Ethel: "Well, Jimmy does the same thing, doesn't he?"

"I don't know about that," Ethel said.

"No, ma'am," Jimmy said, "the attorney general's right. I've been accused of looking at people like that, too. I've got to admit, though, I like 'a coon peering out of a henhouse.' " He laughed.

"We're not very formal around here, as you've probably noticed," Bobby said. "Call me Bobby, and I don't think anyone else has ever called my wife ma'am."

"Well, everyone should," Ethel said, laughing. "Now, are you ready for the surprise, before it gets dark?" She gave Bobby a significant look.

"Sure," Bobby said, and they all retired to the dining room, which was now brightly lit.

Betsy stood by the curtains, and Mary, outraged, jumped up and down and said, "Mommy, you promised that *I* could do it!" The children were all laughing and wrestling about the room. Neither Bobby nor Ethel seemed the least bit concerned.

"Okay, you can do it, honey," Ethel said.

Betsy looked at Jimmy, smiled, then helped Mary pull the cord. Everyone screamed and shouted as the curtains opened. Jimmy was shocked to see a theater-sized signboard poster of *Rebel Without a Cause* sitting on a scaffold on the patio. The poster depicted Jimmy in a red jacket with his hands in the back pockets of his jeans. Above the image: "Jim Stark—a kid in the year 1955—what makes him tick . . . like a bomb?"

"Holy cow," Jimmy said. "Where the hell did you get hold of that?"

The kids were laughing, and Ethel said, "Language, Jimmy." Then she smiled and said, "We have our ways of finding things. Welcome to Hickory Hill. We want you to feel at home here."

Ethel seated everyone in the dining room and went into the kitchen. The children kept giggling and laughing until they were crying. When Bobby and Jimmy realized that there were two huge green bullfrogs in the centerpiece, it was pandemonium. "Jesus Christ," Bobby said.

"Watch your language!" Ethel called from the kitchen.

"Frogs?"

"They're green—for Saint Patrick's Day."

"But Saint Patrick's Day is a week away."

"Mr. Dean will be in California on Saint Patrick's Day," Ethel called from the kitchen. "So we're changing the date for him. Is that okay, Jimmy?"

"Fine," Jimmy said, laughing, as the kids prodded the frogs to jump around the table.

Ethel entered the dining room and took her seat at the far end of the table, opposite Bobby.

"How'd you get them to just sit there?" Jimmy asked.

"Drugs," Ethel said, grinning.

A dark, puffy, nervous-looking woman brought in a large, covered silver platter and put it down beside Bobby. Jimmy was surprised that Betsy didn't bring in the food, and that there wasn't a place set for her at the table.

"Okay, what's this?" Bobby asked, suspicious.

"Open it up and find out."

Something moved inside. It was, of course, the green chicken. When Bobby lifted the cover, it ran around the table. Joe caught it and told Mary that this was the chicken that they really were going to eat. She started crying but calmed down when a bowl of clam chowder was put in front of her.

"We're making a very bad impression on our guest," Bobby said.

"Then he'll always be a guest," Ethel said. "If he wants to join the family, then he'll have to get used to it." She nodded at Jimmy approvingly.

Jimmy just shook his head and tucked into the chowder, which was delicious.

While they ate, Bobby tested the children on current events. "It's a family tradition," he told Jimmy. "You're welcome to join in—no holds barred." He grilled the children about the Peace Corps; his brother Jack had announced its formation yesterday. "And who's in charge of it?" Bobby asked.

"Uncle Jack," said Robert Frances, who was seven.

"The president is in charge of everything, but I asked who's in charge of the Peace Corps. Come on, before the main course comes in."

"Uncle Sargent," Kathleen said, meaning Sargent Shriver, Bobby's brother-in-law. "That's easy."

"Very good," Bobby said. "Now tell me who Uncle Jack said was going to be the first volunteer."

"That's no fair," Kathleen said.

Bobby shrugged. "It's in the paper. You're supposed to read at least *one* newspaper. Is that too much to ask?" Kathleen looked properly cowed.

The atmosphere at the table had changed. Bobby rather than Ethel was certainly in control, and the children were subdued and polite now. Dinner at the Kennedys' had suddenly turned into serious business. "I'll give you a hint," Bobby said. "It's an athlete."

"Is it a girl or a boy?" Joseph asked.

"If you knew the answer, you wouldn't ask such a dumb question."

When it became obvious that the children couldn't answer the question, Jimmy said, "It's Rafer Johnson. He took gold in the decathlon last year in Rome. He won it by only some sixty points, though."

Bobby nodded and looked at Jimmy with respect. Jimmy winked at Kathleen, trying to diffuse the tension.

"What else about him is important?" Bobby asked Kathleen.

"He's a nigger," said Joseph.

"We say Negro," Bobby said. "And what's that got to do with the price of beans?"

"Because he carried the flag," Kathleen said.

"That's right," Bobby said. "He was the first Negro"—he looked at Joseph when he said "Negro"—"ever to carry the American flag in an Olympic procession."

Kathleen looked relieved, vindicated, but Bobby kept hammering away with more questions about the Peace Corps, economic aid for Latin America, the Twenty-third Amendment—"So who can now vote in a presidential election?"—and Leakey's sensational discovery of the bones of a child in the Olduvai Gorge of Tanganyika.

There was a nasty edge to Bobby, Jimmy thought, tuning out the questions. He felt tired, drugged, as he digested the good steak and strawberry shortcake dessert.

"Bobby learned how to ruin dinner from his father," Ethel said. "Every time the children take an exam, they expect the school to serve them food."

Bobby just looked at her, as if he hadn't heard a word or simply didn't get the joke. He turned to Jimmy, gave him his coon-in-a-henhouse look.

Jimmy gave it right back to him.

It was time to do business.

THEY WALKED ACROSS THE LAWN IN THE MOONLIGHT. BEHIND THEM the house was aglow, the windows butter yellow, warm and welcoming; outside, it was cold, uncomfortable.

"You okay in that jacket?" Bobby asked Jimmy.

"Yeah. I'm used to cold weather."

Bobby walked briskly; it was obvious that he could navigate around his extensive property blindfolded. He was wearing a bomber jacket like Jimmy's over a button-down shirt. His tie was pulled loose. "If you like, we'll go riding tomorrow before you go. You ride—you have your own horses, right?"

"Had. I had a horse, but it died."

"Sorry."

"Who told you about the horse?"

Bobby shrugged. They walked down to the edge of the road but kept to the property.

"I'd like you to act in a movie I'm making," Bobby said, as if it had taken him all this time to work up his courage. "It's an adaptation of my book, *The Enemy Within*." He clasped his hands together as he walked, pressing hard and staring at them—obviously a nervous habit.

"*You're* making the movie?" Jimmy asked.

"Well, I'm involved in it," Bobby said. "Jerry Wald is the producer. He came to me with the idea. Budd Schulberg is working on the screenplay."

Jimmy nodded. "What's it about?"

"I was chief counsel for the Senate's Rackets Committee. Some of the proceedings were televised. You probably saw some of it?"

Jimmy hadn't, but he said, "Yeah?"

"It's about how organized crime has taken over the labor unions. It's about a conspiracy of evil that's poisoning our institutions. Our entire society." He walked faster but didn't look at Jimmy. "It's about greasy hoods in eight-hundred-dollar suits who prey on the weak and destroy anyone who gets in their way."

"You mean Hoffa," Jimmy said.

"And others," Bobby said. "But think about it. The Teamsters drive the trucks that clothe and feed us and provide the vital necessities of life. They control the pickup and deliveries of milk, frozen meat, fresh fruit, department-store merchandise, newspapers, railroad express, airfreight, and cargo to and from the sea docks. Quite literally your life—the life of every person in the United States—is in the hands of crooks and murderers like Hoffa."

Good speech, Jimmy thought sourly.

"When I first started investigating labor racketeering, I learned how the Teamsters keep things sweet with the trucker associations. I interviewed a union organizer from Los Angeles who'd gone to San Diego to try to organize jukebox operators. The Teamsters told him to stay out of San Diego, or they'd kill him. Well, he went back anyway, and union goons beat the living shit out of him. When he regained consciousness the next morning, he was covered with blood and had terrible stomach pains, which were so bad, he couldn't drive back to Los Angeles. So he stopped at a hospital, where he was operated on immediately. The doctors found an entire cucumber shoved up his ass.

Later on he was told that if he ever came back to San Diego, it would be a watermelon."

"I take it he didn't go back," Jimmy said.

Bobby smiled mirthlessly. "No, I don't believe he did." They continued to walk along the edge of the street. Jimmy could see his breath in the air; it was getting really cold. "Schulberg is writing a terrific script," Bobby said. "Jerry Wald thinks this film could be as important as *On the Waterfront*."

"Well, he would," Jimmy said.

Bobby chuckled. "I guess you're right. I've read the first draft, but what the hell would I know?"

"It sounds like your story *is On the Waterfront*."

"Except mine's real," Bobby said.

Jimmy shrugged. "So why me?"

"I'd like you to play me."

"I don't even look like you."

"Yeah, you do. At least everybody agrees that you'd be perfect. It would be great for the film—and great for you."

"How so?"

"You'll become identified as a modern-day hero." Jimmy laughed. He wasn't quite sure whether Bobby was kidding. "And you'll make a shitload of money," Bobby continued.

"So why didn't you just tell me what you wanted when you called me on the phone?"

Bobby shrugged. "Because it's not the way I work. It's not a comfortable way to do business."

"I think you're holding something back," Jimmy said cautiously. "Anyway, I'm not the person you should be talking to. You need to call my agent. Jerry Wald should have told you that. He knows better." Jimmy gave Bobby a sidelong glance, but it was too dark to judge any subtlety of expression. "I hope I'm not sounding ungrateful or anything. I really enjoyed spending time with your family."

"Yeah, they're terrific," Bobby said. "And what'd you think of our girl Betsy?"

"She's a sweetheart."

"She's more than that," Bobby said, chuckling. Jimmy thought it best to let that go. He followed Bobby, who was cutting back across his property.

"I wanted to talk to you about Marilyn, too," Bobby said abruptly. He didn't glance over at Jimmy but gazed straight ahead at the trees silhouetted flatly against the milky darkness of the sky. "She's still in the hospital."

"I saw her today, but you probably know that," Jimmy said.

"Yeah, she calls Jack."

"So?"

"She calls him all the time," Bobby said.

"What does this have to do with me?" Jimmy asked warily.

"You're a dear friend of hers, and . . . look, I don't want this to get all fucked up. I'm afraid that if she keeps calling Jack, it's going to make trouble for both of them. If any of this gets out to the press—"

"You got the wrong guy, Bobby. You should never have asked me over here on the bullshit pretense of a movie to get me involved with whatever Marilyn and your brother got going. I'm not one of your fucking—"

"Jimmy, please, just *listen* to me." He sighed. "I knew this was going to get all fucked up. I wanted to see you because you're the one I want to play me in the film. I figured if I left it up to everybody else, it wouldn't happen, and I'd end up with Paul Newman in the lead. He'd be okay, he's a good actor, but he'd just be wrong for this part."

"Is he in the running?" Jimmy asked, taking the bait.

"He's interested," Bobby said.

"Then he got called first, right?"

"I got into an argument with Jerry because I wanted to talk to you. Otherwise, we would have gone through channels and called your agent. I should have left it to him."

"Who's your director?"

"That element isn't attached yet," Bobby said.

Jimmy couldn't help but laugh. "They've already got you talking the talk. You'd better watch yourself, or you'll end up in the business."

"I assumed that since you've been working with Nick Ray—whose work I also admire—that you might be interested in directing, or codirecting. Whatever."

"But this is really about Marilyn."

"No, it's about you. But I—" He laughed. "Politicians always have agendas. I guess I couldn't resist combining business with pleasure."

"Which is which?" Jimmy asked.

"I know Marilyn is your friend, and my brother is crazy about her. But she's got to stop calling him every five minutes."

"And if she doesn't?"

Bobby hunched his shoulders, as if there was a gale-force wind blowing. "Then she's going to get hurt."

"Is that a threat?" Jimmy asked coldly.

"No, of course not. I didn't mean she'll get hurt physically. I mean Jack will have to stop seeing her."

"He's been telling her he's going to marry her," Jimmy said.

"No, he hasn't. Jack might be a fucker, but he wouldn't lead her on like that."

"Well, that's what she's getting. Does he love her?" After a beat, Jimmy continued, "Well, you brought it up. I figure it was never any of my business in the first place."

"He cares about her," Bobby said. "More than he cares about any of the women he sees. But Jack never really gets involved."

"So he'll drop her and it'll be over," Jimmy said.

"If it could be that simple, I wouldn't be dragging you into it. Look, Jack doesn't know I'm talking to you about this. He cares about her, but it's never going to be serious with Jack. He'd never drop Jackie. Never."

"I still don't get all this," Jimmy said. He could see the lights of the house twinkling through the pale, snow-gray branches of the trees.

"There was an . . . incident," Bobby said. "Marilyn uses another name when she calls the White House, and she had Jack's private line, so when she calls in, Jack's secretary knows what to do. But his regular secretary wasn't there when Marilyn called, and when the substitute secretary wouldn't connect her with Jack, she started screaming at the poor woman, telling her she was Marilyn Monroe, and if she didn't let her talk to the president, she was going to get her ass fired."

Jimmy shrugged.

"She was in one of her states," Bobby continued. "She finally tracked me down and threatened that if she couldn't get ahold of Jack right away, she was going to call a press conference."

"She was just putting you on," Jimmy said.

"I don't believe that for a minute. She was out of her head. Who knows what she's telling people."

"What she's been through would make anybody crazy. Look, I saw her this morning, and I can tell you she's doing really well."

"The incident I just told you about happened today," Bobby said. "After you saw her. Do you see the problem now?"

Jimmy shrugged. He wasn't ready to give anything away to Bobby just yet. "Even if you're right, what can I do?"

It was Bobby's turn to shrug. "I thought you should know. She confides in you. Maybe you can talk some sense into her. I really don't think, in her more rational moments, that she wants to bring down the president of the United States." After a beat he said, "Maybe she does."

Jimmy laughed. "That's all a bit melodramatic."

But Bobby was serious. "She's acting crazy, Jimmy."

"She's *not* crazy."

"Okay."

"This is a threat," Jimmy said. "Or you wouldn't be telling me anything."

Bobby stopped when he reached the back porch. An overhead light sharpened his features, making him appear worn and older than he was. He laughed and said, "Oh, yeah, we've got threats, but they don't have anything to do with Marilyn."

"What are you talking about?"

"There are people who don't want *The Enemy Within* to get made. Nasty-ass people, Jimmy. Jerry Wald has already been threatened once. And Fox may chicken out of the deal."

"And you figure that's an inducement for me to get involved, right?" Jimmy asked.

"I figure that since you crash racing cars and turned Frank Sinatra's jaw to glass, you have a death wish." He held the back door open for Jimmy. "So, do you think this project might interest you?"

No. Get fucked.

I got to talk to Marilyn.

He's right about one thing, though—she's in over her head.

Jimmy stepped into the fireplace-warm house, which was lit up like day, and heard himself mumble, "It might . . ."

TWELVE

■

Twisting

"Marilyn?"

"Yeah?" A sleepy voice.

"It's me, Jimmy. What did you want?"

"You." Marilyn let out an audible yawn, then giggled. "But your little wopster playmate didn't seem keen to let you talk to big bad me."

"Don't talk about Pier like that." Jimmy spoke in a low voice, even though he was downstairs in the library. He hadn't turned on the lights, and the large, high-ceilinged room seemed to be floating in shadows. A night-light cast a red halo around an electrical outlet near the door. Every room in the house had a night-light—both Pier and Jimmy were afraid of the dark, although Jimmy would never admit his fear.

"Last month you hated her. Now she's living with you."

"She's not living with me," Jimmy said. "She's just staying over. She has her own apartment. Why? You jealous?"

"Yeah," Marilyn said, giggling again. "But I think she's more jealous of me."

"So what's up? Why'd you call? You all right?"

"I'm fine," Marilyn said matter-of-factly, which meant she wasn't. At least she didn't sound cotton-mouthed from too many tranquilizers, as she often did. "Jimmy, I really am sorry if I got you into any trouble with Pier. I just figured you'd be alone, except for Marty."

"Marty's gone."

"Why?"

"Pier doesn't like him."

"So you kicked him out?"

"Yeah, I guess."

"For good?"

"He's got to get his own life," Jimmy said. "I've been trying to get rid of him for years. I can't have him hanging around all the time. People will think I'm queer or something."

"You mean Pier will think you're queer."

Jimmy laughed mirthlessly. "She already does."

"What happened to Mr. I Won't Live My Life with One Hand Tied Around My Back?"

"Is this what you called to tell me?"

"I called you to tell you that I love you. Do you love me?"

"Yes."

"Then tell me a secret, and I'll tell you one back."

"I asked Pier to marry me." Marilyn didn't respond. "Hello? Did you hang up?"

"No, I'm here."

"Well?"

"That's a shock."

"You know how I feel about her."

"Yeah." There was something tentative in Marilyn's voice.

Jimmy giggled. "That doesn't change how I feel about you, little sister."

"I know," Marilyn said in a small voice.

"Well, then?"

"I did a terrible thing tonight, Jimmy."

"Yeah, what?"

"I've probably screwed everything up, but it had to be done. Now

Jack won't let me go to the party for Bobby. I'm sure he won't, and I want to go, I—"

"Marilyn, you're not making any goddamn sense. It's almost morning and—"

Marilyn started sobbing.

Jesus Christ, turn it on and turn it off. Jimmy tried to calm her down. "Just tell me what happened."

"I can't. It's too terrible. I called to tell you something else, too, but I'm not going to upset you. It's too terrible, it's *all* too terrible." With that she hung up.

Jimmy called her right back, lest she try to ring him and wake up Pier.

"Yeah?" she said.

"Look, are you going to be all right?"

"No, that's why I called you. Come over here and stay with me, Jimmy. Please."

"I've got Pier here. I can't."

"Fuck Pier. She doesn't love you."

"Well, fuck you, Marilyn."

"I'm sorry, Jimmy. Forgiven?"

"Just go to sleep and we'll talk tomorrow."

"Everything has gone wrong, Jimmy. I need to see you now. I need you to help me."

"Call your shrink. You said he was your goddamned Jesus."

"I did, but it rang through. Please, Jimmy, I just need to see you for a little while. I'll tell you something about Pier if you come over."

"What about Pier?"

"Are you coming over?"

"No, I can't."

"Then fuck you, James Byron Dean. I'm going over to Googie's, and I'm going to eat banana cream pies until I'm fat as a house and fart when I walk. Unless I decide to stay here and just kill myself." And she hung up again.

Jimmy tried to call her back, but the phone just rang and rang.

GOOGIE'S WAS PRACTICALLY EMPTY. ALL THE WANNABES AND COOL cats were sleeping on this Wednesday morning, the dykes and greasy hair and leather crowd were somewhere else, and the hippies were being hip in their freak pads with pop art posters and black lights.

Marilyn sat at the back booth near the jukebox, which was playing Del Shannon's hit song "Runaway." She was wearing white slacks and a silk leopard-pattern blouse, which looked slept-in. Her unwashed hair was mostly hidden under a kerchief, and she wore no makeup. Her eyes were red, her face pasty with a sheen, as if she'd been sweating—what Jimmy always thought of as fear sweat.

When Jimmy walked in, she was, indeed, eating a slice of banana cream pie, her second. She looked up at him and grinned; for an instant, she was Marilyn, white-light charismatic and astonishing, the most beautiful and vulnerable woman in the world, but the light faded just as fast, leaving her wan and spent, just another pale, ectoplasmic spirit who inhabited late-night diners and truck stops. Jimmy waved to Skinny, the counterman, who seemed excited to see him, and sat down beside Marilyn. He ordered pie and coffee.

"You look like shit," he said.

"Thanks for that," Marilyn said, wiping her mouth with the back of her hand, then wiping her hand with a napkin that she worried out of a tin receptacle. "So do you."

Jimmy looked around. "I haven't been here for dog's years. Hasn't changed, except there isn't anyone here."

Skinny brought over pie and coffee. He was in his late forties, maybe older; the dark shadow of a day's growth covered his long and too-angular face, and his kinky gray-streaked hair was pulled back into a ponytail.

"Place is dead," Jimmy said.

"See what happens when you leave," the counterman said, smiling. He turned to Marilyn and asked, "Can I get you anything else, Miss Monroe?" She shook her head and gazed down at the table. Skinny walked away.

Jimmy took a sip of the coffee and said, "So tell me what's going on." Marilyn just looked down at the table. "Marilyn!"

"Sorry. I'm just tired." She laughed. "Can't sleep, but I'm tired. How's that for a conundrum?" She savored the last word, as if it was round and delicious.

"You're a regular dictionary," Jimmy said. "You take any pills?"

"Yeah, a few, but it's not that." She shook her head. "They're out of my system by now, anyway. I'm stone cold sober, and I can't stand it. I want to fucking die, Jimmy."

"Why?"

"You got all night?" She looked at the pie and made a face, as if she'd just discovered that she'd eaten too much and didn't like banana cream pie anyway.

"We ain't got much left of all night. What did you do?"

"I called Jackie," she said in almost a whisper.

"Who?"

"Jackie Kennedy."

"Jesus Christ. What for?"

"To tell her that Jack's going to divorce her and marry me."

"You're absolutely bug-fuck crazy," Jimmy said.

Marilyn shrugged. "Somebody had to do it. I'm not a coward, and I can't stand being a sneak. It was time for her to face up to the truth. No way she hasn't known what's been going on, and my call proved it."

"How?"

Marilyn smiled at Jimmy, which chilled him. "Jackie knew I was going to call her. She had to know."

"Yeah . . . why?"

"Because she wasn't upset. She was calm as could be, and she said that if Jack wanted me, then she'd step aside. So Jack will be able to divorce her and marry me. She talked to me like she was my friend and told me that if I'm serious about Jack, I'll have to take on all the responsibilities of being First Lady. She said otherwise I should forget about it and stay on the sidelines. But that's not me."

"She's as crazy as you are." Marilyn shrugged and drew cross-hatching lines in her pie with her fork. "So what's the problem? Looks like everything is jim-dandy."

Marilyn spoke so low that Jimmy couldn't hear her.

"What?"

"Bobby called me and told me never to call the White House or Jack or anybody ever again."

"Yeah."

"I called Jack's private number, but it was dead, and I couldn't get through to Bobby. I thought . . . maybe you could call him and explain."

"Explain what? That you've just blown the president of the United States out of the water?"

"You're working with Bobby on that picture of his. I don't really even know him."

"Yes you do," Jimmy said. "Calling the president's wife was a really stupid thing to do, Marilyn."

She looked up at him, furious. "Well, if Jack thinks that's the end of it, he's in for a big surprise. I'll hold a fucking press conference and—"

"Calm down, and lower your voice."

"Will you call Bobby?"

"It won't do any good."

"Will you try?"

"I'll mention it to him when we talk."

"Jimmy, you've got to call him. I can't wait."

"Okay. Jesus Christ. Tomorrow."

Marilyn beamed at him, as if the deed was done and he'd fixed everything up, Jimmy the fixer, the quintessential, impossible fixer.

"Why don't you just let it all go? The president can only mean trouble."

"I can't."

"Why? You're seeing other people, aren't you?"

"Maybe," Marilyn said cautiously.

"You're seeing me."

She grinned. "I'll always see you."

"And what about Old Glass Jaw? He's crazy about you. Christ, you were all excited about that diamond pin or whatever it was that he gave you."

"Don't call Frankie that," Marilyn said, "and they were earrings. Diamonds and emeralds. They cost him thirty-five thousand dollars."

"Proves my point."

"About what?"

"That he's in love with you."

"He wouldn't expect me to be a housewife like Joe wanted. We could both have our careers. It would be perfect."

"Well, then?"

"He's not ready, and I'm in love with Jack."

"No you're not."

"Yes I am."

"If Sinatra asked you to marry him tomorrow, would you say no?"

She shrugged. "What do you think I'd say if *you* asked me?"

"I don't know. I'm afraid you'd marry all three of us."

Marilyn laughed. "Wouldn't that make me a bigamist or a trigamist or something?"

"Marilyn?"

"Yeah, Jimmy?"

"Why are you fucking around with Jack Kennedy?"

"I told you. Because I love him. Because . . ."

"Because why?"

"Because he makes me . . . important," she said ever so softly, shyly, and then she resumed staring hard at her plate. After a beat she said, "You promised you'd fix it with Bobby." Frustrated, Jimmy just shook his head. "You promised. Now take me to the Santa Monica pier. I want to ride the merry-go-round."

IT WAS RAINING, AND THE BOARDWALK PIER WAS DESERTED. JIMMY and Marilyn climbed over the locked gate and sat on the floor of the carousel between two gaily painted wooden horses.

"I wonder if you could turn it on," Marilyn said.

"And get us both busted. I don't think so. It's going to be light soon. I've got to get back home. What were you going to tell me about Pier that was so important?"

"I didn't say it was so important."

"Cut the shit, Marilyn."

"You only think about yourself, don't you? Nobody else is important."

"Marilyn! We've been talking about you all night."

"Haven't been together all night. You didn't want to spend the night with me, remember?"

"First it was that shit with the president, now it's . . . what? What else is wrong?"

"I can't make *The Little Prince* with you anymore."

"What?"

"My agent told me I can't contract for any new projects until I fulfill my obligation to Fox. It's legal stuff."

"Who told you that, Mickey Rudin? I don't trust that little prick. I didn't trust him when he was just your lawyer, but that wasn't enough; you had to go and make him your goddamn agent, too."

"You don't trust anybody, Jimmy. Mickey's good. He just wants what's best for me. And Dr. Greenson agrees with him. He talks to Mickey, and he thinks I've got to make this film, too."

"So, you make the film, and then we do ours. What's the problem, except for your agent? You've got to put something in place for the next year anyway."

Marilyn raised her knees to her chest, as if trying to protect herself. She whispered, "Mickey says we can't sign anything because of the contract with Fox. It would leave us too exposed or something."

"Well, thanks for telling me. What the hell am I supposed to tell Warners? They're interested, and they're supposed to be contacting your asshole agent. How long were you going to wait before letting Nick and me know?"

"I thought I could get out of this shit with Fox. You know how much I hate them. Every time I get a letter from them, I puke. I'm getting sick just thinking about them, but there's nothing I can do. I've got to make this last picture. They've been sending me these legal letters, and Mickey says they're threatening to tie me up in court for ten years, and nobody will go near me while that's going on."

Jimmy groaned in frustration, took a deep breath, and inhaled the smell of the sea; he looked out at the sky and imagined that it was getting a bit lighter.

"I tried," Marilyn continued. "Mickey tried to cut a deal so we could do our picture, too, but they're bastards, Jimmy, fucking bastards. They're making me do that stupid piece of fluff—*Something's Got to Give*—the one I already turned down three times."

Marilyn pushed herself closer to Jimmy and snuggled against him. "I hate it all. I was going to tell you, Jimmy. But Mickey told me to wait until he could see what he could do."

"And he couldn't do anything," Jimmy said sarcastically but softly.

"Yeah, that's about it."

"You should have told me. Now I'm going to look like an asshole."

"You could just do the picture without me," Marilyn said.

"That wasn't the deal, and I'm not everybody's favorite person, thanks to your friend Bobby."

"He's not my friend." After a beat, Marilyn asked, "What do you mean?"

"The picture I'm working with Bobby on—*The Enemy Within*—it's all fucked up." Marilyn shrugged and waited for him to explain. "Fox is getting pressure from the labor unions and who knows who else."

"Why?"

Jimmy laughed. "There're a lot of nasty people who don't want to see Bobby's picture get made. Jerry Wald was threatened, and Schulberg told me that an A-line actor who read the script and loved it pulled out because he was afraid he'd be killed."

"Killed? Who'd want to kill him?"

Jimmy shrugged and said, "Jimmy Hoffa. Your gangster friend Sam Giancana. How the hell should I know?"

"Christ, it's only a movie," Marilyn said, subdued. She cuddled against Jimmy, as if afraid for her own life. "Has anything happened to you?"

"I got a call, that's all."

"From who?"

"A concerned friend." Jimmy laughed.

"What did they say?"

"It was a broad, if you can believe it. Sandra Burns. Pier knew about her. Said she was a groupie girl who used to date your pal Frank—and Sam Giancana. Ivy League college girl. You probably know her." Marilyn shook her head. "She was oh so worried that I was setting myself up to get blacklisted and wanted to meet me for a drink to explain how she could help me."

"What did you tell her?"

"I said no. So she put another concerned friend on the phone who had a deep voice and a wop accent, and he was worried my arms were going to get broken."

"You can't do that film, then, that's all there is to it," Marilyn said.

"I'm doing the goddamn film. Fuck them! I talked to Bobby and Jerry Wald and Schulberg about where we could shop the script if Fox chickens out." Jimmy laughed. "Get it?"

"This isn't funny, Jimmy."

"If we have to, we can make the picture in Europe. Nick's hot to be in on the project. We'll have to do something. *On the Road* is stalled."

"I'll have to talk to Jack about this," Marilyn said. "He'll know what to do."

"You told me you can't get through to Jack."

"I'll be able to after you talk to Bobby. Now hold me."

Jimmy put his arms around her. The sky was smeary gray; it was getting light. "Now, what were you going to tell me about Pier?"

"Nothing. I just wanted to see you."

"So you lied to me, right?"

She nodded and pressed her face against Jimmy's shoulder. "That's me—liar, pliers, sitting on a telephone wire."

"I don't believe you. It was something. Now tell me."

"No."

"Tell me."

"Fuck you, Jimmy." She pulled away from him.

"Tell me."

"I can't."

"Yes, you *can*."

"If I do, will you promise to stay here with me?"

"I shouldn't be here now."

"Yes you should, Jimmy," Marilyn said softly. "Because she's seeing someone else."

"Who?" Jimmy suddenly felt like he was wrapped in something cold and slippery and repellent.

"Pier."

"I meant who's she seeing?" Jimmy felt something change, as if time was tilting or something; he was in the same place and only a second two seconds three seconds had ticked by, yet everything was different now, everything looked different now, and he knew that feeling, had felt it over and over again when his mother died, when he was alone empty fucked up and now it was back again, that hungry empty aching in his chest, all emptiness and anger. He'd been fucked over, again, goddamn you, you wop pizza pie whore, maybe it wasn't true, it could be nothing, but everything was twisting around him now, cold filaments twisting tighter and tighter, gagging him, strangling him, and he focused himself into a space just on the edge of the translucent black frames of his eyeglasses, as if looking at that black mirage spot was his only security, bodhisattva bliss, Jack Kerouac Zen; he'd discovered the diamond focus of quiet, and he was calm, calmness itself.

"She's seeing a painter."

"What's he do, paint houses?"

"He's an artist."

"What's his name?"

"Domenicos Theotocopoulos," Marilyn said softly.

"What? What the fuck kind of a name is that? You know him, don't you? Or you'd never remember."

"Fuck you, Jimmy, just fuck you! I'm not stupid. I remember everything I see or read or hear, so just fuck you. I don't know him. Just his pictures. He does those pop art cartoon-strip paintings. He works with Andy Warhol and Roy Lichtenstein. You probably don't even know who Lichtenstein is. It's not me who's stupid—"

"I don't think you're stupid. I'm fucking stupid, okay? So how do you know about him and Pier?"

"I just know."

"How?"

"Jesus, who cares about how?"

"Because I need to know, that's why."

"All right, Frankie told me, but he didn't want you to know where it came from because he figured it would—"

"Would what?"

"Embarrass you."

Jimmy laughed. "What's to be embarrassed about? Just everybody in the fucking world knew but me, right?"

"Maybe it's just a rumor," Marilyn said lamely.

"Oh, yeah, right. Come off it! Where did Frank see her?" Marilyn didn't answer. "Where did he see her?"

"At a party at a gallery or something, he walked into one of the rooms and—"

"You mean she was fucking him at a party?" Marilyn nodded. "Then it wasn't a goddamn rumor, was it?" Jimmy said viciously.

Marilyn started crying. "I shouldn't've said anything, I knew it was wrong, I talked to Dr. Greenson and—"

"Great, Dr. Greenson again, the busybody to the stars."

"He told me it wasn't my place to say anything, and that if I did, it could be because I was being possessive and trying to spoil a good relationship for you."

"A good relationship? Oh, that's great, she wants to marry me so she can fuck her boyfriend at parties and make me look like an asshole."

"No, Dr. Greenson says it's perfectly plausible that she was seeing someone else, someone on the side, because of your unpredictability."

"My what?"

"That maybe Pier doesn't believe you're serious about her, that she thinks you'll leave her, so she's seeing somebody else as insurance, but Jimmy, he probably doesn't mean anything to her, and now that you asked her to marry you, she'll probably tell him to fuck off."

"Marilyn, go to hell. You know that's bullshit. You said she doesn't love me."

"I'm sorry," Marilyn whispered. Her eyes became wet, but she wasn't crying or shaking; she was vulnerable but obviously in control. "That was me being a cunt. Dr. Greenson says that that's the other side of me, the bad side, that part of me is like a kid while the other is . . ."

"Is what?"

She just shook her head. "Like I was telling you that Pier doesn't love you. I'm sure she does, Jimmy."

Jimmy cradled Marilyn's face in his hands and said, "Just once, right the fuck now, tell me what you really think." Marilyn tried to pull away. "Tell me."

"You're hurting me, Jimmy. Let go."

He did, and she said, "I don't know."

Jimmy moved away from her and leaned against the metal post of a golden horse with its front legs in the air. He looked into the center of the carousel, at the pipe organ and operating mechanism.

"Jimmy?"

"Yeah."

"She's not for you." She paused. "That's the truth. That's what I think."

"And who's for me?" Jimmy said softly, talking to himself.

"Me," Marilyn said, crawling over to him. "What are you going to do?"

Jimmy felt numb, stoned, quiet; everything was wrong. He should be ranting and shouting. His heart should be pounding, and he should be tasting liver bile at the back of his throat. He should be screaming his way home, tearing the front door from its hinges, rushing up the stairs, and throwing Pier out, throwing her down every one of those steps, throwing her and every one of her cute little porcelain dolls out, throwing out her frilly dresses and blouses and nightgowns, *fuck you fuck you fuck you Pier*, but Jimmy was cold calmness, eye of the storm, centered—dead. *That's it, I'm dead, cold fucking dead, Momma I'm* dead, and he listened, half expecting to hear her voice, or perhaps she would just rise up out of the painted plank floor of the carousel. "I'm going to hot-wire this merry-go-round," Jimmy told Marilyn, which he did. Once the engine started turning over, once the lights and music were on and the carousel revolving, he pressed Marilyn against a big white horse and slid his hand between her legs.

"Oh," Marilyn said softly, giggling. "This should give Fox and the newspapers something to think about." But Jimmy wasn't listening. He was caught up in the yowl of the pipe organ, the electric light music, the long, hard-on moment, the klieg-lit, agonizing moment, and the whispering of his mother's voice.

A voice that became the urgent yet distant siren of a police car.

JIMMY WANTED TO DRIVE HIS NEW CUSTOM, PLUM-COLORED XKE Jaguar, but Marilyn had already made arrangements to rent a huge, white Phantom V Rolls-Royce limousine. They sat in the backseat, looked out through darkened windows at the other cars whizzing past, inspected the polished mahogany cocktail cabinet; made small talk with the chauffeur, who was dressed in white livery and had written a screenplay and was "taking meetings" and *Hey, maybe I could send you a copy, hey,* drank champagne in crystal glasses; shared Marilyn's stash of pills, and argued.

"So how the hell are we supposed to get back?" Marilyn didn't answer. "You could have him come back and pick us up."

"I can try to set something up when I get back to the garage," the chauffeur said, cheerfully breaking into the conversation, "but I'm off after I drop you. You've really got to set those things up in advance, but who knows, hey? Maybe they'll accommodate you, being who you are. Hey, I got it, if you'd be willing to take a look at my—"

Jimmy told him to stop eavesdropping and shut the fuck up.

Marilyn started crying. "This is going to be all fucked up, I'm going to fall flat on my face, and all you can do is argue with the driver. We'll get a ride back. We can always call a cab."

Jimmy started laughing.

"What's funny?"

"You. Your crocodile tears. Me. This car. Everything. We're both shitfaced, and you're worried about making a good impression."

"I'm not shitfaced," Marilyn insisted.

"Okay, stoned."

"That's different. And they're not crocodile tears."

"What are they, then?"

"You're a shit, Jimmy. I'm upset and need your help and all you can do is make fun of me." Then in a low, tiny voice, "Jimmy?"

"Yeah?"

"Will you promise to stay with me all the time?"

"Sure."

"And sit next to me?"

"What do you mean?"

"Sit next to me at dinner."

"You didn't tell me this was a sit-down dinner. You said it was a *party*."

Marilyn shrugged. "I don't know what it is, but if it is dinner, will you sit next to me?"

"Don't you want to sit next to Bobby? Isn't Bobby the point of this whole thing?"

"I want you to sit next to me, too."

"Okay," Jimmy said, shaking his head and grinning.

"And if I fuck up, will you help me look smart?"

"Jesus, Marilyn. What's to fuck up?"

"I don't know." She fumbled for her purse in her handbag and unfolded a square of yellow notepaper. Relieved that it was there, she refolded it and said, "Jimmy?"

"Yeah?"

"Do I look all right?"

Jimmy laughed. She looked stunning, and she knew it. She was made up to look perfect. Her face was flawless. Her lips poison red. Her hair coiffed, blond as light, smooth. She wore a long, tight, black-lace dress, which barely covered her powdered and rouge-shadowed breasts. "You look good enough to eat. I'll tell you what, let's have a quickie right here, right now. Come on, I'll smear your lipstick, get jizz all over you, make you—"

"Leave me alone, Jimmy, you bastard."

The image of his mother flashed through his mind. "See. I told you so," he said.

"You missed your chance." He just nodded, suddenly lost in a childhood memory of being in his mother's kitchen, the smell of onions and bacon sweet and strong in the air, the profound sense that everything was secure.

"Jimmy, are you okay?"

"Oh, you've suddenly realized I'm here."

"Are you?"

"Here?"

"Jimmy, cut it out. You know what I mean. Are you okay?"

"Pier's history, if that's what you're getting at. Like I told you—"

"Have you talked to her?"

"She calls me, but I don't talk to her." Jimmy laughed. "She told me she didn't think I loved her and she felt unloved and all that shit, so she was just keeping one little painter on the side, just in case. Bitch."

The chauffeur opened their door, but Marilyn couldn't move. She just sat and looked straight ahead.

"Come on, Marilyn," Jimmy said. "Time to get out." She blinked. "It'll be okay."

"I can't. Tell the chauffeur to drive us back home."

"Marilyn."

"Tell him."

"Welcome!" shouted a husky yet refined voice. Peter Lawford, looking tanned, athletic, and slightly flushed, strode down the driveway. He wore a khaki suit, the stiff-collared shirt open to reveal a heavy gold chain and chest hair. He motioned the chauffeur aside and then extended his hand to Marilyn. Marilyn came to life. Turned herself on. Took Lawford's hand and shimmered out of the limousine. Awkward, fumbling, yet graceful. She was beautiful blond movement, her tits bobbling, her eyes flashing, focused, radiating charisma and help-me-I-feel-faint vulnerability.

"You look good enough to eat," Lawford said.

"You're a pig, Peter, but that's what everyone loves about you."

He tried to tweak her breasts, but she pulled away from him. "I'll tell your wife."

Lawford laughed. "*I'll* tell my wife."

"Hey, Jimmy, you coming out or what?" Marilyn asked.

Jimmy slowly, reluctantly got out of the limousine. He felt suddenly small, and dirty. He *was* dirty. He hadn't showered, his hair was greasy, and he needed a shave. He was wearing jeans, sneakers, thick-rimmed glasses, and a white T-shirt that was soiled under the arms. He had no business being here. He didn't want to be here. Marilyn didn't need him. She was all blond now, all light, and he was withering. *Fucking withering.*

"Jimmy, you've met Peter. Peter Lawford?"

Jimmy nodded, put his hands in his back pockets, and surveyed the sandy white expanse of Lawford's beach house. Beyond was the ocean, dark blue and shadowed purple. It was almost dusk.

"Bobby's been raving about you," Peter said to Jimmy. "Everybody wants to meet you. Kim Novak's here. She's been asking about you."

"Do you know her?" Marilyn asked.

"Nope," Jimmy said.

"Well, you will in a minute," Peter said, and they walked into the house, which was bustling with servants setting up a grand buffet in the dining room that opened onto the deck and swimming-pool area. Three sides of the pool were enclosed in a white picket fence, and two wire-mesh fences separated the property from the perfectly clean, white sand beach. There were about fifty people in suits and gowns standing around and sitting on deck chairs while others in bathing suits and casual clothes were walking along the beach.

"Is Bobby here?" Marilyn asked shyly.

"Who do you think we're having this party for?" Peter said as they walked into the pool area. "He and Ethel are on their way to the Far East on . . . government business. Any excuse for a party."

"I'm sorry, but I got to go," Jimmy said, turning.

"Jimmy!" Marilyn called.

"You haven't even got here yet," Peter said. "Give us a chance. Have a drink, and if you still think the party sucks, then you can cut out." Peter smiled at Jimmy, who felt caught. *I just can't fucking do this, I can't—*

"Please, Jimmy." Marilyn suddenly lost it all, the brightness, the focused charisma—the look.

Jimmy turned away from her, nodded, and followed them into the party, which was hot with ego and energy. They were introduced to Kim Novak, who was excited about her new house in Big Sur and had big eyes for Jimmy. She was tall and Nordic-looking, her straight, white-blond hair cropped short, her oval face almost as perfect as Marilyn's; she had the same strong sexuality but none of the vulnerability. Her blue eyes were hard, her gaze powder-soft. Jimmy would fuck her, but it would be by rote. She wasn't giving anything away. She was on. Marilyn was on. Everybody was on—except Jimmy, who slouched and looked around, glaring at the world, his head down. Kim Novak drifted away—*"Hello, darlings, just give me one sec and I'll be there. See you later, Jimmy?"*—blinking, beckoning, waving, promising; and Peter introduced Jimmy and Marilyn to James Bacon, the journalist; Tom Braden, the columnist, and his wife, Joan; and Gloria Romanoff. They chatted with Angie Dickinson, and Marilyn made a fuss when she saw her friend Jeanne Carmen.

"It's going to be all right now," she said to Jimmy. "Peter, where's Frankie?" Marilyn asked, looking around. "Wasn't he supposed to be here, too?"

"No, he couldn't make it." Peter looked uncomfortable and impatient— it was obvious that he was eager to get to his other guests. Jimmy guessed that Lawford wanted to try an inning with Kim Novak.

"So the coon's still peering out of the henhouse." A familiar voice, the vowels decidedly flat, Boston flat, and Jimmy couldn't help but smile at Bobby Kennedy.

"Hey."

"Pete wasn't sure whether you were coming or not," Bobby said.

"Yeah, well, I've been . . . working."

Bobby nodded as he stood awkwardly before Marilyn. Now that Bobby had appeared, Peter seemed suddenly reluctant to leave. "It's very nice to see you again," Bobby said to Marilyn. Marilyn blushed. "I've never really had a chance to talk to you. My brother always hogs your time."

"Well," Marilyn said, giggling, "I'm all yours now." A servant stepped onto the patio and gonged a bell to indicate that dinner was ready.

"Can I buy you a drink?" Bobby asked Marilyn, cupping her elbow in his hand. Then he gave Peter a quick look *(Leave!)* and asked Jimmy if he wanted to accompany them back toward the house and buffet. Marilyn looked nervous, shaky, but for that matter, so did Bobby. It was obvious that he was putting on a show, that he was excited to be holding the arm of *the* Marilyn Monroe.

"No, man, I'll be here when you get back," Jimmy said.

"You've got to eat," Marilyn said, not very convincingly. She was in control. She didn't need Jimmy now.

"Maybe after I check out the beach."

"Okay." But as Jimmy turned toward the beach, Marilyn cried, "No, Jimmy! You've got to eat."

"Oh, sure, Mom."

I need you. Please please please . . .

Jimmy nodded, and Marilyn smiled beatifically at him.

He followed her and a bemused Bobby up the stairs, across a deck, and into the open, glassed-in dining room. Others were also moving toward the long table of food—close-eyed, shiny, sleek, gill-less sand sharks in natty suits, in slacks and shorts and bikinis and revealing, skin-tight, glittering gowns; but none more glittery or spectacular than Marilyn's. Ever solicitous, Bobby prepared a plate for Marilyn, and she yea'd and nay'd for shrimp Kiev, lobster Newberg, soufflé oysters, salmon, beluga caviar, sour cream, smoked trout, fried chicken, duck with mangos, potato, broccoli, saffron rice, and then Bobby held his plate and hers before the tuxedoed carver—braised pork with calvados? Roast turkey with pine-nut stuffing? Prime rib?

Belatedly, Peter announced that dinner was on and that guests could eat by the pool or in the dining room, after all, *there're no formalities here, and on behalf of my darling wife, Pat, and myself, wel-*

come, everyone, and if you're shy and need an introduction to the attorney general of the United States who's taking a nice around-the-world cruise on taxpayers' money, just ask me, and I'll introduce you, if he ever gets done fidgeting over Marilyn . . . oh, Bobby, your wife's watching.

Laughter, milling around, shouting, catcalls, introductions, toasting, schmoozing, the band warming up on the far side of the pool, fairy lights and pool lights and decorator-designed deck lights blinking on. The house was lit in yellow-blond light while dusk turned the rest of the world gray.

Everything was Marilyn, and she felt good. She felt like Marilyn. Good-bye, Norma Jeane, her alter-ego plain-Jane self; and right now, as she sat down at a white-linen-covered table with Bobby, she would show him she was smart. She would play him. She would delight him with her faltering, but everything would come out right. *Jimmy, where are you? Oh, there you are, piling up your plate. Okay, okay,* and that goddamn Peter couldn't keep away from Bobby for five seconds, and he brought people over for introductions until the table was filled with beautifully dressed, smart, sophisticated gawkers. Bobby stood up when Ethel arrived.

She told him to sit down. "I've got to help Pat get everything under control," she said pointedly. "Certainly Mr. You Know Who won't help." Peter smiled at her. He was standing behind Marilyn's chair. "Well, you two, are you going to introduce me to Miss Monroe, or do I have to do it myself?" Ethel asked. She laughed nervously, and Marilyn smiled at the rather dowdily dressed woman, who was plain-faced yet cute in an athletic sort of way. *So this was Bobby's wife. Why would he marry her?*

"Hi," Marilyn said, then looked down at her plate. She didn't feel nervous, but her body did. She felt that she was watching herself, that she was distant from it all, safe and protected. But that sense of safety could disappear in a second. She glanced around but couldn't see Jimmy.

"I'm a big fan of yours," Ethel said.

"Thank you."

"I told Bobby that I wanted *you* to play me in his movie."

Marilyn smiled at Ethel and said, "And I wanted to do it, but"—she shrugged—"there were some problems with my contracts."

"Maybe you still can."

Marilyn was about to explain but thought better of it. "Yeah, maybe. That would be great."

"Bobby, make sure you get her autograph for me."

"Come and sit here with us," Marilyn said. *This is stupid, I don't want her here, but what can I do? Dammit, Jimmy, come over and help me.* "We can just pull over another chair."

Looking flustered, Bobby started to stand up again to give Ethel his chair, but she said, "No, Bobby, I told you, I've got to help Pat." Then she said good-bye to everyone at the table and rushed off.

Bobby grinned at Marilyn and said, "Well, that's Ethel."

Marilyn fumbled with her black purse. She put on horn-rimmed glasses, unfolded a lined, yellow piece of notepaper on her lap, squinted down at the list of questions she had written, and read her first question to Bobby. "What does an attorney general do?"

Bobby was taken completely by surprise. A woman wearing a taffeta gown giggled, and Marilyn distinctly heard the man sitting beside her say, "Don't. She's had a sad and lonely life, and she has no self-confidence at all."

You bastard. Jimmy, where are you? I can't do this. I can't—

But Bobby patiently explained his job to Marilyn. When she pushed her glasses against the bridge of her nose, he smiled. He doted. He answered her questions about the House Un-American Activities Committee, civil rights, support of the Diem regime in Vietnam. She looked at him as if there were no one else in the room. He blushed when she caught him looking down her dress; and she imagined him touching them, fondling them, then sliding his hands lightly all over her skin; she thought about that as she listened to him; she thought those thoughts at him; and it was as if he heard because he spoke softly, moved closer to her, seemed shivery nervous. *Like me,* she thought. *Like me.* And she had him, right now she had him; and the band started playing "Let's Twist Again." Peter insisted that they play it over and over. "Mr. Attorney General," Marilyn said.

"Bobby, call me Bobby." His face seemed large. It was so close to her. There was noise all around, yet they could be private, personal . . . alone. The others had left the table to dance and mingle. They made their nasty comments, and Bobby and Marilyn ignored them. *Go away!*

It was just Bobby and Marilyn.

"Are you going to fire J. Edgar Hoover?" Marilyn asked. "I think he's a fascist. He thinks there's a Communist under every pillow—and he doesn't believe there's such a thing as organized crime. I'm right about that, aren't I?"

Bobby nodded. He wasn't looking down her dress. He was looking straight at her, thinking, *The president and I would like to get rid of him, but we don't feel strong enough to do it. Not yet, anyway.*

"He's no friend of yours—or the president's."

Bobby blushed. "I'm sorry. Jack had—has a lot of respect for you. He liked to talk to you."

"Among other things," Marilyn said, looking steadily at Bobby. This was the moment. No coquettishness now. No wet parted lips. She took off her glasses. That part was done. "And your job tonight is to let me down easy. That's what Jack told you to do, didn't he." It was a statement, not a question.

Bobby seemed to be at a loss for words.

"You mean he still does want to . . . continue?" Marilyn asked.

"He cares a great deal about you, Marilyn, but—"

"But what?"

"But it's too dangerous."

"Who says so? You?"

"Yes, I'm afraid, me. And others."

"Like Hoover?"

"It's not about who, Marilyn. You know that it's dangerous, that—"

"Isn't *this* dangerous?" Marilyn asked, softening, feeling the fear, letting it take her. *Bobby, help me, please help me.*

Bobby smiled sourly. "I suppose it is. Point taken."

"People will gossip about everything, but you and me, here, what could be more innocent?"

"Do you think I'm the most handsome man in the room?" Bobby asked. Marilyn giggled. He looked as serious as a schoolboy in an exam. "You don't?"

"Yes, of course I do." After a beat. "Are you going to stop Jack from seeing me?"

"I can't stop Jack from doing anything he wants to do."

"So *he* doesn't want to see me."

"I didn't say that."

"Will you help me?"

"No, Marilyn, I can't. I've got to be honest with you. It can't work."

"Will you try?"

"I'm telling you—"

"Just promise you'll talk to him," Marilyn said. "I know if you talk to him, everything will be all right."

"I'm not that good."

"I bet you are." Then Marilyn hesitated, looked crestfallen. "You mean, he really doesn't want to see me—"

"I didn't say that. I'm sure he—"

"What?" Marilyn asked, anxious.

"Nothing."

"Tell me, please."

"I'll talk to him, okay?" Bobby said, looking irritated.

"Promise?"

Bobby started to turn away from her, but she took his hand and held it just under her breast. "Please . . . promise?"

Bobby grinned and said, "I'll try. That's as much as I can do. No promises."

Marilyn beamed at him and said, "That's good enough for me. Now, let's give everyone something to talk about. Do you know how to twist?" Bobby shook his head. "Well, come on."

Marilyn gulped down the wine in her glass and stood up. She was a bit unsteady, just a little stoned and drunk, but she didn't have to keep herself so tightly in control now. She'd won. She had Bobby, and Bobby was cute, not handsome like his brother, but sensitive and good-looking in a smaller way than Jack. She could make him fall in love with her, and maybe she could fall in love with him a little; but it would all be perfect and platonic and wholesome, and she would get Jack back. She dragged Bobby down the stairs to dance. She showed him how to swivel his hips and turn on the balls of his feet, taught him how to move his arms one way while his body twisted the other way, and then she was dancing all around him, almost jiggling herself out of her dress, and he was transfixed, and she was the black-lace snake, and everyone was watching and applauding. Somehow she ended up sitting on the drummer's lap, and then she was in Bobby's arms, more drinks, champagne, dancing, swirling, shouting, applause, and she drank even if Bobby didn't, and then they found themselves in a bedroom.

The music was muffled. Marilyn was exhausted. She fell onto the bed.

"No, you've got to come over here, Marilyn," Bobby said. He dialed a number and waited, the illuminated dial of the princess phone illuminating one side of his face.

"You look ghoulish," Marilyn said, giggling. "Like a monster."

"This is important," Bobby said earnestly, and Marilyn thought that he really was like a schoolboy.

"Hello, this is Bobby. How's Dad doing?" Beat. "Okay, that's good. Can you put him on the phone, just for a minute? That's okay, I'll wait." Beat. Marilyn began to say something, but Bobby shushed her. "Hello, Dad, it's Bobby. I'm in California. I had to call you. Guess who's standing next to me?" Before his father could possibly answer, Bobby said, "Marilyn Monroe. Can you believe that?" Then he handed the receiver to Marilyn and said, "Here, say hello to my father." Bobby covered up the speaker. "He's had a stroke, so he won't be able to answer you, but he can hear you."

Marilyn took the phone and said, "Hello, Mr. Kennedy, I hope you're feeling better," and went on to describe the party, how excited everyone was to meet his son Robert; and Bobby was a little boy, and Marilyn gave him back the phone and patted him, and, pleased, he said "Good-bye, Dad," and then he was on top of her; he was very light, he didn't dig into her, and his breath tasted meaty and she let him kiss her and fumble with her dress and she had to help him inside her *Don't you want to get undressed?* and he was crying in her ear and she closed her eyes and thought of Jack and Jimmy and being the queen of the White House with everything painted white and she would wear nothing but white gloves which she would sweep along the tables and antiques to make sure that everything was perfectly and absolutely clean.

Bobby came quickly, there, it was over, and he was even quicker than Jack.

He stood up, smoothed out his clothes, and said, "We'd better get back." He looked awkward and embarrassed, as if he'd just been caught out.

Marilyn smiled at him. But she was in no hurry to get up from the bed.

ETHEL KENNEDY FOUND JIMMY SLOUCHING AGAINST A WINDOW IN the dining room. "Have you seen my husband?" she asked him.

"Well, hello and how do you do," Jimmy said.

Ethel blushed. "I'm sorry, Jimmy. I don't know what's gotten into me. She patted his arm and said, "You look tired. Are you all right?" Jimmy nodded. "You sure?"

Jimmy smiled and said, "I'm fine."

"I looked for you. Peter said you were with Marilyn Monroe. I was introduced to her. I've seen all her pictures and was excited about meeting her." She shrugged. "She's been hanging all over Bobby, and now I can't find either one of them."

"They're right down there," Jimmy said.

"Where?"

"Dancing, right there by the pool beside all those trees."

"Well, they weren't there a minute ago," Ethel said. It was dark, and the pool and patio lights seemed soft, out of focus. The trees looked preternaturally green; the blue water in the pool was the stuff of light itself. Everything was limned with mystery—the perfect party, perfect people, perfect music, perfect lights. The band played "Mood Indigo," the players no doubt relieved to be playing cool jazz instead of monotonous chewing-gum rock. "I know she's your friend," Ethel continued, "but I just think she's a big phony, and if I'm never around her again, that would be fine with me. Look at her, the way she's dancing with Bobby. She's all over him, for crying out loud. Women like that make me so mad, trying to seduce a married man. I'm furious about this, I really am."

"She doesn't mean any harm," Jimmy said, lying.

"She means something," Ethel said. "What should I do?"

Jimmy shrugged. "They're only dancing. It doesn't mean nothin'."

"It means somethin'." Jimmy grinned at her for mimicking his speech pattern. She smiled back. "You're right. I've just got to learn to ignore it. Women always try to get clingy with Bobby because he's got an important position in government." She laughed. "I guess he's sort of like a movie star. Like you."

"Yeah, pretty much the same," Jimmy said.

She watched Marilyn and Bobby, her face tight; and she moved a little closer to Jimmy. "You know, you and Bobby are alike in some ways."

"I really don't think so."

"No, really."

"Just because we both do that bull stare, or whatever he calls it . . . that doesn't mean anything."

"It's just the way you both are. You both put on this tough front, but underneath you're . . ."

"What?"

She turned to him and took his hand. "Frightened, I think."

"Of what?"

"Everything." After a beat Ethel said, "I shouldn't have said that. I think I need another drink." She looked out at the dancers on the patio. "Marilyn's obviously shitfaced. What's good for the goose is good for the gander." But she didn't move away from Jimmy. "Jimmy?"

"Yeah?"

"What are you doing here? You're not mixing, and you look like you've just come off a bender. You smell like a horse." Jimmy snorted. "I'm sorry, Jimmy, I'm being too forward. We hardly know each other, except—"

"Yeah?"

She shrugged. "Except I feel like I know you. I felt that when you were at the house."

"I felt comfortable there," Jimmy said. "I've decided I'm going to get a place like yours, with horses and land and everything. Maybe around your way, or in Connecticut or Westchester or something. Get away from all this phony shit."

"So why'd you come to this party? Was it for Bobby?"

"Yeah, well . . ."

"Somehow I didn't think so. Why'd you come? Certainly not to talk about the movie you two are working on. How's that going?"

"It's okay."

Ethel squinted at him; she knew he was lying. "Bobby tells me there's trouble."

"We'll sort it out."

"There's trouble with everything," Ethel said philosophically. Her words were slightly slurred, as if now that she was exposed, revealed in front of Jimmy, she could no longer hide her state of inebriation. "So tell me, I want to know why you're here at this phony-baloney party of my sister's and her lecherous bastard pimp of a husband?"

Jimmy sensed that Ethel could become dangerous very quickly, which he found endearing. "To take care of Marilyn."

"Doesn't look like she needs *anyone* to take care of her." Jimmy shrugged. "Why does she need taking care of?"

"Because she's like me, I guess." He smiled.

"What does *she* have to be scared of?"

"Everything. Like you said."

PART THREE

1962–1964

THIRTEEN

∎

Bought and Sold

Jimmy answered the door.

Elvis stood on the porch.

"This is a surprise," Jimmy said, after shaking Elvis's moist hand. "To what do I owe this visit?" Elvis didn't answer. He looked painfully uncomfortable. "Where's your entourage? They in the car?"

"No, sir, I left the boys back at the house."

Jimmy laughed. "You're still doing that sir shit. You ain't in the army no more, remember?"

Elvis smiled. "Sometimes I forget."

"You living here in L.A.?"

"I just finished making another film for Mr. Wallis, and I got a place near the little park on Beverly Glen. But I need to get back to Memphis bad, back to Graceland. You know, you been there. This place ain't no good for nobody. No offense."

Jimmy nodded, remembering Elvis crying and carrying on and fondling his mother's feet in her casket. "How's your dad doin'?"

"He's good. Got himself a new woman." Elvis's face hardened, and he went on. "He's down here, with us. All the guys are down here, too. Like I said." He shook his head and looked down at his feet.

"So how come you're here by yourself?" Jimmy asked. "That ain't like you, not to have Jerry and the other guys all over you like gravy on rice." There was a nasty edge to Jimmy's voice.

Elvis shrugged. "Yeah . . . well."

"Come inside," Jimmy said. He took Elvis into the paneled library and cleared a stack of scripts from the couch. Empty pizza boxes were piled high on an end table; tapes and records were scattered everywhere, as were books, scripts, papers, and unopened mail. There were paintings on the walls. His bullfighting cape was hanging between a set of landscape paintings. Underneath the cape were two sets of bongo drums neatly stacked one atop the other. The place smelled of stale cigarettes, rising damp, and sweat. A black-and-white photograph of Pier Angeli was propped up against one of Jimmy's clay sculptures— a rough, agonized self-portrait—elbows resting on knees, face covered with large, spidery hands.

"So what brings you here?"

"I guess I came here to . . . to . . ."

"Yeah?"

"To apologize."

Jimmy laughed. "Apologize for what?"

"For breaking my promise."

Jimmy stared at him, head down. "Yeah . . ."

"About goin' against the Colonel to work with you and Nick Ray."

Jimmy shrugged and said, "Look, man, you do what you have to do. Who am I to shit on your parade? You're the man now. What did *Blue Hawaii* do? Something like number one on *Variety*'s list of top-grossing films for the year. Not bad, man. So what the fuck do I know?"

"It was number two, same as *G.I. Blues*."

"Oh, right. Sorry." Jimmy grinned at him, but Elvis was working his way through something of his own.

"So what's happening with *On the Road*?" Elvis asked.

"Nick's in Europe trying to put financing together," Jimmy said, his face tight.

"I thought Fox was going to do it."

"Yeah, well, I thought you were going to do it, too. And Marilyn."

"Marilyn?"

"Jesus, Elvis, Marilyn Monroe. There's only one."

"Yeah."

"Like there's only one Elvis," Jimmy said, seeing that Elvis had recoiled at his remark. This was the old, pimply-faced, uncertain Elvis Presley sitting in front of him, not the Elvis who wore shades and black mohair suits and dressed all his Memphis Mafia bodyguards in sunglasses and matching black jumpsuits.

"I had people who believed in me as a real actor," Elvis suddenly said, as if talking to himself, trying to convince himself. "One of them was Jerry Wald. You been workin' with him on that picture with the president's brother, ain't that right? Jerry knows the president, too. You know that? And Phil Dunne, he was my director, he believed in me, too. He wrote speeches for the president. Did you know that?"

Jimmy shook his head. Elvis was working himself up to something.

"I read everything about the president," Elvis continued. "I think he's a great man, like Douglas MacArthur. Better even. I dunno if you saw me in *Wild in the Country*, but Jerry was my producer and Phil was my director." He paused, musing, realizing that he was repeating himself but going on just the same. "And they believed in me as an actor."

"So you said."

"They worked for the president, and they believed in *me*. They were going to make me click in the movies. They weren't going to make me sing stupid songs or play stupid parts like in the other pictures. Them and Buddy Adler at Fox were going to give me the chance to be a real actor. The Colonel told me I was gonna do serious acting, and he said that's why he got me them two films—*Flaming Star* and *Wild in the Country*—which had serious scripts, not like the other ones. They were going to be a showcase for me as a serious dramatic actor, you know?"

"Yeah," Jimmy said tentatively, trying to be helpful. Elvis was so obviously uncomfortable.

"But he said he didn't want me fuckin' with you and Nick. He told me that he had a plan and a special way of going about business, and that if I messed with it, then everything would go all to hell. He said he wasn't going to tell me how to act, but I would have to trust him with the business, and to prove it he was going to get me these serious pictures." Elvis shook his head and laughed. "And you know what he did?"

Elvis stared hard at his hands, which were tented on his lap; he seemed to be trying to block everyone else out. His face was contorted, in anger. "You know why I listened to the Colonel and broke my promise to you? It was because of this dream that I kept having over and over. I dreamed that everything was gone, the fans, the money, the Colonel. I figured it was a sign." He laughed. "It was . . . it was a sign from the devil."

"What do you mean?" Jimmy asked. *Maybe the poor kid has gone off the deep end.*

Elvis shrugged but sat up straight on the couch and began to fidget. His face was still tight with anger, and Jimmy suddenly felt uncomfortable. There was something menacing about Elvis, something dangerous, unpredictable. "I figured that the dream meant if I went against the Colonel, everything would fall apart like he said it would. But he lied to me. He didn't have no intention of letting me do serious pictures. He started having meetings with everybody and tellin' them that I had to sing songs just like in all the other pictures, and they all looked to me to do something, but I couldn't do nothing with the Colonel because he had it all worked out. He told me he couldn't get rid of the songs 'cause we'd been paid, and we was locked in." He shrugged. "Everybody just gave up after a while, but the Colonel got all pissed off at them for trying to make good pictures for me, and so we didn't even go to the opening of *Wild in the Country*."

"*You* could've gone, for Christ's sake," Jimmy said. "You didn't need the Colonel."

"You know what Phil Dunne told me after it was all over and we weren't working together? He said that he was impressed with my talent as an actor and how I could understand what was going on in the scenes. He said he thought he was creating a new star."

"Must be a virus," Jimmy said.

"Huh?"

"That's what Nick and I thought we were going to do."

"So now I'm doing all these fucked-up films the Colonel contracted for. They're all cheap and stupid and embarrassing; and you know what?"

"What, Elvis?"

"The songs ain't worth a rat's ass—my singing is going all to hell, too—and the pictures ain't makin' no money. Or not as much as they were supposed to."

"Don't look like that from the outside," Jimmy said.

"Well, I ain't on the outside." Elvis stood up. "And I ain't no cow for the Colonel. I'm never going to be anything at this rate. Never going to learn to act or direct." Jimmy chuckled; he couldn't help himself. "What's funny?" Elvis asked.

"No offense, Elvis. But sometimes I think I'm not ever going to direct, either."

" 'Cause of me?"

" 'Cause of a lot of things."

"I heard about the trouble with the film you're doing with Jerry Wald and the attorney general."

"What have you heard?" Jimmy asked.

"You know, that people don't want you to do it. But you shouldn't take shit from nobody. You got to deal with the Mafia like *you're* the Mafia, you know what I mean?" Elvis stood up and wandered around the room, inspecting the posters and paintings, and Jimmy knew what he was doing. He could see Elvis relaxing back into himself, into the cool, groovy, smooth-skinned, rich, famous, beautiful, perfectly controlled Elvis. "You want me back in *On the Road*, just say so," Elvis said to the wall.

"What about the Colonel?" Jimmy asked. "And your pictures you're sold out for until 1965?"

"Fuck the Colonel," Elvis said quietly, and without making eye contact with Jimmy, he walked out of the house.

FOURTEEN

■

Twinkle, Twinkle, Little Star

The phone rang again.

It had been ringing all night, the same nasal voice, the same filthy words: "Leave Bobby alone, you fucking tramp, you fucking slut, you—"

Marilyn shouted back, but the caller had already hung up. As Marilyn held the receiver to her ear, she could hear clicks. She always heard clicks, and she was sure *someone* was tapping her line: Joe DiMaggio, the Mafia, Fox, the press, maybe even Bobby or her Dr. Greenson; it could be *anybody*. She had told Frank Sinatra about it, and he had ordered that fat prick Budd Schaap to do a sweep of the house. Nothing. No bugs. What was it the private eye had said? "Clean as a whistle."

But still, there was that clicking.

"Hey, phone tappers," she shouted into the receiver, "if you can hear this, fuck you, and your old man, too!" She was sitting up in her bed, looking into the flat, absolute blackness. Shaking with fear and anger and frustration. Shaking with memories. *Shake rattle and roll, you bastards, you're all bastards, every single one of you; and I'm alone on a Saturday night, on my own, you bastards, you fuckers. You're all users, even you, Bobby, you're just not as bad as the rest, like your brother and that shit Peter Lawford, but I love you, Bobby, you buck-toothed, come-in-a-minute little boy, you fucker, I love you, and nothing that your wife can do will ever get in our way. Ethel can pay a thousand cunts to call me, and it won't make any goddamn difference to you and me at all.*

The phone rang again, as if on cue, and Marilyn picked it up to hear "Leave Bobby alone, you—"

She hung up. She giggled. Maybe it was a tape recorder or something. But she was seething, out of control. It was as if she'd been suddenly split into two people: Marilyn thought it was funny, silly really; but Norma Jeane, the other, the real Marilyn who was always submerged, always drowning—*she* knew the truth, that the caller or the recording was right. She was a slut a loser she was being used she had been used by Jack, who was such a goddamn coward that he had Peter Lawford call her—*You won't be able to speak to the president ever again you're never going to be First Lady look, Marilyn, you were just another one of Jack's fucks.*

But Bobby made it better. Bobby explained, held her, told her how much he cared about her. *He loves me he'll marry me he'll protect me.*

The phone rang.

"Look, you stupid cunt!" Marilyn shouted into the phone.

"Jesus H. Christ, Marilyn. Hello . . . Marilyn?"

"Who is this?"

"It's Jimmy. Are you completely messed up or what?"

Marilyn giggled, changing persona instantly, pulling her knees to her chest for security. She blinked and saw purple spots in the total darkness; she always saw the purple spots in the dark and imagined they were the glowing buttons she had to push to get into heaven. "Or what."

"Marilyn?"

"Well, if I have to choose between 'or what' or being completely fucked up, I think I'll choose 'or what.' "

"Yeah, right. Look, Marilyn, maybe I'll call you another time, okay?"

"No, Jimmy, don't hang up," she said, desperation evident in her voice. "I'm glad you called. Certainly took you long enough."

"Yeah, well . . ."

"Don't get mad," Marilyn said. "It's okay. You can call when you want."

"Sorry," Jimmy said. "I guess it's me who's messed up. What time is it?"

"I don't know. It's dark in here."

"I shouldn't've called you so late."

She giggled again. "I was awake."

"What was that stupid cunt business?"

"I've been getting nasty phone calls about Bobby."

"From who?"

Marilyn shrugged. "I don't know, but it's the same voice all the time."

"Probably his wife."

"No, it's not her voice, but she probably put someone up to it." The phone clicked. "There, did you hear that?" Marilyn asked.

"What?"

"The clicking. Someone's tapping my goddamn phone, I don't care what Frankie says."

"What are you talking about?"

"Can you hear it?"

"All I hear is you talking crazy."

"I'm not crazy," Marilyn said.

"I didn't say you were."

"Yes, you did."

"Oh, shit, look, Marilyn, I'll call you another time."

"No, please, don't hang up. Frank told me that—"

"You mean Old Glass Jaw?"

"You're not nice, Jimmy, but yeah, Frank had everything checked over here, but if the phone isn't bugged or anything, then what the hell are all the clicks I hear?"

"Static, maybe, I don't know," Jimmy said.

"You can hear more in the dark."

"Marilyn?" But Marilyn had taken the receiver away from her ear. She held it in the air like a barbell and listened in the cloaked darkness. She had thick blackout curtains installed to help her sleep. Of course, nothing helped. "Marilyn?"

"One sec, Jimmy," Marilyn whispered into the darkness. She heard the floorboards in the hallway squeak. Goddammit, her housekeeper— the housekeeper Dr. Greenson had selected for her, his spy, his spook, his snoop—was at it again, sneaking around in her white crepe-soled shoes. Marilyn whispered, "Hold on, Jimmy;" then laid the receiver down next to the phone base on the night table. Carefully and quietly, she stepped over to the door. She pulled it wide open and caught her housekeeper listening by the door.

"What the hell do you think you're doing?" Marilyn asked.

Mrs. Murray, severe in a faded housecoat, her coarse gray hair pulled back into a frizzy bun, said, "I was just going to the toilet."

"Your toilet's right off your room, for Christ's sake. You can do better than that."

"I was going to use the bathroom in the guest cottage so I wouldn't disturb you. I *thought* you were sleeping."

"That's bullshit, Mrs. Murray, and you know it," Marilyn said. *I've done it again goddammit I've called her Mrs. Murray and she'll call me Marilyn like she's the boss and I'm working for her.*

"I'm not used to being talked to that way, Marilyn. I expect at least a modicum of respect."

"You're fired, Eunice. I want you out of here tomorrow. Is that clear?"

"We'll see about that. I'll be talking to Dr. Greenson tomorrow, Marilyn."

"Well, I'll tell you what, Eunice, you can talk to him all fucking day if you want to, and you can tell him for me that he's fired, too."

"I think you're ill, Marilyn. I think you're having an episode due to lack of sleep and your sinusitis, I think—"

"I don't give a rat's ass what you think!" Marilyn screamed. "The only sick I am is sick of you. Now, get out of my house."

"It's four o'clock in the morning, Marilyn," Mrs. Murray said calmly.

"You don't think I know about all your bullshit, Eunice, but I do." She tried to inject Mrs. Murray's first name everywhere she could to prove that she, Marilyn, was in control, was the boss. "I know you're spying for Dr. Greenson, Eunice. I know you used to work as a psychiatric nurse. I know fucking everything, Eunice. Now get out of my house right now. You can stay the night at the Château Marmont. I'll pay for it. Call a cab. And tomorrow I'm sure Dr. Greenson will be happy to take you in."

"You can be a nasty piece of work, Marilyn," Mrs. Murray said. She turned on her heel and headed for her bedroom.

"I thought you had to go to the bathroom!" Marilyn shouted. Satisfied, she closed the door. She felt for the light switch, and the room blazed with light. The walls and ceiling of the relatively bare room were painted white on white, white the color of light, of life and everything good and safe and eternal, and although Marilyn needed blind darkness to fall asleep for a few jittery, dream-shot minutes, she was afraid of the dark. Darkness and death and growing old and becoming crazy like her mother and her grandmother . . . no, she needed all the lights on, God's light, God's countenance shining upon her, she needed God and light and Jimmy, *oh, shit,* "Jimmy, Jimmy, hello? Are you still there? Jimmy?"

The phone was dead.

Marilyn tried calling Jimmy back, but the number was busy. She started to panic and took a few Nembutals to calm herself down. She washed the capsules down with champagne, which had gone flat. The phone rang.

"Yeah?"

"That's no way to answer the phone," Jimmy said, laughing because "Yeah" was his salutation. "It's almost morning, and you just left me hanging on the phone. What the fuck is that about?"

"I just fired my maid."

"While I was on the phone?"

"She was eavesdropping. I fired Dr. Greenson, too." Marilyn giggled.

"Jesus Christ. I thought he was supposed to be your Jesus, remember?"

"You want to come over?" Marilyn asked. "Please . . ."

"What the hell happened with you and Greenson?"

"Come over and I'll tell you."

"It's too late."

"You haven't even seen my new house, Jimmy. You just disappeared. I tried calling, but the phone just rang and rang."

"I been right here. I just disconnected the phone for a while. I couldn't deal with anybody. Your little pal Marty would've told you. You guys are always talking, right?"

"Poor Marty, he worries about you all the time. You were mean to him, Jimmy. Very mean."

"Well, I made up for it."

"How?"

"I saw him, and apologized."

"Jeez."

"What the fuck is that?"

"You apologizing, and admitting it. Good for you, Jimmy. Now, what about me? You were mean to me, too."

"No I wasn't."

"You just said so. You said you couldn't deal with anybody. You don't care about me. You left me to die."

"What?"

"You're leaving me again right now. Come over and I'll tell you everything."

"It's almost dawn."

"We'll go for a swim. I've got a pool."

"Too cold."

"It's not cold, and the pool is heated, anyway; and I can't talk on the phone with all the goddamn tapping. Jimmy, please."

"Did you talk to Pier, too?"

"Come over and I'll tell you. I'm afraid, Jimmy. I don't know what Mrs. Murray will do to me. I don't want to be alone with her. She's supposed to be leaving, but I don't hear anything. Come over and help me, please."

"I'm not going to help you kick out an old lady at five in the morning."

"She's not an old lady. Please come over."

Marilyn yawned and started to fall asleep.

THE NEW HOUSE WAS A SINGLE-STORY, MISSION-STYLE HACIENDA IN Brentwood. It was protected by seven-foot whitewashed walls and concealed by high stands of eucalyptus trees specially imported from Australia. It was surrounded by a full acre of neatly trimmed lawns and secret gardens, Marilyn's secret gardens. Her gardens were like her diaries, her books of terrible, beautiful, funny, frightening, dangerous secrets. Her gardens were filled with red and gold and white memories, white-hot memories and numbing cold memories, mnemonics to trigger her thoughts, bring her closer to the white light that she knew was heaven, and make her remember how white and good everything was now and how horrible, dark, and terrible everything had been when she was brown-haired, big-chested Norma Jeane, factory worker and pinup girl for *Yank* and *Laugh* and *Peek and See*.

Marilyn turned on all the exterior lights, then stood between two backlit flowering bushes outside her front door and waited for Jimmy. She watched her little white poodle run through what looked like puffs of cloud—baby's breath—along a winding, softly lit, flagstone pathway. "Hey, Maf. Hey, boy. Here, boy."

The dog was a present from Frank Sinatra; she had named it Maf as a joke . . . Maf for Mafia. It ran across the lawns and stopped just in front of the gate; vines of blood-red bougainvillea spidered across the protective white walls and seemed to radiate their own light. Maf started barking and yipping and jumping at the gate. Marilyn heard the sound of an engine. A door slamming. "Hey, Jimmy!" she called. "That you?"

"Yeah, how do I get in?"

"The gate's open."

"Hell if it is."

"Oh," Marilyn said, then reached inside the doorway to activate the electronic lock release. "Try it now."

Jimmy opened the gates wide, petted the dog—which then disappeared into the gardens—and drove around the circular brick driveway to the front of the house. Marilyn hugged and kissed him when he got out of the car; but he wasn't responsive. He looked terrible. He had lost too much weight—his clothes were hanging on him; and he needed a shave, a haircut, and probably a bath.

And then there was the car.

"So what the hell is *that*?" she asked, looking at the black Phantom V Rolls-Royce. Jimmy shrugged. "I thought you were a racing-car kind of guy, like your friend Paul What's-His-Name."

"Newman. And you've got it the wrong way around. He's like me."

Marilyn smiled. There was a slight flash of the old Jimmy, but Christ, he looked awful. "So you're both racing Rolls-Royces now?" she asked sarcastically.

Jimmy looked down at the ground, as if embarrassed. "I got rid of the two Porsches and the Jag. I kept the truck . . . and got this."

Marilyn laughed, and her blue-and-red kimono slipped open. Although it was a balmy night, she pulled the kimono tight around her as if she was cold. Her white-blond hair was mussed; Jimmy always took her as she was; he didn't care. Her skin was whale white, for she never stayed in the sun. She once said she needed a tan and a man. But she had Bobby. He was tan and a man.

"Pier hated racing," Jimmy said. He shrugged again. "So I gave it up." Marilyn waited for him to continue. "I did it after we broke up. Crazy, huh?" Jimmy stared at Marilyn's face, as if he desperately needed her approval. "How'd you get that bruise? Looks like it was bad."

"I fell in the shower."

Jimmy watched her, his head lowered, his gaze steady and hard. "Yeah, right."

"Joe came over. We had an argument. We talked about getting back together—he really wants me back, but it was the same old shit. He still wants me to give up my career. I told him he should give up *his* career. I could support him. I make more money."

"So he hit you for that?"

"I guess I deserved it. I humiliated him."

"You don't deserve that. He's an asshole."

"He's the only person who ever loved me, I mean really loved me. He still loves me."

"So?"

Marilyn jerked backward. She heard something. A branch crunching underfoot. *Someone's out there, watching me.* "Jimmy, go close the gates, please." She saw Maf running toward her. *It's nothing, Maf made the noise. You just need to get sleep. What did Dr. Greenson call it? Sleep fright.*

She shivered. "Jimmy, close the gates!"

MARILYN INSISTED THAT THEY JUMP INTO THE POOL.

"What about your sinusitis, or whatever it is?" Jimmy asked.

Marilyn shrugged out of her kimono. She was the color of moonlight. Her nipples were erect from a slight but sudden chill in the night air. "It'll be warmer in the pool. I keep it really hot." She waded into the water from the shallow end. "Best thing I ever did was that nude scene for *Something's Got to Give*. Best publicity in the world. Did you see any of the photos? They were in all the magazines. All over the world."

Jimmy took off his clothes and slipped into the pool. He slouched beside her, leaning against the blue parquetry sidewall.

"Well, did you?"

"Did I what?"

"See any of the photos."

"Yeah, I think so," Jimmy said.

Marilyn made a face. "Well, everybody else did, but I didn't show anything. At least I didn't wear a body stocking like Elizabeth Taylor did in her bullshit nude scene for *Cleopatra*. What a fake." Her eyes narrowed and she grinned. "You can also see all the flab under her arms."

"You're a bitch," Jimmy said.

"Well, this bitch is what's going to save Fox's ass. All the money they've been pouring into that *Cleopatra* turkey. They're just about bankrupt. But all that's going to change. Because of me."

"I heard a lot of shit went down."

"You could have called me. I was dying."

"Don't look like it to me," Jimmy said. "You look pretty good . . . to me."

"You weren't there when I needed you, Jimmy. For the first time ever you weren't there."

"I told you, I was fucked up."

Marilyn nodded, then tickled him. "I won, Jimmy. I beat all those bastards. You saw the campaign Fox ran against me. That's when I needed you, when your ugly-faced, bitch friend Hedda Hopper wrote that I'd gone around the bend, that I'm no good and insane and washed up as an actress. Did you see that?"

"I heard about it, but she was quoting your director, what's-his-face, who's an asshole anyway."

"George Cukor," Marilyn said, as if she'd just bitten into something rotten. "Those fuckers at Fox spent a hell of a lot of money trying to make me out to be crazy. But I'm not crazy, Jimmy." She pushed herself against him. "I'm not."

"Of course you're not."

"They hurt me, Jimmy. That was the worst thing they could have said."

"Well, like you said, you won."

"I fought back, and they had to rehire me, for a million bucks." She giggled. "A two-picture deal, and they're bringing Nunnally Johnson back to rewrite the script that Walter Bernstein ruined, and *I* get to pick the producers. And Cukor, that sniveling little shit—you know, he wouldn't even let the crew give me a birthday party. Everybody chipped in to buy me a little cake, and I had to practically shove a piece down Cukor's throat. He was shouting that there'd be no party and no champagne on his set. Well, Georgie, you're gone, fired, bye-bye. It's *my* set now."

Jimmy smiled at her. "Is this the new tough Marilyn? I better be careful."

"You better," Marilyn said.

"So how'd you do it?"

"You mean, win?"

"Yeah, win."

"Well, you know about the takeover." Jimmy didn't. He didn't nod or shake his head. "That prick Milton Gold and his Wall Street cronies bought up tons of stock so they could control the board of directors. I called Spyros Skouras—he's always looked after me—to find out why he fired me, and he said it wasn't him. He didn't fire me. He still was president but didn't have any power. It was all Gold, John Loeb, and Sam Rosenman, they're Wall Street thugs. They're the board now, and they don't give two shits about motion pictures. They want oil."

"Oil?"

"Yeah, would you believe it, there's an oil field under the back lot. That's what they're all about."

"So they're gone now?"

Marilyn smiled conspiratorially. "No, Jimmy. They're all still there."

"Then how did you win, if Skouras doesn't have any power?" Jimmy shivered, but that was because of the breeze blowing on his neck and shoulders. The pool was warm as a bath.

"They were getting thousands of letters from my fans who wanted me back. And Dean Martin walked off the set. He told them he wouldn't work with anybody but me. You know who they were going to replace me with? Lee Remick. Who the hell knows Lee Remick?"

Jimmy knew Lee, but he didn't say anything.

"They tried getting Kim Novak, but she told them to fuck off. So did Shirley MacLaine and Doris Day. Oh, God, could you imagine Doris Day playing my role?" Marilyn giggled. "Anyway, it was all good publicity for me, and bad publicity for them."

"Okay," Jimmy said, unconvinced. "It's just that none of it makes any sense. It was stupid of Fox to try a smear campaign. You make them a lot of money. They just hurt themselves by making you look bad."

"My lawyer thought maybe they were running some sort of an insurance scam to get money, you know because of my sinusitis and not being able to be on set like I should have. But he said they'd have to prove I was malingering, and the doctors all said I was sick, so it couldn't be that. I think it was Jack."

"Kennedy?"

"That bastard."

"Why? How?"

"He probably thought that getting me fired would stop me from holding a press conference and blowing his ass out of the water. I was going to hold a press conference, too. Teach him not to treat people like trash. He's an inconsiderate bastard . . . and a lousy fuck." She slapped the surface of the water, smiled sweetly, and said, "I know a lot of secrets about the Kennedys."

"What kinds of secrets?"

"Dangerous ones. They're all in my diary. I should let you see it."

"I don't think I want to," Jimmy said.

"Jack had the wrong girl, if he thought he could fuck with my career."

"How?" Jimmy said, frustrated. "What the hell could he do?"

"He's the president of the United States," Marilyn said.

"So?"

"I found out that Gold and his cronies were all in bed with Jack." She laughed. "Gold was a partner in one of his father's companies. Jack made him ambassador to Peru."

"Then he should be in Peru, and not in L.A."

Marilyn didn't smile. "And Rosenman was in the Justice Department. Jack used him as a labor consultant."

"Sounds like your friend Bobby was involved then," Jimmy said. "The Justice Department is Bobby's turf and—"

"And you know what else?" Marilyn said. "Rosenman sold Fox's back lot to be developed into Century City or something like that. You know who bought it? Alcoa Aluminum. You know who owns Alcoa? Ethel's family."

"Bobby's wife?"

Marilyn nodded.

"That's what I was trying to say. Bobby's involved."

"Not in getting me fired. That was Jack."

"How do you know?" Jimmy asked.

"Because Bobby saved me. When he found out what Jack was up to, he shut it down. He called everyone and made it right."

"And you promised you wouldn't go public, right?"

"It's my trump card," Marilyn said. "And do you know why Ethel's got somebody calling me all the time? She *knows* Bobby loves me, not her."

Jimmy shook his head and watched the steam rise from the water; the air was getting chilly. "I wouldn't trust any of them."

"You don't get it, Jimmy. Bobby made it right and went against Jack to do it. He told me everything." She paused. "I thought he was your buddy, anyway."

"I wouldn't exactly call us buddies."

"What, then?"

Jimmy shrugged. "I think Bobby just did what was best for his brother."

"Bobby did what was best for *me* . . . but there's stuff that Bobby doesn't even know."

"Like what?"

Marilyn giggled. "It's a secret."

"We been in here too long," Jimmy said. "It's too hot. You got towels?"

"Nope. Forgot them. You want to know the secret?"

"If you want to tell me."

"I haven't signed the new contract with Fox. You know why?"

"Why?"

"Because there's going to be another takeover there. And when that happens, then I'm *really* going to win."

"This winning thing has gotten really important to you," Jimmy said.

"Yeah, it has. Everybody's been trying to make me lose all my life, even Joe. Especially Joe. That's why Joe's out of my life. That's why Dr. Greenson's out of my life, and Mrs. Murray, too. She was just working for him, anyway."

"Why'd you fire Dr. Greenson?"

"Because he's no different than Arthur. He's using me like Arthur did with *The Misfits*."

"How?"

She laughed. "He wants to be in movies. He started becoming my agent instead of my psychiatrist, and all his goddamn loyalties are with all the assholes at Fox." She looked toward the house and shouted, "Hey, Eunice, are you gone yet?"

"Stop it," Jimmy said.

"I fired her and told her to get out. You were on the phone. You heard me."

"Yeah, well you can fire her tomorrow."

"She's probably recording everything we're doing right now," Marilyn said.

"So, let her record."

"Do you like the new me?"

"No," Jimmy said flatly.

"Jimmy, they were all fucking me over while you were off somewhere feeling sorry for yourself. Are you still feeling sorry for yourself?"

Jimmy smiled. "Yeah, probably." After a beat, he asked, "You said on the phone that you and Pier talked."

"You want some champagne? I do, but we'll have to go inside to get it." She opened her eyes wide in a mocking expression. "And we'll have to sneak around the horrible Mrs. Murray."

"What about Pier?" Jimmy insisted.

"Marty told her to call me," Marilyn said. "He asked me if it was okay. So she called."

"And?"

"And nothing. She told me how much she loved you, and asshole that I am, I tried to call you to tell you, but nobody could get through. She said something crazy, though. I told her she was off her nut."

"Yeah?"

Marilyn giggled and pressed her pelvis against Jimmy. "She thought you were in love with me instead of her. That's why she behaved like she did. So I set her straight."

"What did you tell her?"

"I told her she was right."

"Thanks," Jimmy said.

Marilyn laughed, touching him. "Okay, I lied. I told her the truth, Jimmy, that you're in love with her. But you *should* be in love with me. Why aren't you, Jimmy?"

"I am."

"No you're not. Not with a prick this soft."

"Nothing's working for me anymore, I guess."

"Oh, poor Jimmy. Pretend I'm Pier."

"You're sick, Marilyn."

"Try it."

Jimmy felt himself getting hard. "What about Mrs. Murray? She's probably watching right now."

"Then let her get all hot and bothered. Serves her right. Are you thinking about Pier?" There was something desperate in her voice.

"No."

"Who, then?"

"You," Jimmy said, and as he held and fondled her, he looked into the illuminated blue water, magical blue pure dream blue water, pure light, pure blue, his favorite blue, the blue of the blue time just before sundown; and then he kissed her. She tasted like almonds and cigarettes and her eyes were as blue as the water and her skin was white against his and she was warm water, glycerin, oceans of glycerin, and he moved inside her, she was the warm bath, the cleansing. They stared at each other, as if they were in love, and Jimmy realized yes yes it was Marilyn, it was always Marilyn; he wanted only Marilyn, even if she was thinking about Bobby and Jack and Joe and everybody else in the goddamn world; and as he fucked Marilyn, as he pushed himself into her, stroked her, lathed her, slid pushed pressed into her warm bathwater glycerin crack, he didn't think of Pier.

He didn't imagine Pier's dark and perfect face superimposed upon Marilyn's.

Marilyn giggled as she came, and he whispered her name. "Pier."

"You're a son of a bitch, Jimmy."

Flaccid Jimmy. "No, Marilyn, I wasn't thinking about her, I swear. Her name just came out . . . because you were talking about her, probably, because—"

"Fuck you, Jimmy. You're not fucking me."

"Marilyn, I swear . . ."

Marilyn got out of the pool. She looked down at Jimmy and asked, "You hungry?"

"Yeah," Jimmy said, looking up at her.

"You going to stay the night with me?"

"It's almost morning." She didn't respond. "Yeah," Jimmy said. "I'll stay as long as you want."

"It's not just what I want, Jimmy. It's got to be what you want, too."

"You look good from the bottom up."

"You think so?" Marilyn asked, grinning and spreading her legs.

"I think so," he said.

"HERE, I'LL PROVE IT TO YOU," MARILYN SAID, AND SHE PICKED UP the phone. The lamp on her night table cast a yellowish light against the wall, curtains, and bed.

"What time is it?" Jimmy asked sleepily.

Marilyn shrugged. "Probably nine . . . or maybe ten, or eleven. Something like that. Mrs. Murray is usually trying to break into my room by this time. But she knows better. Maybe she's left. You think she's left?"

"How should I know?" Jimmy sat up in the bed. "You want me to check?"

"In a minute. You got to talk to Bobby first. He'll tell you what happened."

"Look, forget it, I believe you. Whatever you say."

"No, I'm going to prove it to you," Marilyn said, still holding the receiver.

"Christ, it's like a tomb in here. You mind if I open the curtains?"

"Watch the snaps. They break easy, and I can't have any light coming in when I sleep."

While Jimmy pulled the blackout curtains open—it was another bright, still day—Marilyn dialed the special, private number that Bobby had given her. It bypassed the switchboard of the Justice Department. The phone rang once, and then a recording cut in: "You have reached a nonworking number at the United States Justice Department. Please check your directory and dial again."

Oh, no, son of a bitch, please, no, it's not happening again, not you, too, Bobby, you fucker, you fucker, you're no better than your brother, but it's not true, it's probably an ordinary mistake, don't jump to conclusions, just dial the number again, calm, be calm, don't let on to Jimmy, it's just an ordinary mistake, it'll be all right . . .

She dialed again and got the same recording. She felt the cold, itchy edges of the old recurring nightmare, of being lost, abandoned— *everyone abandons me—my father, Arthur, Jack, Jimmy*—but she couldn't tell Jimmy, couldn't let on, not now, not yet, not until she was certain; and she needed wanted had to be alone. She couldn't let

Jimmy see her grief, and she knew that's what was coming—grief and darkness and anger. The hollow, hungry aching in the pit of the stomach. Grief.

"No answer?" Jimmy asked, turning from the window.

"Just a minor screwup," Marilyn said. She had to fix this by herself now, right now this minute, and she didn't want anyone near her, overhearing her, eavesdropping on her. She wouldn't allow herself to be distracted, not even by Jimmy, who came back to the bed. She dialed the main switchboard. *And fuck you Bobby, I'll use my own name, too.*

"Justice Department, may I help you?" A male voice. Well modulated, professional.

"Yes, this is Marilyn Monroe, and I'm having trouble reaching the attorney general on his private line."

"That line has been disconnected on orders of the attorney general, ma'am. I'm sorry, but there's no referral."

"What the hell do you mean, there's no referral?"

"We haven't been advised of another number."

"Transfer me over to his office. I'll get this taken care of."

"Yes, ma'am. I am sorry for the inconvenience."

"Marilyn?" Jimmy asked. "Is anything wrong?" Marilyn shook her head and turned away from him, as if he was making too much noise for her to hear what was being said on the phone.

"Attorney general's office, may I help you?" A woman's voice, thin, reedy.

"This is Marilyn Monroe, and I need to speak to the attorney general. So don't fuck me around. This is important, and I need to speak to him now."

"I'm sorry, Miss Monroe, but Mr. Kennedy is in conference all afternoon."

"Then let me speak to his secretary."

"I'm sorry, but she's not available just now. If you give me your phone number, I can ask her to call you back."

"I don't want her to call me back. I want Bobby to call me back. You got that?"

"Yes, ma'am. If you'll just give me your phone number—"

"He knows my phone number. Tell him that unless he calls me today, *I'm* calling a press conference tomorrow. You got that?"

"Yes, ma'am."

Marilyn hung up the phone. "Jimmy, would you get Mrs. Murray for me?"

"What's going on?" Jimmy asked.

"It's just a glitch with the phones in the Justice Department."

"And that's why you're going to call a press conference, right?"

"Jimmy, please, just get Mrs. Murray for me."

"I thought you fired her."

"Please, and don't shout from the door. Just knock on her door." Jimmy shook his head and got up from the bed. "I'll tell you every-thing, I promise."

But when Jimmy returned with a very smug Mrs. Murray, he found the door locked.

"Marilyn Monroe, open this door right now," Mrs. Murray said.

"Call Dr. Greenson on the other line and tell him I have to see him right away."

"Marilyn, let me in," Jimmy said.

"Go home, Jimmy. I'll call you later."

"Open the door or I'll kick it down."

"Jimmy, please, go home."

"I'm counting to three. One . . . two . . ." Jimmy paused, waiting. Marilyn opened the door a crack and then got back into bed. "How many pills did you take?" Jimmy asked.

"Just a few. To take the edge off. But don't worry. Everything will be all right in just a few minutes."

"I'll get the doctor," Mrs. Murray said wearily. "No doubt she's overdosed herself again. I knew this was coming, I just knew it."

"I didn't do any such thing," Marilyn said as she slid into deli-cious, white oblivion. "But I do need Dr. Greenson. I need my Jesus." She smiled and yawned at Jimmy, as if, indeed, nothing in the whole wide world could ever be wrong. "Jimmy, close the curtains and come to bed."

FIFTEEN

■

Bug Fuck

LOS ANGELES: AUGUST 4–5, 1962

Roses.

That's what Jimmy's mother used to say when everything was going well—*it's all roses, my Jimmy, and you're the big rose, the biggest most wonderful most beautiful rose*—and she would laugh when Jimmy would pinch his nose and puff out his cheeks to make his face red and prove conclusively that he was indeed the biggest best rose in the entire world.

Roses, Jimmy said himself, to the ether, to Pier, to Marilyn, and to his mother deep in her rotting earth-moist grave. It was Saturday, and Jimmy was thirty-one years old and still roses. He made his rose face, showered, and put on fresh jeans and a white T-shirt.

He should call Marilyn and tell her that she was

right, that everything was roses and that Pier loved him and everything was going to work out and they were getting married. *You're right, Marilyn, I'm happy. I should call you right now and tell you. Thank you, Marilyn, for the contact with the pizza-pie boys in Milan—they want to do everything, all your movies and* On the Road *and maybe even Bobby's film, and baby, I got news for you . . .* Jimmy reveled in the idea of starting work Monday on *The Hustler*. *But that ain't the news. The news is you and me doing the film version of* Sweet Bird of Youth. *All you got to do is say yes, sweet blond beautiful sister, sweet confessor, sweet fuck, sweet downy radiant mirror twin sister I do love you.*

He'd call her now.

But his phone rang.

"Yeah."

"Jimmy?"

"It's mental telepathy," Jimmy said, excited. "I was just this minute going to call you. I got news. Beautiful news."

"Bobby—"

"Yeah?"

"Jimmy, I'm afraid." Marilyn's breathing was ragged, as if she'd been crying.

"Afraid of what?"

"Bobby, he's going to do something to me, Jimmy, he hit me and pushed me, he ransacked my house, he threatened me, he's going to do something horrible to me, but I'm not going to let him win, Jimmy, I'm not going to, he won everything, and I'm going public, I'm going to tell the whole fucking world what he and Jack did to me, but I know he's going to do something terrible to me, I just know it. He said he would, he said so."

"Whoa, slow down," Jimmy said. "What do you mean he hit you?"

"He did," she whispered into the phone. Sobbing. "He hit me . . ."

"Why would he hit you?"

" 'Cause he wants . . ."

Jimmy waited for her to continue, then asked, "Marilyn?"

"Yeah?"

"Wants what?"

"Everything. Me on a plate, all diced and sliced." Then she sighed and started breathing heavily into the phone, as if in a deep sleep.

"Marilyn? Marilyn? Hey, are you there? Talk to me. Are you okay?"

"Yeah, I'm fine. Jimmy?"

"Yeah?"

"I love you." Then just the stentorian sounds of heavy breathing.

"Marilyn?" Jimmy asked again.

"I love you, Jimmy," she said, her voice muzzy, barely audible. "Come over. We'll go to Chasen's. You're too skinny. You need to eat."

"I'm coming over right now."

Her breathing like sighs, deep and regular.

"Marilyn . . . Marilyn? Can you hear me?"

Deep breath in, glottal catching rattling sighing, then deep breath out.

HE TOOK THE TRUCK AND DROVE TO BRENTWOOD. HE RANG THE buzzer on the gate, but there was no answer. *She's definitely O.D.'d,* Jimmy thought, and he found the nearest phone booth. *Who to call? The police? No. Call her doctor.* But someone had torn the phone book in half, and the half he needed was missing. He called 411 for information, then called Dr. Greenson's number. His wife answered the phone. No, Dr. Greenson isn't home, he's with a patient. *Click.* He fished out another dime and called Marilyn again, just to be sure. Then he'd call the police.

A man's voice, well modulated, with a slight European accent.

"Is Marilyn all right?" Jimmy asked.

"I'm sorry, but Miss Monroe isn't here just now."

"I just talked to her, goddammit. Don't fuck me around. Is she all right?"

Click.

That was Dr. Greenson, her Jesus, to be sure.

JIMMY DROVE TO PIER'S APARTMENT IN BEL AIR.

"What's wrong?" Pier asked. She was wearing pink short shorts and one of Jimmy's white T-shirts. Her lustrous black hair was pulled back from her heart-shaped face and tied with pink ribbons into two ponytails. No shoes. No makeup. Pier the doll-collecting tomboy.

"What makes you think anything's wrong?"

"Because you're two hours early for our date. Because you look upset. I ought to know that look by now." She lowered her head and squinted, mimicking him.

"Very funny, Pier. Christ, it's like a goddamn refrigerator in here."

The air-conditioning unit was wheezing and sighing, and Jimmy thought of Marilyn. *I should have gone over to her house again instead of coming here. I'll call her . . . but not from here. Her shrink is doing something over there, so she must be okay. He's probably fucking her or something.* Jimmy felt suddenly angry and vulnerable but wouldn't couldn't admit jealousy.

"In case you haven't noticed, we're in a heat wave," Pier said.

Jimmy looked around her living room. Her dolls were everywhere, in every corner and cabinet, on every bookshelf and tabletop. "It's coming off the desert," Pier continued.

Jimmy nodded and looked out through her windows at the slate-roofed houses that seemed to waver in the heat. But he shivered in the air-conditioned chill.

"So did you make a reservation at Chasen's like you promised? It's Saturday night, and *you're* not dressed to take me out."

"Do you really want to go out?" Jimmy asked. "Let's just stay home and watch television. I'll get takeout."

"No, Jimmy, absolutely not. Did you make a reservation?" Jimmy shook his head. "Well, *I* did, so we're going."

"What's the big thing with Chasen's? It's just a restaurant, for Christ's sake."

"It's the restaurant you always go to with Marilyn."

"So?"

"So that's where I want to go. I want everybody to see us. Like you said, the golden couple. We'll go back to your house after I get dressed, and you can change." She sat down on a white velour couch and patted the cushion, indicating that Jimmy should sit beside her. "Now tell me what's the matter, and Mommy will make it all better." She grinned at him, her signal that if he was a very good boy, she would go down on him. But Jimmy was too preoccupied to be interested.

When they first met, she had taunted him about liking that kind of pervert sex. Now Pier had become the aggressive partner. Jimmy wondered if her artist boyfriend had taught her that, and he felt angry. Angry at Pier? For what?

Angry at Marilyn?

"Okay, Jimmy. Just tell me."

"Tell you what?"

She sighed. "What's bothering you, and then we can get on with our life."

"If I tell you, you'll only get all pissed off."

"Jesus, Jimmy. Give me a break. Just tell me."

"No, I don't need a fight."

"Jimmy, tell Mommy."

"Marilyn called me. I think she's overdosed or something."

"What?"

"Oh, she'll be okay. Her asshole psychiatrist is with her."

"How do you know?" Pier asked.

"Because he answered the phone when I called back. But he wouldn't tell me anything, except that she wasn't home, which is a lie."

"Maybe she's not."

"I *know* she's home."

"Well, why don't you just call her back and find out?"

"I'll call her later, once the drugs wear off and her psychiatrist leaves." After a beat: "I think she's in real trouble this time. She said something about being threatened."

"By who?"

Jimmy shrugged. *Don't tell her any more.*

She stared at Jimmy, studying him, then asked in her little-girl voice, "Do you want me to call Marilyn?"

Jimmy shrugged. "Do whatever you want."

"Will that rest your mind?"

"I'll call her."

"No, Jimmy," Pier said, "I think *I'll* call her."

"HELLO?" MARILYN'S VOICE WAS SOFT AND BREATHY, AS IF SHE'D just been awakened by the phone.

"It's Pier."

"Hi, Pier." Marilyn's voice brightened. "What's up? Everything okay?"

"Oh, everything's fine. But Jimmy's been worried about you."

"Why?"

"He said he called you and someone answered the phone and said you weren't home, but he knew you were home."

Marilyn laughed softly. "That was Dr. Greenson. I should hire him as a flacker. He tells everyone who calls that I'm not home. He's thinks everyone who calls me is a mugger and a rapist. Of course, in Jimmy's case . . ."

This time they both laughed.

"Is Jimmy with you?" Marilyn asked.

After a brief hesitation, Pier said, "Yes. But he was afraid I'd get jealous if he called you, so *I'm* calling."

"God, men are so fucking weird."

"You can say that again."

"He said something about you being threatened."

Marilyn giggled. "Oh, he always blows everything out of proportion. No, just problems with men. But I'm *always* having problems with men."

"You're not alone."

"Is everything all right with you and Jimmy?" Marilyn asked, concern in her voice.

"Everything's great . . . thanks to you for getting us together."

"I didn't do anything but whisper in that lovesick fool's ear." Pier giggled. "I think Jimmy is coming over later," Marilyn said. "We're going over to Chasen's for a quick bite. You're coming, aren't you?"

"Jeez, I don't know. He just wandered into my apartment a few minutes ago, and he looks like he needs a shower and a suit."

"That figures."

"I'll check with him and call you back."

"Okay," Marilyn said.

Pier could hear her yawn. "You're sure you're okay?" Pier asked.

But there was no answer, just the whisper of distant breathing.

"WELL, IS SHE ALL RIGHT?" JIMMY ASKED WHEN PIER HUNG UP. "I thought you were going to let me talk to her."

"She's fine. She just sounds sleepy, and we've got to call her right back, anyway."

"For what?"

"Is there anything you want to tell me?" Pier asked brightly.

"Like what?"

"Like why you didn't tell me you made a date to take Marilyn to Chasen's."

"I didn't make a date. Marilyn mumbled something about me being skinny and needing to eat, and then she fell asleep on the phone, for Christ's sake. You got to get over this, Pier."

"Get over it? Who do you think you are? Mr. America?" Then she shifted back to sweet-voiced sarcasm. "Seems like you two are such big stars that you don't even need a reservation at Chasen's."

"Pier . . ." Jimmy reached over to caress her, but she jerked away.

"So once again I just made a fool out of myself."

"Nobody's made a fool of anybody. I thought you and Marilyn were friends."

"Marilyn's everybody's friend. She means well and wouldn't hurt a fly. But if you go out with her, you'll fuck her, I know you will, and she'll let you. She'll encourage you. You know why?" Pier didn't wait for an answer. "Because she's in love with you."

"That's bullshit, and you know it."

"And you're in love with her."

"No, I'm not, Pier. I'm in love with *you*. If she was in love with me, why would she have done so much to get us back together?"

"Because she loves you, stupid."

Jimmy rolled his eyes and shook his head.

"Don't give me that shit," Pier said, getting up from the couch. "I'll call your girlfriend back. I told her I would. She wants to know if you're bringing me along to Chasen's. Are you?"

"Pier, don't get into this weird shit. I'm not going to see Marilyn. I came here to see you."

"Then we'll go over to see Marilyn, and you two can work out your thing."

"You just want to fuck everything up, don't you?" Jimmy asked. "Why? What are you feeling guilty about? What have you been doing?" Then it struck him. "You're still seeing that artist, aren't you? That's it, isn't it? So you figure that I'm doing the same thing with Marilyn." Jimmy raised his voice.

Pier blushed, giving herself away, or perhaps it was just the flush of pure anger because she threw an engraved Stiegel tumbler at him. He raised his arm to deflect the glass, which landed on the carpet.

"You *are* seeing him," Jimmy said, panicking. He could feel it, the terrible familiar slippage into nightmare and emptiness. Pier started to cry. "Did he give you that thing you just threw at me?"

"No," Pier said, almost in a whisper. "My mother gave it to me. She thought it was cute."

"Tell me, did you see him or not?" Jimmy demanded.

"Did you fuck Marilyn? You tell me that, Jimmy."

"I told you, she's just a friend. But that's not how it is with you and that asshole artist, is it?"

"I only saw him to tell him good-bye, it was over, that's all," Pier said softly. "That's what we agreed."

"We didn't agree for you to see him again."

"What'd you want me to do, do it over the phone?"

"Or a letter, that would have been better."

"You're crazy, Jimmy."

"Did you see him again after that?"

"No, I told you." But her face was still red.

"Swear that you didn't fuck him after that, or go down on him, or hold his goddamn hand. Swear on your mother's life."

"I won't swear like that. It's against God."

"It wasn't against God when you swore you loved me."

"I do love you, Jimmy."

"Then why are you still seeing him?"

"Because—"

"So you *are* seeing him." Somehow that shocked Jimmy. Although he was intimidating her, browbeating her, he hadn't really believed that she was still carrying on with her old boyfriend.

"I'm not seeing him. I just tried to do the right thing. He's such a mess. I couldn't be cruel like you, like you are, Jimmy." She glared at him, as if she could still turn the situation around and blame him, but then she looked down at her hands and cried. "I was just trying to make it right, so everything would be all right with us."

Is she acting? "So that's why you're fucking him, and that's why you just threw his vase—or whatever the fuck it is—at me?"

"It's not his vase," Pier said in her little-girl voice. "And I'm not fucking him. Jimmy, please . . . hold me."

Everything had gone wrong again, and Jimmy was standing up, turning, rushing toward the door, escaping, running. *Turn around. Make it stop.* "Jimmy . . ."

But he couldn't. He couldn't get rid of the image of Pier screwing her square-faced Russian artist boyfriend. Jimmy was sick, revolted with himself, empty; and he could hear his blood pounding in his head, the hollow choo-chooing of the *Silver Challenger,* the ghost train that had taken his mother back to Illinois, back to her grave, and he wanted to stop and turn around and tell Pier that everything was all right, but it wasn't all right, she was fucking that artist, she really was, how could she do that and look so small and pretty now? How could she do that?

He whispered "Momma" as he ran out into the hot, empty street.

HE DROVE TO MARILYN'S, THE TRUCK'S AIR-CONDITIONING SIGHING, whispering, for he was back in the nightmare again, the nightmare where everything was hollow and shaky and whispery, but Marilyn would know what to do, she would get him out of it, she would make it right, maybe Pier hadn't fucked her boyfriend, and so what if she did? *So what if she did?*

He rang the buzzer at the gate, but there was no answer.

Not even Maf barking. Just the hot, hollow whispering of the evening, twilight, catsup-red light bleeding into the dirty ash of the sky. Jimmy rang the buzzer again, insistently.

A gray-haired man stepped out of the house. He was dressed in a gray suit; his gray-and-red-striped tie was neatly knotted, but his white cotton shirt was wrinkled. He walked across the lawn to the gate but didn't open it. "Yes, may I help you?"

"Yeah, you can open the gate for a start."

"You're James Dean, am I right?"

Although Jimmy knew who this man was, he asked, "Yeah, and who the hell are you? I want to see Marilyn."

"I'm her doctor, Dr. Greenson. She said you might come over and asked me to tell you that she's feeling a bit under the weather and won't be able to see you tonight."

So this was her Jesus. Hair thin on top, black, bushy eyebrows, hawk nose, black Errol Flynn mustache, tight mouth. Big pores, and he was sweating under that starched shirt and gray-as-your-day suit. He was the quintessential tight-ass, and Jimmy knew that this tight-ass was in love with Marilyn. He was in love with her money, too. Marilyn practically lived at his home, and it seemed that he spent more than a little time in hers. Marilyn had told Jimmy that she bought her house in Brentwood because it was close to her Jesus.

"So you're her Jesus."

"What?"

"Nothin'."

Dr. Greenson smiled mirthlessly. "I heard what you said, son. I'm her doctor, that's all."

"Well, I want to see her."

"I just gave her a sedative, and it wouldn't be a good idea to disturb her. Are *you* all right?"

"What do you mean?" Jimmy asked, hostile.

Dr. Greenson shrugged. "When she wakes up, I'll tell her you were concerned and stopped by." With that, he turned and walked back to the house.

Jimmy called to Dr. Greenson but was ignored.

He heard Maf bark when Dr. Greenson opened the front door, but the noise was muffled and distant, and suddenly it was dark. There was no intervening blue time, no transition from day to night, from real to dream.

Jimmy got into his truck. He had a plan.

He was going to get blind drunk.

HE CALLED MARILYN. HER PRIVATE NUMBER: GRANITE 6-1890. NO answer, still no answer, not even that fuck Dr. Greenson.

He called Pier, then hung up. Finished off the bottle of Johnny Black. Broke his sculpture of himself. Tore up his photographs of Pier. Searched for pills, popped two small purple capsules—he couldn't remember what they were—and fell into electric, snapping sleep. Pier used to say he'd been "monstered" when he told her about his recurring nightmares of his mother rising from her grave. She'd wake him up when he screamed in his sleep. She'd touch him fuck him suck him whisper him back to sleep, so he could dream again.

Dreaming . . .

I'll kick those monsters out, Jimmy.

You're the monster, Pier.

No, Jimmy, you're the monster, and the train clatters, clacks, whis-tles through his head, whistling through his mouth and his eyes and his ears and—

The phone was ringing.

Drugged out, wheezing, trying to catch his breath, Jimmy picked up the receiver.

"Jimmy? Jimmy? You there? Answer me. That fucker Bobby came back again and ransacked my house. Twice. I called Dr. Greenson, but he's . . . unavailable."

"I saw him at your house."

"He was here. He gave me a shot and . . ."

"And what?"

"And then he left."

"Are you fucking him?"

"Jimmy, please come over. I'm really scared."

"Maybe you should try your Jesus again."

"Jimmy? What's wrong with you? Jimmy?"

But it was Jimmy's turn to fall asleep on the phone. When he woke up, guilty, sweaty, queasy and muzzy-mouthed, head pounding, eyes aching, it was almost 3:00 A.M. He remembered Marilyn's call. His re-ceiver was off the hook; he had cradled it to his ear all night, and not even the beeping of the phone had awakened him. He dialed her num-ber. It was engaged, which meant that she was either talking with someone or had fallen asleep on the phone. Either way, he was going to find out.

He had to make things right, lest she think he didn't care about her, didn't love her. He wanted to sleep with her, too, comfort her, and make everything better. And she would tell him what to do about Pier.

But he knew what she would say.

Forgive her and stop being such an asshole. You're fucking me—how is that different from Pier trying one on?

It's different, Marilyn.

How?

It just is . . .

HE TOOK THE ROLLS BECAUSE ITS AIR CONDITIONER WORKED BETTER than the truck's, which emitted a burning smell. The Phantom V's lac-quered expanse of hood swallowed the road ahead, swallowed the soul-silent darkness.

Marilyn's house looked ghostly in the hazed moonlight. The gate was wide open. Cars whispered up and down Fifth Helena Drive with their lights off. A dozen cars and a white ambulance were parked in the cul-de-sac. There were Lincolns and black and white police cars with their dome lights turned off. There were a few nondescript panel vans. Figures hurried in and out of the house and across the lawn. Everyone silent. Everyone busy. Jimmy turned his headlights off, parked the Rolls in a concealed driveway, and stumbled outside. The dry, hot wind coming from the Mojave Desert almost choked him; the trees around Marilyn's white stucco home rustled and swayed. Jimmy could hear the clinking tinkling of the wind chimes that the poet Carl Sandburg had given her. Above, a helicopter wheeled, then, making a *chock-a-chock* rotor noise that cut through the wind and dark, it landed on a nearby golf course.

Jimmy's head pounded and his eyes ached. He was hungover and felt like he was going to be sick. But he was focused on Marilyn, on getting to Marilyn.

Two burly men in dark suits stood by the gate; they chain-smoked cigarettes, spoke in hushed voices, and were probably armed. Jimmy would never get by them. He climbed over the white wall, using vines to gain purchase. *Oh, shit, I'm too sick for this.* He fell, landing in shrubbery in one of Marilyn's secret gardens, crushing flowers, bruising his right arm, which pulsed in metronomic time with his headache and nausea. The smell of the flowers was sweet, cloying . . . nauseating. At first he thought he had broken his arm—he had felt a thrumming when he hit the ground—but he could move it in all directions. It would hurt later.

Son of a bitch . . . everything would hurt later.

A high-pitched woman's voice. Screaming.

"Murderers! You murderers! Are you satisfied now? You bastards. You fucking bastards!"

Jimmy watched two men supporting the distraught woman, holding on to her as she tried to break free. She looked like Marilyn's publicist, Pat Newcomb. Long, well-cut, blond-streaked hair. Suit. High heels. She was crying, sobbing, inconsolable.

He made his way across the lawn, keeping to the long shadows cast by the light from the windows. Hearing men's voices—*We're done here, Mac. Shit, I've had the course. Let's leave it, it's clean as it's going to get. Let the Fox assholes finish it up*—he staggered to Marilyn's bedroom window. The window was broken. A shard of glass crunched under his foot. He stood frozen, but the men inside didn't hear him. They left, their voices fading as they walked into the hallway.

One of the voices had a Boston accent. Damn Bobby, Jimmy thought as he peered through the window.

He saw Marilyn lying facedown on the bed. Her color was wrong: white and blotchy. Her legs were straight, and her arms were by her sides, as if she was a soldier at attention. "Marilyn," Jimmy said, then again, louder. "Marilyn!" he shouted. *She's overdosed. Why isn't anyone helping her?* "Marilyn . . . Marilyn, goddammit, Marilyn, wake up!"

A tall man with prematurely gray, short-cropped hair stepped into the room. Startled to see Jimmy, he turned on his heel.

Jimmy recognized him. He was one of Bobby's aides. Jimmy shouted to Marilyn again, but she didn't move. Panicked, he smashed at the window with his arm, Cutting himself. He didn't feel any pain, but there was blood all over the sill. He pulled off one of his penny loafers, swept it along the edges of the window to remove the jagged, knife-sharp bits of glass, and climbed into the room.

"Marilyn, dammit, wake up." He tried to shake her awake, but she was ice cold, ice-cold rigid frigid dead cold, blue blotchy dead, a stiff, bleach-blond soldier standing lying dead at attention.

Jimmy heard screams but only dimly realized they were his own; and then he was throwing punches at a tall, red-haired, freckled man who had entered the room with other men. All shadow figures. He tried to punch the familiar face of Bobby's gray-haired henchman, as if the skinny lawyer was Bobby himself. *You did this, Bobby, you son of a bitch shanty-Irish bastard,* and then for an electric, white-pain flash of a second he was playacting with his mother, pretending, and this room was a stage, and there was just Jimmy and his mother, everything else was pretend, and he was acting all the parts for her, and she said, in a man's voice, that she was sorry and—

"I didn't hit him hard, but Jesus Christ he was going wild." Bobby's aide was calmly talking to two uniformed policemen who were holding Jimmy.

Jimmy stared at Marilyn, transfixed. "Marilyn, wake up." He tried to pull away from the policemen but couldn't. "What'd you do to her?" he shouted at Bobby's aide. "She's dead, isn't she? I know what's going on here." He lunged for the aide, but the police held him firm. "I'm going to tear your face off, you scumbag. Marilyn was scared that cock-sucker Bobby was going to hurt her. Where is he?" Then Jimmy started shouting for Bobby.

"I'll get the doctor," the aide said.

"I know who you are," Jimmy said to him, and then he called to Marilyn, shouted at her to wake up, told her he was sorry he'd fallen asleep when she called, sorry that he'd accused her of fucking her Jesus, that asshole doctor of hers, "Oh, God, I'm sorry, Marilyn, but I'll make it up to you, I'll get you out of here, you're going to be all right, everything is—"

"Jimmy. *Jimmy!*"

"Yeah?"

"I'm Dr. Greenson."

"What the hell's going on here?"

"Get him out of here," Dr. Greenson told the police.

"Where're Bobby's henchmen?" Jimmy asked as the policemen dragged him out of the house. Dr. Greenson walked ahead of them. "You ain't her Jesus!" Jimmy shouted. "You ain't nobody's Jesus!"

Outside. The breeze still hot. Wind chimes tinkling. "Let go of me you're hurting me." The policemen smelled like Old Spice aftershave and rotten food. *Let me go. Marilyn* . . .

"I can give you a sedative, but I need to know if you're on anything else," Dr. Greenson said. "I'm sorry that man had to hit you."

"You're not giving me anything. What did you do to Marilyn?"

"Marilyn took an overdose, Jimmy. She's dead, and the police are conducting an investigation. I'm very sorry. Sorry for all of us."

"She didn't take any overdose. I talked to her, and—"

Then he was in the police car. He couldn't remember how he got there—his right hand and arm were bandaged and aching, and he was missing a shoe—but he remembered what Jesus had said.

"Sleep it off."

He was in the backseat, stretched out, cold as Marilyn. Policemen were driving him home.

He felt the caressing chill of Demerol needling through him, numbing him, sweeping him back to his secret place of safety, even as he cried for Marilyn.

SIXTEEN

■

Book of Secrets

Los Angeles: August 5, 1962

The clock radio, tuned to station WBOP, had been blaring for hours.

Jimmy slept through "Loco-motion," "He's a Rebel," "Mashed Potato Time," "Limbo Rock," "Walk Like a Man," "Duke of Earl," "The Wanderer," and new songs by Roy Orbison, Ray Charles, Bobby Darin, Del Shannon, and Elvis; he woke up when the disc jockey replaced "Sherry" with Ray Anthony's tuneful and symphonic "Marilyn," recorded in her honor in 1953. After a few seconds, the deejay interrupted the recording. His voice was low and scratchy, his trademark: "Marilyn Monroe dead of suicide at age thirty-six. We grasp at straws, as if knowing how she died will bring her back. Not since Jean Harlow have the standards of feminine beauty been so embodied in one woman. Marilyn Monroe, dead at thirty-six. Let's take a moment of silence in her honor."

Jimmy clutched the base of the telephone to his chest, as if it was a teddy bear. He coughed, stirring up the dust balls on the floor. Had he fallen off the couch? His back and neck ached. He was in a fetal position.

Marilyn?

The phone was dead. He had tangled the line in his sleep and pulled it out of the wall socket.

Jesus Christ, you asshole, she's not there, she's dead, no more Marilyn sleeping on the phone, no more choking breathing overdoses, you're dead, Marilyn, and it's all my fault.

Take your medicine, Mr. Big Rose.

Face it.

She called you for help, and all you could think about was whether she was fucking her Jesus.

Jimmy opened his eyes; they felt gummy, granular. The light was incandescently bright, and the deejay resumed the music, playing "Sherry" by the Four Seasons.

Marilyn had had her minute of silence. Time to turn on the world.

Jimmy tapped the plungers on the phone, as if that could give him his direct line to Marilyn up in heaven. He crawled along the floor to reconnect the line. His hand was seeping blood through the bandages, discoloring the carpet. His arm ached, his head ached, he needed drugs, but he couldn't get up just yet to find them; and they probably weren't there anyway. Jimmy started laughing. It was time to take his medicine, but he couldn't overdose if he tried. He didn't have enough booze or pot or pills. Not even rat poison.

Only some aspirin and Alka-Seltzer.

He could fizz himself to death.

The phone rang, and Jimmy dropped it, surprised. He picked it up again and, impossibly expecting it to be Marilyn, said, "Yeah . . . that you, Marilyn?"

"Jesus, don't you know? You don't know, do you? Oh, my God . . ."

"Pier?"

"Yes, Jimmy, it's me." She sniffed and in a quavering voice said, "I've been trying to call you for hours. I just had to call you. I've got something to tell you, Jimmy, I'm so sorry, but—"

Jimmy felt the light the room the world pouring into him. His lungs hurt as he took a deep breath. He must have smoked three packs of Chesterfields last night. His fingers were yellow with nicotine. "I already know, Pier, it's all right."

"Oh, Jimmy, oh, my God, I just can't believe it. It was all my fault, I should have let you go and help her, I should have helped her, I should have called her, we should have done something, you tried, you did everything you could, but I was just jealous and stupid and—"

"Pier, it's not your fault, it's not anybody's fault." But Jimmy didn't believe that.

"Jimmy?"

"Yeah."

"I'm so sorry we had a fight."

"So am I."

"I forgive you if you forgive me."

"Yeah, okay," Jimmy said.

"Do you want me to come over?"

"No, you don't have to."

"But I want to." Jimmy didn't respond. "Jimmy, are you there?"

"Yeah."

"I love you, Jimmy. Everything will be fine, I promise. I won't ever be jealous like I was, and it's all over between me and Dom."

"Dom?" Jimmy said sarcastically.

"Jimmy, cut it out. You know who I mean. It's been over for a long time. You never had anything to be jealous of, Jimmy, never ever, but I understand why you were. So?"

"So what?"

"So I'll come over, okay?"

"Okay." Jimmy hung up the phone and stared at it, as if willing it to ring, as if he could concentrate so hard that he could melt the phone and boil away the morning—or was it afternoon?—boil everything away until all there was was Marilyn, Marilyn calling him, asking for help, and he would save her and make everything right, and *fuck you, Dr. Greenson false Jesus bastard, and fuck you, Mrs. Murray, you troll, and fuck you, too, Pier, fuck your boyfriend Dom, fuck everything because I love you, Marilyn.*

Jimmy held the phone in his lap and started laughing, crying; it was like throwing up, as if something was caught in his lungs, in his throat, and he tasted bile, bitter, as if there would never ever again be sweetness, sweetness was gone, boiled away. Sweetness was Marilyn, and Jimmy squeezed his eyes shut because he flashed back to Marilyn lying at attention, cold sweet dead, smelling like bile, *and there you are, Jimmy, there's your karmic godhead crystal dharma Kerouac Buddha epiphany; it's not your mother rising out of the ground to condemn you, it's Marilyn. Not Pier. Marilyn.*

Jimmy howled and roared. Pier was right. He had always been in love with Marilyn, *and now she's gone, and you've got nothing but the telephone, that's all Marilyn had, now you got it, you stupid fool clown, that's all you got, the phone and no Marilyn,* and Jimmy was laughing crying at himself when the phone rang again, jolting him, and he opened his eyes to the burning light and said, "Yeah?"

"Jimmy, it's Joe." The voice quiet, without affect.

"DiMaggio?"

"I didn't know who else to call. Funny, huh?"

"I guess."

"But Marilyn would have wanted it this way."

"What do you mean?" Jimmy asked.

"You and me, like when we got her out of that hospital. You know what she told me later?"

"What?"

"She made me promise that if anything bad happened . . . to call you." He laughed mirthlessly. "An' we don't even like each other."

"Yeah, well, thanks for calling," Jimmy said.

"We've got to get Marilyn released."

"What the hell's that supposed to mean?"

"From the morgue," Joe said. "We got to get her out of the morgue."

"You just call a funeral home or something."

"Got to be immediate family."

"Her mother's still alive. In a nuthouse in Norwalk or someplace like that."

"I already tried to call her. An official at the sanitarium told me that her mother said she never heard of Marilyn Monroe. So there you are."

"Try her half sister. What's her name, Berniece something?"

"Miracle, that's her last name. I called her. No answer. I'll keep trying."

"So what can I do?" Jimmy asked, his tone soft; Joe sounded shattered.

"We got to make the funeral arrangements. It's Westwood Village Mortuary on Glendon Avenue." Then Joe DiMaggio's flat affect changed, and his voice became louder. "But I should tell you right now that it's going to be a small funeral so she can go to heaven in the quiet she always sought. None of those asshole reporters are going to be there. No way. No photographers, producers, executives, stars, none of them, only some family and friends. They all sucked her blood when she was alive. They're not going to now. I'll make sure of that. I'm going to make up a list. None of the people who hurt her, none of those Kennedy fuckers, or Lawford or Sinatra or—"

"Joe, where are you now?"

"At the morgue, but they won't let me see her. They said—" His voice broke.

"Why don't you go over to the funeral home? I'll meet you there."

"Because I got to release Marilyn."

"Okay, I'll go over to the home and get things started."

"No!" Joe said. "I got to do it."

"But you just said—"

"You'll invite everybody to the funeral. You won't say no to nobody, I know you, you and your friends—"

The doorbell rang. *It must be Pier.*

"Joe, you want to hold on a minute, someone's here. Just one minute."

Jimmy opened the front door. His postman grinned at him and handed him a package. "You hear about Marilyn Monroe? Terrible thing, terrible. Go figure."

Jimmy took the package inside, dropped onto the couch, and picked up the phone. "Joe? You there? I got something. Shit, I think it's from Marilyn. Joe?"

But the line was dead.

IT WAS MARILYN'S RED DIARY, HER BOOK OF SECRETS, THE DIARY she'd always promised to show him sometime. She'd wrapped it in brown paper; and there was a note inside, written on a torn piece of the wrapping:

> *Dear Jimmy when you get this if everything is okay call me, but if you get this and something bad happened to me then you'll know who did it. Everything's in the diary this is what those bastards want to get their hands on and Bobby's no better than his brother or the rest of them, for that matter. After Bobby hitting me and tearing everything apart in my house with Peter Lawford that pervert I don't know what he might do next. He told me there was more than one way to keep me quiet. I'm afraid, Jimmy, and I can't trust anybody but you, not even Dr. Greenson, probably especially Dr. Greenson, even though he knows everything in the world about me, but he's probably working with Bobby or Fox, everybody but me.*

Okay I'm getting this out to you. If you don't hear anything bad, give me back the diary. If you don't hear anything, don't read it. Just give it back. I'll trust you to do that. Maybe it'll work out. Bobby said he was sorry after he threw everything at me. Somehow I still think he loves me, but

That was all. She didn't sign it or finish her sentence. *Maybe Bobby came back. No, then he'd have the diary.* It was typical Marilyn, typical goddamn Marilyn. *You fell asleep, didn't you? Fell right asleep, sleepy-time girl, and now you don't ever have to wake up, do you? Do you?* Bobby held the faux-leather diary and cried. He could never get her back now. He wanted to smash his head into the wall, bang his forehead bloody on the floor, knock himself unconscious, punish himself for stupidity, supreme deaf dumb and blind stupidity. *I loved you and didn't know it.*

No, I love Pier.

Pier, where are you? Come and save me.

Like you saved Marilyn? That voice was hollow, a deep, man's voice, the voice he used to hear inside in his head when he was an adolescent. Reverend De Weerd had told him it was the voice of his conscience.

Numbed, hungover, strung out, grieving yet denying, he smiled as he read the first page of the diary. PRIVATE PROPERTY DO NOT READ OR *YOU WILL DIE I MEAN IT.* On the opposite page, Marilyn had drawn an angel with an elongated neck and arms and small smiley faces for breasts. She had written below, GOD IS LOVE.

As Jimmy turned the pages, getting used to reading Marilyn's crabbed scrawl, he understood why Bobby wanted to get his hands on this. *Had she kept this thing to blackmail the Kennedys?* He remembered her telling him that she always took notes on everything, it was a way to be smart. *Write everything down, that's what you have to do, Jimmy.* But this was too ordered, too focused on politics and inside events.

But Bobby wants me to be able to talk about political things with him. Jimmy could hear Marilyn's voice, as if she were still alive.

He read. Page after page of notes and anecdotes, some carefully written and coherent, some dated, some not, some just a few lines to jog the memory.

I have notes about everything, Jimmy. About Fox and all our projects, and you, Jimmy, I have notes about you, but you don't have to worry, they're just about how fucked up you are and that you don't even know you love me, but you love Pier, you love Pier, too, I know you do . . .

BOBBY, YOU SHANTY-IRISH BASTARD, YOU KILLED HER. YOU, NO-*body else, not Jack, not the Mafia, not the CIA, you. I saw your aide there. I punched his fucking face in.* Jimmy clutched the diary while the doorbell rang incessantly. *I'm going to get you for this.*

He raised the diary, as if he was about to throw it.

Indeed, it was a weapon.

SEVENTEEN

■

Possession

LOS ANGELES: AUGUST 8–10, 1962

Even from inside the chapel you could hear hundreds of cameras clicking and whirring. The cameras and crowds outside the cinder-block gates and chain-link fence of the Westwood Memorial Park sounded like cicadas or locusts—voracious, chittering, buzzing. It was another hot, sunny, cloudless day, and the small, run-down chapel was bright with color and sound. Huge bouquets of pink carnations and white roses were piled around the open casket, and the organist, stepping on the notes and playing too fast, finished Tchaikovsky's *Sixth* and started on "Over the Rainbow," Marilyn's favorite song.

Jimmy sat with Pier and Joe DiMaggio in the front row. Pier was beautifully dressed in black taffeta, and

Jimmy wore a dark suit and the monogrammed red silk tie Marilyn had given him for his birthday. Jimmy's head ached, and Lee Strasberg, who was also sitting in the first row, next to his wife, Paula, nodded to him. Jimmy nodded back and turned away.

Then the minister stepped up to the podium and began his eulogy—"How wonderfully she was made by her Creator"—*yeah, sure, buddy,* and on and on, platitudes pouring, until it was Strasberg's turn, *goddammit, Joe, you're such a gullible fool, Strasberg couldn't even be bothered to see Marilyn the last time he was in town—and now he's acting up a regular storm, trembling and crying, his voice quavering, fuck you, man*—"We knew her as a warm human being, impulsive, shy, and lonely, sensitive and in fear of rejection, yet ever avid for life and reaching out for fulfillment."

Pier was sobbing and clutching Jimmy's hand, and Jimmy felt drawn to look at the open bronze casket, but he averted his eyes, as if something perverse was entombed in there, not Marilyn. He felt numb, as though he was watching himself and everyone around him from a great distance, as though this had nothing to do with him because Marilyn, the real pulsing luminescent flesh-and-blood Marilyn, wasn't here, wasn't dead, but *yes she was, just like you, Jimmy, everybody here is dead, I got to get out of here, let go of me, Pier,* and Jimmy moaned. Pier leaned toward him, then rested her head on his shoulder, *no, I need to get out of here, there's nobody here that gives a shit—gave a shit—about Marilyn, Joe invited all the wrong people, and the fucking minister standing with the stick up his ass beside Lee Strasberg, he never even met her, and the others*—Jimmy turned around to look at the impeccably dressed men and women Joe had invited—*they're not Marilyn's friends, just users, her friends are all being kept out, goddamn you, Joe, you poor deluded schmuck . . .*

He grimaced at Eunice Murray, who was sitting beside Dr. Ralph Greenson and his family. *Greenson, you're some Jesus.* Sitting on the other side of the aisle was Walter Winchell. DiMaggio had kept out the press corps but invited Winchell because they were buddies.

A room full of gray-faced, black-suited hangers-on.

Where is that bastard Arthur Miller?

Joe had invited him, at least.

Then Jimmy was standing up; and Joe was sobbing, saying, "I love you, my darling, I love you," as he leaned over the casket, kissed Marilyn's powder-white forehead, and pressed a nosegay of roses into her cold hand.

"Don't you want to say your last good-bye, Jimmy?" Pier asked softly. "I know how much you loved her. It's all right."

Jimmy watched the attendants close and screw down the casket lid. Everyone was standing. Jimmy stole a look at the pews behind. The invited guests were all there, staring at the casket, crying crocodile tears, preparing for the photo opportunities to come; but Jimmy couldn't cry. He had no sense memory left. He had failed all Strasberg's lessons. He had failed the Method. He was dead, free, just like Marilyn. Pier took his hand—hers was cold—*everybody really is dead here*—and they followed Joe and the casket out into the buzzing noise and the stifling heat rising from the concrete. Everyone silently walked behind the old, battered hearse, which was flanked by white-gloved Pinkerton guards, to the garish pink Mausoleum of Memories. Jimmy glanced at the gate and saw Frank Sinatra standing between guards who were keeping him out; behind him were the crowded bleachers erected for the press.

Frank saw Jimmy, too, and gave him the finger.

Fuck it, they're all going to blame me, not Joe.

Inside the pink mausoleum. Sweating. The air close, dry as dust, the phony pastor intoning "Ashes to ashes," one of the black-suited attendants parting the curtain that concealed the vault, three others lifting the coffin into the vault, into the obscene dark hole surrounded by its curtained dress. The vault was about three feet from the ground. The attendants were sweating. Jimmy was sweating. Pier was crying, wailing like a child, as were Joan Greenson and Pat Newcomb.

An attendant attached a bronze plaque to the variegated-marble wall and polished clean his fingerprints

MARILYN MONROE
1926–1962

Jimmy didn't watch. He tried to read the notes on the wreaths of flowers set against the marble wall. There was a huge wreath from Sinatra, one from Arthur Miller, another from his children; there were wreaths from Jack Benny, the Lawfords, the Dean Martins, Rupert Allen, and Spyros Skouras, her patron and protector at Fox. Jimmy gazed sadly at an anonymous wreath. Its large, handwritten card bore a sonnet of Elizabeth Barrett Browning.

How do I love thee? Let me count the ways
. . . I love thee with the breath,
Smiles, tears, of all my life!—and, if God choose,
I shall but love thee better after death.

*   *   *

JIMMY LOOKED AROUND IN DISBELIEF.

His house had been ransacked, trashed—door casings torn off, carpet pulled away from the floor, walls broken. His desk had been taken apart, books pulled off shelves. The floors were covered with papers, ornaments, and paintings, which had been roughly cut away from mats and frames. "Jesus Christ," Jimmy said.

"What's this all about, Jimmy?" Pier asked. She was shaking, and Jimmy held her; but he was shaking, too, shivering with anger.

Bobby, you cocksucking son of a bitch, I'm going to get you. You did this, you bastard, you killed Marilyn and you figure I got the diary, which tells it all.

"You're in trouble, aren't you?" Pier asked.

Jimmy had given the diary to Pier for safekeeping. *I've got to get it back. I don't want her involved. She's in danger now. She's in danger here. She's in danger as long as she has the diary, as long as she's around me. Oh, shit, Marilyn, you were right about everything, but I'm going to get him for you, I'm going to string him up by his balls.* "No, everything's going to be fine," Jimmy said. "I'm going to take you home, baby." *And get the diary.*

She looked terrified. "You're going to stay with me, aren't you, Jimmy? I don't want to be alone, not with all this." She looked around the room. "Jimmy, what if . . . oh, no," and she started crying again.

"What is it?" Jimmy asked. "It's going to be all right, I promise."

"What if they've done the same thing to my house? All my dolls and everything."

"Everything will be fine at your house, I promise."

"This is about the diary, isn't it?"

"I don't know what it's about, Pier, but we're going to get rid of the diary."

"No, *I'm* going to get rid of it. And you'll stay there with me, okay? Promise me, Jimmy."

"Yes, I promise," he lied.

"CAROLINE TUCHMAN, *L.A. TIMES.*"

"Hey."

"Who is this?"

"Me, Jimmy."

"Dean?"

"Who else?"

"I've been trying to call you, Jimmy, but I've been either getting a busy or it rings through."

"I pulled it out of the wall. I didn't want to talk to nobody. Anyway, I'm not home. I'm calling you from a phone booth."

When Jimmy didn't say anything else and just breathed quietly into the phone, she said, "Jimmy, talk to me and tell me what's wrong. It's Marilyn, I know, but if there's something else . . ." He didn't respond. "Jimmy?"

"What makes you think something's wrong?"

"Because you called me, and you've been silent for the past I don't know how many seconds."

"I'm always quiet when I'm pissed off."

"What are you pissed off about?"

"You want the biggest story in the fucking universe?"

"Is the pope Catholic? Of course I do. Is it about Marilyn? I was calling about Marilyn, to see how you're doing, I know how close you were to her."

Jimmy imagined he could see afterimages of Marilyn, as if he had been staring at her in the casket, and she were life and light, so bright she had burned herself into him. He remembered reading something about the eyes being the windows of the soul, and now the windows were open, and he couldn't close them, couldn't shutter them; and he suddenly thought of Pier, remembered holding her, comforting her in the ruins of his living room; and he visualized—hallucinated—the console table that Pier had bought him at an antique auction. Bobby's henchmen, or whoever they were, had overturned it and pulled off bits of its gilt wood scrolling. He didn't know why, but just thinking about that table made him want to cry.

You mean, malicious bastard, Bobby. You cocksucker.

"Jimmy, Jimmy? You okay? Don't cry. What did you want to tell me?"

I don't care if you try to kill me. I'm going to take you down. You and your asshole president brother are going to twist in the wind.

"Jimmy, whatever it is, it'll be all right. Look, I'll come over to your house."

"No. Meet me at the Santa Monica pier in an hour. By the merry-go-round."

"What's this all about?"

"Marilyn. Just like you thought."

"Yeah?"

"She didn't commit suicide like everybody thinks."

"How do you know?"

"I've got proof. Fucking Bobby Kennedy killed her."

"Jimmy, don't you think that's—"

"I told you, I've got proof. You want the story, meet me in an hour. If not, I'll give it to somebody else."

"No, I want the story, but, Jimmy, really, it's better if we meet at my house. It's safer, more private, and—"

But Jimmy had already hung up.

FRIDAY MORNING AND THE PIER WAS PACKED WITH AUGUST crowds—students who had been hanging out by the beach bunched up early in front of the concession stands for popcorn, hot dogs, and strawberry-flavored cotton candy; teenagers in revealing T-shirts and cutoffs bicycled around mothers with their screaming broods and senior citizens strolling in impossibly bright polyester pants and suffocating-neckline blouses; businessmen sipped coffee out of Styrofoam cups and had meetings outside the office; and the bums and street people begged and hung out and watched, watching, watching, just like Jimmy. It was already blisteringly hot, and all the young bodies on the beach were glistening with commercial lotions and home-brewed fast-tan combinations of baby oil and iodine. Jimmy leaned against a concession stall, grasped Pier's Bergdorf Goodman shopping satchel, which contained Marilyn's diary, and watched the walkers. A young man with a JAMESDEAN scar, white-blond hair, and white T-shirt and jeans sauntered by Jimmy and nodded without recognizing him. Jimmy smiled. What had Nick Ray said about the continuing scarification fad? "The scars have legs."

And then Caroline appeared, dressed in shorts and a rough-weave cotton blouse, her hair shoulder length and luxurious, her eyes green and intense. A smear of pale lipstick, pink sneakers. Heads turned toward her. She was busty babe beautiful when she wasn't zipped up in a reporter's frock.

Jimmy smiled at her. He was relaxed now, and cold inside, ice-cold amphetamine cold, death white snow cold, as if he'd just swallowed a Benzedrine and was buzzing with death. He was focused, deadly cold focused; it was as if the deed was done and Pier was safe and he was safe because once Marilyn's diary became public, they *would* be safe.

Or relatively safe.

Jimmy laughed at the thought. He didn't care about being safe. After all, everybody always said he had a death wish. *Bet your respective asses, and I'm taking all you fuckers with me.*

As long as Pier is safe . . .

"Hi. What's so funny?" Caroline asked nervously.

"Nothing," Jimmy said. "Private joke."

Caroline looked at him suspiciously. "Were you bullshitting me about Marilyn and the Kennedys on the telephone?"

"No bullshit. Come on, I'll take you for a ride on the merry-go-round. It's my favorite thing here."

Jimmy paid for two tickets, and they stood together on the carousel, holding on to a post beside the white horse where Jimmy had once made love to Marilyn. The music played. "Here's Marilyn's diary. Take a look. It's all in there. It's yours. You finally got your big exclusive."

Caroline seemed agitated, distracted. She looked around nervously and then started reading. "Jesus Christ, you weren't kidding, were you?"

"No" Jimmy said. "It's dynamite. She had the goods on Bobby and Jack."

"I guess she did." And then someone grasped Jimmy's arm, someone else grasped his other arm, big burly bastards standing too close to him, two of Bobby's errand boys, brush cuts, blue button-down shirts, wrinkled suits, the smell of sweat and chewing gum; and he turned, recognizing the skinny, gray-haired aide he had seen—and tried to punch—at Marilyn's house.

"Hi, Jimmy," the aide said as he took the diary from Caroline. "I'm Frank Waters, and I'm sorry about what happened last week. I only hit you in self-defense." He smiled at Jimmy, a warm, boyish smile, a Bobby Kennedy I-can-win-you-over smile. But Jimmy ignored him and tried to shake free of the men beside him.

Jimmy shouted at Caroline, "You're a fucking bitch!"

"I think you should get out of here," Waters said to Caroline. "Now."

"You're in bed with Bobby, too, aren't you?" Jimmy screamed, feeling his glands open up—the cold trickling sensation of adrenaline in his chest, cold, everything cold, and he didn't care about anything but breaking that smirking freckled face of Bobby's aide. *It's all over they're going to get me and Pier no you're not I'm going to rip off your fucking faces I'm going to—*

"I'm sorry, Jimmy," Caroline said, "but there are some things you just can't—"

break your fucking bones tear out your beady squinty eyes you shanty-Irish catamite fuckers, you slimy small-prick faggot bastards oh Momma Momma help me give me strength—

"Let go of me!" Jimmy shouted, berserk—that's what he wanted to be, stoned out and crazy on adrenaline, that was his only chance of escape—but before he could stomp on the shiny black wingtip of the goon on his right, before he could break away to punch the other, one of them got him first, pressed two fingers against his neck, and then a sudden, nauseating sensation of falling, sudden light bright then dimming, darker, darker, darker *no no no you son of a bitch bastards* as Jimmy blacked out.

"CAROLINE, YOU TWO-FACED, LYING BITCH," JIMMY MUTTERED AS he came to in the backseat of a gray Cadillac limousine.

"Mrs. Tuchman did the right thing for her country," Frank Waters said. He was seated opposite Jimmy.

"Fuck you," Jimmy said, elbowing Waters's men for more room. He felt nauseated, and his head was pounding, aching. "I think I've just run right out of flags and tickertape."

Waters smiled at Jimmy. "I greatly admire your work as an actor."

"And I greatly admire your work as a catamite lapdog ass-sucker. So what now? Drop me into the ocean? What?"

Waters chuckled and shook his head. "Not exactly. You've been invited for dinner."

"How nice, I'm going to be dinner. And will you be there, too?"

"Since you asked, yes."

"I get it. Marilyn got to overdose at home alone. I get to overdose in someone's toilet at a dinner party. I think Bobby needs some advisors who are a little more creative than that. Don't you?"

"Well, you'll have your chance to tell him exactly what you think because Bobby will be there, too."

PETER LAWFORD GREETED FRANK WATERS AND JIMMY AT THE FRONT door of his beach mansion. He was wearing jeans and a yellow golf shirt. The house was chalk white in the sun, and Jimmy was marched through to a den on the second floor. A large balcony overlooked the blue-eye ocean and empty, combed, private beach. Several well-worn chairs were scattered around a casual, pale-patterned sofa, all oriented toward the high windows and balcony. On one side of the room was a billiard table; on the other side was a television and stereo system surrounded by the mirror and glass of a well-stocked bar. Waters's men stood outside the door while Lawford mixed drinks.

"How about gin and tonics all around? Beat the heat."

"Sounds good to me," Waters said.

"And you, too, Jimmy?"

"You know what Marilyn used to call you?" Jimmy asked Peter.

"Look, Jimmy, we're all upset," Peter said. "Bobby's going to be here in a little while, and he'll explain everything. It's not anything like you think—"

"Marilyn told me she couldn't stand the sight of you. She always called you the pervert, never used your name. Can I call you the pervert, too?"

Lawford's neck and face turned red, mottled red. He handed Waters a gin and tonic. He put Jimmy's on the butler's table.

"I won't hurt you," Jimmy said, then stood up menacingly.

"Larry," called Waters softly, and his men came through the door and were instantly on either side of Jimmy.

"Is the other one called Moe?" Jimmy asked, sitting back down. "Let's see, that would make you—"

"You should watch your mouth," Peter said to Jimmy.

"Peter," said Waters, warning.

Just then Bobby entered the room. He was wearing a blue blazer, white duck trousers, and brown Docksiders. He looked exhausted and old; there were shadows under his pale blue eyes, and the crow's feet in his face looked deeper, whittled. "Hey, Trash," Bobby said to Waters, obviously forcing bonhomie, "good to see you." Bobby looked at Jimmy and nodded, as if they both shared and understood a dirty secret. "Hey, Jimmy." He shrugged and said, "I've known Trash since we were in the navy together. That's where he got his nickname. Ask him about it sometime."

"You cocksucker," Jimmy said, and tried to stand up, but Waters's men held him firmly in his chair. "You killed her, you shanty-Irish son of a bitch, you and your brother."

"No, Jimmy, we *didn't* kill her."

"I saw your fuckstick friend Trash at Marilyn's the night she was murdered. You were probably hiding in the closet."

"You got the diary?" Bobby asked Trash, who handed it to him. He leafed through it and said, "Believe it or not, Jimmy, now that I've got the diary, you're safe."

"Yeah, how's that, you piece of shit?"

Bobby gave Jimmy his coon-peering-out-of-a-henhouse look. "Because it's going to be destroyed."

"Oh, that'll save us all."

"The people who would kill you just as soon as look at you will know," Bobby said. "And that's all that's important." Jimmy looked away from Bobby, as if he was completely uninterested. "You want to hear me out? If you still think it's bullshit, you can have the diary back."

Jimmy turned back to him and laughed. "You're so full of shit."

"You got nothing to lose."

"Just my life. Like Marilyn. She had nothing to lose either, did she?"

"We just *saved* your life," Bobby said softly. "Well?"

"Talk away all you want. You got Larry and Moe here to protect you, and Trash and the pervert to wipe your ass. I guess you're safe enough."

"You little prick," Peter said, but before he could go on, Bobby told him to leave the room. "You, too," he said to Trash. "And you guys too," he said to the men.

"Bobby, do you really think that's wise?" Trash asked.

"Everybody out. Now." He turned to Jimmy. "I suppose you can take your shot at punching me out and jumping two stories from the balcony, or you can listen to what I have to say." He sat down in Trash's seat opposite Jimmy and said, "I was there, at Marilyn's house, the day she died. Twice. I tried talking her out of holding a press conference, which is what she'd threatened to do. I tried getting her diary, too, and any other incriminating papers before anybody else did."

"You said the word. Incriminating."

They stared each other down, Jimmy gauging whether he should indeed take his shot and kill the son of a bitch. *What do I have to lose?*

"You okay in there?" Trash called from behind the door.

"Don't ask me again," Bobby said, looking at the door. "Go downstairs. Everybody, and take Peter Pan with you."

"Peter Pan?"

"Pete's not as bad as you think," Bobby said. "I know Marilyn couldn't stand him. He's not good with women." He made a face. "He's an asshole. But he's loyal."

"Like a dog."

"He's loyal. Sometimes that's enough." He stared hard at Jimmy.

"You want to continue your bullshit speech?" Jimmy asked.

"You want to know what happened, I'm telling you."

"I didn't ask to know anything, remember? I *know*."

"It all got out of control at Marilyn's. I went there with Pete. Late afternoon, and I was upset. I acted like an asshole. I broke into her filing cabinet. I took some papers. Shit, Jimmy, she was taking notes on everything she heard, on national security matters, everything."

"So you killed her to shut her up."

"We got into a fight. I lost my temper, threw something or other at her in the kitchen, I can't even remember, and she came at me with a knife." He paused, stared into space, as if he'd just remembered the incident. "I took it away from her and left. Look, I admit it; I went beyond the pale. I got crazy. But when I was holding her, and she started crying, Christ, I don't know. You know what she wanted?"

"Yeah, you." Bobby nodded. "And you used her and threw her away."

Bobby didn't flinch. He looked right at Jimmy, nodded, and said, "That's what she said. Exact words. I was a bastard. I can't undo it. I'll live with it for the rest of my life, what she said to me, her crying in my arms. But I didn't kill her."

"Were you there . . . when I was?"

"No, I didn't go back. I sent Trash after we got word she was dead. Trash burned the files, cleaned up. The studio—Fox—worked along with him. They wanted everything squeaky clean, too."

"And who else?" Jimmy asked.

"Dr. Greenson and Marilyn's maid. Some people from Justice. The police."

"She had no friends at all," Jimmy mumbled. "Nobody. So if you didn't kill her, who did?"

Bobby shrugged. "You know how I've been going after organized crime and the unions. If it's them, they were after me."

"After *you?*"

"I'm the target. They'd be looking to get me, implicate me. Blackmail me. If word got out, which it would, I'd be finished politically, and so would Jack. End of problems for Hoffa and Giancana and the rest of them."

Jimmy snorted. "Wouldn't want to fuck up your political careers."

"It could have been Hoover. He's been looking for something to use since we tried to fire him and reorganized his department. Yeah, Jimmy, welcome to politics. Or the CIA. It's their way of doing business, and they fucking hate Jack and me. They hate Jack for what happened in Cuba during the Bay of Pigs assault. They think we should have sent in airpower to save their sorry asses, and they've been leaking to the media that Jack promised support and reneged. It's all bullshit. It was their poor intelligence that fucked their operation. Jack was crystal clear on his position of nonintervention. But he carried the can. He accepted the blame. It's probably in the diary. You read it, right?"

"Yeah," Jimmy said, remembering something in the diary about Jack saying he was going to splinter the CIA into a thousand pieces and scatter it to the winds . . . and something else about how the CIA was acting illegally. "So you're trying to tell me that the CIA killed Marilyn to get you?"

Bobby shrugged. "To get both of us, Jack and me. I think they could have sent their mechanics in to do the job. We know that the group associated with the Bay of Pigs was making plans against us after it all went pear-shaped." He paused. "We know they had Marilyn under surveillance." Jimmy remembered reading something in the diary about how one of the CIA factions blamed Bobby for the debacle; they thought he was making the decisions because Jack was having back problems. "They were working with organized crime to assassinate Castro," Bobby continued. "So they could have been working together on this."

"You mean Marilyn."

"Yeah, I mean Marilyn."

Jimmy shook his head, suddenly overcome with that rushing blowing crashing sensation that something was rolling over him, some wet, sticky, inchoate memory that threatened to transform him into a helpless child who couldn't hold back tears, couldn't control his breath, couldn't form the proper words. But Jimmy held his gaze on Bobby, Bobby who somehow just now, in the cool shade of this room, looked like Jimmy; they were improbable look-alikes, two predatory birds staring at each other, and Jimmy held himself tight, stared through the gauziness of tears, but wouldn't touch his face, wouldn't wipe the wetness away, wouldn't expose his grief anger hatred; and Bobby, looking stricken and weak, gave his speech, explained that all his people did was clean up the mess, get rid of the incriminating evidence, and make the murder look like a suicide, thus foiling their enemies and protecting the government and the security of the United States of America. *There is, after all, a cold war going on . . . going public would only bring disaster to the whole country . . . the CIA could not be implicated . . . their tracks would be well covered . . . you'll be safe from further interference, Jimmy, blah blah blah,* and Jimmy remembered the pastor blathering at Marilyn's funeral, *"How wonderfully she was made by her Creator,"* and that asshole Strasberg, *"I did not know this Marilyn Monroe,"* and Jimmy and Bobby were looking away from each other. They were lost and trying to conceal their emotions.

"I think you're full of shit," Jimmy said softly. Bobby nodded. "So now you give me the diary back, right?"

They stared at each other, heads lowered, gazing upward.

Coons peering out of a henhouse.

Bobby started laughing first, and Jimmy stood up, walked to the glass doors that opened onto the balcony.

"You going to jump or come down for lunch?"

Jimmy gazed out at the swelling, rolling, pounding ocean.

It frightened him and fascinated him, and he could feel the drowning undertow of hatred and grief, *I'll get you, I'll get you you bastard if you killed her I'll get you Momma Momma Marilyn Pier help me.* Jimmy felt the cold dangerous focus of a new resolve.

"Well?" Bobby asked softly. Jimmy shrugged. "Might as well die on a full stomach."

EIGHTEEN

■

Maya

LOS ANGELES: SEPTEMBER–NOVEMBER 22, 1963

"Pier, will you save me?"

"Yes, Jimmy."

"Pier, will you marry me?"

"No, Jimmy."

"Why?"

"Because you're still in love with Marilyn."

"No I'm not, Pier. I swear. I only love you."

"Then marry me right now and swear on your mother's grave that you don't still love Marilyn . . ."

May she rest in peace.

"ENOUGH IS ENOUGH," PIER SAID TO JIMMY AS SHE cleaned the paneled library where Jack Kerouac had spent most of his time drinking, editing, and revising the script for *On the Road*.

He'd stained the Persian rugs and chipped the Socci writing table, and all the embroidered armchairs were sticky with Benedictine, which he had been imbibing with religious fervor. The room still stank from sweat and liquor and hash. "He's a pig, a complete fucking pig," she continued, and she swore in Italian as she examined her porcelain dolls, which were carefully displayed in front of the leather-bound books. "There, look, he broke one, I knew it, I knew he would, now tell me, why does he have to spoil everything he touches?"

"We have cleaners to do the cleaning," Jimmy said. "Leave it alone. Everything will get cleaned up on Monday."

"He's a pig, and he tries to make you a pig. He takes you away from me. He gets you drunk, he tries to introduce you to whores, and he probably wants you himself, he probably—"

"Pier," Jimmy said softly, controlled—he was always controlled now—"don't go there."

Pier turned the vacuum cleaner on, pushing it furiously over the carpet, and then she turned it off and faced Jimmy. "I'm sorry, Jimmy. You've got enough on your mind. You told him to go. It wasn't like with Marty, and I should be ashamed of myself. I'm a terrible wife." She lowered her head and wrapped her arms around herself, which made her look small and vulnerable; and although Jimmy knew the trick well, he responded. She was anything but small and vulnerable; she was like him, an intent child pretending to be grown up. As much as he loved Marilyn, as much as he craved her and missed her yet, he never could reveal that part of himself to her—he shared that only with Pier—and Pier, for her part, hated company, hated anyone other than Jimmy to see her dolls, which were tangible reminders of her past, each a mnemonic for a treasured memory. She told Jimmy stories about each doll and said that *if you put all the dolls together you'd have me*.

"Jack broke one, look, Jimmy. Look at this." She held up a cloth doll with a porcelain face. "Jimmy, you, of all people, understand, but I'm sorry, Jimmy, I didn't mean to take everything out on you. Jack's gone, and you evicted him because you could see, you could see he was hurting me—"

"Evicted him?" Jimmy said, chuckling. He held her, patted her thick, dark hair, felt her tight body against his; but she wasn't shaking. If she were truly upset, she would be trembling. No, she wanted something.

"We're happy, aren't we?" she asked.

"Yeah, of course we are."

"You don't regret getting married?"

Jimmy pulled away from Pier, laughed at her, and kissed her. She drew him close, huddled into him.

"And . . . Marilyn?" she asked. Jimmy stared out at the window, which was lined with books and Pier's dolls. He could smell her shampoo and perfume. A wisp of hair tickled his face. "I know you loved her, Jimmy, but are you feeling okay about . . . about . . ."

"I love *you*," Jimmy said. "The past is over. It's a dream."

"That's Jack talking, not you."

"Well, sometimes he's right. Not often, but sometimes."

Pier giggled, and Jimmy felt numb, cold, as he remembered staring at Marilyn through the bedroom window he had broken, Marilyn white and blotchy and lying facedown dead on the bed, and he remembered Bobby's aide Frank Waters stepping into the room as if he was just getting on with a routine errand. *They killed her, they killed her, not the Mafia, not the CIA or the FBI or who knows who else, but Bobby, he was dirty, even if he wasn't there, Bobby you bastard, it's not over yet . . . yet, and yet Bobby had made sense that afternoon at the pervert's beach house, had made a case. They'd all killed her.*

I killed her. He groaned.

"Everything's going to be all right, isn't it?" Pier asked in a small, practiced voice.

"Everything's fine," Jimmy said, imagining that he was holding Marilyn, then feeling immediately guilty because he loved Pier, *I love Pier.* "I love you, Pier."

"I love you, too, Jimmy, and everything's really going really well for you, isn't it?"

"Yeah, I guess."

"I mean with *The Hustler* and *Hud* and you're done with *On the Road* and everybody loves you, and you're a big star and—"

"We're not done with *On the Road* by a long shot," Jimmy said. "I'm gonna be living in the editing room since Nick's pissed off back to Europe."

"And you're going to do *Sweet Bird of Youth* with Geraldine Page."

Jimmy began to feel uncomfortable holding Pier. She was up to something. He tried to pull away, but she held him tight and said, "No, hold me, Jimmy."

"Where are you going with all of this?"

"All of what? I'm just talking to my husband."

"Let's sit down on the couch."

"In a second." After a beat, Pier asked, "Jimmy?"

"Yeah?"

"When are you starting *Sweet Bird of Youth?*"

"Jesus, Pier, I don't even know if I'm going to do it. MGM has the rights now, and I don't know if they want me, and I don't know if I'm interested. It was a project I was going to do with Marilyn, remember? I think maybe someone else should do it. Paul Newman's been biting for it." Jimmy laughed. "Like he bites for everything." He successfully pulled away from Pier and sat down on the leather couch. This was his favorite room, a man's room, all dark wood and old, deep-brown cracking leather, a smoking room. It was the only room in the house where he could be comfortable.

"Jimmy?" Pier asked, sitting down beside him. "Everything good is happening for you, and although I'm so happy being married to you, everything isn't happening for me. I want to work. I want to work with you."

"What do you mean? We're a team. You're involved with everything."

"I want to play Alexandra in *Sweet Bird of Youth*, and I want you to be my Chance Wayne. I want to play opposite you, like Marilyn was going to. That would be right. I know she would have wanted that."

"Gerri Page already has the part," Jimmy said.

"Not if you wanted it to be different," Pier said. "I talked to Dick."

"Clayton?"

"He's my agent, too."

"The hell he is."

Jimmy expected Pier to start crying, but she could play him better than that. She stared at her hands, which were folded on her lap, and said, "I want this, Jimmy. It's been all about you for the last year. That's okay. You were hurt, broken. You're still hurt, I know that, but I'm here, too. Now I need your help, because nobody knows who I am. Except as your wife. Jimmy's wife."

"You said you wanted to stay home and take care of Perry, be a good mother."

"He's eight years old, and he has Carla. She's a good nanny, and I *am* a good mother." She stiffened as she said that.

Jimmy nodded. "Of course you are. I never said you weren't."

"And you are a wonderful father to him," Pier said, brightening. "I love you for that."

"I thought we were going to have a baby," Jimmy said. Then, catching himself: "Another baby." Jimmy had always been convinced that he, rather than Vic Damone, was Perry's father. But blood tests proved otherwise.

Two small spots of color came to Pier's cheeks. "We will, and when the time comes I will stay home and be a mother—for a while. It will happen, Jimmy." She smiled shyly, almost slyly, at Jimmy.

"There's nothing wrong with me."

"I know that." Jimmy nodded again. "You and Nick can make your own films now with your company. I want to be part of it. Like you."

"You *are* part of it!"

"As an actress. Like we were in *Somebody Up There Likes Me*."

"I wasn't a director then."

"You're everything now."

Jimmy grinned, in spite of himself, but it was Pier's turn to become aggressive—and distant at the same time. She stood up and walked to the window. "As much as I love my child, that's not why I stayed home. I stayed home to take care of *you*. You were my child, too. Now it's my turn, Jimmy. I want to be a star, as big as you. I want everyone to know who I am, not remember who I was—oh, yeah, isn't that Jimmy's wife, wasn't she good in that movie, what was it called?"

"Okay," Jimmy said.

But Pier wasn't finished. "I waited for you to ask me, to help me. I was too proud to ask for even a small part in *On the Road*. But you didn't think about me, did you?" Her voice started to rise. "But I made a promise to myself. I promised myself to take care of you, no matter what because . . . because it was my penance for what happened to Marilyn, and you . . . and don't think I don't know what you're doing. What role you're playing."

"What are you talking about?"

"Being cold and quiet and not losing your temper like you used to. You're playing your character Fast Eddie and the other one, Hud, because you're scared."

"I'm not scared of anything," Jimmy said.

"You're scared of what could happen to me because of what you know, and what could happen to you; and you're angry, all that hate and grieving, and you turn it all on me with coldness, Jimmy, not love, coldness."

"I'm not cold to you."

"You just *act* like you love me. You just act." Pier picked up one of the dolls from the shelf and suddenly threw it hard at Jimmy. He blocked it with his forearm. The doll smashed and pieces skittered onto a low mahogany table.

"Jesus Christ, Pier."

She cried, as if *she* was broken. "You see, you just sit there. The old Jimmy—"

"What, what would the old Jimmy do? Shout at you. Jump up and slap you?"

"Better than what you do to me now. I gave up everything for you, Jimmy—my family, my mother. Now I'm dead to her. I'm dead to them all."

"Your mother's a bitch."

"She's still my mother, even if she won't talk to me," Pier said softly.

"I'll try to get you the part," Jimmy said.

Pier stood in front of him, her hands fidgeting, waiting for him to stand up and embrace her. "I have something else to tell you."

"I can hardly wait."

"Stand up and hold me." Jimmy just shook his head. She sat down beside him, twisted herself against him, and said, "Jimmy, I'm pregnant. So it looks like you'll get what you want, and I'll get what I want."

"Are you kidding?" Jimmy asked. He felt giddy. "You're kidding, right?" Pier shook her head.

Jimmy couldn't stop smiling. *A baby, God, that would make everything right, Momma, if it's a girl we'll name it after you—Mildred—no, you wanted your granddaughter to have your middle name, Marie, but if it's a boy, we'll name it Wilson, your maiden name, Momma, it's going to be all right now, everything is going to be all right, this is what I wanted, all the rest everything else is maya, like Jack said.*

Hugging her tightly, Jimmy asked, "Why didn't you tell me this before, you manipulative bitch?"

"So I could get what I want," she said matter-of-factly. "Remember, Jimmy, you made promises."

"I didn't really *promise*," Jimmy said, teasing. He caressed and tickled her, and she laid her head on his lap, teasing him back, exciting him. "So what do you want, Mrs. Mommy-to-Be?" Jimmy asked playfully.

"Everything." She nibbled at him through his trousers.

"Name one thing."

"Oh, that's a big mistake to do that, Jimmy," she said, giggling. She lifted her head to watch him as she unzipped his fly and worried his penis out of his briefs.

"Ouch."

"Oh, poor Jimmy, he'll be all black and blue. Here, I'll make it better." And she went down on him, teasing him, but lifting her head before he could come. Watching him again, gazing up at him, her porcelain-doll face perfect, elegant, childlike. "You know the property you just bought, that thriller about brainwashing?"

"You mean *The Manchurian Candidate?*"

"Yeah."

"Well?"

"I want to play Mrs. Shaw, the mother of the killer."

"Who?"

"The mother of the guy you—or Elvis—is going to play. Raymond Shaw."

"Jesus, we haven't even started the script. How do you know about Raymond Shaw?"

She giggled, playing with him, keeping him hard, which was difficult now. "I read the book. I do read, you know."

Jimmy nodded and closed his eyes, the signal for Pier to continue fellating him. "You're too young and beautiful to play the mother. I can't believe you're going to have a baby." He giggled. "Holy shit. I just can't fucking believe it. You're bullshitting me, right? It's not real."

"It's real, Jimmy, it's all real." She squeezed him and said, "But I've got you now and I'm not giving up. Mrs. Shaw is the most interesting role in the film, and I'm thirty-one years old. Makeup can do the rest."

"Can we talk about this later?" Jimmy said. "The only thing that's important right now is the baby."

"That's the problem with our relationship," Pier said. "Right there. I'm not important."

"You're the *most* important," Jimmy insisted, pulling himself straight on the couch, away from Pier. "Anyway, I don't think that role would be good for your career."

"It will do *everything* for my career. So go tell Angela Lansbury to fuck off, she can be in another role. And she's the same age as me."

"She's older, and you're getting way ahead of yourself. This isn't the right time for this discussion. Anyway," Jimmy said, grinning, "you can't give me a blow job to get a part in my movie, you dark-haired slut. We're married."

She giggled. "Doesn't matter. You're a producer, and I think it's the perfect time to have a discussion. Tell me you and Nick didn't discuss who'd be in the film?"

"But Nick wasn't giving me a blow job."

"I hope not."

"Pier, Angela *looks* old. You don't. She's perfect for the part."

"No, *I'm* perfect for the part. It needs a sweet old lady to be the monster. I can play it, Jimmy. And you watch, I'll win an Oscar for it."

"I'll talk to Nick," Jimmy said. "Only you could fuck up a wet dream—and you just did."

"I already talked to Nick."

"Son of a bitch."

"He thinks I'd be perfect for the part."

"I'll bet he does. Isn't this baby important to you?"

"It's everything to me."

"Then why the fuck are we talking about this shit?"

"Because it's important to me, too, and you won't do anything about it if I ask you later."

"You're crazy, Pier. Let's go out and celebrate."

"I thought that's what we were just doing."

"Until you brought up all this I-wanna-be-a-star shit, and what about the baby? How are you going to do a film pregnant?"

"Won't matter for the old-lady role. Make me look better, and the other stuff will work out."

"You should be taking care of the baby."

She laughed and started to get him excited again. "I am working on the baby."

Jimmy dreamed about being a father and dreamed about his mother. He remembered how she used to put his little yellow boat with two smokestacks in the water and create a whirlpool with her finger; he remembered how it made him dizzy, how it made him laugh, and he would insist on making the boat turn and turn like Mildred did, but the boat would always flip on its side and sink and Mildred would fish it out and start again. Jimmy would show little Wilson the trick (but he would call him by his middle name, Nick, after Nick Ray); and he would build him a swing, and he would buy a farm, somewhere away from L.A., Upstate New York, maybe, where his son could grow up with hay and horses and fresh air, like he did.

And as he dreamed, as he floated into the future, which mingled with the past, Pier made everything warm syrup, secure and safe, secure and safe, *oh, Marilyn, and Bobby you murderous son of a bitch, stay away from my family.*

Just as Pier brought him toward the warm whiteness of orgasm, the doorbell rang. Jimmy tensed, frightened.

"Forget it," Pier whispered.

But it rang, insistent, incessant. Jimmy went to the door and found Jack Kerouac drunk and weaving in the doorway. "Jesus Christ," Jimmy said, "what do I got to do, call the fucking police?"

"Did you hear?"

"Hear what?"

Jack pushed past Jimmy. "You gotta turn the television on."

"Why?"

"Because John F. Kennedy has just been shot. And I need a drink."

NINETEEN

■

Lions and Lambs

LOS ANGELES: MARCH–JUNE 1964

"You ever play the slots?" Jimmy asked as he led Elvis downstairs.

"Yeah, but I don't get a kick out of them like some of the guys do, Jerry especially. You remember Jerry? Poor fat bastard. I was going to fire him, he don't do nothin', but Bit talked me out of it because the poor bastard don't have no one but me. But, man, whenever we're in Vegas, he eats and sleeps in the casino. It's a wonder he don't pee in his pants, the length of time he sits in front of those machines."

Jimmy laughed. "I don't mean those kinds of slots. I mean *these* kind of slots," and he opened the door to his basement rumpus room. A huge plywood table filled up most of the room. Atop the table a wildly winding four-lane racecourse ran across perfectly modeled hills and rills and suspension bridges, over papier-mâché pastureland and crinkled aluminum-foil streams, through matchstick woods and neon tunnels and tiny towns with electrically lit municipal buildings, stores, cinemas, and porched houses. The racecourse was more than fifty feet long, and it twisted into Möbius-strip fantasias of cloverleafs and figure eights. Above, fluorescent lights shone bright as day.

"You never saw one of these?" Jimmy asked, handing Elvis a palm-sized replica of Jimmy's old flat-four 547 Porsche Spyder. The little car had an extension under the front bumper that would fit into the groove—the slot—of the H.O.-gauge racetrack.

"Shit, the guys would love this," Elvis said. "This is the car you crashed, huh?"

"No, I drove a bigger one," Jimmy said, joking. "I had these made specially by the Aurora Plastics Corporation." He handed Elvis a tiny black Rolls and a plum-colored XKE Jag. "Exact replicas of all my cars. Now I also just happen to have"—and with a flourish he produced a model of a white Rolls-Royce. "Look familiar?"

Elvis laughed, delighted; it was a replica of his own car, right down to the yellow-striped black leather seats.

"I always beat the hell out of your Roller, even when I race it against my truck," Jimmy said, and he handed Elvis a scale model of his truck. "Who knows, maybe you can do better."

"How do you work it?" Elvis asked.

"I can't believe you haven't gotten into this," Jimmy said, and he clicked a switch under the table. The lights went on in the miniature towns and along the highways, and the room was filled with the soft, barely audible hum of transformers.

"Looks like I'm goin' to. Now I guess the guys just weren't into it or something." Elvis walked around the table, fascinated. "Looks like they're going to get into it, though. I'll break their necks for keeping this a secret from me."

"You got to be living in a box or something, not to know about the slots."

Elvis gave him a hard look and felt the anger, his hair-trigger anger, which always surged through him like something hot, scalding. *I don't live in a box, asshole, but I protect myself, so I see what's important, not the bullshit, I know what's happening, and I could beat the shit out of ten James Deans, you don't fuck with a black belt, and I'm learning things that would blow your fucking mind, Jimmy.*

He had, in fact, brought Jimmy a copy of Joseph Benner's *The Impersonal Life*. That book had indeed changed Elvis's life. Thanks to his guru and hairdresser Larry Geller, Elvis had been born again. His heart was pierced; he had seen the face of Christ in a cloud near the Grand Canyon. He had seen even more profound things, had seen the Grand Canyon cloud face of Joseph Stalin turn into a perfectly chiseled, beneficent Christ. He had seen the very truth of existence, and now Elvis would have to be in control, in control of everything. He remembered a line from Benner's book, a profound, life-changing line, which had become the mantra he used when he boiled over, when he wanted to shoot everyone around him with his silver-barreled .45-caliber pistol.

Be still!—*and KNOW,—I AM,—God.*

His anger dissipated into a warm oatmeal sensation in his stomach.

"How's it work?" he asked Jimmy, meaning the slot cars.

"Here." Jimmy gave Elvis a handheld rheostat and fitted the two model Rolls-Royces into the track grooves. "They got brushes that make electrical contact with metal strips in the track. You up the current, and the car accelerates. You know how fast these suckers go? Somewhere around six hundred miles an hour. That's at scale, but it's fucking fast, man, and you make one mistake, and your car's careening off the track."

"I guess you stopped racing real cars after your accident."

"As a matter of fact, I still race," Jimmy said testily.

"Sorry, man, I didn't mean nothin'."

"Yeah, I know. I guess you hit a nerve."

"What do you mean?"

"Oh, I promised Pier I wouldn't race until she had the baby. She said she couldn't stand it if anything happened while she's pregnant."

"So what happens after the baby?"

"I'm sure she thinks she's gonna do some kind of shit to make me give it up, but I can tell you, I won't."

"She got you to stop for a while."

"Yeah, but she had to pay for that."

"Yeah?" Elvis backed away from Jimmy and looked down at the ground. "I'm sorry, man, I don't mean to be into your business."

Jimmy laughed. "Hey, you *are* into my business."

"Yeah."

"Pier wanted a part in a film I'm doing, but it was already promised to a good friend of mine." Jimmy laughed. "You got to watch my little Pier—she's a hustler. She knew she wasn't going to be able to do that part pregnant—it was Alexandra in *Sweet Bird of Youth*—but she really ground me to get it. Then when Gerri Page was mad as hell at me, Pier cut her deal."

"But she's still in the new movie?" Elvis asked.

"Yeah, that's the role she really wanted. She was blowing smoke for the rest."

"Worked."

Jimmy laughed. "Yeah, it did. She's good. Now, what about you? You got something on your mind, right?"

Elvis felt his face get hot. He was in control. He had his own Mafia. He could buy anything he wanted. *Even the Colonel knows not to fuck with me.* So what was it with Jimmy? Why did he always feel awkward, as though only Jimmy was filled with the light? Elvis shrugged.

"You didn't come over here just to play the slots," Jimmy said, grinning at him. "The Colonel's up to something again, isn't he?"

"Nothin' I can't handle," Elvis said.

"Okay, then this is just a social visit, right?"

"Not exactly."

"Well?" Jimmy asked.

Elvis slowly turned the knob on the rheostat he was holding, and the white Rolls-Royce slot car began moving.

"Hey," Jimmy said. "You can't win by being a sneak," and he caught up with Elvis's car. "You got to go slow around the curves, or you'll fly right off the track." He turned the knob on his rheostat, and the black Rolls shot forward.

"Holy cow, these things really move," Elvis said, delighted. He followed Jimmy around hairpin turns, and they opened up on the straightaways. Elvis was a natural, and he maneuvered his car alongside Jimmy's. Indeed, the speeds, given the size of the tiny models, were ferocious, and the race became serious. Elvis had too much speed going into a cloverleaf and his car snapped off the track and smashed into an adjacent train station but missed an American Flyer locomotive sitting on its H.O.-grade train track.

"I guess I win," Jimmy said, walking to the middle of the table, leaning over, and picking up Elvis's car. The plastic chassis had cracked, and the station would need repair, too.

"I didn't mean to break it," Elvis said. "I'll get it fixed."

"No problemo," Jimmy said.

"I'll get it fixed," Elvis repeated.

Jimmy shrugged and handed him the car. "Now, what can't you fix with the Colonel?"

"Who said I couldn't fix somethin'?"

Jimmy shrugged. "Come on, man, I know he's jerking us around. He don't want you to do the film, right?" Jimmy sped his black Rolls around the track until it was within reach. He removed it and put the

Jag and the Porsche on the tracks, side by side. "You break the Jag, and you're in deep shit, Elvis."

Elvis smiled at him, that crooked, charming, bright-light, privileged smile. "No," Elvis said. "The Colonel thinks *The Manchurian Candidate* could be a big-money film. That's how he grades everything. Big money or nothing."

"Yeah, I know. So what's the catch?"

"He told me that he's been letting me do what he's callin' artsy-fartsy films because they're important to me, but he thinks we got to make the same percentages that we make with the films I'm doin' with Hal Wallis. He says that was the problem with *On the Road.* He says it would have made money if it was done right." Embarrassed, Elvis looked away from Jimmy. "I mean that's what he says, man. I don't know nothin' about that part, the business part."

"You mean the Colonel wants a bigger percentage for himself."

"No, he told me if the film is done right, then it would be fine. He says that his problem ain't with our contract but with—" Elvis stopped in midsentence, as if he didn't quite know how to go on, as if he had confused himself.

"What do you mean, done right?" Jimmy asked.

"Oh, shit," Elvis said, "I'll just tell the Colonel to fuck off."

"Yeah, we've been through that one before." After a beat, "What's he want?"

"He wants to bring in Sam Katzman to produce the picture."

"*I'm* producing the picture. Who the fuck is Sam Katzman?"

"He's—"

"I know who he is, man. He's a cheap hack. Jesus Christ almighty. He produced one of your latest pictures, didn't he? What was it?"

Elvis stared intently at the slot-car table and mumbled, "*Kissin' Cousins.* It's a piece of shit. Man, I was embarrassed just bein' on the set. Wearing that stupid blond wig. But that probably ain't Katzman's fault."

"Then whose fault is it?"

"The Colonel told me that maybe Katzman has lousy taste, but that don't matter, according to the Colonel. The grosses were dropping on our pictures, and Katzman's fixing that. He don't need to know which is a bad script and which is a good one. The Colonel says that Katzman saves us money whether it's a good picture or a bad picture. He says it's up to you, Jimmy, to make the script good."

Jimmy shook his head in disbelief. "He wants the King of the Quickies to produce our picture? A major motion picture?"

Elvis continued to stare at the table, as if trying to burn a hole in the tiny plastic paddock exactly in front of him. "The Colonel said that Mr. Katzman could be on as sort of an advisor."

Jimmy laughed. "What do *you* think?"

"He made *Rock Around the Clock* for three hundred thousand, and it grossed four million."

"You can't compare that piece of shit with our film," Jimmy said. "And I thought you said you don't know anything about the money side."

Elvis didn't answer. *Don't keep fuckin' with me,* he thought. *It ain't my fault.*

"Okay, look, I'll check with Nick, and then I'll call the Colonel," Jimmy said. "We'll work something out. We don't have much of a choice, do we?" Jimmy watched Elvis, waiting for a response.

"I know what you're thinkin'," Elvis said. "We been around and around it before. But if I tell the Colonel to fuck off, then what?"

"Then you make good pictures, and you get to do what you want with your records. He's not helping you, man."

Elvis nodded. "It just ain't that easy, Jimmy."

"No, I guess it's not," Jimmy said.

"You want to race?" Elvis said.

"And if I win, what?"

Elvis shrugged and said, "Then you win."

"This ain't the old Elvis who would make a bet because win or lose, it would be a sign."

"No, Jimmy, I been betting everything on signs and portents. When we go upstairs, I got a gift for you that will change your life. A book."

"Hasn't seemed to change yours," Jimmy said.

"Yeah, man, it did. *Everything* is changed."

"It doesn't look like anything's changed with you and the Colonel."

"Are you ready?" Elvis asked, looking meaningfully at Jimmy, and then he quoted *The Impersonal Life*: "In order that you may learn to know me, so you can be sure it is I, your own true self, who speak these words, you must first learn to *be still* . . ."

"What?"

"It's all in the book," Elvis said, "but that's only a start. Doesn't matter about the Colonel, or whether we do this picture or that picture or no picture."

"Well, it matters to me. If you don't give a shit, maybe you shouldn't be in the picture." Jimmy was testing him, carefully.

"You read the book, we'll do the picture."

"You mean I got to read the book or no dice?"

Elvis smiled. "No, man, whatever, I'll do the picture."

"Maybe we got this all wrong," Jimmy said. "Maybe the Colonel's right. Maybe you should just keep doing those fucked-up pictures with the Colonel. Maybe serious acting isn't that important to you. Maybe you shouldn't do this picture." He leveled his eyes at Elvis, his head down. "Maybe you're out of this one."

"Don't fuck with me," Elvis said in a low voice, seething.

"Don't let the Colonel fuck with me," Jimmy said. Then he asked, "Well, you want to race or what?"

That broke the tension, and Elvis, who had been nervously toying with the rheostat, turned the knob, giving his Jag a head start.

"Son of a bitch," Jimmy said, trying to catch up to the Jag with his Porsche. He regretted using that particular swear word because Elvis hated it and took it personally.

"My momma ain't no bitch," Elvis said, as if she were still alive and watching over the goings-on in this room.

"Sorry, man, I didn't mean—"

"I know you didn't," Elvis said, slowing his car. "Momma was crazy about you. She told me you're a good man and I should trust you." Then Elvis laughed and twisted the black, grooved, plastic knob on the rheostat. His Jag flew forward on the straightaway, gliding into the first figure-eight track, past glowing houses, leaving Jimmy behind. Elvis whooped and focused completely on the little racing car skittering and jittering along the track. Jimmy tried to catch up, and there was a loud crackling in the room: Pier's voice overloading the house's intercom system, which sounded like a radio tuned just off-channel. Too loud and staticky.

"Jimmy, Jimmy, help me! Something's wrong here, terribly wrong!"

Elvis was concentrating so hard he didn't seem to hear. Jimmy was catching up with the Jag, and if he could navigate the third cloverleaf faster than Elvis, he would overtake him; and that would be the race. One more second. He couldn't leave now, and Pier was always calling him about something being terribly wrong. This morning the drapes in the baby's suite were terribly wrong; this afternoon Carla, the nanny, was terribly wrong because she wanted to take a week off during Perry's school term, and now, now—

"Jimmy!" she cried. "It's the baby! I'm bleeding all over, oh, God, in the toilet, in the toilet—"

Jimmy threw the rheostat onto the table, and the tiny silver Porsche didn't make the next figure eight but slipped its track and smashed against the wall. Elvis slowed his car down and looked up at Jimmy.

"Come on," Jimmy said, "Pier's in trouble." They dashed up three flights of stairs to the master bathroom. Jimmy rushed in, but Elvis stayed behind in the bedroom. "I'm ready to help if you need me," Elvis said, but he was speaking to Jimmy's back. He stared at the closed bathroom door, heard Pier wailing, crying like a child who can't catch its breath, and he remembered his mother's feet, her "sooties," as he called them, remembered kissing them when she was lying in her casket, her lips red with lipstick, her face clown white with powder, and he wondered why he was thinking of that when Jimmy's poor wife was crying and carrying on.

"Elvis, come in here and help me!" Jimmy called, desperation in his voice. He was holding Pier upright. "We're going to get a doctor, honey, it's going to be all right." Elvis came into the bathroom, looking embarrassed, and they gently carried Pier into the bedroom.

Jimmy's face was pale. "It's going to be all right, honey, I promise." But son of a bitch son of a bitch there was blood everywhere, all down her legs, bleeding through her dress, which was sopping red, trailing red along the white carpet; there was blood in her hair and on her hands and even on her doll-white face, and Jimmy wanted to squeeze his eyes shut, sew them shut forever with black thread, because he had looked into the toilet bowl and had seen the fleshy pieces floating turning in the stringy red water. "It's going to be all right, honey, I'm here. I'm here . . ."

"YEAH," JIMMY SAID INTO THE RECEIVER. HE SAT ON HIS LEATHER couch in the library that Pier had tried to redecorate as a doll's house and gazed out the window. It was a gray, rainy day, and the eucalyptus outside the window was wet and green and swaying in the gusting winds.

"Jimmy, is 'at you?"

"Who were you expecting, Marlon Brando?" Jimmy hated Marlon, perhaps because he had idolized him so when he was a kid.

"Uh, sorry." The woman who had called seemed flummoxed, and Jimmy sensed she would hang up unless he said something.

"Who's this?"

"Ethel."

"Ethel?"

"Kennedy. Bobby's wife."

"Hey, hi, Ethel," Jimmy said, his voice softening. "I'm sorry about . . . you know."

"Yeah," Ethel said. "It's been pretty rough around here lately."

"How's Bobby doing?"

"Not good, Jimmy. He's . . . not himself. He just mopes around. He doesn't even seem to care about being with the kids. He says he goes to the office, but I don't know." She paused and Jimmy heard a scratching noise as she muffled the phone. "He says he goes to the office, but I think—"

"What, Ethel?"

"I dunno. It doesn't matter. Nothing matters."

She was slurring her words ever so slightly. Jimmy guessed that she was drunk. Somehow that softened him to her, as if their pain was mutual, as if they'd always shared it. "This doesn't sound like the Ethel who serves green chicken *avec* frogs even when it's not Saint Patrick's Day."

But Ethel didn't respond. After a beat she said, "I was going to call you and congratulate you on your marriage." Her voice was flat, as if devoid of affect. He waited for her to go on; the pause was awkward. "I felt so guilty, I guess I did what I tell my kids never to do—I didn't do anything, and now all this time has passed. But did you get the tea set we sent?"

Shit, how the hell am I supposed to remember that? "Yeah, it's beautiful. Pier keeps it right on the dining room table, all the time. Pride of place, you know?"

"Good, I'm glad."

Another awkward pause.

"How's Pier doing? I just wanted to call when I heard, er—"

Jimmy felt his face begin to burn and he wanted to cry. Since Pier had the miscarriage and the follow-up D and C, Jimmy could not shake this feeling of constant sadness. Pier seemed okay; she'd launched herself back into her acting career and was perfect as Mrs. Shaw, the quintessentially evil mother in *The Manchurian Candidate*. Sweet and fragile, stone hard and implacable. Jimmy was sure she'd take an Oscar for her role. She was perfect.

Elvis might even pick something up for his role as her son Raymond.

Elvis . . . Pier . . . everything just goes on, and Jimmy flashed back to the scene with Pier in the toilet, Elvis helping him carrying her out, Jimmy glancing back, glancing into the white porcelain bowl red hole, filled with—

"Pier lost her baby," Jimmy said. "That's what you heard, right?"

"No, Jimmy. I didn't know. I'm so sorry."

"Well, everybody else does. The magazines have been having a field day with it."

"Jimmy," Ethel said, "I better confess, I did know. I read about it. I'm ashamed to say so. I'm so embarrassed. You've got your own tragedy. I shouldn't be bothering you with my problems."

"We could always talk, Ethel. What's going on?"

Ethel laughed and said, "Oh, you mean besides Jack getting shot and Bobby carrying on with Jackie and my entire family falling apart and—"

"Ethel, I know you're upset, but that's really not—"

"I know, I know, I'm sorry, Jimmy. God forgive me, I shouldn't be bothering you at a time like this, but I called about Bobby. As I said, he's not himself anymore. He needs help." She laughed again. "Or maybe it's all me. Maybe I'm the one who needs help. Old Moms, who's about as interesting as cornflakes."

"I think cornflakes are very interesting."

Ethel giggled.

"Maybe you should get him a doctor or something," Jimmy said. "I don't know . . ."

"No, he wouldn't have any of that, and that's not what he needs. He needs . . . you, Jimmy."

"Me?"

"He needs a friend to talk to. You know, hang around, smoke cigars, do whatever it is that you guys do behind closed doors."

"Ethel, there's bad blood between Bobby and me. We . . . we don't like each other much."

"Because of the Marilyn business."

"Because of a lot of things," Jimmy said, but Ethel had caught him with that last remark. "What . . . what do you know about Marilyn?"

"I know what was going on between them. Remember how upset I was at that party when he was all over her? God, it was the most humiliating night of my life. And you, you were probably as upset as I was. You just hid it better and weren't such a crybaby."

"It wasn't all that bad, Ethel," Jimmy lied. "If you hadn't told me how upset you were, I wouldn't have thought anything of it."

"Bobby was a mess when she committed suicide. God rest her soul and forgive her. She was a poor lost thing, Jimmy, and I think Bobby fell in love with her. Do you think he was in love with her?"

"I don't think so, Ethel," Jimmy said, soothing her.

"She was your girl, everybody knew she was crazy about you. Bobby had no business coming between you and her. No wonder you're mad at him. Oh, God, I'm drunk, Jimmy. I'm drunk as a goddamn skunk. There, you see? I never swear."

Jimmy shook his head and chuckled. *Ethel doesn't know anything.*

"But I couldn't call you otherwise, Jimmy. I couldn't humiliate myself like this if I was sober."

"Ethel—"

"No, let me finish this. Bobby keeps talking about you and that movie you're doing together. I think you should come for a visit and talk to him about it."

"There's nothing to talk about. We're not doing the picture."

"Bobby thinks you are."

"If he thinks that, maybe he *is* crazy."

"Will you come to Hickory Hill for a visit, Jimmy? I know you felt at home here, and you fit right in. Most people don't, but you do."

"Ethel, really, I'd love to, but I'm in the middle of editing a picture—"

"Jimmy, please," Ethel pleaded. "I don't know who else I can ask. Bobby doesn't . . . relate to anybody, to any of his old friends and the men he works with, but I know it would be different with you."

"It wouldn't, Ethel, believe me."

"It *would*."

"How do you know?" Jimmy asked, frustrated.

"Because God spoke to me."

Oh, shit, she's worse than Elvis.

"And you and Bobby are so alike."

"No, we're not," Jimmy said. "We're not alike at all. Except we have that—what's Bobby call it?—that henhouse look."

Ethel giggled. "I don't think that's what he called it, but I know what you mean. Come up this weekend."

"Ethel, I'm in California."

"I'm going to tell him you're coming. Can you bring your wife? I'd love to meet her."

"Ethel, look, it just isn't—"

"Stop torturing that poor woman, Jimmy." It was Pier's voice; she had been eavesdropping. "Yes, Mrs. Kennedy, please excuse me for intruding, but I couldn't help but overhear Jimmy abusing you. He tries to do that to me, but I won't stand for it for a second, and neither should you. Jimmy and I would be honored to visit your home this weekend."

"Goddammit, Pier!" Jimmy shouted, holding the phone away from his face. He put the receiver back to his ear. "Pier?"

But Pier and Ethel were busy making plans.

TWENTY

■

Cross-Eyed Boys

MASSACHUSETTS: JUNE 1964

In typical Kennedy fashion, Ethel suddenly changed the
venue. She'd forgotten that Bobby was taking the
family to the compound in Hyannis Port, and so
they wouldn't be at Hickory Hill. But Massachusetts was only a little bit farther away, wasn't it?
Never mind, Ethel had fixed up the airline tickets,
limousine, and driver, and Pier was delighted with
the casually fashionable little town of some hundred
shingle-and-clapboard homes. The cottages were
cute, and the estates, separated by hedges and
stone walls, looked weatherworn, private, and comfortable. Neatly trimmed lawns stretched out to
dune grass, rippled-sand beaches, and emerald-
green water.

"Now, don't you dare spoil everything," Pier said as the limousine drove down Scudder Avenue toward the compound and the sea.

"*I* wasn't going to come, remember?" Jimmy asked.

"Yes, you were, and watch your mouth; the driver can hear everything you say."

"I don't give one fuck what the driver can hear, and I've taken just about all the shit I'm going to take from *you*, too."

"Please, Jimmy, I'm sorry. I just want this to be nice, for Ethel's sake." Pier was wearing a blue sundress and looked like summer itself.

"You don't even know Ethel."

"I know her well enough," Pier said.

"After talking to her for five minutes on the phone?"

"It was an hour. It was enough."

"I don't know why you forced this."

"I forced it for you, Jimmy. And for Bobby."

"Oh, Christ, now it's Bobby. I suppose you talked with him for an hour, too?" Jimmy shook his head. Pier folded her hands on her lap and looked small and fragile and perfect. "We're going to put the past behind us. All of it. I've got my reasons." And then they were inside the compound. The chauffeur—a young man suited up in the Bobby Kennedy Justice Department uniform of button-down shirt, thin tie, slept-in suit, and brush cut—opened the door and smiled at Pier. He was beefy enough to be a bodyguard, which he probably was. Jimmy was uncomfortable here, although the sea air smelled fresh and salty; and he took a deep breath, as if he'd just escaped from a fetid room. Then dogs ran toward them, followed by children. Ethel waved from the porch and called the dogs back. She was wearing rolled-up jeans and a white, embroidered blouse. Jimmy couldn't help himself: he grinned at her, and Pier glanced sideways at him, as if evaluating whether she needed to be jealous of Ethel. But then Ethel was shaking Pier's hand; and they laughed and hugged each other, as if they were relatives who hadn't seen each other in years.

A six-year-old boy goggled at Jimmy, as though a monster had been washed up by the sea. A freckled, brown-haired girl who was a little younger pushed the boy. Jimmy thought she was the little girl he had carried to the house when he'd visited Hickory Hill. Then an eight-year-old said, "That's my sister, Mary. She's named after *me*."

"You're Mary, too, hey?" Jimmy asked.

"Don't you remember me?" she asked petulantly. "Well, *I* remember you. You came over that time Mommy fixed us a green chicken for Saint Patrick's Day. You're an *actor*." She said that as if being an actor was something quite loathsome.

"It's good to see you, Jimmy," Ethel said. She hugged him chastely and kissed him on the cheek. "I'm really happy you could come for a visit. Bobby's in the house. He'll be so happy to see you."

"You know what my daddy says about you?" eight-year-old Mary asked Jimmy. "He says you're a damned bastard."

The younger Mary shrieked with laughter.

"Mary Courtney, I'm going to wash your mouth out with soap!" Ethel shouted. "Go straight to your room this very minute! Go on, and you, too, Michael. All of you, get out of my sight." She turned to Jimmy, her cheeks reddening. "I don't know where they hear these things. Certainly not from us."

"I heard it from Daddy, I did so," Mary said, impenitently.

"Oh, God, I'm so embarrassed," Ethel said, but Jimmy was giggling.

"Don't be," Pier said. "Kids say the darndest things."

"I guess." Ethel seemed somehow deflated, and Jimmy put his arm around her and said, "I've been called a lot worse. Ask anybody."

Ethel shook her head and looked like she was about to cry, then recovered herself immediately. "Come on," she said cheerfully. "I've got a barbecue started in the back, on the patio. You eat burgers and hot dogs, Pier?"

"I sure do."

She ordered the chauffeur to take the luggage up to their room. Then, in barely a whisper: "Jimmy, Bobby's waiting for you in the den. Just go straight through."

WHEN JIMMY KNOCKED ON THE BRASS-HANDLED DOOR OF THE DEN, Bobby said "Enter," as if he were allowing a servant into the room.

Damned bastard, am I . . .

Jimmy walked into the sunny room. He looked out the windows of the sunporch. There was a broken basketball hoop lying on the lawn. Beyond the lawn was the ocean, now blue. Dark, angry clouds drifted across the sky. Looking past the huge, ash-stained fireplace to his right, he could see the green shading of oak and scrub pine through the windows.

Bobby sat on a green lounge chair and gazed out at the sea. His hair was unkempt, and he was wearing an old man's four-button gray sweater that looked too large for him. Jimmy stared at the back of his head for several seconds.

Bobby turned around, smiled wanly at Jimmy, and said, "Grab a chair. You want a drink?"

"Yeah, I guess." Jimmy was surprised at how much Bobby had aged. His face seemed thicker, coarser; there were shadows and wrinkles under his eyes, but it was the eyes, the deep-blue eyes, that seemed to be squinting in pain.

"You still drinking Scotch?" Bobby asked.

"Yeah."

"Johnny Black do you?"

"Yeah, anything's fine." *Fuck the small talk.* "Did you get pissed off when you found out that Ethel had invited us?"

"You want it neat or with soda?"

"Neat."

"Ethel talked to me before she called you," Bobby said, handing Jimmy a cut-crystal tumbler filled with a few fingers of the deep amber liquid. "That surprise you?" Jimmy shrugged. "I was thinking about calling you anyway," Bobby said as pulled his chair beside Jimmy's and sat down. "About our film."

"We don't have a film," Jimmy said. "We got a script, some promises, a lot of scared people, and no financing."

Bobby grinned. "Sounds like life."

"Not *your* life."

"You're a bastard, Jimmy."

Jimmy chuckled. "That's what your daughter just told me."

"What?"

"Your daughter called me a damned bastard. She said that's what you call me."

"Son of a bitch."

"Make up your mind, Bobby. Which is it to be? Bastard or son of a bitch."

Bobby shrugged. "Take both, my compliments."

"Yeah, well, I'm going to go out and see how Pier is doing."

"You still think I killed Marilyn?"

Jimmy shrugged. "Ethel thinks you were in love with her. Were you?"

"Were *you,* Jimmy?"

"Cut the shit. I asked you first."

"Yes, I was, and you know what sticks in my mind, it was—oh, fuck it."

"What, tell me." Jimmy said.

"It was the last time I saw her, when I was going through her house and she came at me with a knife. I took it away from her, and we were wrestling each other, and then we were holding each other, and it was too late, it was all over, and she was crying and trembling in my arms, and I was saying 'I'm sorry.' That's the moment I'll take to my grave. I can't undo that."

"I know. You told me before, remember?" Jimmy got up and walked around the room. "But why are you telling me this shit?"

Bobby looked at Jimmy and gave him a tentative smile, a crooked half smile that those who knew him well would recognize. "Because you're safe."

"Don't bank on that."

"Because you love your wife. Because there are people who would do us harm. For lots of reasons."

"What did you do with the diary?"

"Like I told you, it's been disposed of. It's not an issue."

"Oh, yeah, it's not an issue. They killed your brother, and it's not an issue." Jimmy caught himself and said, "I'm sorry, man. I shouldn't have said that."

Bobby laughed, but it was hollow, a lamentation. "They—whoever they were—should have killed me. I'm the one they wanted. I'm the one who went after the racketeers hammer and tongs. I'm the one who kept after that cunt Castro. I'm the one who suggested that Jack ride without a bulletproof bubble top on the car. You know what I told him? I told him, 'It will give you more contact with the crowd.' " He smiled at Jimmy, a hard, nasty smile. "Well, I was right. He certainly had contact with the crowd. The fuckers, the dirty fuckers. What do you think is going to happen to Jackie and her children?"

Jimmy shrugged, feeling awkward and embarrassed. "You can't blame yourself. Who do you think—"

"Who gives a shit who did it," Bobby snapped. "Will it bring Jack back?"

"How the hell should I know?" Jimmy said. "You're the head of the Justice Department, not me." Then after a beat: "Sorry, man, this was a mistake. I just knew it was going to be a mistake. I got to get out of here."

"You want another drink?"

"I haven't even finished this one." But Jimmy understood that Bobby was making a gesture of conciliation; he nodded and sat back down. The Scotch was making his mouth numb. "Oh, what the hell. Yeah, sure."

After refilling Jimmy's drink and sitting down with his own, Bobby said, "I'm sure that little pinko prick Castro had something to do with it, but he certainly didn't mastermind anything. He should've shot me, not Jack."

"They got Lee Harvey Oswald. He was a Communist. Wasn't he a member of that Be Nice to Cuba Committee, or whatever it was called?"

Bobby guffawed. "The Fair Play for Cuba Committee."

"So who do you think it is?" Jimmy asked, insistent.

"Who do I think it is? You, me, everybody, anybody. It could be those Cuban cunts, the anti-Castro exiles. They're all working for the mob. They blame us for the Bay of Pigs, and they're trying to make this look like a Castro-Communist hit. And I don't trust those guys at the CIA. They're worse than the Mafia." He laughed. "As I said, everybody wants to get us. But you know what, Jimmy? I don't give a shit. I don't even want to know. What good will it do to know?"

"You ain't going to be safe until you know and deal with them," Jimmy said.

Bobby laughed. "You're starting to sound like General MacArthur. He told me the same thing. But if you said 'ain't' in front of Ethel, she'd be all over you like gravy on rice." Jimmy chuckled. That was an expression he himself often used. "No, Jack died for my sins," Bobby continued as he stared hollow-eyed at the sea, which was simultaneously comforting and threatening, its still depths filled with all the grotesque and crippled monsters of Bobby's tortured soul. "And now we're safe. You know why? Because I'm out of the picture now. Like Jimmy Hoffa said, I'm just a lawyer now."

"You're still the attorney general."

"You keep saying that. But it means shit. That asshole Hoover couldn't wait to disconnect his phone line to my office. No, everybody got what they wanted. Organized crime and the unions are free to go back to raping and pillaging the country. Hoover can go back to jerking himself off over Communists. Castro and the CIA should be satisfied. Everybody's satisfied. Especially Colonel Corn Pone and his Little Pork Chop."

"Who?"

"Johnson. Your new president and his charming wife, Lady Bird. Jackie gave them that nickname. Fits, huh?" After a beat, he said, "I wouldn't put it past Lyndon."

"Put what past him?"

"He hated Jack."

Jesus Christ, he really has gone off the deep end. "You don't really believe that the president was behind the assassination?"

"Nixon's the true slime bucket. And I should have investigated Howard Hughes years ago."

"You're kidding, right?" Jimmy asked.

Bobby glanced at him, grinned, and said, "Yeah, of course I'm kidding. So tell me, you been to any good funerals lately?" Jimmy just shook his head in consternation and took a sip of his Scotch. "I guess I'm not making a very good impression, am I?" Bobby asked.

"Why on earth would you care?"

Bobby shrugged. "Before . . . before the events of November twenty-second I wouldn't have, but now . . . now everything is different."

"How?"

"Camelot's over, Jimmy. All gone. Johnson isn't going to do shit for the poor in this country, and he doesn't give a shit about civil rights. Now that we're out, the Negroes don't have any voice in government. Nobody gives a damn about them. My brother cared, but this guy couldn't care less. It's up to us to finish Jack's unfinished business."

"*Us?*"

"Yes, Jimmy. Us." Bobby suddenly seemed completely focused, alert; it was as if he had simply shaken off his grief, paranoia, and cynical morbidity. "The essential thing is not to lose oneself, and not to lose that part of oneself that lies sleeping in the world."

"What the hell is that supposed to mean?"

"I thought you read Camus."

Jimmy sighed. "Yeah, right."

"Well, have you?"

"Yeah, matter of fact, I have."

"We are faced with evil. I feel rather like Augustine did before becoming a Christian when he said, 'I tried to find the source of evil and I got nowhere.' But it is also true that I and a few others know what must be done. Perhaps we cannot prevent this world from being a world in which children are tortured. But we can reduce the number of tortured children. And if you believers don't help us, who else in the world can help us do this?"

"Is that Camus or you?" Jimmy asked. *Jesus H. Christ.*

"Camus."

"Well, I'm not a believer."

"Bullshit."

"And what am I supposed to believe in?"

"Well, you believe in the purity of film," Bobby said.

"There ain't no such thing."

"There will be if we do *The Enemy Within*."

Jimmy burst out laughing. "God, you're so full of shit, Bobby. Why do you want to do the film now?"

"Because we can. We've got a script. All the rest will be taken care of."

"Yeah? How's that?"

"I've got the money sourced, and the people involved—no one will fuck with them . . . or us."

"Who are they?" Jimmy asked.

"Just people," Bobby said dismissively. Then, earnestly, "We *have* to do this film. Because it will make a difference."

Jimmy just shook his head, and Bobby said, "I'm going to run for the Senate seat in New York. I've decided. Jackie knows, we've spent hours discussing it, and she thinks it's the right thing to do. But I haven't told Ethel yet. Or anybody else, for that matter. Ethel thought I should go for the vice president position." Bobby laughed. "She thought Johnson would need me, and he would have, if Goldwater had lost in California. All Johnson has to do now is shut his mouth and stay alive until the election's over. Goldwater's such a right-wing nut, he doesn't have a prayer—except in the South, where he plays on their fear of the nigger." He smiled at his own thought, which he didn't share with Jimmy. "The Republicans do seem to have a death wish."

"If you think Johnson had something to do with your brother's assassination, how could you even consider—"

"I don't really think Lyndon had anything to do with it," Bobby said softly. "I just hate the fucker. I do think he'd turn the other cheek, though, if he did know. Ask me sometime about what he said about Jack being cross-eyed. You know what he said?" Jimmy looked at him blankly. "He said that Jack's eyes were crossed and so was his character, and that was God's retribution for people who were bad. He said that what happened to Jack was divine retribution. Divine retribution."

"Then what would ever possess you to run as his vice president?"

"To keep Jack alive, to finish his unfinished business—the War on Poverty, nuclear proliferation, civil rights, the Alliance for Progress. We've got to do something about apartheid in South Africa, and we've got to get out of Vietnam. Jack and I talked about that before . . ." His voice trailed off, and he stared at Jimmy, his coon-peering-out-of-a-henhouse stare. "I'm the keeper of the flame for Jack. There's nobody else."

Jimmy couldn't help but grin at Bobby, who scowled back at him.

"But I could never do it as vice president. I wouldn't have any influence. Jackie and I are in agreement about that. And I would lose all ability to ever take any independent position. Aside from all that, Johnson would keep me too busy wiping his ass." He laughed at that, gallows laughter.

"What makes you think you could do any better as a senator?" Jimmy asked.

"I just told you . . . I'd be independent."

"You'd be a junior senator. One out of a hundred. You'd have about as much power as the stenographer."

Bobby looked at Jimmy with new respect. "I wouldn't be a junior senator. I'm a Kennedy. I'd be the senator from New York and the head of the Kennedy wing of the Democratic Party."

"You'd be the carpetbagger from Boston."

"I thought you didn't understand politics."

"I don't," Jimmy said.

"I think you do. That's why we've got to do the movie and get it out in the next few months."

Jimmy laughed. "You're crazy."

"We need this movie," Bobby insisted. "To win."

"You mean, *you* need it to win. I'm not running for anything, re- member?"

"No, I know what I mean. *We* need it. There's a war going on in Vietnam, the niggers are about to riot, we've got an asshole running the country, and you're too afraid to get involved."

Jimmy laughed. "You'd fail salesman school, Bobby. You want to get elected, go get a publicist, or whatever the hell you guys use."

"This isn't about me, or you. It's much bigger than all our selfish, greedy bullshit."

"I got to go," Jimmy said, standing up.

"This would be the hottest film you've ever done," Bobby said, standing up, too. "Fox is back in." He paused for effect. "It's a done deal. You'd have full control. And whatever monies that would flow to me, will go to you. You can produce, direct, whatever. But *you've* got to play me."

"Me? What happened to the idea of using Paul Newman?"

"I can't tell you what to do, but I think Newman would be wrong. You and I are . . ."

"Are what?" Jimmy asked.

"We look alike."

Jimmy shook his head. "Bullshit we do, and you might think the Republicans have a death wish, but it's you, Bobby. Haven't you pissed off the Mafia enough? It's too dangerous. I'm not putting Pier in any more danger than she already is—than *you've* already put her in. And I don't want to be a target for everyone who wants to shoot your ass off."

Bobby nodded. "Of course, you're right. Point taken."

"Even if I wasn't stupid enough to be afraid for myself. I'm afraid for Pier, and you should be afraid for Ethel and your family."

"Yessir," Bobby said.

"I'm serious."

Bobby nodded. "Of course you are. So then I should get out of pol- itics entirely. Hide under the bed. Become the complete coward."

"Maybe you should."

"I don't believe Ethel would have very much respect for me if I did that."

"Yeah, well, none of this is my problem."

"You want to play some football?" Bobby asked.

"No. I got to go."

"The long days store up many things nearer to grief than joy. Death at the last, the deliverer. Not to be born is past all prizing best. Next best by far when one has seen the light . . . is to go thither swiftly whence he came."

Jimmy smiled. "Sophocles."

"*Oedipus Tyrannos,*" Bobby said. "I've been reading a lot lately. It helps. Jackie's been my mentor. She has a classical education."

"Did you ever read *The Little Prince*?"

"Yeah, and I reread it. It reminds me of Marilyn . . . and Jack." Then he quoted from the book. " 'I shall look as if I were suffering. I should look a little as if I were dying. It is like that. Do not come to see that. It is not worth the trouble.' Do you know the next line?"

"Very funny," Jimmy said.

"Well?"

Jimmy quoted the next line. " 'I shall not leave you.' "

BOBBY AND JIMMY ATE LEFTOVERS AND PLAYED WHAT WAS SUPPOSED to be a very nonphysical game of touch football, using a soft foosball, with the kids in the dining room. Jimmy slipped and broke the table. Ethel yelled at Bobby, who thought it was funny, and Ethel told Pier— in a voice loud enough for Bobby to hear—how delighted she was that Bobby was so much better now and finally playing with the children again, no matter how many tables they broke.

The phone rang, and Ethel answered it.

"Oh my God, Bobby. Ted's been in a plane crash!"

Bobby took the phone from her. After a short conversation, he hung up and said, "Ted's seriously injured. He might not make it through the night. His back has been broken in three places, and his legs are paralyzed." Then he turned to Jimmy, as if his brother's accident was somehow all Jimmy's fault.

IN THE DARKNESS AND THE RAIN, OVER THE MECHANICAL WHINE and whistle of the engine and the whispering and plashing of tires over slippery macadam, Jimmy said yes. He would do the picture. He would play Bobby Kennedy the G-man attorney general James Cagney hero, but there was no way, no way that the picture would be out in time to help Bobby's race for the Senate. "It takes months to do a picture, usually years to set it up, so if this is to make you feel better, okay, that's one thing, but . . ."

Bobby didn't seem to hear a word Jimmy said, and Jimmy wondered if he'd been talking or just thinking the words in his head, musing as he watched the shadow trees on either side of the road become glaucous green in the harsh white high beams of the headlights.

"Thanks for coming with me," Bobby said.

"You already thanked me. No problem."

"Ethel will come in tomorrow, but I just couldn't stand to have her in the car with me." Bobby shook his head, as if admonishing himself. "I know that sounds terrible, but I just can't deal with her easy answers to everything. She's one of those people who knows there's a god and just what he looks like." He laughed. "Gets on your nerves after a while. But she's a wonderful mother and loyal as the day is long."

"Do you love her?"

"Of course I do," Bobby said.

"Like you did Marilyn?"

Bobby didn't respond, but Jimmy couldn't help himself; if he was ever going to get through to Bobby, discover what was there, who he was, it would be now.

Did you kill Marilyn, you son of a bitch?

"Are you in love with Jackie?"

"Ethel tell you that?"

"Nobody told me anything," Jimmy said.

"Ethel's crazy about you. She thinks the sun sets in your ass." Jimmy grinned. "Yeah, she's right. I guess I am in love with Jackie. I've always been in love with her a little. But it's not what you think. I always felt like she was my sister, and then when Jack . . . when all that happened, someone had to take over, help her and the children."

"Are you fucking her?"

"You're a cunt," Bobby said, and he stepped on the brakes and pulled over to the side of the road.

"You want me to get out, I'll get out right here," Jimmy said.

"Why would you give a shit who I'm fucking?" Bobby stomped down on the accelerator.

Jimmy shrugged. "Maybe I like your wife." Bobby didn't respond, just kept on driving. "You never answered my question," Jimmy said. "About Marilyn."

Again, Bobby didn't answer, and they drove on for another hour, Jimmy nodding in and out of sleep, dreaming of Ethel, Pier, Marilyn, and his mother, as if they were all aspects of one another, pieces of some neon jigsaw puzzle he could only see while he was asleep.

"Of course I was in love with her," Bobby said.

"What?" Jimmy asked, snapping awake, tasting salt and cotton dryness in his mouth.

"She was the only woman I ever loved—like that."

"And Jackie?"

"You can't get off that, can you? I might as well have taken Ethel."

"Think of me as her emissary." Bobby laughed, and something nasty, dark, and dirty passed away.

A tension neither recognized dissolved.

"I didn't kill Marilyn," Bobby said. "And my relationship with Jackie is none of Ethel's fucking business. Or yours. Especially yours."

Fifteen minutes passed; time expanded in the metronome darkness, contracted when oncoming headlights scoured everything white for a blinding, migraine instant.

"My brother is probably dead, and you're acting like a one-man Warren Commission," Bobby said.

"Sorry."

"Well, at least our picture is back on the burner."

"What makes you think that?" Jimmy asked.

"I heard you say yes." Jimmy giggled. "There's something else I'd like to ask you, though."

But Jimmy had already slipped back into the dark, into the itchy, jangling, dangerous sleep of dreams where his mother waited for him, waited to council him and wrap her cold, fish-skin arms around him like a lover in need.

THEY ARRIVED AT THE COOLEY DICKINSON HOSPITAL IN NORTHAMPton, Massachusetts, at three in the morning. Bobby sprinted up the stone steps to the lobby, and Jimmy followed; but Jimmy was in no hurry. He wasn't going to see Ted. He wasn't family. He was along for the ride, and in the empty and soiled-looking waiting room he wondered about Bobby. *He killed Marilyn. He had something to do with it* . . . yet Jimmy felt an unhealthy empathy with Bobby, with his grief and anguish, his existential angst bolstered and enflamed by Aeschylus, and Euripides's "giant agony of the world."

"Well, are you coming?" Bobby asked, returning for Jimmy, as if he'd momentarily forgotten something.

"You don't want me up there," Jimmy said. "It's only family in intensive care."

"I can't go in there alone."

They went up together. Ted was in an oxygen tent. There was a tube in his right nostril; a tube in his chest, for his lung was collapsed; and another clear plastic tube, transfusing him with bright red blood. His square, pugnacious Kennedy face was battered, black-and-blue, his hair greasy and clumped. He tossed in pain, but he was awake. He looked at Bobby and said in a voice hardly louder than a whisper, "I'm okay, Bobby, I'll be fine." He smiled wanly. "I saw Jack. I went to Arlington, to the grave, and I told him that the bill passed."

"That's great, Ted," Bobby said, looking uncomfortable. "You need to get rest now." He reached inside the tent and clasped his brother's hand. "As you said, you're going to be fine."

Ted's hooded eyes glanced at Jimmy, then back to Bobby.

"That's James Dean," Bobby said. "The actor."

Suddenly Ted's eyes opened wide and he asked, "Is it true that you're ruthless?"

Jimmy didn't know whether he was speaking to him or to Bobby.

IT WAS JUST DAWN, AND BOBBY AND JIMMY STRETCHED OUT ON THE dew-damp hospital lawn. They gazed up at the constellations, which were being leached away by the grayness in the east and the ambient lights of the city.

"Ted's going to be okay," Bobby said.

"Yeah," Jimmy said, although he was pessimistic about his chances. The doctors said that even if he lived, he would likely be a paraplegic.

"He said he was going to be fine, and he will be," Bobby insisted.

"Well, I hope so," Jimmy said. "What did he mean about that ruthless shit? Was he talking to you or me?"

"He's all drugged up. He doesn't know what he's saying." Bobby chuckled. "I'll ask him about it when he's feeling better." After a beat, he said, "You know, there was something I was going to talk to you about in the car."

"Yeah, what's that?"

"My campaign."

"What about it?"

"You know, when I first got the news about Ted, I thought, fuck it, it's time to give it up. Somebody up there doesn't like me. Or us." He blinked at the sky, as if waiting for a sign. Then he continued, "But that was wrong thinking. No matter what happens to Ted, it's up to me to keep going, to finish what Jack started."

"That's a good sentiment," Jimmy said.

"It's more than sentiment. It's going to be my life."

"Hallelujah."

Bobby smiled. "I guess it does sound like a conversion, but what else could be more important than the war against poverty? That was Jack's last wish."

The sun had come up, promising another muggy day. The sky was the color of slate, cloud upon cloud, striations of gunmetal gray.

"Bobby, I'm getting my ass soaked in this grass, and you're giving me a fucking speech."

"You're a pussy. A little dampness won't hurt your ass."

Jimmy reached over, and suddenly they were wrestling, trying to pin each other. Jimmy had to win, had to press Bobby's head into the ground, beat him until he was too weak to cry uncle. He remembered wrestling with his basketball teammates at Fairmont High School, and he used to wrestle with his mentor, the Reverend De Weerd, who was the scoutmaster of the team, a war hero who helped all the guys, who smelled like grass and cologne and bacon; and Jimmy remembered teaching his little cousin Markie how to wrestle, but all that was just for fun. Benign family, fraternal fun.

This . . . this was something else.

An older couple stopped to watch them. Bobby went limp, giving up, and said, "Hey, hey, let's call a truce, or we'll end up in the goddamn papers. 'Robert Kennedy Wrestles with Famous Actor While Brother Fights for His Life.' "

"I had you pinned," Jimmy said, panting. "Fair and square."

"Bullshit you did."

They stared each other down, as if ready to go at it again.

"You should help me, Jimmy," Bobby said.

"What do you mean?"

"Get political. Take a stand."

"I just beat *your* ass."

"I'm serious, Jimmy." They started up the hilly incline toward the hospital. Bobby nodded to the elderly couple. The old woman shook her head and turned away. "You should get your feet wet."

"Everything else is wet."

"Get involved."

"I think I'm involved enough."

"Your wife doesn't think so."

"What the hell is that supposed to mean?"

"Ask her. She'll be here in a few hours. In the meantime, I'm going to see if my brother's still alive."

PART FOUR

1964–1968

TWENTY-ONE

■

Windows of the Sea

The wives stayed home.

Ethel was suffering from particularly severe morning sickness—she had never had a problem with that before—and Pier was meeting with Bob Wise, who was interested in having her star in his new film, *The Sound of Music*. But he was also interested in Julie Andrews. "So I *have* to be here," Pier said.

"That's not your kind of picture," Jimmy said in a low voice, almost whispering into the phone. He was staying with Bobby in New York at the Carlyle.

"I'll make myself scarce so you can talk," Bobby said, leaving Jimmy alone in the large, well-appointed living room. Jimmy gazed out the window. A light snow was falling, and East Seventy-seventh Street looked gray and cold and lifeless.

"You said that about *The Manchurian Candidate,* too," Pier said. "You said I wasn't right to play Mrs. Shaw, remember?"

"Yeah," Bobby said grudgingly.

After a pause, Pier said, "Bobby?"

"Yeah."

"You know I want to be there with you more than anything else."

"It looks like it's going to be just us boys out on the campaign trail," Jimmy said.

"I talked to Ethel," Pier said. "She called me from Hickory Hill. She's pretty sick."

"That's what Bobby told me. He's disappointed she can't be here, and he's worried that maybe something will go wrong with the baby."

"No, she's going to be fine."

"If you say so," Jimmy said.

"I say so," Pier said. "And I'm going to get this part."

"I think you're crazy. It's a musical, isn't it? You're no singer."

"I'm as good as Andrews," she said, losing her temper.

"Sorry."

"You'd better be, buster."

"Buster?"

Pier giggled. "Are you going to be okay up there?"

"Yeah, I think I can handle New York."

"I mean all those bad neighborhoods. I talked to Ethel, and she said that without us, you guys could go into the slums and get votes. She said you and Bobby would be too nervous to take us along."

"I don't know where we're going. Johnson City and Glens Falls or someplace. I don't think they've got slums in Upstate New York. Just good old farm boys who'll rob you and rape you and then shoot you."

"Jimmy!"

"Sorry," Jimmy said. "But all the exposure will be good for the picture"—Jimmy glanced around the room to make sure he was alone—"and that's what I'm doing it for."

"What about for Bobby?"

"What do you mean?"

"Don't you think we need him in government?" Pier asked. "All that stuff you told me about helping the poor and the blacks, and do you want Perry to be over in Vietnam fighting when he's eighteen?"

"God, you bought the speech hook, line, and sinker."

"Didn't you mean what you said?" Pier asked.

"Yeah, I mean everything I say, but I'm not a politician. I'm an actor."

"I think you'd make a great politician."

Jimmy laughed at that. "Yeah, right."

"I've seen you talk to the crowds. They love you."

"Bullshit."

"You know, rebel with a cause."

Jimmy laughed. "Yeah, it makes good copy."

"And it's for a good cause."

"Pier, you really are a Mickey Mouse."

"A Mickey Mouse that loves you."

"Then come to New York. I don't want to be here alone, doing this shit with Bobby."

"You're just jealous because you can't sing and nobody wants you in a musical."

"You're just going to get depressed again," Jimmy said. "Wise is just fucking around, trying to get Julie Andrews hooked."

"Fuck you, Jimmy. That's a terrible thing to say. I've worked with Bob, and so have you. He's not that kind of man. He's always telling me he wants to work with me again, and in case you haven't noticed, Jimmy, I'm a big star now. You're not the only one in the family, you know."

"I talked to Hedda, and she told me that Wise is hot for Andrews."

"Thanks a lot," Pier said, crestfallen.

"But I asked her to see what she could do."

"Well, that's something," Pier said.

"Do you want me to call Wise?"

In a tiny voice: "If you think that might help."

The doorbell rang.

"That's probably Lem Billings and some of the other guys at the door," Jimmy said, "so I'll have to go."

"Jimmy?"

"Yeah?"

"I really think you're doing a good thing with Bobby," Pier said, "and I don't mean just for the picture."

"I know about your little talks with Ethel," Jimmy said. "I'm an actor, and that's all I want to be. If you want to be First Lady, you're going to have to knock off Lady Bird." Jimmy laughed at that, but Pier didn't.

Jimmy heard guffaws and Lem's voice loud in the hallway.

"Jimmy?"

"Pier, I really got to go now."

"Do you think I'm a good actress?"

"What the hell kind of question is that?" Jimmy asked. "Of course I do."

"Do you really?"

"Are you okay or what? You keep telling me you're the best thing since sliced bread, so what's this all about?"

"I don't know, I just feel sad."

"About what?"

"About losing the baby, and not being with you, and maybe not getting this new part."

"We'll get you the part you want."

"Promise?"

"Promise."

"Jimmy?"

"What?" Jimmy asked, impatient.

"Do you think I'm a good person?"

"Yes, Pier, I think you're a wonderful person."

Then, with a click and a sigh, the line went dead.

THE CROWDS, THE NOISE, SHATTERING CRYSTAL COLD AND INDIAN-summer dirty brown slush, the marching bands, the same overcrowded well-policed Main Street in Ithaca Binghamton Endicott Oswego Potsdam Cortland Schenectady Watertown; banners, confetti falling like snow from skyscrapers in the greater cities, in Syracuse and Albany, in Rochester and Buffalo and New York, shirtsleeves torn and black to the elbows from pressing the flesh—it was pure and absolute adoration for Bobby and Jimmy. The crowds screaming and shouting *Jimmy Jimmy Jimmy* even when Bobby stood up to talk, the crowds screaming and shouting *Bobby Bobby Bobby* when Jimmy gave his speech, the special Bobby-booster speech, the speech that changed every time he gave it—but when he gave it, he believed every hokey word of it. Believed it absolutely. For the moment.

Recreation Park in Johnson City, New York. A cold November morning, the sky low with soiled gray clouds promising snow or drizzle. Behind Bobby and Jimmy, who were standing on a jury-rigged podium, was a beautiful turn-of-the-century merry-go-round, which reminded Jimmy of Marilyn, sweet white Marilyn, who would never visit a town like this, who would curl up and wither and die in a town like this.

"Bobby's the *man*," Jimmy said, speaking into a microphone.

Jimmy in a greasy gray overcoat; underneath, a V-neck cashmere sweater, white T-shirt, and tight jeans. Bobby with a floral tie pulled loose under an open collar, tweed jacket, slacks, and a cream-colored woolen overcoat.

Jimmy standing at the podium: "Who else do you think is going to be there for all of you? Who else is going to be there for the decent working man and the unemployed and the schoolkids and the Negroes and everyone else who isn't getting a decent break in our society?"

Cheers from teenagers and Negroes and everyday regular working people, cheers from staunch Democrats and old, cool, groovy fans with JAMESDEAN scars and leather jackets.

Bobby Bobby Bobby

Jimmy Jimmy Jimmy

"No, man, it ain't me. It's Bobby. I'm just the actor who plays Bobby." Laughter.

"So who's going to make sure that New York remains the most important state in the Union?"

Bobby Bobby Bobby

"So you . . . and you . . ."—pointing—"and you will have the security of knowing that you'll have a job tomorrow and the best education for your children. Who's willing to go up against big corporations and big business and big unions to protect *you?*"

Chanting. *Bobby Bobby Bobby*

"Whose record consistently shows that he's for the underdog?"

Bobby Bobby Bobby

"It certainly ain't that shit Keating."

"Jimmy, we don't say bad things about our opponent," Bobby said, reaching for Jimmy's microphone.

Jimmy blocked him. "No, man, the deal is that *you* don't say bad things about your opponent. I'm just the actor here, remember?" Jimmy continued. "That son of a bitch accused Bobby of trying to help a Nazi corporation when it was Keating himself who introduced the bill. Keating didn't lose his brother in World War II. Bobby did. Keating's a politician, man. He may look like everyone's Dutch uncle, but underneath all that Lorne Greene white hair, he's slick and slimy and dirty."

"That's an exaggeration, Jimmy."

"And although he'd have you believe his civil-rights record is great, it's just the opposite. You check it out, and if I'm wrong, *I'll* go into politics." Laughter. "You all know who the underdog is here. It's Bobby, and do you know why?"

The crowd huddled together like a Greek phalanx, spears with red, white, and blue posters waving in the air, all the posters bobbing up and down to Jimmy's rhythm, and somehow this was better than acting, better than theater because he, Jimmy, was out there, on his own without a script (or so he thought), and now it was about intuition, sensation, and being in the moment. This was perfect focus, for him and for the crowd, perfect laser-straight connection; and Jimmy could feel that the people rocking and smiling and shaking before him were really doing the talking, that he was just saying their words. He was the medium. He was the pastor. He was the enlightened one. He was Reverend De Weerd showing the crowd his private parts, and it didn't matter that everything Jimmy said might be bullshit, it was true just the same, true right now, this instant, which was pure synchronization, the incandescent point of everything. Jimmy was high. Jimmy was perfect. Jimmy could do no wrong. He'd switched the power on so high that he might burn out at any moment.

Like Marilyn.

Just like Marilyn.

But he was just the opening act.

It started snowing, great white flakes, perfect crystalline shapes, God's own torn bits of tickertape.

"You know why Bobby is the underdog? It's because he doesn't kiss ass like Keating to get your votes. His family's suffered for what they believe in. Two of his brothers died for what they believed in. Your president—Bobby's brother—died because he wouldn't kiss ass to the Communists and the labor unions and the FBI—oh, yeah, Keating will tell you that Bobby is tight with every right-wing organization in the world, but it's bullshit. J. Edgar Hoover hates him. Did you know that? And you know why he didn't go on LBJ's ticket as vice president?"

"Jimmy," Bobby warned.

"Hey, Bobby. You want me along, I'm going to tell it to these people like it is. Hey, reporters, you takin' notes?" Indeed, the reporters were taking notes. "Bobby didn't want the vice presidency because he'd have to go along with everything Johnson's doing, whether he agreed with it or not. He wouldn't be able to speak against what Johnson's up to in South America, he couldn't push for civil rights, he couldn't push to protect *your* rights, he'd have to kiss ass. Well, if you vote for Bobby, he'll fight for you. Your wants and needs and ideas will get out there." Bobby grinned at the crowd. "Anyway, I figure if Bobby's got to kiss anybody's ass, it might as well be yours."

To laughter and shouting, Bobby took the mike, saying, "I'd better come clean and tell you right now, I'm not going to kiss *anybody's* ass."

Flags waved. Huge posters of Bobby bobbed, as if he was nodding in assent in two dimensions. More cheering. Bobby joked and smiled at the warmed-up crowd of reporters, shoe-factory workers, administrators, party apparatchiks, the Democratic youth of America, hippies, hangers-on, Jimmy's fans, Bobby's fans, and the middle-aged house-

wives and old ladies who loved him, just as they loved his brother
Jack. Bobby had done his homework. He knew the issues important to
Upstate New Yorkers. Although he still wasn't comfortable speaking to
crowds (but he was learning from Jimmy, perhaps even imitating him
a bit), he worked his audience. And later the ladies would have a tea
for him, the ladies who were the mechanics of grassroots politics, the
little white-haired blue-haired old ladies who got out the vote and determined who would be out and who would be in.

Bobby opened with a put-down of Barry Goldwater, who was running against Johnson. "The Catskills were immortalized by Washington Irving. He wrote about a man who fell asleep and woke up in
another era. The only other area that can boast such a man is Phoenix,
Arizona, Barry's birthplace." More waving, laughing. "But you should
vote for me for two reasons. First of all, I have eight small children who
need a lot of shoes. Second, I'm the one who popularized those fifty-
mile hikes . . ."

Then Lem Billings rushed up the rough, wooden steps of the
podium and said something to Bobby. Bobby gasped and said, "Oh,
God . . . oh, God."

"What's going on?" Jimmy asked.

"We'll have to cut things short," Lem said, looking away from
Bobby. Lem with his long face and dark-framed glasses, Lem all gangly arms and legs, Bobby and Jack's wiry fighter and boyhood com-
panion, trusted confidant and aide. Then for one long second he stared
at Jimmy with haunted eyes while Bobby told the crowd that he was
sorry, *"but we have an emergency and . . ."*

"It's *something*," Jimmy said pointedly and angrily to Lem, but
Lem turned away, led Bobby and Jimmy past the officials and honored
guests, through the police lines, to the waiting black Lincoln limousine; and they drove through God's white snow, through the nasty and
poor part of town, past ramshackle factories and miner cottage-style
houses, past the railroad terminus with its long mottled green roof, and
Bobby sat next to Jimmy—"Oh, God, Jimmy, there's no way to tell you
this, but Pier's—" He stopped, then continued. "Pier's had an accident, Jimmy. She overdosed."

"She *what?*"

"That's all we know. We're getting you to a plane."

"Is she in the hospital? Which hospital? Is she okay?" Thoughts
sailed, floated like the snow dropping and then bouncing off the windshield.

Jimmy, do you think I'm a good actress?
Jimmy, do you think I'm a good person?

Jimmy . . .

Jimmy . . .

Jimmy . . .

"Jimmy." Bobby's voice.

"She's not all right, is she?" Jimmy said flatly.

"No, Jimmy," Bobby said. To his credit, he didn't glance away. He looked Jimmy in the eye and said softly, "She passed away, Jimmy. She passed away."

"Passed away? Fuck passing away, she didn't get on a goddamn train or anything, she fucking died, she's fucking dead you son-of-a-bitch bastard, it's your fault, you son-of-a-bitch bastard, you did this, or the fucking CIA did it, or the Mafia, all because of—" Jimmy was shaking and jolting with seizures. Everything felt like it was moving in slow motion. It was a motion picture. It wasn't real. Pier was fine. He'd call her. She'd be there. She was always there.

He was flailing about, trying to punch Bobby. Lem caught him, held him tight, skinny-ass gangly Lem was stronger than he looked, Jack's old army buddy or something, *let me go you fucking freak,* then to Bobby, *it's because of that fucking diary, you killed her, you—*

THREE DAYS AFTER BOBBY WAS SWORN IN AS THE JUNIOR SENATOR from New York and four days before she would give birth to her ninth child, Matthew Maxwell Taylor, Ethel Kennedy was ringing Jimmy's doorbell.

He didn't answer.

She had called him, told him she was coming; he sounded vague, stoned, but said, "Yeah, okay."

She kept pressing the doorbell and was about to give up in frustration when Jimmy opened the door. She was shocked that he looked as good as he did; he had shaved closely, his hair was washed and combed, and he was dressed in slacks and an open shirt. The perfect creature to inhabit this mansion, she thought. But his eyes looked glazed, haunted; she had seen that same look when she had visited patients in sanatoriums, the patients all Sunday fresh in pressed clothes as if they were spending their days in quiet contentment rather than struggling with the scratching, biting, writhing demons of the soul. She hugged him. He responded but only barely.

"Come in."

"Wow," she said, staring up at the beau monde ceiling mural over the great staircase. There were paintings, lithographs, and posters on every wall; and there were dolls everywhere, in cases, on bookshelves and nooks, and standing life-size on the floor, every kind of doll imaginable: Jumeau bisque dolls, English boy dolls with waxed heads, Indian bazaar dolls, Chinese mandarin dolls, Indian kachina dolls, Dresden dolls with china heads, pedlar dolls with kid heads and wooden bodies, Dutch dolls with wooden limbs, leather Kafir dolls, ivory dolls, corn-husk dolls, terra-cotta dolls, and a beaded buckskin doll sitting over the architrave of the library.

"You want a drink?" Jimmy asked, leading her into the library and gesturing for her to sit down on the leather couch. "Martini, isn't it?"

She smiled, nodded, and sat down. "You're looking well, Jimmy."

Jimmy nodded, mixed the drinks in a shiny tumbler, then sat down beside her. "You expected me to be stinko drunk or high, didn't you?" Ethel nodded again. "And unshaven and filthy dirty."

"I suppose I did."

"Well, you would have been right. I was so bad I was pissing myself."

"So what changed?"

Jimmy put his arm over the top of the couch but didn't touch Ethel. "You. Your call. You gave me notice. I figured I was going to have to come back sometime, so I started getting ready for the part. It's all in the method." He giggled. "First I called the cleaners, then I took a bath, then I shaved." He grinned at her. "Then I called all my friends and apologized."

"For what?"

"For treating them like shit."

"You didn't call Bobby."

"He wasn't here for me to treat like shit. Lucky for him, huh?"

"He wanted to be here."

"Now you're full of shit, Ethel. Another drink?"

"I haven't finished this one yet."

He poured her another martini anyway, then handed her a folded, handwritten note. "Here, read this. You might as well. I ain't shown it to nobody else."

"Haven't shown it." They smiled sadly at each other. "Why are you showing it to me?" Ethel asked.

"Because you're you, because . . . how the hell should I know? Because you understand. Bobby wouldn't, but you do. Don't get pissed off at me, but the only other person I'd show it to is Marilyn, and that would be a little difficult." He laughed mirthlessly.

Ethel started reading, then said, "I shouldn't be reading this, Jimmy. It's wrong."

"Please," Jimmy said, imploring.

Ethel read Pier's suicide note and said, "Holy mother of God, Jimmy."

"Yeah, my sentiments exactly."

"What can I—"

"Did you read where she wrote 'I love you, Dom.' What the hell's that about? What the hell's that about?" Jimmy folded his hands together, pressing hard palm to palm, as if he could just squeeze the past into oblivion.

"I don't know. Maybe . . ."

"Yeah, maybe what?"

"Maybe she just wrote the wrong thing, like she meant to write your name, but was confused because of the drugs. She did write that she loved you more than anyone."

" 'Anything.' That's what she wrote. I got the letter memorized."

"I saw the pictures in *Photoplay*," Ethel said almost in a whisper. "They weren't much. Just Pier sitting with that artist. Big deal."

"I guess you missed the ones where he was pressing her flesh."

"What?"

Jimmy laughed grimly. "They were in *Whisper*. So much for politics, hey?"

"I don't understand."

"Pier wanted me to be like Bobby. I told her she'd have to kill Lady Bird Johnson, or you, if she ever wanted a shot at being First Lady. I didn't expect her to kill herself."

"If you ever want to go into politics, Jimmy, what happened . . . it wouldn't hurt you."

"That's the last thing I'm ever going to do, Ethel. So tell Bobby he doesn't have to worry."

"Bobby mentioned you in his victory speech."

"That's nice," Jimmy said dismissively.

"He told everyone that he believes you have so much to give and that he thinks you'll be doing much more than making movies."

Jimmy laughed at that. "I won't be doing shit, Ethel, and the last thing I want to be is like Bobby. No offense."

"None taken."

Jimmy stared straight ahead, holding himself as still as a statue.

"Jimmy?"

"Yeah?"

"It's going to be all right. If you believed in God, it would be so much easier, everything would be so much clearer, and—"

"Don't even bother me with that Bible-pounder shit, Ethel. That's what you came all the way over here to tell me? That God is going to make everything all right?"

"If—"

"Don't."

Ethel nodded, and Jimmy leaned toward her, put his arm around her, brushed his hand intentionally against her right breast.

"No, Jimmy, that's not what I came here for. Bobby would probably try that sort of thing, but I expect something different from you."

"I'm sorry," Jimmy said. "It was an accident. No, it wasn't an accident. I'm sorry, Ethel. I just wanted to be close, that's all."

"We can be close," she said, her voice surprisingly husky. "That's why I'm here. You just can't do that, that's all."

"Would you have wanted me to if circumstances were different?"

Ethel laughed nervously. "Jimmy, you can't ask me such a question."

"Would you?"

"Maybe, Jimmy, but circumstances aren't different. I've got a husband who I love. I took vows, which I don't take lightly."

"And I've got a friend."

Ethel smiled and allowed Jimmy to nuzzle her. "Yes, you do."

"How could I have missed it?" Jimmy asked. "She was seeing him right under my nose. I'm a fucking fool."

"No, Jimmy, you're anything but a fool."

"Then how could I not know?"

"She was an actress," Ethel said, "and a very good one. Of course she could fool you, just as she fooled herself."

"What do you mean?" Ethel stared at her hands, and Jimmy could feel her tremble. "She told you about it, didn't she?"

Ethel nodded. "She talked to me when he threatened to blackmail her. She said she couldn't trust anyone else. I told her to tell you, I begged her, but she was sure that she would lose you if she did. Like she told you in her letter. That was all true."

"Something could have been done," Jimmy said, "but . . . she loved him. She didn't want to stop seeing him." Jimmy looked like he was in physical pain. He pulled away from Ethel.

"She was just in too deep," Ethel said. "He was a nasty piece of work. She did want to stop seeing him, Jimmy. She just didn't know how to get out of it. I tried to help her."

"How?"

"There just wasn't enough time," Ethel said.

"What do you mean?"

"Lem Billings was putting something together."

"Like what?" Jimmy asked, surprised, angry, and humiliated.

"Something to scare the man away from Pier. Pier didn't know . . . nobody knew, but everything happened so fast, Pier taking her own life, I don't know, Jimmy, I'm so sorry for you."

"Bobby knows, doesn't he?" Jimmy asked. "You told him."

"I'm sorry, Jimmy. We just wanted to help." She shrugged, helpless. "But we were too late."

"You should have told *me*. Everyone knew but me. Son of a *bitch!*" Jimmy stood up and paced around the room. "I wanted to break every one of these fucking dolls, did you know that? But I couldn't. Just like I wanted to break that asshole artist's face. Did you read her last request—that I shouldn't hurt him? What bullshit. I should break his face. I'm *going* to break his face." Jimmy moved toward the door.

"Bobby got mad at me, too," Ethel said.

"For what?"

"For telling him about Pier, for asking him to help you."

"You should have told *me*," Jimmy said, pacing around the room again.

"Pier made me promise. I knew I couldn't win, that whatever I did would be wrong. But I care about you, Jimmy, and so does Bobby."

"Bobby only cares about Bobby."

"He made me promise not to tell you anything. He said it would only make it worse. He was right. He said you wouldn't want him to know. He said that you think he killed Marilyn. He said you probably think he had something to do with Pier's death, too, and that I was never to tell you that he was trying to help."

"Why?"

"Because he said you wouldn't believe it. It would just make it worse. Do you believe me, Jimmy?"

After a beat, Jimmy said, "Yeah . . . about Pier, I do."

"And Marilyn?"

"This isn't a conversation we should be having."

"Now you sound like a lawyer," Ethel said.

Jimmy sat down beside her. "I can't talk to you about Bobby. You're his wife."

"Yes, you can. I've broken all my confidences to be honest with you. You can tell me what you think, your feelings."

"How do I know you won't break my confidence, go back and tell Bobby everything?"

"I guess you don't," Ethel said in a voice so low it was barely audible.

"I don't know what I think. I saw Bobby's men in Marilyn's house the night she was killed . . . died. What do you want me to say? That because Bobby's my friend, I think he's innocent?"

Ethel was shaking. Not with anger. Perhaps fear. "He's not a murderer, Jimmy. And neither are you."

"What do you mean?"

"It's not your fault."

"You're right about that. It's Pier and that fuckhole of a boyfriend of hers." He hugged Ethel and cried. "No, it's not Pier. It's . . . everything."

He fumbled with her white satin blouse.

"Jimmy, please don't." Her voice seemed to catch in her throat. She pulled gently away from him and whispered, "Bobby's not a murderer."

"I'm sorry, Ethel," Jimmy said, staring hard at her. He needed and desired her. He wanted to kiss her and be safe. He wanted to be inside her. But he had broken a trust. He was as self-serving and unethical as that asshole Domenicos Theotocopoulos, and she was plain as vanilla ice cream . . . yet she was beautiful, radiant in bulging pregnancy— her breasts full; her stomach round with life, her face tight; eyes wide, almost goggly, nose slightly too large and flared; mousy brown hair flat against her neck and forehead. No makeup. She smelled of milk and mint and soft perfume. With a shock Jimmy realized it was Joy, Marilyn's perfume.

"Do you want to feel the baby?" Ethel asked.

Jimmy let her guide his hand to her stomach.

"There, feel it?"

Jimmy giggled and nodded. He left his hand on her stomach. "Pier didn't even want me to take care of Perry."

"You could fight it. Would you want to?"

"He's not my son, not physically, anyway. Pier never knew that I knew."

"Does that matter?"

"I wouldn't stand a chance in court."

"I'm sure you'll be able to see him whenever you want," Ethel said.

"Pier's mother won't let me near him. She's got good lawyers, too."

"I'm sorry, Jimmy."

"How do I get past all this?" Ethel shook her head. "You ever been to the Santa Monica pier?" Jimmy asked. Ethel shook her head again. "I used to go there a lot. Something about seeing the ocean makes everything else seem . . . small. You eat cotton candy?"

Ethel laughed, and Jimmy imagined he was walking into the sea, into the cold froth of the breakers, into the deep lithium darkness.

TWENTY-TWO

■

Methods and Martyrs

LOS ANGELES: FEBRUARY 1965

Jimmy met her at Berkeley, after he gave a speech in front
of the Sproul Hall steps. She wore her hair in an
Afro, a huge kinked halo that framed her face as a
perfect oval. Her eyelashes were thick, her black eye
makeup even thicker. She had a perfectly straight
nose, and faint laugh lines shadowed the corners of
her full, sensual mouth. Her skin was powder dark,
her neck long and regal. She wore a very long bead
necklace and an emerald-green sheath dress, and
she carried a honey-colored acoustic guitar with a
white, beaded strap.

"I liked what you said," the woman said to Jimmy.
Jimmy nodded. There was something cruel and hard

about her features. She was stunning. "You want a toke?" She handed him what was left of a marijuana cigarette.

Absentmindedly, Jimmy took it. He inhaled deeply and held it in his lungs. There were thousands of people behind him, mostly students. Heads nodded at him as he gazed around, young people making eye contact, congratulating him, making the connection, and that was enough; they didn't need to press him for attention and autographs; they were too cool for that. Here he was famous yet somehow anonymous. Here he was safe and calm in this dreamless, crowded, noisy place. Here everything was solid, tangible, hard, like the Nubian student princess beside him, who was probably one of the free-speech-movement leaders.

"How come you're here?" she asked.

Jimmy gave her back the joint and shrugged. "Somebody asked me to come and say something. Probably someone from the student union."

"It's not organized like that, and that's not what I asked you."

Jimmy snorted. *I don't need this shit.*

"But I did like your 'students are just citizens caught in the machine' speech. You're the only old person who seems to give a shit." That said sarcastically, not innocently. Jimmy laughed. "I mean who's over thirty."

"There're hundreds of people here who are over thirty," Jimmy said.

She shrugged. "Yeah, I suppose. I probably should stop smoking these silly cigarettes."

"How old are *you?*"

"Over twenty-one. Old enough to know."

"You a student here?"

She shook her head and smiled grimly. "Just someone who cares about freedom of speech."

"You a folksinger?"

"No, but I sing a little."

"I think you're older than you look."

"You do, do you?"

"Yeah," Jimmy said, and then the crowd began shouting at a thin, wiry, dark-haired student leader. Framed between Corinthian pillars, Mario Savio stood on the steps of the administration building. Shaking with energy and conviction, he thanked Jimmy for his support and then gave his speech. The amplifier made his voice so loud that it echoed around the square.

". . . and you know, James Dean is absolutely right, we're all caught up in the gears of the government machine. But there's a time when the operation of the machine becomes so odious, makes you so sick at heart, that you can't take part, and you've got to put your bodies upon the gears and upon the wheels, and you've *got* to make it stop."

The crowd went wild and kept shouting, "Make it stop Make it stop Make it stop!"

"Claudia, you want to come up here and help us out with a song?" Savio said in a resonant voice as big as the crowd; and the woman Jimmy had been talking to stepped in front of the microphone and began to sing "Blowin' in the Wind." After the first chorus, the student leader interrupted her and shouted, "Are you ready to march into the administration building right now and sit down on the gears?"

The crowd surged forward. *"Fuck, yes!"*

Claudia continued to sing, her contralto voice a combination of gravel and molasses; and then, when all the students who were going to participate in the sit-down had disappeared into Sproul Hall, she looked at Jimmy and spoke into the microphone, "You going inside, Jimmy?"

The plaza was almost empty, and Jimmy felt deflated, enervated, as if he was a vampire who had taken the blood energy from the crowd, and now there was nothing left, no crowd, no pounding deafening screams, no mass bobbing, heaving, swaying to capture and fill his field of vision; and once again he felt the crushing weight of memory. Pier was dead. Marilyn was dead. "I'm a ghost," he said to himself.

"What?" Claudia asked, her voice large in the plaza that had nearly emptied; there were still students about, students standing around talking and smoking and passing out political leaflets.

Jimmy laughed and said, "I'm a ghost." People watched him, listening.

"What the hell is that supposed to mean?" Claudia asked. Jimmy shrugged. "So are you going in or what?"

"No," Jimmy said. "My work is done." And he turned and started walking through the plaza.

"Hey, you want to have coffee?" Claudia asked, still using the microphone.

"No," Jimmy answered, but dark, sleek, cool, self-possessed, over-twenty-one Claudia couldn't hear him.

"Hey . . ."

SHE SAID SHE HAD A CRASH PAD IN WATTS, BEHIND THE PROJECTS on Imperial Highway. Jimmy considered the slums in L.A. to be rather nice, candy-ass, working-class black neighborhoods; they certainly weren't anything like the South Bronx or Bed-Stuy in New York. Now *those* were slums. War zones that smelled of fear. You knew you were a target there, but Watts didn't feel that way.

Jesus Christ almighty, this could be any neighborhood in Indianapolis, Indiana. But Jimmy wasn't taking any chances. "You got a garage?"

"You think nobody here ever saw a Jag?" Claudia said, teasing him.

"I'd just like it to be in one piece when I leave."

"I thought you said this ain't no ghetto, just pretty little ramshackle houses all in a row. Nigger heaven, eh, Jimmy?"

"Yeah, yeah," Jimmy said.

"Turn right at the next corner. My house is the brown one right after the grocery store, and, yes, I have a garage."

"So it's a house."

"Yeah . . . what'd you expect?"

"You said a crash pad."

"Well, that's what it is."

"You own it?"

He stopped in front of the grafittied two-car garage, and without answering, she got out of the car and opened the roller door. "Yeah, I own it," she said, leading him through a narrow hallway to the living room, which was as messy as Dean's house used to be. The room was dark, the windows covered with dirty eggshell-colored pull shades. She picked up a pile of newspapers and magazines to make room on the couch for Jimmy. "You want a joint?"

Jimmy shrugged.

She fumbled around for a half-smoked joint in a large, porcelain ashtray, which was overflowing, and said, "I'm never here."

"Where are you, then?"

"Working, mostly down South. I'll be moving to Selma. That's in Alabama."

"When you going?" Jimmy asked, ignoring her condescension and making small talk, accepting the little fuzzy high that the marijuana would give him and wondering what the fuck he was doing here. She had wanted to talk to him over coffee, and there were a hundred coffee shops and restaurants around Berkeley, but here they were, in her crash-pad house, in the candy-ass slums, and for a terrifying instant he couldn't remember the sequence of events, how he got here—yes, yes, the car, but why not the coffee shop? Why did he accept her invitation? Did she invite him?

"I'm leaving in a few days," Claudia said. She sat beside him but kept her distance. He glanced at her breasts, which made interesting wrinkles in her tight-fitting dress. She wasn't wearing a bra.

"You know, maybe it's the dope, but I don't know why I'm here. I thought you wanted to have coffee. I thought I said no."

"Yeah, you did."

"Then how am I here?"

She laughed. "You gave a pretty good speech at the university for someone who was stoned out of his head."

"I wasn't stoned then," Jimmy said.

"Then what was all that 'I'm a ghost' business, and all that jive about being a vampire?" Jimmy shrugged. "Maybe I shouldn't have brought you back here, but you seemed completely fucked up."

"*I* drove us here."

"Yeah," Claudia said. "So what's your point? That I'm stupid?"

Jimmy grinned at her. If he hadn't been stoned at the rally, he certainly was now. "This is good shit. I'm practically hallucinating."

"Panama Red. Expensive."

"I can see squiggly lines going through your furniture."

"Terrific."

"Was that what you gave me earlier? This Panama Red?"

"No," she said, making fun of him. "That was Acapulco Gold."

So it *was* the pot, he told himself, but he'd only taken one toke at the campus—no, he had finished the entire joint while she was singing, and then he walked away and—

"You were a mess, man. What was that shit about being a vampire?"

"I was talking out of my head," Jimmy said. He noticed that her mouth turned down at the corners. He felt a sudden urge to suck on her bottom lip. She wore dark lipstick, and stoned-out Jimmy thought of plums.

"Yeah . . . but it was about *something*. You said you could only get close to your wife when you were in a crowd. You remember that?"

"No," Jimmy said, suddenly focused and sensing danger, "I don't remember nothin'. Are you the goddamn FBI or what?" *She could be the FBI.* "What about you? What were you doing at the rally?"

"Singing, remember?"

He snorted. "Yeah, I remember."

"Oh, it was that bad, eh?"

"No, you have a beautiful voice," Jimmy said, softening. "Really mellow."

"Thank you." Her voice still gravelly, husky.

"I meant, why were you at the rally?" Jimmy said. "You one of the organizers?"

"I help out when I can."

"You're not going to give me a straight answer, are you?" Jimmy felt the dope working through him, cooling him, chilling him, exaggerating everything he saw heard felt—his heart was banging in his chest and throat, banging in the hollows, and his blood was pumping in time with it, a deafening red ocean, pulsing, everything was pulsing with it: the furniture, walls, Claudia.

"Why are we both dancing around here?" she asked.

"Why'd you want to have . . . coffee with me?"

"Touché," she said, smiling, gazing at him as if she were miles away and high. Jimmy imagined she was twenty feet tall and looking down at him. He was small and vulnerable, a fucking bug. She laughed and said, "Maybe I'm a starfucker."

"You don't strike me as the groupie type."

"What type do I strike you as?"

"I dunno, one of those people who have the truth all sewed up, some sort of political activist on a mission."

"Got it in one, honey," Claudia said.

Jimmy felt the tension between them, could actually feel it vibrating, and he reached toward her. She pulled away. "Watch your hands, white boy."

Jimmy grinned. "Some of my best friends are—"

She covered his mouth with her hand. He licked her palm, and she pulled it away.

"I was going to tell you that some of my best friends are singers," Jimmy said, feeling suddenly merry, as if Claudia's good pot had segregated all his bad memories, freed him from guilt, from Pier.

"Oh, yeah?"

"You know Eartha Kitt?" Jimmy asked.

"She's your friend, is she?"

"Yeah, she is."

"So some of your best friends *are* niggers."

"What's this thing with you?"

She sighed and said, "Look, Mr. Dean, I'm sorry I wasted your time."

"Mr. Dean?"

She stood up, and in that instant Jimmy felt cold sober—but pot had that effect on him; he would slip in and out of the numbing, glowing fog.

"Okay, Miss Claudia, I'll get my ass out of here," Jimmy said. "What did you want? What was all this about? What did you want to ask me over for, coffee?"

"I wanted to ask you to come to Selma and help us out," Claudia said.

"How?"

"Just by your presence. You're quite the symbol, didn't you know?"

"Symbol of what?"

"Rebellion. You're the G-man Robert Kennedy who fights crime and injustice. That's what you do in the movies."

"Then why not ask Bobby Kennedy?"

"Oh, Bobby, is it?" Claudia sat back down next to Jimmy. "Because he's not the hero, you are. He's a prick who's only interested in what will make him look good, and I can tell you, being in Selma ain't going to do that for him. And it will be dangerous, and that's not the Kennedy brief."

"Tell that to his brother Jack."

That caught her. "What happened to John F. Kennedy was"—she sighed, shook her head—"I'm sorry, but it doesn't change anything. Robert Kennedy is the consummate politician, just like his brother was. He doesn't give a shit about blacks or civil rights, any more than Johnson does. Do you know what that prick did when Fannie Lou Hamer was testifying before the Credentials Committee at the Democratic Convention?"

"You mean Bobby?" Jimmy asked.

"No, I mean Johnson."

Jimmy just shook his head. "Who's Fannie Lou Farmer?"

"It's Fanny Lou Hamer. Shit, you really have been living in white-bread bliss, haven't you? Don't you even watch television? She was national news. She was on all the networks." Seeing the look on Jimmy's face, Claudia changed her tone. "Fannie's the leader of the MFDP, and we challenged the official delegation at the Democratic Convention. All we were asking was to be recognized."

"What's the MFDP?"

"Mississippi Freedom Democratic Party." Claudia continued. "Fanny was telling her story, she was rolling, she was telling the whole fucking world about how she tried to become a registered voter in the Delta, how she lost her job and was evicted from her house, and how the pigs tortured her in jail; and then jive-ass Johnson figured that was real bad for his southern votes, so he got her pulled off the air by calling an impromptu press conference. You know, one of those 'We interrupt this program for a special announcement from the dickhead president of the United States.' But a lot of what she said was replayed on the evening news anyway. You really never saw it?" Jimmy shook his head. "You *do* know about the civil-rights movement?"

"Look, you're right, I should piss off out of here."

"Do you know about the civil-rights movement?"

"Yeah, of course I do."

"Well?"

"Well, what?" asked Jimmy.

"Are you going to do something? Like you did today for free speech?"

"You want me to go and be part of your sit-in, right?"

Claudia laughed. "Man, you're too easy to disrespect."

I don't have to take this shit. But he did because he was lucid now, cold burning cold seeing, ice cold, razor cold sight. He would analyze her and break her. "You want to tell me or what?" he asked in his softest, boyish voice, and she told him that the Alabama Project, as she called it, was a campaign to secure new legislation that would ban discriminatory poll tests and insure that voting rights were federally protected.

She told him that Selma was the seat of Dallas County, "and you know how many black people are registered to vote in Dallas County, even with all the effort of the Dallas County Voters' League—those are black people I'm talking about—and the NAACP? At last count, it was about one percent. Now, I'm sure that wouldn't have anything to do with the fact that the registration office is open only two days a month, or that when it is open, the registrars are somehow always out to lunch, or that if you're a Negro, you have to fill out endless complicated forms and take a test on reading-and-writing comprehension and knowledge of the Constitution that I'll bet *you* couldn't pass. And any Negro who gets involved in anything to do with voting in Dallas County usually gets to meet Sheriff Jim Clark and his merry posse of civic-minded citizens who take care of Negro troublemakers with guns, clubs, whips, and electric cattle prods. They're the most sadistic, violent racists in the South. That's why we're targeting them."

"What are you going to do, go down there so they can beat the shit out of you?"

She shrugged, then smiled. "Think of it as a photo opportunity. We expose what's going on to the media. That puts pressure on politicians. That's the only way anything's ever going to change. It sure as hell isn't going to happen because politicians are naturally kind and good."

"You're fucking crazy."

"We fought a war in Mississippi this summer. You heard about Mickey Schwerner, Jim Chaney, and Andrew Goodman, right? They disappeared on the first day of Freedom Summer."

"You mean the volunteers who were murdered?" Jimmy asked. It had been all over the news in July and August.

"You think their disappearance would have been major news if we didn't have organization? Before we sent volunteers out there, we trained them, got the names and addresses of their local newspapers and media contacts? Every volunteer had to provide four photographs and had to pledge five hundred dollars as a bond in case they got arrested, and at every training session we had reporters. No one could fart without a reporter being there."

Jimmy shook his head. They *were* fucking crazy.

"I knew those guys," Claudia said, almost in a whisper. "I trained Jim Chaney. He was a baby, a rich white kid who wanted to do something good. He was beaten so bad his own mother wouldn't have recognized him. You think Johnson would have sent two hundred soldiers to try to find the bodies if we didn't have organization?"

"Dead is dead," Jimmy said.

Maybe it was the dope, but something Claudia said seemed to have color and shape, and a special coded meaning for him. *Wanted to do something good . . .*

"No, they're martyrs. The good old boys can still kill us, but they can't do it in secret anymore. We're lighting our own crosses now in their yards, and when we're done, they're not going to be able to beat us and kick us and murder us anymore, and if they're still stupid enough to call us nigger, then it fucking well better be Mr. or Mrs. Nigger."

"Well, that straightened me out," Jimmy said.

"I wouldn't want to scare you," she said sarcastically. "But you'd be pretty safe marching with us in Selma, not safe as houses, mind you, but the bigots probably won't kill James Dean in front of the press corps. And if you came out, you'd have company—it looks like Joan Baez and Bobby Dylan will be coming, and the writer James Baldwin. You heard of him?"

"Yeah. Of course I have."

She nodded. "We need all the media magnets we can get—it will ensure the kind of coverage we need. You could really make a difference, James."

Jimmy giggled. *James, I like that.* "Is this being organized by Martin Luther King?" he asked.

She looked at him warily. "Yes, his SCLC people will be there; they're involved."

"What?"

"Southern Christian Leadership Conference. And he'll certainly be there when we march."

"March where?"

"I don't know where yet," she said impatiently.

"So you're with King's organization?"

"There will be a lot of organizations involved," Claudia said.

"What's yours?"

"SNCC. There, does that help?" After a beat she said, "Student Nonviolent Coordinating Committee."

"So it's run by students?"

"Started off that way, but not so much anymore."

"So you're for nonviolence, like King, the way of Gandhi."

"I see nonviolence as a tactic, and a very powerful one; but for most of the people involved with the struggle, it's their whole philosophy."

"So what's your philosophy?" Jimmy asked. She smiled at him. "I'm serious. I want to know."

"Do these questions mean you're interested in overcoming fear?"

Jimmy laughed, but it was forced. "Yeah, right, you read my mind."

"You want to smoke another joint?"

"No," Jimmy said. "I want to learn about overcoming fear."

"My philosophy? Struggle, resistance, self-sufficiency. The global rebellion of the oppressed against the oppressor, the exploited against the exploiter."

"You sound like Malcolm X."

She shrugged and smiled. "Some of my best friends are—"

Playfully, Jimmy covered her mouth. When he pulled his hand away he asked, "Will he be there?"

"Maybe. I haven't asked him, but a lot of people will be in Selma, and they probably won't all be turning the other cheek."

"Are you a Black Muslim?"

"Well, I'm black," she said, holding her hands in front of her, as if to make sure, "but not Muslim, although I respect them and their program. If I was a Muslim woman, I wouldn't be here with you."

"Why?"

"You've used up your questions, James. It's my turn. Now tell me why you think you're a vampire."

"I don't."

"You want a joint to help you out?"

This time he accepted. It was dark, and the room was shadows; outside was quiet, and then harsh, unearthly lights and noises—screams, sirens, the scything of a low-flying helicopter—and Jimmy thought of his record of *War of the Worlds*. He shouldn't be smoking, not stuff this strong—it would make him paranoid, make everything worse. But he found himself talking; it was as if he was watching himself from across the room, and the talking Jimmy was lying back on the couch talking about Pier, about how she wanted him to be a politician instead of an actor, that she wanted to be Jackie Kennedy, but he didn't want any of that shit, although he . . . although he . . .

"Yes?" Claudia asked, her voice honey, her voice bright brittle light.

He was a vampire, and he told Claudia he was going to bite her neck, but she'd be safe because he was only a vampire in crowds, taking their sweat and smells and bovine pushing and shoving, because in crowds he could forget Pier yet Pier would be with him, she'd take the aching longing away, and Jimmy sucked at Claudia's neck, working up a perfect hickey, red and delicious, a sordid mouth; and she pulled herself away from him even as she pressed herself against him, and she reached behind her and unzipped her dress, and he massaged her small breasts and sucked on her lower lip before going down on her, down, down, down, her pubic hair curly, her scent sharp, olives and pears, and his face was wet with her, wet with forgetfulness and forgiveness, and then she was on his lap, facing him, staring at him. He hardly moved inside her.

"Well?" she asked.

"Well, what?"

She smiled and asked, "Are you coming or not?"

TWENTY-THREE

■

The Egg Trick

Claudia rang him and asked, "You hear about Jimmie
Lee Jackson?"

"The kid who was shot?" Jimmy wanted a cigarette, but he couldn't reach the pack of Salems that he had tossed on the library desk. He had started smoking menthol cigarettes after Pier died.

"Yeah, well he died. State trooper shot the poor little fucker for trying to protect his mother from a beating. Point-blank range."

"So what do you want me to do?" Jimmy asked.

"If you're still up for overcoming fear, this is the time, James. We're going to march. We're going to Montgomery to lay Jimmie Jackson's body at Governor Wallace's front door. Call all the media you got; tell them we're marching for our lives and the right to vote, and get your ass down here."

"And if I'm not up for overcoming fear?"

"Then congratulations on all your nominations for the Academy Award." Her sarcasm and impatience were evident.

"Yeah, but *The Manchurian Candidate* didn't do shit," Jimmy said.

"Say what?" asked Claudia.

"I expected it would sweep," Jimmy said, goading her, "but it's only up in two categories. Now *The Enemy Within,* that did a *lot* better."

"Are you really that self-absorbed?" Claudia asked, rising to the bait.

"I'm an actor, remember? Like I asked you before, why not just get Bobby Kennedy?"

"We tried that, James, and he suggested we call you."

"You're kidding, right?"

"Are you coming or not?"

ANDREW YOUNG, A CONFIDANT OF MARTIN LUTHER KING, LED THE prayers outside of Brown Chapel African Methodist Episcopal Church, and everyone kneeled and cried and sang "Amen," and then they were walking. Jimmy walked behind John Lewis, the chairman of the Student Nonviolent Coordinating Committee, and Hosea Williams of the Southern Christian Leadership Conference. Beside him were Claudia and SNCC leaders Albert Turner and Bob Mants. Claudia had introduced him to all the activist leaders, who were dressed in their Sunday best.

It was a chilly, cloudy afternoon in Selma, Alabama; and Selma, to Jimmy's mind, was nothing but a shithole of fast-food emporiums, gas stations, and used-car dealerships. Good old boys with their wives and children jeered at Jimmy and the five hundred marchers walking quietly toward the Edmund Pettus Bridge to cross the Alabama River and march onward to Montgomery, the state capital.

It was going to get very nasty. Jimmy could feel it.

"So where the fuck is King and all the rest of the so-called stars who were supposed to be here?" Jimmy asked Claudia.

"What we heard," said a tall black man of about twenty wearing a peaked cap, white turtleneck, and what Jimmy would call high-water pants because they were so short, "is that Dr. King's advisors thought it would be too dangerous for him to be here because he was receiving death threats."

"No," said someone else. "He has an evening service at Ebenezer, and if they put him in jail, he won't be able to keep his promises to his congregation. If we were doing this march tomorrow, he'd be here, that's for certain."

"Where'd you hear that?" asked someone from behind.

"From someone close to Dr. King. They believe that after all the criticism of the troopers in the press, we should be pretty safe here today. And Dr. King has other obligations, you know. He can't be everywhere."

"There you go," Claudia said to Jimmy. They'd been sniping at each other all day. "You done thinking all about yourself, James?" she asked.

"Yeah, and fuck you, too."

She took his hand, pulling him closer to her. "I asked you to be here with us in good faith. You didn't have to come. You could have just said no if you were so worried and nervous."

"There you go again with the jibes."

"What jibes?"

" 'If you were so worried and nervous.' "

Frustrated, she exhaled sharply. "I didn't mean it like that, and you know it."

"You didn't just phone me and ask if I'd come to your march."

"It's not *my* march."

"You had to get in all that overcoming-fear shit and tell me how self-absorbed I am."

"Well, you are. You were more interested in how many nominations you got than that kid who just got shot."

"*You* brought up the Academy Awards, remember? I just led you down the path after that."

"Yeah, right."

"All you had to do is ask me to come down," Jimmy said, his voice sincere.

"That's what I *did*."

"And here I am."

She tried to pull her hand free from his, but he held on playfully. "This isn't exactly the place to be holding hands, James. That's a hanging offense around here."

"You took my hand, remember?" Jimmy said. She looked straight ahead and smiled, and they walked hand in hand. "Since we're not in any danger according to whoever's behind us, and since we're not going to Birmingham."

"Who told you that?" Claudia asked.

"Your friend John Lewis. He figures since we're not taking tents and camping equipment, we won't have anyplace to camp, so the idea is that we march out of Selma and then come back, and then we do the big walk tomorrow. So maybe Dr. King will make the march tomorrow."

"Maybe he will."

"You knew all about this, didn't you?" Jimmy asked. "You could have mentioned it."

She shrugged. "Not important. What's important is ahead of us."

A force of blue-uniformed troopers was positioned at the bottom of the arched steel bridge. Each man wore a helmet, carried a nightstick, and had a holstered sidearm and a gas mask. Along the edges was Sheriff Jim Clark's posse with silvery badges affixed to their helmets. Some were standing, some were on horseback, and all brandished nightsticks or cattle prods. Sullen, hateful faces.

"John, can you swim?" Jimmy heard Hosea Williams ask John Lewis.

"No."

"I can't either," said Williams, "and I'm sure we're gonna end up in that river." He turned around to Jimmy. He had a wide face and a neatly cropped mustache. "What about you, Mr. Dean? We might *all* be taking a dip in the river." The river was a few hundred feet below.

Then he turned and led the marchers right up to the police line.

The troopers began removing their gas masks from their belts and putting them over their faces. An officer stood in front of his troops— stood right in front of Hosea Williams and John Lewis—and spoke into a loudspeaker. "You are all ordered to disperse. Go home or go back to your church. This march will not continue. You have exactly two minutes to comply."

"Major, may we have a word with you?" Williams politely asked the officer.

The major appeared not to have heard him and glared straight ahead at Jimmy. *That son of a bitch certainly knows who I am.*

The marchers and the troopers faced one another. Only the wind and the rustling of clothes could be heard. Barely a minute passed— Jimmy could feel the blood pounding in his temples like a clock— and, still staring directly at Jimmy, the major shouted, "Troopers, advance!"

Jimmy heard the distant clomping of horses, as if they had somehow dropped out of the sky, and the troopers rushed the marchers in a coordinated attack. Swinging, kneeing, kicking, beating everyone in their way. Marchers were falling all around him.

Jimmy had lost Claudia.

He had just been holding her hand.

He shouted "Claudia!" as a trooper clubbed a woman to the ground a few feet away from him *It's not her* and Jimmy could smell the trooper's cheap cologne, could smell that through the bitter dust and sweat and blood, and it was as if he was standing still in the sea as breakers of blue-uniformed, white-helmeted troopers were surging and boiling past him, stepping over bodies, rushing after the marchers, who were running, retreating, and then, only then, did Jimmy hear the howling, terrified screams of the marchers. It was as if he had been deaf for those first seconds, and he realized that none of the troopers *not one* came near him. He was a ghost. Protected. *No, it wouldn't do for Sheriff Jim Clark's men or the troopers to bloody a movie star,* and then there were *pop pop pop* sounds and the air turned hot white, frosty white, tearing white, dust and tear-gas white, and the cloud settled over Jimmy, even as he ran away from it, and his eyes burned and his throat was raw meat, and there were screaming, crying specters all around him. *"Claudia Claudia Claudia!"* Jimmy shouted, and she called him.

"James!"

He'd found her, even as he heard the whapping sound of clubs against bone, as another trooper clubbed another woman, another figure, a specter, and Jimmy shouted *Claudia!* again, but there was no answer, and he punched the trooper who had taken down the woman, pulled off the man's helmet, head-butted him, kneed him, took his nightstick, stood his place, and started swinging.

Cameras were going *click.*

Jimmy had found her, was holding her, Claudia. But how could she be so light? He carried her away from the dust and smoke and jaw-breaking screams, pulled her dragged her helped her out of the scorching biting pounding whiteness to safety.

Click. Click. Click.

Then realized he was carrying a stranger.

Click. Click. Click.

He heard a hollow crack, felt a warm numbness in the back of his head.

You're not Claudia, you're not Pier, you're not Marilyn. His thoughts faded into a mushroom-white explosion. He felt a tickling sensation all over his scalp, and as he fell through perfect whiteness, he remembered the "trick" he always used to ask his mother to perform—the egg trick—and Momma was once again gently rapping her knuckles on his head (breaking the egg), and then ever so slowly and gently, she would spread out her hand and just barely ruffle his hair, and Jimmy would shiver and squeal in disgust and delight because indeed it always felt as if a raw egg was gelatinously spreading right across his skull.

Momma . . .

TWENTY-FOUR

■

Sooner or Later

Los Angeles: May 1965

"Yeah?"

"Well, I'm glad you're back home safe and sound."

"Who the hell is this?"

A pause. "Caroline. Caroline Tuchman. Jimmy, please, don't hang up."

"Why shouldn't I?"

"Because I've got something you want."

"Yeah? Well, give it to somebody else. You had your chance, and you ran a game on me. You only get one chance, honey."

"I gave you up to Bobby for your own good, to protect you. I was trying to do the right thing."

"For my own good?"

"It wasn't a game." Then, gently, "Honey."

Ordinarily, that would have softened Jimmy, but not now, not after Selma, not after Pier. "So what do you have that you think I'd want?"

"Information."

"You want to tell me what you have or what?"

"Or what." Jimmy didn't respond. "Can I come over?" That said in a tiny, almost childish voice.

"You got something to tell me, tell me."

"Not over the phone."

Jimmy hung up the receiver. The phone rang immediately.

"Jimmy?" Silence. "I really do need to talk to you."

"Fuck off, Caroline."

"I talked to Pier a few weeks before—"

"You *what?* What the hell was she talking to *you* for?"

"We used to talk every once in a while."

"Behind my back."

"She trusted me, Jimmy. She needed to talk about her hopes and fears—and about you."

"Shit, she must have been crazy toward the end."

"I was going to get in touch with you before, but—"

"But what?"

"My own life sort of fell apart. My husband and I are separated." Silence. "I was also in the hospital."

"For what?"

"Can I come over, Jimmy?"

"What did Pier talk to you about?"

"Can I come over, Jimmy?"

CAROLINE MUST HAVE CALLED HIM FROM A NEARBY PAY PHONE BEcause the doorbell rang a few minutes later.

"You look like hell," Jimmy said as he let her into the house. He had intended to ask her about Pier immediately, but now that she was here, he didn't want to know. *Not just yet . . . not just yet. I need to breathe, I need to get my head straight, then I'll be ready, then I'll be all right.*

"Thanks." She looked around, obviously awed by the paintings and the cracked beau monde ceiling mural. "A bit over the top. I wouldn't have expected it from you and . . ."

"Pier. You can say her name." *Ask her.*

Caroline nodded, and Jimmy led her into the library.

She looked around the room and said, "Jesus Christ, you once told me that Pier collected dolls, but I had no idea. God, I've never seen anything like this."

Caroline looked hollowed out, wasted. Her hair was cut shorter than when he last saw her, and her face was thin, waiflike; she had lost a layer of softening fat and appeared anorexic. In fact, she looked like a haunted child. Yet she had aged.

"You lost your tits," Jimmy said, realizing only then how cruel that sounded.

"And the rest," Caroline said as she sat down beside him on the couch. She seemed mesmerized by the shelves of dolls, by the porcelain-white relics of the dead.

"You want a drink?" he asked. *Jesus Christ, she looks like Pier somehow.* She shook her head. "Dope?"

"No. Thanks." She glanced nervously around the room. "It's like all the dolls are watching you. Doesn't it bother you?"

"I sold the house once," Jimmy said, ignoring her question, lighting a joint, musing, nattering on. "And then when Pier and I got back together, she had to have it back. Nothing else would do, and I had to buy all the paintings back at double their value. A sheikh from Iran or Iraq or somewhere around there bought the house, and he didn't care about any of the stuff." After a beat, he said, "He just wanted to fuck over a movie star. Sound familiar?"

"I imagine you sold it to him for a good piece of change in the first place."

Jimmy laughed. "That's why he wanted to fuck me over. At least *he* had a reason."

"Stop it, Jimmy," Caroline said. "If I was smart and doing the right thing for my career, I would have published Marilyn's diary. It would have been *the* story of the year."

"So how is your career?"

"I left the *Times*."

"Yeah?"

She looked directly at him. "Okay, I was fired. When I was going through the divorce. I was acting a bit . . . out of character. I pissed a few people off, fucked up a few stories, and now I'm making more money freelancing."

"*That* sounds like bullshit."

"Okay, I'm making the same money, and I'm my own boss."

Jimmy kept the curtains drawn in the library, and the light in the room was dusty, subdued. This had become a quiet place, a reliquary, a memorial for Pier. "You know, in this light, you . . ."

"What?" Caroline asked.

"Why were you in the hospital?" Jimmy asked, quickly changing the subject.

"Because my husband . . . my ex-husband beat the hell out of me."

"Why?"

She forced herself to look Jimmy in the eye and said, "Because he found out that I was fucking Bobby."

"What?"

She chuckled darkly. "Now *you* sound like Bobby."

"Yeah, thanks." Talking to himself. "So *that's* how he got you to get the diary."

"No, nothing was going on then. I did that because—"

"Because he convinced you it was for my own good."

"And Pier's."

"Tell me about Pier," Jimmy said softly.

"Bobby is a bastard," Caroline said, seething. "When I needed just this much support"—she made a broken circle with her thumb and forefinger—"he had his numbers changed so I couldn't reach him. Just like he did with Marilyn, huh?"

"So is this why you're here, to get some phone numbers?" Bobby asked.

"No," Caroline said. "Bobby promised me a job when he became a senator. I'm good at what I do. You know that."

"Oh, yeah, sure."

She let that pass and said, "I want the job."

"What job?"

"To be his press secretary. For all that I think he's a prick, I also think he's going to be the next president."

"Yeah, and I'm going to be governor."

Caroline smiled at him, as if she knew something.

"What?" Jimmy asked. "Tell me what you were talking about with Pier. Now."

"In a minute, Jimmy. Let me get this off my chest."

"You don't have a chest."

"Fuck you, Jimmy." After a beat, Caroline continued. "Bobby and I were friends. We had an affair, that's all it was, but I never was in love with him. I thought he was sensitive and smart. My husband was a prick." She laughed. "Like Bobby, I suppose. I just needed . . . something." She sighed. "I guess I always just need something. Anyway, Ethel caught us."

"Caught you? Jesus Christ."

"In the proverbial act. Or almost. Just the same, she knows."

"You're crazy, Caroline, absolutely bug-fuck. Of course he changed his phone numbers. What the hell did you expect him to do?"

"I expected him to be a man. At least close the circle, call me and say good-bye, it was nice knowing you, bitch."

Caroline looked at him, and all Jimmy could think was that she was a ghost, the ghost of a beautiful woman he had once known, and soon, like Pier, she would disappear, just dissipate into the air and become entirely spirit. "I want the job Bobby promised me."

"So you do want his number."

"No, I want you to talk to Ethel. Bobby told me how much Ethel likes and respects you."

"What do you want me to tell her, 'Oh, Ethel, remember the broad you caught screwing your—' "

"Jimmy, if you do me a favor, I'll do you a favor."

"Caroline, just tell me about Pier, like you promised, and then go home."

"Remember the woman you were seeing in Selma?"

"What about her?" Jimmy asked warily.

"Her name is Claudia Clemson, right?"

"Yeah."

"She's big in the Black Panther Party. Very big."

"What about it?"

"Ever wonder why you don't see her anymore?"

"She told me she was going to be moving around down South trying to register voters," Jimmy said, lying to protect her.

Caroline shook her head. "She's in New York. I can give you her address, if you want it."

In New York? Jimmy shrugged. "What kind of a game are you running now?" He waited for her to give more away.

"Did you care about her? Do you care about her?"

"I don't know," Jimmy said. He had felt something for Claudia, some sort of closeness. "We didn't have enough time together." *Too close to Pier's passing away.* He made a sour face. *Passing away—as if Pier had gotten into a cab and left town. But Claudia took the pain away a little. Another ghost.*

"The scandal magazines were certainly having a heyday with it."

"Yeah. So what else is new?"

"And you being front-page news and on the covers of *Time* and *Life* for saving that woman and standing up to those troopers on Bloody Sunday. Bloody Sunday in Selma. You can't buy that kind of publicity, Jimmy. And you shaking hands with Martin Luther King when he came to visit you in the hospital. All that. Heady stuff." Then she said, "Bobby thought that your relationship with the Black Panther woman would hurt your career, and I think for all his concern with civil rights, it went against his grain for you to be seeing a Negro."

"Seeing a Negro? Who the fuck cares whether it goes against his grain or not?"

"Well, your girlfriend was in some very nasty trouble, and Bobby fixed things up so she wouldn't have to go underground like the rest of her friends did."

Caroline certainly had Jimmy's attention. Claudia had said something about having to go underground, going to Europe for a while— "*Just part of the gig, Jimmy*"—and that she would call him when it was safe. "What do you mean, 'fixed things up'?"

"Called in favors, I don't know. Whatever he does."

"Why would he bother?"

"To get you out of harm's way. That's what he told me."

"Harm's way?"

"He thought it would hurt your political career."

"I don't have a political career. I'm an actor, remember?"

"Okay, your political future." Jimmy shook his head in disbelief. "The deal was she doesn't see you." She paused. "You want to check it out, I told you I'll give you her number and address in New York."

"Bobby, you little son-of-a-bitch bastard," Jimmy whispered. "Who do you think you are?"

"Yeah, tell me about it," Caroline said.

"I'm going to break his fucking head," Jimmy said. "Manipulative bastard."

"He was only doing what Pier would have wanted. She used to call him."

"Are you going to tell me that—"

"No, Jimmy, nothing like that. But when we talked, she would tell me about how she wanted you to be more like Bobby."

"Be like Bobby? Son of a *bitch*."

"No, she wanted you to be a leader."

Jimmy laughed. "No. *She* wanted to be the star. I told her once that if she wanted to be First Lady, she'd have to marry Bobby. I guess she took me seriously."

"She wasn't interested in Bobby. Not in the least bit."

"Yeah." Even now Jimmy felt the hot juices working through his chest; he was jealous of his dead wife. *The dead can't fuck.*

"But she seemed obsessed with the idea of you being—"

"Something I'm not," Jimmy said.

"I'm not sure she was so wrong. You've been giving a lot of political speeches these days." She looked smugly at him. "Actually, you're already a politician. You've been putting your ass on the line for politics. Heady stuff, like I said, especially when you combine it with winning two Academy Awards and—"

Jimmy snorted. *Academy Awards* . . . and he thought about how he felt in crowds. In possession. Being possessed. In control. Not thinking. Being. Just being and forgetting Pier and Marilyn and maybe even Claudia a little.

"And you know that Pier really wanted to be your support person. She wanted to make you cookies and have your babies."

"You're talking about some person I never married."

"Maybe you needed to talk to her."

"Maybe I did," Jimmy said. "Okay, you done?"

"Will you talk to Ethel for me?"

"No fucking way."

"If I'm working for Bobby, I can find things out."

"Like what?"

"Like about Marilyn. Do you still think he had something to do with her death?"

"No," Jimmy said, although in truth he wasn't sure about Bobby. Sometimes it seemed impossible that Bobby could have been involved in Marilyn's murder. But sometimes Bobby treated people like they were just things.

But maybe Marilyn had just been another "thing" to Bobby. . . .

Caroline shrugged. "All right, then. I'm out of here."

"What did you talk about with Pier?"

"I told you, Jimmy."

"You know what I mean. Why?"

"She thought Bobby was right to take back the diary. She figured that saved both your lives, which it probably did, and she thought that Bobby was the way out for you."

"Way out?" Jimmy asked. "Way out of what?"

"She thought you hated acting. She said you're always unhappy when you're working, bitching at everyone, throwing things, pissing everyone off."

"I think I've done all right for someone who hates to act."

"She thought you were the most talented actor in Hollywood or New York, but she figured if you kept going, you'd end up killing yourself like you almost did in that Porsche."

"She's a good one to talk." He laughed, the bitterness obvious. "I was a kid when I had that accident, and I was probably safer in the Porsche than in Selma."

Caroline shrugged. "I'm only telling you what she told me, Jimmy.

I don't know you that well. But what you were doing in Selma was a good thing, and it was political. But it was grandstanding. I'm sure it wasn't what Pier had in mind."

"Maybe if Bobby's brother was an actor, he'd be alive today."

"Maybe he would."

"So what do you think Pier had in mind?"

"Jimmy, I don't *know*. She thought if you went into government or something, it would be better. You would be better. Happier."

"And what was she going to do? Stop acting?"

"I suppose."

"No, Pier was bullshitting you. She was good at that."

"She seemed sincere."

"Yeah, so sincere I'm sure she would have given back the Oscar she just won for *The Manchurian Candidate*."

"You're still really angry at her, aren't you?"

"For killing herself, yeah. Wouldn't you be?"

"I guess."

They sat in silence for a few minutes, each lost in thought. It was getting later, and the light coming through the curtains and blinds changed from pale white to gray, and shadows seemed to come alive in the room, the dolls shimmering, their painted eyes blinking in surprise, as if they were some sort of unnatural trompe l'oeil.

"Pier told me how much she loved you, Jimmy."

"Do you think she fucked Bobby?" Jimmy asked, obsessed.

"Is that really what's on your mind?"

Jimmy shrugged. "God, I can't believe she's gone."

"You know, Bobby really likes you."

"Why are you changing the subject?"

Caroline shrugged. "I don't think he likes anybody, but he always talks about you."

"Yeah? What does he say?"

"That you're willing to take risks. That you have courage—that's very important to Bobby, that's why he respects John Glenn and that boxer José Torres and Martin Luther King. You're all willing to die for what you believe in."

Jimmy laughed until his eyes became wet. "I don't believe in anything, and I'm not willing to die for *any* goddamn cause."

"Then what about what happened in Selma?"

Jimmy shrugged. "I was just there. It happened. It wasn't about courage. It was about not taking shit from assholes." He laughed again. "And even if I had been trying to be a hero, I saved the wrong girl. I was looking for Claudia, and I ended up dragging some poor woman I never saw before over to the side of the road."

"You and Bobby are always doing macho stuff. Bobby told me all about that. What are you guys trying to prove?" Jimmy didn't respond. "Well?"

"Always do what you're afraid to do," Jimmy said.

"Bobby always quoted Emerson at me, too."

"You asked."

"Are you going to climb that mountain with him?"

"How'd you know about that?"

"I'm still a reporter. I've still got my contacts."

"Are you interviewing me, then?" Jimmy asked.

She chuckled. "No, Jimmy, I'm not interviewing you. I'm just trying to figure it out. You keep telling me you hate Bobby, yet you've both got this . . . thing with each other."

"We don't have any *thing*," Jimmy said.

"Then what is it?"

Jimmy shrugged. "Most of the time, when I see him, it's because of Ethel. She always sets everything up."

"Why does she do that?"

"How the hell should I know? Ask her. She thinks I cheer him up or something, and it became some sort of a conspiracy between Pier and Ethel to get us together."

"I think it's more than that."

"Yeah? Like what?"

"Some sort of weird attraction, maybe because of Marilyn and all that."

Jimmy shook his head. "Like I said, I saw him for Ethel."

"Do you have any idea how fucked up that sounds?" Jimmy shrugged. "What's it between you and Ethel. Are you—"

"No. Don't even go there, Caroline."

"Maybe she's some sort of mother figure for you."

"Cut your Freudian bullshit," Jimmy said.

"You know that Art Buchwald is writing a story on you and Bobby for *The New Yorker*?"

"How the fuck would I know that?"

"He's calling it 'The Odd Couple.' "

"We'll see about that."

"So what are you going to do? Call Bobby?"

"Fuck you, Caroline." After a pause, Jimmy asked, "Do you believe Bobby had anything to do with Marilyn's death?"

"No," Caroline said firmly. "But he would have done anything for

Jack, for the family, and maybe to protect himself. I guess sometimes I think absolutely not, and at other times I think . . . maybe." She shrugged.

And Jimmy touched her breasts. Out of curiosity.

She didn't resist.

"They're still there," he said.

She smiled sadly and relaxed, leaning her head back against the couch. "Maybe I will have one of those . . . cigarettes."

Jimmy rolled a joint, lit it, and gave it to her.

TWENTY-FIVE

■

On Top of the World

MOUNT KENNEDY, CANADA: MAY 1965

The Royal Canadian Air Force helicopter pilot turned back to Bobby and shouted, "It looks like the end of the world, don't it?"

Bobby looked up, as if startled, and then went back to reading the sixth volume of Winston Churchill's *The Second World War*. He leaned against the window, holding the thick, leather-bound book on an angle to maximize the light. The other men who were going to climb Mount Kennedy with Bobby were looking out the windows and exclaiming, "Holy shit!" and "Wow, look at this!" Below were glacial valleys, enormous slides, and cascades of rock and ice and snow. The high peaks of Mounts Hubbard, Alverstone, and Kennedy were lost in cloud, and as the helicopter dipped and shook and rose over ridges and glaciers, over sheer rock faces and vertical gorges, Bobby continued to read. If he read, he could pretend he wasn't here. Although he had tried, he just couldn't look out the window. He couldn't look into that cold, vertiginous nothingness. If he looked out the window, he would feel as if he were falling, and he didn't have to see the mountain peaks and knife-sharp edges to know that they would make him want to jump, to end it all in screaming, howling fear. How the hell was he going to climb "the peak worthy of a president"?

That was the tentative title of the article he was going to write for Mel Grosvenor, the publisher of *National Geographic,* the magazine that was sponsoring this expedition. He looked over at Jim Whittaker, the leader of the seven-man expedition, and Jim nodded to him. Whittaker was tall and bony, quiet and secure. He had a long face and a hairline that had receded, leaving only a small bushy island on his high forehead. Bobby knew he'd be all right with him. Bobby and Jimmy had trained for a day in Whitehorse, an outpost in the Yukon, with Jim Whittaker and Barry Prather, the youngest member of the team. Jim and Barry had both climbed the summit of Mount Everest.

Bobby smiled at Jim, remembering the look on Jim's face when he asked Bobby what he had been doing to get in shape for the climb; Bobby had answered, "Running up and down the stairs and hollering 'help!' " It was the only time he had seen Jim scowl.

Bobby looked at Jimmy, who was sitting across from him and gazing out at the sky and mountains. Whittaker didn't seem to like Jimmy at all; they hardly spoke to each other. But Jimmy hardly spoke to anybody. Bobby figured it was about Pier, about coming to terms with her suicide. He had asked him in Whitehorse, but Jimmy just shook his head and mumbled something about being another person now.

"Hey, Jimmy, what do you think? You think it looks like the end of the world?"

Jimmy looked at Bobby, shrugged, and then went back to looking out the window.

Same old shit, Bobby told himself. *Why did I bring him along? Ethel. Christ, you'd think she was in love with the little asshole. She's always pushing him on me.* But Bobby knew that was bullshit, complete bullshit. It was good politics to bring him along, what with all the publicity Jimmy had been receiving after Bloody Sunday; Jimmy was somehow speaking to people, speaking better than Bobby ever could, *and everyone but Jim Whittaker loved him, especially the press . . . especially that cunt Caroline, who—*

Jimmy suddenly turned to Bobby and glared at him for what Bobby thought was no apparent reason. "We'll talk later," Jimmy said.

The helicopter was descending.

"There's base camp," Whittaker said, and Bobby forced himself to look.

I can do anything. I'm doing this for Jack, I'm overcoming this for Jack . . . for Jack.

Base camp was nothing more than two tents in what looked like an amphitheater of ice and snow and granite. Icefalls created eerie, grotesque shapes. The glacier looked as if blocks had been cut out of it. Bobby blinked as the carved white snow mass rose up to meet him. *I can't do this . . .*

"Base camp's at eighty-seven hundred feet," Whittaker said. "Tomorrow we go to High Camp, which is about eleven thousand five hundred feet. Then it's only twenty-five hundred feet to the top." Whittaker smiled at Bobby; whether that smile was ironic or genuine, Bobby didn't know. He repressed the urge to cross himself.

"YOU'RE ON BELAY!" WHITTAKER SHOUTED DOWN TO BOBBY. "NOW you climb."

It was a sharp, sunny day, and Whittaker's voice echoed, as if they were in a gigantic white tomb. The sky, not so far above, was a painted blue ceiling, and Bobby craned his neck to look up at the steep sixty-five-degree cliff face. If he was to get to the summit, he would have to "climb the pitch." This was it, the last and most dangerous part of the climb. Bobby was sweating. He wore a down vest and hood, rubber Korean overboots and crampons, a nylon parka and pants. He wore goggles and a face mask, and a hat; his pack weighed more than forty pounds. He carried an ice ax and a Prusik sling, which would help him should he fall into one of the seemingly bottomless crevasses.

He shivered, but that was fear; he was quaking with fear, quaking and sweating, and behind him was Jimmy, who hadn't said more than two goddamn words since they'd begun the climb. Not that Bobby was talking either. He was focused. That was the only way he was going to do this. Even now, if he looked out at the surrounding peaks wreathed in mist and cloud, he would be lost. He had only been able to come this far by taking the climb in small, discrete bits. He'd divided it into sections and counted the steps in each, concentrating only on the count, *one step, two step, three step, four,* putting everything else out of his mind; there were no crevasses, no bottomless openings, no hell mouths, no sheer falls into sharp, empty, freezing nothingness, just the count. He was thirsty from perspiring, and his lungs were giving off water vapor, which didn't help either; but this was no time for water, no time for anything but to finish climbing Jack's mountain—for Jack and Jackie. It might be time to fall and die—or to climb to the summit like a spider on the wall and plant the flag for Jack.

Helicopters were circling above to verify the event.

But whatever was going to happen—death or success—Bobby just wanted it over with. He felt dizzy looking up at Jim Whittaker, who had swung his ice ax as deep into the snow as he could, then tied a rope to it: the same 120-foot nylon rope that was tied around Bobby's waist. Behind him and below was Barry Prather, making sure that everything was tight and going according to procedure. *What the fuck am I doing here?* Bobby asked himself.

It would be Jimmy's turn to climb next.

Cold comfort.

Jim Whittaker was leaning against the ax with his chest and shoulders, using all his weight to hold it in place. If the rope slipped, Bobby would fall—and then Bobby was scrambling and hanging and crawling, pulling himself up the sheer face. He seemed to find the right toeholds and handholds by instinct.

Now he wanted to scream, not in terror, but in defiance. Defying his own overwhelming fear.

Bobby didn't use the kick steps that Jim had gouged out for him; he was just moving climbing defying, and he heard himself scream, finally letting it go; yet he was silent, silent and wordless as the glacier, quiet as the rock face; and this was it, he told himself, this was the dance, the dance with death, *oh, Jack, you'd fucking love this, wouldn't you?* and up and up, everything pure and concentrated, pure and perfect, every breath the last, fear curling and uncurling in his throat; and Bobby suddenly remembered blowing an accordion whistle at midnight on New Year's Eve, *Jack, you were there, goddamn you for dying;* and perhaps it was just the frozen white snow fear, but Bobby could swear that the rock was moving, bending, undulating; but he didn't lean into it. Jim told him that if he did, he would be at the wrong angle to climb and could easily fall. So he leaned out, out into the void, into nothingness, into death, *fuck you, death, Jack, look at me, look at me, Jack,* and Whittaker shouted, "Remember to breathe!"

Then it was Jimmy's turn, but Bobby couldn't bring himself to watch. He was exhausted. He closed his eyes and told himself, *I just want to stay right here.*

*   *   *

BOBBY WALKED TO THE RIDGE, TO THE SUMMIT, ALONE; IT WAS
only a twenty-degree incline. It was sunny and cold. The air was thin,
and Bobby stared ahead through the tunnel of a pulsing headache. He
planted the flag with the Kennedy coat of arms—three gold helmets on
a black background. He pressed a leather-bound copy of Jack's Inau-
gural Address into the hard-crusted snow. He positioned Jack's Inau-
gural Medallion in front of it, set it at an angle; his brother gazed up at
Bobby with unblinking bronze eyes. Then Bobby rested three of his
brother's *PT-109* tie clasps in the snow. He could hear Whittaker and
Jimmy and the others behind him, and he crossed himself as he spoke
to his brother in heaven, *in the name of the Father, the Son, and the
Holy Ghost, oh, Jack . . .*
      And he raised his head, splayed his legs for support, leaned forward,
and looked down. Six thousand feet below was the Lowell Glacier. He
looked out at mountains wreathed in clouds; it was a 14,000-foot drop
to the ocean, and he could see for 150 miles. He could hear the wind,
a lyre playing on the cold, translucent blue silence, and he felt a
numbing sensation work down from his groin to his toes. For an instant
he felt the terrible, crippling urge to jump, to end it all, but when that
passed, he was left with a sensation of soaring, of bliss. *Jack . . .*
      Then Jimmy and Jim Whittaker and Barry Prather were standing
beside him.
      "Can you feel it?" Bobby asked.
      "Mountaineers grow to like that feeling," Whittaker said didacti-
cally, "when they know they can handle it." But Bobby had been
speaking to Jimmy, who stared straight ahead into the cloudy blue
void.

AS THE PARTY CLIMBED DOWN THE MOUNTAIN TO THE BASE CAMP
Bobby and Jimmy trudged along together without speaking. The experienced men seemed to push the novices together, as if to protect them
by encircling them, but that wasn't enough, for no one noticed the slight
irregularity in the snow. They had been moving down an incline, all
wearing crampons; except for occasional gusts of fifty-mile-an-hour
winds, it was relatively warm. Scudding, gray-shadowed clouds filled
the sky; the mountains and ice and snow all around them were just
slightly refracted into the blue; and it was quiet but for the creaking of
the pack frames and the occasional bellyache groaning of the ice.
Bobby noticed a little hole in the snow, but the glacier was full of holes

and furrows and little winding ice forms. Jimmy was walking beside him, and suddenly Bobby was falling, sinking, and he shouted, "Whoa!" as if he were reining in a stallion, but this was no stallion; he was sinking into the snow, sinking up to his chest, falling, slipping, slipping; and then Jimmy shouted, but Bobby couldn't make out what he said; it sounded so far away. Bobby was reaching, grasping, gasping. He clawed himself out of the crevasse, which had opened up beneath him; indeed, like a hell mouth, and he saw Jimmy's clenching hand exposed a few feet away. Rolling onto solid ground, he reached for it. He pulled Jimmy up, but Jimmy was scrambling up himself, gaining purchase on the ground, even as he coughed and choked and sputtered.

The others were all around him—Whittaker; Prather; James Craig, a lawyer from British Columbia; Dee Molinar, who had welcomed them at High Camp; and Bill Allard, a *National Geographic* photographer from Minnesota—all pulling Bobby and Jimmy to safety, even though they had already pulled themselves to safety. Jimmy shrugged off the other men and carefully crawled back to the edge of the abyss. "Give us a minute, fellas," Bobby said, and he positioned himself beside Jimmy. They both looked down what had been a little hole but was now a fistula the size and shape of a Volkswagen Bug. The pit was so deep they couldn't see to the bottom.

"I didn't need your help," Jimmy said. "I had everything under control."

"The only thing that was above the surface was your hand."

"Yeah. Didn't mean nothin'. I had it under control. You didn't save my life."

"I didn't say I did."

"Good. After all this, you still afraid of heights?"

Bobby smiled, gazing down into the twilight that descended into blackness. "I don't think the climb changed anything. I didn't enjoy any of it. Henceforth I'm going to stay on the first floor of my house." He looked over at Jimmy for a reaction. When none was forthcoming, he asked, "Why have you been such a prick on this trip?"

"*I've* been a prick? What the fuck is that supposed to mean?"

"You haven't said more than ten words the whole time."

"Neither have you," Jimmy said.

Bobby nodded. "Maybe I needed to concentrate."

"Maybe I did, too."

"Yeah. Why was that?"

"Maybe I'm afraid of heights," Jimmy said, trying to cover the truth with sarcasm.

Bobby nodded, understanding. "What was all that crap you were telling me on the plane about how you're a different person now?"

"Just what it sounds like."

"Cut the shit, Jimmy."

"No, you cut the shit, Bobby. It's none of your fucking business who I am or what I do."

Bobby started crawling backward, away from the crevasse.

"Why did you want me to make this climb with you?" Jimmy asked.

Bobby stopped where he was, and remaining on his hands and knees, he stared hard at the cake-frosting snow beneath him. "Because you . . . know."

"Know what?"

"What it feels like to lose everything."

"You haven't lost everything," Jimmy said, his voice flat.

"No. But it feels that way. It will never be the same."

Jimmy stood up at the edge of the crevasse, as if daring the earth to swallow him.

"Anyway," Bobby continued, "I couldn't very well ask Jackie to climb a mountain. She'd still be looking for the elevator." The other guys laughed at that, but it was none of their business, and Bobby gave them a cold look. Surprised, they turned away and began to talk among themselves, but Bobby said, "Gentlemen, shall we continue the descent?"

JIMMY DIDN'T REALLY KNOW HOW THE FISTFIGHT BEGAN, NOR DID he care. It was inevitable. Bobby was cruising for it, had been ever since he shoved his Catholic nose into Jimmy's personal affairs. Breaking him up with Claudia was the last straw. "Nobody fucks with me like that, and you, you son of a bitch, you had something to do with Marilyn that night, I don't give a shit what you say and how much you cover it up with money and bullshit."

"This isn't the time or the place," Bobby said.

"No? Is that what your mommy taught you?"

The other men standing around outside the supply tent at Base Camp, the high walls of the glacier glittering in the late-afternoon sunshine, the glacier a natural amphitheater for the gods who would deign to sit in frozen comfort and watch the foolishness of tiny mortals. Jimmy and Bobby's voices echoing, but this wasn't the time yet for humiliation. Jimmy had already taken a swing at Bobby. A right hook.

Bobby ducked reflexively and parried with a sharp punch that caught Jimmy on the chin.

Jimmy pulled Bobby to the ground, taking the punches while doing so, and then he was inside, choking Bobby, smashing the air out of him, pressing him into the snow. *I'll kill him now, kill him for what he did to Marilyn and Pier. You fucked Pier, you bastard, I know you did. And I know what you did to Claudia, I know all about your deal with her, and I know how you turned Pier against me. You're a snake, Bobby, a thin and wiry snake.* And Bobby pulled away from Jimmy. Bobby coughed and wheezed and caught his breath. The two men-boys stood up, trying to stare each other down, weaving warily back and forth in front of each other.

"So this is the new Jimmy, you hold everything in, you don't say word one, and then you try to kill people. Oh, that's good, Jimmy. That's a good new look for you." Bobby turned and shouted at the other men, "Get out of my sight! This is private."

"You fucked Pier, didn't you, Bobby?" Jimmy said.

"What? You dumb, stupid bastard, of course I didn't."

"No, of course," Jimmy said sarcastically, "you would *never* fuck a friend's wife."

"Well, I didn't fuck *your* wife," Bobby said, his ragged breath visible in the cold air. "Pier used to call me just to talk, that's all, and it was always about you."

"About me? Fuck you, Bobby."

"She wanted more for you."

"More than what?"

"What?" Bobby turned his head, as if the answer could be found in the distant mountains. "I don't know, Jimmy, she—"

"She didn't want me to be an actor, did she? She wanted me to be . . . you." He said that with such disgust that Bobby actually took a step back.

"No, she didn't want you to be me."

"Then what?"

"She was always asking me what I thought."

"About me?" Jimmy asked. "She wanted to know what you thought about me?"

"Yes, Jimmy, and yes, she wanted you to get out of acting. She said it was eating you up alive."

"So if I became like you, I'd be fine, right? No more eating myself up alive, just untold happiness every day, right?"

"How the fuck should I know? I'm not a psychiatrist. She told me about a dream you always had about your mother, and she thought—"

"She shouldn't have been telling you *anything*. You know what she wanted? She wanted to get me out of the way. She didn't want any competition. She wanted to be the star. She didn't want to be the star's wife, and that's what she was going to be, that's why—" Jimmy caught himself. *Oh, God, no, I can't talk about her like that. But she was like that. No, she wasn't.* Jimmy brought himself under control. "You fuck with people's lives, Bobby. Like you did with Marilyn. Like you did with Pier. But you won't fuck with mine." He spoke in a low voice. "Now tell me why you bought off Claudia. Did you want her, is that it?"

"No, Jimmy," Bobby said. "She was in trouble. I helped her out."

"So you could take her from me, like you did Marilyn."

"You know better than that, better than to even say that." There was a meanness in Bobby's face now, and he watched Jimmy through cold, controlled eyes.

Jimmy was determined to do the same, *but, no, I can't be like Bobby, no, no way . . . Still and all,* Jimmy told himself, *the new me is calm. Not cold. Calm. (I'm going to break his fucking face.)*

"I made a promise to Pier," Bobby continued. Jimmy waited, holding his breath. "I promised her I'd look out for you."

"Like I need you to look out for me," Jimmy said.

"I don't break my word," Bobby said.

"Oh, how manly, and you promised her to fuck up any relationship I happen to be involved in, is that it?"

"I did Claudia a favor. I kept her out of jail. Isn't that enough for you, Jimmy, or would you have preferred it if I let the authorities lock her up?"

"Knowing you, you engineered the whole thing," Jimmy said. "And what about the deal that she never call me again?"

"That wasn't in the deal."

"You're a liar, Bobby."

"You should keep better company."

"What's that supposed to mean?"

"Caroline is a manipulative bitch. That's why she's out of my life. Now she's wheedling her way into yours. Doesn't that give you just a little pause?"

"You're the manipulative bitch," Jimmy said.

"Wrong sex."

"Why did you stop Claudia from seeing me?"

"I thought you were supposed to be mourning Pier."

Jimmy went for Bobby, but Bobby deftly stepped out of the way; and Jimmy slipped. "I'm sorry," Bobby said. "That remark was out of order. Claudia is trouble. She's going to end up with a bullet in her head."

"Answer my question, Bobby."

"Because she's a nigger, because she'll fuck you up, because I promised Pier to—"

"That's bullshit," Jimmy said, and he went for Bobby again. This time they both went down into the snow, wrestling, rolling down a slope, punching and pulling at each other. "You fucked her, didn't you, you shanty-Irish prick?"

"Are you talking about Pier like that?" Bobby asked, gasping for breath, as if his words were solidifying, freezing in his lungs. "Are you fucking Ethel? You're talking on the phone with her every two minutes. You took her to the goddamn Santa Monica pier. You didn't think I knew about that, did you? Did you?" He was choking Jimmy, but Jimmy broke his hold.

Jimmy coughed and caught his breath. "No. I never touched Ethel."

"And I never touched Pier." After a pause, Bobby said, "Get rid of Caroline. She's poison."

"Fuck you, Bobby." Jimmy tried to push Bobby away from him, but Bobby was heavier than he looked; he was a dead weight on top of Jimmy.

"Say uncle, and I'll let you up."

That broke the tension, and Jimmy couldn't help himself. He started laughing, then Bobby did, too. "Well?"

"Uncle."

"So *that's* the new Jimmy," Bobby said, releasing him.

"What else did Pier tell you?"

"How much she loved you. What she wanted for you."

"That's so much bullshit, and you know it, Bobby."

"No, it's not, Jimmy. I swear on Jack's soul."

That gave Jimmy pause. He said, "I have Claudia's phone number in New York."

"So?"

"So all your Machiavellian bullshit was for nothing."

"My conscience is clear. I paid my debt to Pier's memory. I'm finished. You're the big movie star."

"Yeah, and she's dead," Jimmy said, feeling suddenly cold and weak and tired.

"Are you going to call her?"

"Not unless you've got a Ouija board."

"I meant Claudia."

Jimmy said yes, but he knew he wasn't going to call her. Bobby just shrugged, as if he knew, too. But Bobby was right about one thing: there needed to be changes. There were going to be changes.

TWENTY-SIX

■

Inversions

LOS ANGELES, SEPTEMBER 1965–JUNE 1966

Jimmy never called Claudia, but four months after his fistfight with Bobby—on the anniversary of Pier's suicide—he did call Caroline.

After his house was broken into, he virtually moved in with her.

The paparazzi were dogging him, and they were much worse than the fans. Caroline lived in a white stucco house in Woodland Hills with two dogs, an Abyssinian cat, and a canary named Perky that belonged to her daughter. Her daughter lived with her father in Rio de Janeiro. Caroline never talked about Liana, except to say that she was coming home for her summer vacation.

But it was already summer.

"If goddamn Marty would just keep his big fat mouth shut and stop talking to the press," Jimmy said. He and Caroline were sitting by her pool. Jimmy could hear the distant sound of traffic whooshing by, and the sky-blue water in the tiled, kidney-shaped pool was perfectly still. Woodland Hills wasn't the leafy suburbs, but it was nice and the house reminded him of Marilyn's white hacienda. He felt safe here, cozy, comfortable. He sipped his beer and felt the sun baking him, but his nose and jaw still ached. At least the doctor had removed the bandages.

"Well, what did you expect?" Caroline asked. "You pissed him off. You used him."

"I used *him?*"

"Probably for the last ten years. He's in love with you, and you treat him like shit."

"What, did he talk to you, too?" Jimmy asked.

"Don't use that tone with me, Jimmy. Yeah, he talked to me. I guess I'm just the kind of girl that people like to talk to." She looked at him coquettishly, and he couldn't help but grin back at her.

"Next thing he'll be doing is talking to the sleaze gossip rags."

"So what?" Caroline leaned toward him. Her sun-bleached brown hair was short, and she had brushed it back from her sharp, intense face. She wore black leotards and a tie-dyed T-shirt and looked like a rather beautiful young boy.

Jimmy turned away from her. "You do care," she said. "This is a new Jimmy. Who are you now, Jimmy?"

"What the hell kind of question is that to ask?"

She shrugged but kept eye contact with him until he shifted his gaze. "It's a legitimate question. You're up to something, whether you recognize it or not, and I'd bet the former."

"The former what?"

"That you know exactly what you're doing."

"I think you're completely full of shit, Caroline."

"All this new you is for Pier, isn't it?"

"Oh, good, I'm shacking up with a pop psychologist."

"You're not shacking up with me, Jimmy. You're hiding out. Do you want to shack up with me?"

"Maybe if you started eating properly."

She smiled wistfully, as if she'd just thought of something sad. "Then we should shack up at your place. I always fancied a grand mansion."

"You really are crazy."

"You've got to go back sometime. You've got to face the press—and your fans."

"I *am* facing the press," Jimmy said.

She giggled and reached out to touch his face where he was bruised. Jimmy didn't pull away. "It looks worse than it is," she said, gently grazing his cheek with her index finger, as if she were spreading purple ink on his face. He pulled on the collar of her T-shirt and looked down at her breasts.

"They used to be bigger," Jimmy said.

She shrugged, still staring at him. "So you keep telling me." Then, after a beat: "I know an agency that will provide you with a bodyguard, someone discreet and savvy, someone you wouldn't mind having around."

"I don't *need* a fucking bodyguard," he said, pulling away from her. He seemed to shrink into the cushioned deck lounger.

"The fans cut through a barbed-wire fence to get to you," Caroline said. "Doesn't that tell you something?"

"It was *your* idea to put the fence up. I didn't have half as much trouble before that."

"No, you just had the fans in to watch us fuck," Caroline said.

"Okay, I'll cop to that. That was my fault. I forgot and left the door unlocked, and they just walked in. But they didn't break in. There's a difference." Jimmy's face tightened. "Okay, so the fans are always hanging around. They hang around Elvis just the same."

"Elvis always had a fence," Caroline said. "And he's got his own mini-Mafia to protect him."

"Maybe the fans are a pain in the ass, but I got along just fine by being a regular guy with them."

"You were never a regular guy. You ignored them. You're still trying to pretend they don't exist."

"No, I don't. I've always talked to them, and asked them to respect my privacy. Most of the time it works."

Caroline guffawed.

"That's not a becoming laugh," Jimmy said. "Anyway, maybe the fans did steal my gargoyles off the roof, but I can tell you it wasn't fans who broke into the house this last time."

"Sure as hell seems like it to me."

"The assholes that broke in—that smashed everything up before I could punch them out—were—"

"You didn't exactly punch them out, Jimmy," she said, looking at his bruised face.

"Yeah? Well, I tried. But there were three of them and one of me. And fuck you, too, Caroline." Caroline smiled. "They were geeks, clean-cut DeMolay and Young Republicans, and I wouldn't put *anything* past Ronnie Reagan."

"DeMolay?"

Jimmy shook his head impatiently. "It's part of the Masons, only for stalwart youth."

Caroline laughed at that, then said, "You can't really believe that Reagan would have anything to do with that. He's much too much the goody-goody."

"He's involved with a nasty bunch of fascists. They're all John Birch crackpots, but Ron has the happy faculty of never knowing what's going on. He just ignores anything that's not nice. Nothing untoward ever happens around Ron. Everyone else might get dirty, but not Ron. I know, I worked with him a few times."

"You're so full of shit, Jimmy."

"Yeah, and I was full of shit about Marilyn, too, wasn't I?"

"I don't know about Marilyn, but I do know that you can't pretend you're just Mr. Average Joe. You need protection, especially now that you're working with the Brown campaign. All your connections with the civil-rights movement and the Berkeley people make you a—"

"Listen to yourself, Caroline. You sound like a Republican."

"How do you know I'm not? And what's with all this stuff, anyway?"

"What do you mean?"

"You know exactly what I mean. You're an *actor*, Jimmy. What's all this bullshit with politics and all these half-assed radical movements?"

"What, you going to vote for Reagan?"

"What if I was? Are you the new voice of America? Is that your new delusion?"

"Just fuck off, Caroline," Jimmy said, his voice hard and nasty.

"Jimmy, is this about Bobby?"

"No, it's about me. Reagan's in politics because he sucked as an actor. But as a politician, he's going to waste Brown. And he's going to take all his aphorisms and that great big toothy smile of his right into the governor's mansion."

"I don't think so, not in a million years. But so what if he does?"

"I'm going to stop him."

"Why, Jimmy? You're a wonderful actor; he's not. What the hell have you got to prove to Bobby? You already climbed his goddamn mountain."

"I don't have anything to prove to Bobby. I told you, it's what I've got to prove to myself."

"What? That you can help a burned-out politician stay in office?"

"That I can do something that's real," Jimmy said, struggling to remember his recurring dream of his mother—

His mother stands beside her grave, cold and damp, welcoming him, reaching out to him. But she's changed. She won't take him anymore. Won't lead him down into the damp, slippery, comforting soil of memory and death. Jimmy knows she would have loved to see him become an actor, but that's all changed. She's become something else. Something rock hard and cold. Something that preys upon him, ever demanding, and for one shocking, vertiginous instant, he realizes that he can't remember her face.

"Although Pat Brown might act like an asshole sometimes," Jimmy said, closing his mind to everything but the here and now, "he still built the best state university in the country, and he built the water system that brings in two billion gallons of water a day, and he got fair-housing legislation passed, and expanded welfare benefits, and—"

"All right, Jimmy, all right. Jesus, you sound more like a politician than Brown does."

Jimmy grinned at her. Although his skin was flushed from the sun, he shivered. But the sun was life; it was warm, protecting; and he could feel it baking into him again, baking in its warmth, baking out his poisonous dreams and memories. If he stayed outside much longer, he would begin to burn. He didn't care.

"Is this all an act?" Caroline asked.

"I told you. This is real."

"And what do you get out of it?"

"Nothing. That's why it's real."

"You've become a true believer, haven't you? You believe in the system."

"Screw you, Caroline."

"Well, don't you?"

Jimmy paused and said, "I believe things can be changed. Maybe. But that doesn't make me a true believer."

"And what about your acting and directing?" Caroline asked.

"What about it?"

"Are you going to do the new film with Nick?"

"What new film?"

"The one about Jack Kerouac's brother."

"I don't know," Jimmy said evasively.

"Nick says you're holding everything up, that you won't give him an answer. Your friend Kerouac's been on a monthlong bender. Is that how you take care of your friends?"

"I can't believe that Nick is talking to you about this. What the hell did you do, sign up as his agent?"

"He's not doing as well as you are, Jimmy."

"He doesn't need me. He can get the funding in Europe."

"You could get it here."

"What do you get out of this?" Jimmy asked.

She laughed. "You."

Jimmy started to laugh, then realized she meant it.

"And if you want to be the next Ronald Reagan, I'll be *your* press secretary."

"Go to hell, Caroline."

Caroline moved over to straddle Jimmy on his plastic lounger, her legs pulled up on either side of him, her bottom pressing against his crotch.

"Cut it out," Jimmy said, laughing.

"And if you're going to be a movie star, I'll be your press secretary."

"I *am* a movie star, and I thought you were going to be Bobby's press secretary."

"You screwed that up for me."

"I think Pat Brown would have a better shot if you were working for him," Jimmy said.

"But I'm working for *you*." She kept moving against him until he became excited and pulled her down on top of him. She was light and fragile, a bony angel. She raised her haunches to allow him to peel down her leotards and panties. She unbuckled his belt and unzipped his fly, and then he was inside her. Her warmth inside, the sun outside, warm in, warm out, in out, in out; and they came together quietly.

"I guess I should call Nick," Jimmy said distractedly. He needed a cigarette.

"Yeah, and?"

"Why are you so hot for me to do this film? It's going to net about minus five cents."

"Because it could be an important film. I think it might be."

"Nick gave you the script, didn't he?" That more a statement than a question.

"No," Caroline said. "Jack gave it to me."

"I'm fucking surrounded."

"I guess that's literally true." And as they laughed, Jimmy slipped out of her. She made a discontented noise, as if he'd hurt her feelings.

"How's it going to look if I'm always surrounded with goons?" Jimmy asked.

"What? What the hell are you talking about?"

"What you said earlier—that you know somebody that can get me some . . . protection."

Caroline shook her head and with difficulty disengaged herself from Jimmy. "You know, Jimmy, a politician thinks in straight lines. You're definitely an actor: you think sideways."

"It's going to look like I'm afraid, that's what."

"So?"

"I'm not afraid, that's why."

"Okay, you're not afraid. Then go back to Sherman Oaks by yourself because *I'm* afraid."

"I didn't invite you."

"Well then piss off."

"Maybe if the bodyguard was someone who didn't look conspicuous," Jimmy said.

"That's better," Caroline said.

"And you can set it up?"

Caroline nodded. "Guy by the name of Budd Schaap has an agency. I've done Budd a couple of favors. He owes me, or owed me."

"That name rings a bell," Jimmy said.

"He's a detective . . . with a lot of connections." After a pause, Caroline said, "He bugged your house."

"He *what?*"

"When Marilyn was alive."

"Why didn't you ever tell me this?" Jimmy asked, enraged.

"Here, have a cigarette," Caroline said, handing him her pack of Salems. "I didn't tell you because I couldn't. And I didn't owe you that."

"You sure as hell do now."

"No, Jimmy, I don't owe you shit. If anything, you owe me, for your life." After fumbling for a cigarette, she said, "Anyway, it was no big deal. He was hired by Joe DiMaggio."

"Now I remember who he is," Jimmy said. "DiMaggio hired him to follow Marilyn, and he followed me, too. He's a scumbag."

"He's the best detective in the business," Caroline said.

"I meant DiMaggio."

"DiMaggio was just a jealous husband. He loved Marilyn—probably more than you did—and wanted to find out what you two were up to. It was innocent, or as innocent as that kind of sleazy shit can get."

Jimmy could only nod. Then he asked, "I'm still being bugged, aren't I?"

"No, not anymore. I asked Budd to clean the place up, which he did. He told me to stay away from you and not to ask too many questions."

"Questions about what?"

"About anything."

"Cut the shit, Caroline. Tell me what you know."

"He pulled his wires three years ago."

"Yeah . . . and?"

"There were other wires in the house."

"This last time, when you asked him to check, what did he find?"

She shrugged. "He told me he found wires and tore them out. That's all I know."

"Who was bugging me?"

"He couldn't tell me."

"You mean he *wouldn't* tell you. But he knows, doesn't he?"

"I think he knows something, a little, which is why he warned me about you," Caroline said.

"I can't believe you didn't say anything," Jimmy said.

"It was in confidence. It could have ruined his career."

"So what's different now?"

"You . . . and me, but maybe down the line he might talk to me. I don't think he'll tell me who was involved, but he might tell me who wasn't."

"That doesn't make any sense."

"That's the closest we're going to get, Jimmy."

"How much does he want?"

"Doesn't work like that," Caroline said. "And if you said anything to anybody . . ."

"What?"

"I think he could do us both a lot of damage."

"He'll blackmail me, that's what you're trying to tell me."

"No, I didn't say that. He's not like that. He's honest and has a good reputation. He doesn't reveal confidences; that's how he stays in business."

"Well, he sure as hell revealed confidences to you."

"I told you, he owed me, and he knows he can trust me. In a way, I'm in the business. I hope I can trust you."

"Don't turn this around on me," Jimmy said, trying to think back, trying to think things through. *Oh, God, Marilyn, they were after you, not only DiMaggio, but—*

"I did ask him one thing," Caroline said. "I asked him if Bobby had a tap on you."

"And?"

"He told me he doesn't think so."

"Doesn't *think* so?"

Caroline shrugged and crushed her filtered cigarette into a metal ashtray. She had been chain-smoking. "That's all I got, Jimmy. I'm guessing it was about Marilyn, her closeness with Jack and Bobby. It could have been Hoover, the Mafia, or the CIA—"

"Or Bobby," Jimmy said.

"Hoover and Bobby hated each other. I don't think the FBI was working for Bobby."

"So why was that shit still in my house?"

"With your involvement with King and Claudia and all the Berkeley business? Why would they take it out? Shit, I'm sure Hoover considers you one of Bobby's close cronies, and I'm sure Bobby's under surveillance." Jimmy nodded, numbed. "Budd told me that Martin Luther King is all wired up," Caroline said. "The FBI is out to get him any way they can. Hoover hates his guts. I can vouch for that myself because one of my colleagues, a dear friend, was offered photographs of King screwing someone who wasn't his wife."

"So? What does that prove?"

"The guy that offered the photographs was an FBI informant. I know who he is. So we need to watch your ass around certain people, Jimmy."

"And what's this *we* shit, anyway?" Jimmy asked.

"Oh, fuck you, Jimmy. Why don't you just get out of my life? I know I called you way back then, you didn't call me, so I've got no right to expect you to act like a human being. God forbid that someone show any vulnerability in front of you. Oh, no, only *you* can be vulnerable." Caroline turned away from him, and as Jimmy glimpsed her face, in motion, that angry flick of the hair, just like Pier . . . just like Pier.

"Pier, I'm sorry," Jimmy said, then catching himself, he said, "Oh, God, Caroline, I'm sorry. I didn't mean—"

"No, Jimmy, that's exactly what you mean. You need a substitute for Pier, that's fine. Go find one. It ain't me, though. Collect your things and get out of here. Be a regular guy to your fans, but I'm telling you now"—she faced him, her face hard and closed to him, her hands trembling—"you ever breathe a word about what I just told you, you ask any questions that get back to Budd, and your ass is grass. You might not give a shit about me, but this time you really are vulnerable, I can tell you that."

"So you do know something."

"Give it up, Jimmy. I told you what I know. You've got everything. Now get out."

"Well, I guess you got your story."

"You bastard," she said. "You stupid bastard."

She stood on the edge of the pool, looking into the water, and Jimmy remembered an argument he once had with Pier, how vulnerable she looked, how alone. He walked over to her, put his arms around her, and said, "I'm sorry, Caroline. It won't ever happen again. I promise. I don't want to lose you."

"Yeah," Caroline said, standing still and stiff and fragile, feeling his erection pressing against her. "Yeah . . ."

She smelled like Pier.

She looked like Pier.

As Jimmy held her tenderly, gingerly, he looked down into the perfect turquoise water and thought of Pier's dolls. "I love you, Caroline."

JIMMY HAD ANOTHER FENCE INSTALLED AROUND HIS HOUSE, THIS one extending right to the edge of the road; and one of Budd Schaap's vendors installed the best surveillance equipment money could buy. Budd vetted the bodyguards; he insisted that Jimmy needed not one but two. Jay and George. Both were skinny. Caroline thought they resembled the "before" photographs in the old Charles Atlas advertisements. They were wiry and incredibly strong (as Jimmy found out when he wrestled them); they knew karate and other arcane Asian fighting techniques; they were licensed to carry sidearms; and, as Budd had promised, they were nice guys "who blended into the woodwork."

Jimmy fired them after a month.

He just couldn't stand having them around. He had argument after argument with Caroline. "It changes all the dynamics," he said.

Later, as a sop to her, he hired Jay back as a "doorman," and used George only when needed, when they attended openings and galas. But Caroline won. It took a few weeks, but Jimmy noticed that George was always nearby, hanging around, within reach, but never in the house. Jimmy thought of Jay and George as well-trained guard dogs. He could live with that.

Pets weren't allowed into the house.

IT WAS ONE BIG HAPPY FAMILY.

Jay and George kept out of Jimmy's way and did their jobs, and Caroline started to gain weight and handle Pat Brown's press relations. Determined to show Jimmy what she could do, she threw herself into the campaign; and Jimmy felt an odd, quiet bliss being with Caroline. He was settled, in a way he had never been with Pier. He could spend the days and nights with Caroline and not feel cornered or claustrophobic, and he imagined that he was quietly and securely in love with her. It was like finding Pier, another Pier, another dark, smart beauty with a mercurial temperament. Another chance.

But he had to admit he was getting tired of Pat Brown, tired of Brown's baby kissing and insincere glad-handing, tired of his gruff humor and shallow philosophizing; but mostly Jimmy was tired of being involved in a campaign with a governor whose apparatchiki had convinced him he was winning when he was losing. None of them could see how strong the new conservative movement was and how estranged voters—and especially traditional labor Democrats—were from Brown's liberal politics. And if Pat called him "another actor like that Reagan" just one more time . . .

Caroline was right: he should be focusing on his real work, on films and perhaps some Broadway or Off Broadway theater. He should be acting and directing, and he should be in Rome with Nick Ray and Jack Kerouac finalizing the deal with their European consortium; but no, he told himself, he was *supposed* to be putting together financing right here. He had also decided to do a film for Warners called *Cool Hand Luke;* he would be the star, a convict who dies but remains true to himself. He would codirect with Nick, and Stewart Sterns, who had written the script for *Rebel,* would be brought on as first writer. Dick Clayton negotiated a double-film deal with Warners; they would also do Marty's *California Beach Red.* That should alleviate some of Marty's anger—and Jimmy's guilt. Nick would direct; Jimmy would star.

Jimmy needed a film that would give him the adulation he had received for *The Hustler, Hud,* and *The Enemy Within.* Dick Clayton had warned him time and again that he was going to lose his position as an A-line actor if he kept up "that political shit." He was probably right. It had started off as a romance but had become more like a one-night stand, Jimmy thought—or, perhaps, a series of one-night stands.

TUESDAY NIGHT, JUNE 14, 1966, NOT EXACTLY BLISS.

George was driving the Rolls. He wore a single-breasted dark blue wool suit, starched white shirt, and paisley tie. He looked more like an account executive than a chauffeur—or a bodyguard. The only thing that might give him away was a hairline scar that ran from the back edge of his jaw down his neck. Whenever Jimmy asked him what had happened, he would laugh and say, "I'm a fan. It's a JAMESDEAN."

But George wasn't laughing. He was staring straight ahead and concentrating on the bumper-to-bumper freeway traffic. Horns were blaring, their noise muted and softened inside the car's cushioned interior.

They were on their way to meet Bobby at yet another rally for Pat Brown.

"You had no right," Jimmy said to Caroline, his voice cold with anger.

"How many times do you want to go over this?" Caroline asked. "You want me out? George can drop you off and take me back to your place. I'll pack. I still have a home of my own, thank God."

"You had no right," Jimmy insisted.

"Tell me, Jimmy. When were you planning on getting rid of Pier's thousand and one dolls? When you're eighty-five?"

"She was *my* wife. It's *my* house. You have no right to—"

"To what? Redecorate?" Her lips curled into a very slight smile, but Jimmy didn't respond. He was staring hard into some lonely, private, unprotected space in his head, into the bright, pooling memories of Pier. *The dolls were Pier . . .*

"It was a test, Jimmy," Caroline said in a voice little louder than a whisper, "and you failed it. Or I failed it, more to the point. I meant no disrespect to Pier, but it was time. *I'm* living with you now. Pier will always be with you, Jimmy, but you can't keep *me* in a mausoleum. I figured it was Pier or me. Well, you've made your choice, and you've made it very obvious." She laughed and lit a cigarette. "But I must confess, I didn't expect you to lock yourself in the bedroom all day."

"I needed to think."

"That was a rather feminine thing to do."

"Thinking?"

"Cut it out, Jimmy. You know what I mean."

"I was just revealing my feminine side to you."

Caroline laughed again, and Jimmy smiled. "The dolls are safe," Caroline said, almost in a whisper. "They're packed away safe."

"Give them to charity," Jimmy said as George pulled into the lane reserved for VIP's behind the Pritchard Vale Industrial College Auditorium. The streets around the auditorium were jammed with people jostling to get one foot closer to their destination. Car horns blared; the air was blue with exhaust fumes. There were police on horses and on foot, police lines to control the crowds, and police with white gloves and shoulder sashes directing the jammed-up traffic on every corner. Jimmy looked out the window as if they were submerged in the sea and he was looking out into the watery purple-blue distance.

George buzzed down his window, and a defiling cacophony of noise blew into the car's cabin. George showed a tall, thin policeman a card, and the policeman nodded respectfully to Jimmy and said, "There's a reserved space near the side door marked DELIVERY. The guard will show you in."

The window sighing shut, the car in slow motion, Jimmy was caught, revealed, and suddenly, inexplicably frightened. "You're right about the dolls. They needed to be . . . put to rest."

Caroline looked at him curiously and then nodded. "I love you, Jimmy."

Jimmy smiled. "You're getting fat."

Inside the plush, secure casket of the gunmetal black Phantom V Rolls-Royce, Caroline leaned against him, gazing at him, possessing him.

Bliss . . .

THE GUARD LED THEM INTO THE GREENROOM, WHERE PAT WAS holding forth to Bobby Kennedy and the aides, both Bobby's and his own. Everyone wore an I'M FOR BROWN button that had a picture of Brown's rather flat, pugnacious face, the nose wide and fleshy, widow's peaks of brilliantine-slick hair, and heavy black-framed glasses. The walls of the claustrophobic room were plastered with GOVERNOR BROWN SPEAKS TO THE FUTURE posters: pictures of a smiling Brown holding a smiling baby, presumably not his own. There was a distant thundering in the soundproofed room—the ocean outside and, in the auditorium, the crowd.

"Hey, Jimmy, you're late," Brown said in a nagging voice, but he was smiling. "Caroline, where were you when I needed you? We got a mob of press out there, and they need sorting."

"Isn't Sheila supposed to be doing that?" Caroline asked, and a thin, pretty, but weedy-looking woman with overly bleached and coiffed hair looked daggers at her.

Bobby looked at Jimmy, breaking away from his huddle with Brown and the others.

"Everything's being taken care of," Sheila said to Caroline, then smiled at Jimmy, her head and perfectly even, capped teeth and rock-solid coiffure bobbing, as if she were nodding to everyone. "But Pat is just a natural sweetie and doesn't like to leave anyone out, does he?" she said, as she pressed his hand and twitched her nose at him; but she had become just slightly too old to be pert. Nevertheless, Brown gave her a very close hug.

"Hullo, Jimmy," Bobby said. "Uh, hullo, Caroline." He looked tired, dragged-out. His natural cowlick had defeated his comb. Wearing a linen jacket and white slacks that accentuated his tan, he looked more Hollywood than Old Boston. "Haven't heard from you," he said to Jimmy. "I called a few times. Didn't you get my messages?"

"I've been . . . it's been really crazy lately," Jimmy said, flushing with embarrassment and wondering why. *Why should I give a shit?*

Bobby glanced at Caroline, then Jimmy. "I hear you two are an item."

"You shouldn't listen to gossip, Bobby," Caroline said.

"Yes, he should," Jimmy said. "Is that a problem?" That said aggressively, the old Jimmy, the thirty-five-year-old Jimmy still pretending to be nineteen.

Caroline giggled nervously, and Bobby looked away from them for an instant, then asked, "Why should that be a problem?" He smiled at Caroline and said to Jimmy, "You need someone to mend your pants and straighten you out?"

"I don't mend pants, Bobby."

"We should talk some business down the line, Caroline."

Jimmy stiffened, and Bobby said, "I mean political business. You've been doing terrific work for Pat."

It was as if Brown had preternatural hearing ability because he suddenly appeared at Bobby's elbow, saying, "It's time, Bobby . . . and Jimmy." He hung possessively close to Bobby. "Bobby, you know how much I appreciate this, how important it is to me and the campaign—and the great state of California."

Bobby laughed and said, "Save it for the podium, Pat."

"Well, let's give the crowd what they want," Brown said, but he seemed to lack his usual enthusiasm; he normally had a ruddy, rather florid complexion, but just now he looked pale, pasty-faced, and sweaty, as if he was nervous about going onstage.

"You go out first, Pat," Bobby said. "I need to confer for just a minute with Jimmy. "You're the one they want. You're the one they're shouting for."

The echoing, repetitive sounds of *"Pat Pat Pat, we want Pat!"* could be heard, crescendos of voices accompanied by stomping feet. All of that orchestrated.

"No, no, Bob," Brown insisted. "It's you they want to see—and Jimmy, of course."

"They see enough of me," Jimmy said.

"Just a few minutes," Bobby said impatiently. He was used to getting his own way and brooked little argument.

Brown's advisors were bunched around them now, and Sheila was tugging at him, ready to go out. The shouts and calls for Brown were getting louder and louder.

"Okay," Brown said to Bobby. "But they want you, they've come here to see you. I'm just some of the icing stuck on the cake." He laughed at that, obviously not able to believe it, although it was absolutely true. He tapped Caroline to come along, and after a beat and the rustle of polyester, linen, and chintz, Jimmy and Bobby were alone. A series of Pat Browns gazed out at them from the walls, Pat Brown the baby kisser, nicknamed "the Giant Killer" because he was popular—because he had been elected for two terms and had beaten two of the Republican Party's Goliaths: Bill Knowland, the Senate minority whip, and former vice president Dick Nixon.

"Do you think Pat looks okay?" Jimmy asked Bobby.

Bobby shrugged. "I don't know. He looks like . . . himself."

"I think he looks sick," Jimmy said, "but Caroline will look after him."

"His wife can do that."

"I didn't see her."

Again Bobby shrugged. "She's around, someplace. Maybe not. I can't remember."

"You wanted to talk to me?" Jimmy asked, feeling awkward and embarrassed, and yet he was happy to see Bobby. Now that they were together, alone, he felt the old bond that always made him uncomfortable, the bond of pain and loneliness. Yet the irony was that he never felt lonely around Bobby. Although he felt warm, comfortable, loving, secure, and positive around Caroline . . . even with all those feelings, he was still hollow. Caroline had probably experienced as much pain as he had—as much pain as anybody—but she couldn't fill him up. She was beautiful, comforting, blissful anesthetic; while selfish, obsessed, condescending Bobby—blinded-by-himself Bobby—was just as hollow as Jimmy. As Bobby had said when they drove together to Northampton, Massachusetts, to see his brother Ted after his plane crash: "It takes one to know one, Jimmy."

Mirroring Jimmy, Bobby, too, looked uncomfortable. "I called because we were having a party, and Ethel and I hoped you'd come out to Hickory Hill as our guest—with Caroline, of course."

"You told me she was a manipulative bitch, remember?"

Bobby smiled. "Yeah, so what's your point?"

Jimmy grinned but turned away.

"I heard you weren't going to be involved in Pat's campaign," Bobby said.

"Where'd you hear that?"

"I have my ways."

Jimmy stepped back reflexively. *I'll bet you do, you son of a bitch, but I just cut your wires.*

"Whoa, Jimmy, it's all around the traps. It's no big secret."

"Yeah, I guess."

"I'm surprised that Pat hasn't heard it."

It was Jimmy's turn to shrug. "He probably has."

Bobby chuckled. "What soured you? Pat's a good politician. He could help you, and he stands to win. You know what they call him—"

"Yeah, Bobby, I know what they call him."

"So he's an asshole. Better he be *your* asshole."

"No thank you," Jimmy said. "We should probably get out there. This isn't the time to discuss this."

"You still didn't answer my question, about this sudden change of mind."

"It's not sudden. Getting into all this weird shit in the first place was sudden. I'm an actor."

"So is Reagan."

Jimmy turned away from Bobby and started for the door.

"Jimmy, what the hell's wrong with you? I'm not trying to fight with you. I'm trying to help you."

"I don't need help, and why would you bother?" Bobby looked away. "I've fucked around long enough," Jimmy said. "I need to get back to work. This is your thing, not mine."

"Maybe so," Bobby said. "But Pier thought—"

"Pier's dead!"

"No, she's not," Bobby said, reflexively and loudly. "And neither is Jack. They own us. I thought you, of all people, understood that. You and Jackie."

"I've moved on, and so will Jackie."

"You don't know shit about Jackie."

"Okay, you're right."

"Okay," Bobby said. "I guess we'd better go out there. This is a waste. I came out here to help you. Pat doesn't need me here to win."

"He sure as hell does," Jimmy said, and explained why. Bobby listened intently. "Reagan's getting the white workers who would ordinarily vote Democratic," Jimmy said, "and no matter how much Pat and his people call him a crackpot and extremist, it just doesn't stick. You know why? Because he's so fucking good on television and in public. He knows how to use the media. Reagan doesn't say *anything* you can nail him on, and he has a bunch of psychologists telling him exactly how to behave. People love him. He'll win."

Bobby nodded and said, "Yeah, you're right, this probably isn't the time to discuss this, or something else I wanted to talk to you about."

"Yeah?" asked Jimmy, his curiosity piqued.

"But since you're giving up on Brown . . ."

"That's not fair," Jimmy said. "I'm not giving up on Brown or leaving him in the lurch. I've done what I can. He's got his advisors, who are advising him. Me, I'm just getting back to my career, which happens to be foundering."

Bobby laughed. "Now, that's bullshit, if I ever heard bullshit."

"You just don't understand."

"Look, Jimmy, what I wanted to talk to you about, there's a congressional seat you might consider. That's part of the reason I called you and wanted to see you. Would be—"

"No," Jimmy said flatly. "Whatever it is, I'm not interested. This"—he looked around the room, as if the essence of his discontent could be found there—"is it. This was a mistake. I'm an actor." *And you're dead now, Pier, sweet, sweet, Pier. I'm guilty enough, but you can't tell me what to do.*

Bobby nodded, and blond, teased, glassy-faced, sweaty Sheila slipped into the room as if dancing on her high heels. The crowds, led by Brown, were shouting, *"We want Bobby we want Bobby we want Bobby."*

"Come on, you two. What on earth can you be doing in here? It's show time."

IT WASN'T THE HOTTEST NIGHT OF THE SUMMER, BUT THE AIR HAD become stale and heavy, redolent with the odors of old men's farts. An inversion had been pushing smog and dirt and grit downward, into hair and nostrils and clothes. Air conditioners would be snapping on, breathing cold, cleansing air back into the city of sweating angels. However, the air-conditioning system in the auditorium had suddenly and inexplicably failed, and the combined body heat of the excited audience turned the room into an oven. It reminded Jimmy of being in church on hot summer Sundays, the air stagnant even with the windows wide open, Pastor De Weerd, blond and square-faced, standing on the pulpit, sweating, his shirt becoming transparent, a miracle of transformation, as he exhorted his flock, and then later, after lunch with Aunt Ortense and Uncle Marcus and cousin Markie, riding around in the pastor's silver-and-ghost-gray convertible, the pastor driving fast over familiar roads, the painted white line snaking ahead, the wind blowing hot in their faces, drying their sweat.

The crowd pressed forward toward the podium. There were no chairs in the room, and Jimmy found himself staring at a distant hinged basketball hoop that was raised to the ceiling. The room was packed. Brown and his planners were probably in breach of a dozen municipal laws. But the audience was ecstatic. Young and old were shouting, reaching out, waving hands and placards as if they were children vying for attention in a huge classroom. The audience was barely in control. Bobby exhorted everyone to "quieten down," as he called it, his voice thin but magnified by the microphone; and when he could hear his own voice again, he stumped for Pat Brown, praised his record, and elevated him into the pantheon of great liberal spirits that included John F. Kennedy. The audience was rapt, hushed into an almost religious awe. Then Bobby read a short speech with particular references to local issues and called Jimmy up to the podium.

The smell, the stink, the heat, the balloons with distended photos of Pat Brown's face . . . the shouting, and the crowd ahead, the ugly, beautiful, sensual, hot, repugnant, sweaty beast, suited up and fitted out, dressed up and dressed down, man, woman, and child, all together bawling screeching screaming howling—for Jimmy.

In an instant those men, women, and children made him a liar. *This was a mistake. I'm an actor. No, it's not.*

They were the lightbulbs, incandescent, and he squinted at them and felt their warmth, absorbed their sweaty warmth and light; the light that was so bright it burned, burned and scoured, scoured out memory, burned out time and pain, and he was the vampire feeding in this place without shadow. But no one got hurt, no one felt the hangover of pain and loss—the cupping and the bloodletting—except Jimmy; and son of a bitch they loved him, they worshipped him, and right now, right this instant, Jimmy could do no wrong; he was perfect; he was the dream of his adolescence; he was the Reverend De Weerd's jerk-off fantasy, and the shouting shifting people before him weren't fans, weren't critics, they were an idea, the *idea* of a neighborhood, a city a state a nation, and Jimmy could change them, shape them, involve them, and if he could get enough of them together, they'd light him up forever and give him the divine gift of amnesia.

He'd never have to remember again.

He could make the world remake the world into . . . into . . .

He shouted, "Think big!" The words that had made Pat Brown famous when he won the race against Nixon in 1962. "And nobody but nobody thinks bigger than our own Pat Brown!"

Cheering, shouts of agreement, and then Jimmy did the speech, his speech, the one that had as many different variations as the people in the audience, the one that seemed to explode in his throat, that was the column and sum of everything he knew believed wanted, and Pat Brown was just a platform to tell the story, to work the crowd, to be in the light; and Pat Brown had good ideas. Brown must win, and as Jimmy spoke, he believed in Pat Brown more than he believed in anyone else in the world, more than he believed in himself because what happened right now in this election would define everything, and although Jimmy knew that wasn't true, wasn't altogether true, it didn't matter because truth was for the moment, and this was the moment; and then he was stepping backward and Pat was patting him, taking his hand and raising it as if he were proclaiming him the winner of a boxing match, and then Pat was stumping for himself, and Jimmy and Bobby were behind, shielded from the light, as rivulets of perspiration rolled down Jimmy's back.

"Think big!" Brown said, and the glistening crowd screamed and shook and waved pennons with balloons and posters of the Giant Killer. "Do you know what I think? Do you know what makes me—what makes *us*—different from our opponents?" Pause, shouting, clamoring. "I believe that the purpose of this thing we call government is to make people's lives better. That's why we've built the greatest university in America, that's why we've reformed labor laws, increased unemployment insurance to make sure that the men and women who are the backbone of this great state have some security from their government that their families won't starve while they can't work, and we established fair-housing legislation and a Fair Employment Practices Commission to make sure that *everyone* has an equal chance to apply for a job or to buy a house."

Applause, but this wasn't an ocean, a waving thundering, breaking over the podium. Jimmy glanced at Bobby, a knowing glance; and Pat went on, exhorting, hoarsely trying to find what he called "the button," trying desperately to find and push the button. "I said no to my conservative opponents over Proposition Fourteen—remember that?—when they tried to repeal the Rumford Fair Housing Act, which I endorsed. The right-wingers, the radicals, the John Birchers, those are the same people who want to take away your Social Security benefits and all federal aid to education. They want to take away from our old, and they want to take away from our young; and these are the same people who are funding and supporting my opponent. They fought me in 1964, and they lost. They fought me with dirty hate and smear campaigns and innuendo—just as they're doing now. And what I said then when they tried to plan gutter politics I'll say again now. And I say this to my opponent, that cowboy actor who got talked into thinking he can play governor."

Cheering—he had pressed the button. Brown turned to Jimmy: "No offense, Jimmy, but sometimes you've got to fight fire with fire."

Laughter, and Jimmy nodded, grinding his teeth. *It doesn't really matter, I'm out of here in a few minutes, back to the house.* But he realized, as his thoughts passed like the train that had carried him to Illinois, that he was home.

This was home.

"And just like in 1964," Brown continued, his face flushed and shiny now, "I can once again hear the echoes of another hate binge that began more than thirty years ago in a Munich beer hall. These echoes come from a minority of the angry, the frustrated, the fearful. They don't represent California or its people. But what they do represent—the spasm reaction of hatred—exists not only here in California, but elsewhere in our nation and in our world. We've got to fight it wherever we find it, and right now we've got a chance to root out that hatred right here at home."

The crowd was stretching toward him, all buttons pushed, as flags waved and balloons burst in the humid, fetid air, and Pat Brown turned to Jimmy and Bobby, who took the cue and were on their feet. It was like standing up in a sauna—Jimmy felt faint and slightly dizzy—but the instant was everything, time compressed into the right now of screaming and waving, and the crowd shifting, eddying, crashing forward, like water surging, seeking, and Brown stood at the podium, not moving, his large red hands grasping the lectern, and then he suddenly fell forward with a woofing sound, banging his chin, Jimmy reaching for him as he collapsed, Brown on his knees as if to pray, Jimmy and Bobby cushioned him, laid him out, shouted for a doctor. The crowd in tumult. Someone with a trembling bass voice at the microphone told everyone to stay in place, to be calm, be calm, please be calm . . .

The doctor—salt-and-pepper mustache and kinky long hair pulled tightly into a ponytail—leaned over Pat, checking for vital signs, and in the sticky heat, in the suffocating heat, Jimmy heard Pat fart, a terrible cracking sound, and he smelled feces and remembered Illinois, fields, cow shit and horse shit, and he heard sirens.

But it was too late.

The Giant Killer was dead.

TWENTY-SEVEN

■

Lap of the Gods

As a wake, it was all business.

It had been raining all day, and Jimmy, Caroline, Bobby, all of Brown's lieutenants—everyone who was anyone in the California Democratic Party and the state's government—and senators, aides, representatives, governors, and dignitaries from many states attended the mass at Saint Mary of the Sacred Heart Roman Catholic Church in Sacramento. Four National Guard helicopters slowly passed overhead and did a loop around the burnished gold cupola dome of the capitol in a "missing man" formation to show respect. Edmund G. "Pat" Brown's casket was draped in a red-and-white California flag and positioned beside the podium.

Jimmy spoke, Bobby spoke, everyone, it seemed, spoke, and then the ride to the cemetery, and ceremony, prayers, heads bowed, relatives dressed in black, and the Lord must have taken mercy on Pat Brown—or, perhaps, on the mourners—because the smeary clouds parted and the skies cleared.

However, the cardinal's speech was much too long.

Amens interjected into the windy susurration, and then everyone hurriedly crowded into cars and limousines. If the helicopters had still been flying in formation, they would have seen those same cars and limousines as tiny beetles moving together, and then, as if suddenly warned of danger, crawling and wriggling away in all directions.

3:00 P.M.

The real party to celebrate who was alive and who was dead, hallelujah, was being held at Pat Ryan's by the river (across the street from a Pick 'n' Pay and under a huge sign for Frank Fat's), a neighborhood Irish watering hole favored by politicians. The bar was packed, and the only way to get to the dining room was to pass through the bar, where there was a conspicuous absence of call girls. Everyone seemed to know everyone else, and most everyone was drunk.

It took almost a half hour for Jimmy, Bobby, and Caroline to run the gauntlet of the bar, then through a heavy closed door: plush maroon carpet, high, peeling ceilings, comfortable chairs, muted lighting, a collection of bad art in overly ornate frames, polished tables, and the best steaks and hamburgers in Sacramento. Five men at the corner table farthest from the door stood up. Jimmy and Caroline knew them; they were Pat's cronies, key old-guard Democratic Party leaders and insiders. A statuesque waitress with shoulder-length teased black hair and piercing green eyes was called to bring another chair, drinks, and three steaks.

"Well, let's raise a glass to Pat," said Matt Marshall, one of Brown's chief aides. He was in his early forties, tan, balding, a college wrestling champion just starting to go to fat.

"Here, here!" came the chorus, and everyone knocked back their drinks.

"Waitress, another round!" shouted Liam Laski, assistant to county executive John Raymond Jones. Jones, who was perfectly dressed—one of those ironed men who never seem to sweat—looked at his aide with distaste and then returned to meticulously spreading twice-baked potato onto a forkful of blood-rare filet mignon.

Then small talk, most of it directed to Bobby and Jimmy, and shop talk; and although Caroline was easily holding her own, the old boys weren't going out of their way to make her welcome. That raised Jimmy's hackles.

He finished his steak, drank the last of an insipid-tasting beer, and said, "Gentlemen, I've got business to take care of at the crack of dawn, so I'm afraid I'm going to have to call it a night. Now, Pat probably wouldn't understand, as he was always the last one to leave the bar, but—"

Laughter, agreement—and consternation.

Surprised, Bobby exchanged a quick glance with Caroline.

"We should stay for another drink, Jimmy," Caroline said. "Or rather you should stay for another drink."

Jimmy stood up and said, "No, these men have important things to discuss, and we're only inhibiting them. Gentlemen—"

Caroline stood up, too. "No, Jimmy, *I'm* inhibiting them. Now, I'm going to go and have one last drink with some very nasty reporters I know back in the bar and—"

The men at the table protested.

Paul Cottrell, who had been Pat Brown's chief of staff, said, "Sit down, Jimmy. And you, too, Caroline. You know why we're here. Please, sit down and hear us out." He looked up at Caroline and said, "Some of these Neanderthals seem to be a bit nervous because of your past professional obligations, but I think we can be assured that anything you hear will be off the record, right?"

"You shouldn't even have to ask her that," Jimmy said. "She worked her heart out on Pat's campaign, and she—"

"Yes, Paul, anything that has to do with this campaign is strictly off the record," Caroline said; she looked at the other men as she spoke. "I'm not a reporter anymore."

Paul nodded, as did some of the others. "Jimmy, please sit down," Paul said.

"I know what this is all about," Jimmy said. "You could at least let Pat get cold in his grave before having this conversation."

"Jimmy, cut the shit and sit down," Bobby said in a low voice. "Stop grandstanding."

Jimmy intended to walk out, but he sat down.

"Unfortunately, there's no time for niceties," Paul said. "It's June. We've got less than five months until election day." Paul was overweight, near-sighted, and rumpled; his eight-hundred-dollar suit certainly could have used a pressing. But he was the consummate insider, and Caroline had once quipped that he wore his clothes baggy just to conceal his dorsal fin.

"As far as I can see, we're screwed," Jimmy said. "Sam Yorty is the natural choice. He almost beat Pat in the primary, and he's almost as right-wing as Reagan." He laughed mirthlessly. "He's probably got the best chance."

"He's worse than George Wallace," Liam Laski said, making a sour face.

"Doesn't matter," said Paul. "Jimmy's right, he was in the primary, so he's a natural choice." He nodded to Jimmy, and Jimmy knew he was being condescended to. Jimmy, in turn, glanced at Caroline, who smiled in acknowledgment that Paul was a dick. "But there's a loophole in the election law in the case where a candidate dies. In that event the central committee of the party can designate someone."

"And that someone will probably be Yorty," Jimmy said. "He's popular, he almost beat Pat."

"So you said," Paul said, watching him intently. "But you could have easily beaten Yorty."

"But *I'm* not running against Yorty," Jimmy said.

Paul smiled, and then the conversation stopped for a moment when the waitress returned to take orders for another round. When she left, Paul said, "He won't have the numbers in the committee. But you do. The party would choose you."

"Is that a fact?"

"Yes, Jimmy, that's a fact. Would you accept?"

"What about Glenn Anderson? He's lieutenant governor. He's running things now, isn't he?"

Paul smiled mirthlessly. "He won't do it, you know that. Personal reasons. He could never win, and he knows it." After a beat he asked, "Well . . . would you accept?"

The others leaned forward in their chairs in anticipation. Paul, the player, the salesman, leaned back, giving Jimmy all the psychological space he might need.

Jimmy embarrassed himself by laughing, but it was a nervous laugh. "I don't think the party would choose me, and anyway"—*I'm not interested, that's what I should say, I'm not interested, get up and leave, like Caroline said, I'm an actor, so what the fuck is she doing playing palsy-walsy with these assholes?*—"I'm overly committed."

"Is that a no?"

Danny Cowles, Brown's campaign chairman, began to say something, but a glance from Paul silenced him.

"Get me the nod from the committee, and then I'll decide."

"We need something a bit stronger than that, Jimmy."

"Well, that's all I've got."

"If you go ahead and run, Jimmy, you'll have all the resources I can muster," Bobby said.

"And what do you get?" Jimmy asked, feeling cornered and somehow exultant, as if everything had led to this point, *life over death, karmic life and karmic death, where are you Jack Kerouac, you should be sitting here, peeing in your goddamn pants and falling off the chair laughing.* Jimmy couldn't help himself. He grinned at Bobby.

"What?" Bobby asked.

"What do you get out of all this?" Jimmy asked again.

Bobby met Jimmy's gaze, blinked once, and said, "California," as if it didn't matter that anyone else heard him.

IN A RENTED WHITE STRETCH LIMOUSINE, DRIVING AROUND THE city, which wasn't much of a city.

Downtown Sacramento was an eyesore, as bleak as any lonely street scene Edward Hopper ever painted: streetlight and shadow, Woolworth's and Doughnut Pride, George circling, driving, the waterfront buildings looking derelict in the darkness, monstrous, as if from some set for a horror picture—there's the ax murderer, just inside that alcove, behind that sign, waiting in the empty parking lots—and back around the capital building bathed in light, the luminous, numinous light of grace and power, white against the ash-scented night, and then George—shaved and fresh-looking and ever-alert—drove into the suburbs, through leafy streets that branched off from smaller downtowns, streets that would become Norman Rockwell streets by midmorning, after the cleansing sun burned away all dark musings, dreams, and nightmares; and for a time Jimmy forgot where he was and imagined he was back in Fairmont; and the Reverend De Weerd was driving, the Reverend De Weerd knew where he was going, the Reverend De Weerd knew all the answers, all the outcomes; the Reverend De Weerd was a bullfighter for God, head down, penis erect; *and now* I'm *a bullfighter for God . . .*

"Bobby for President," Jimmy said, shaping and tasting the thought. Chuckling. "Of course."

"You shouldn't be worrying about Bobby just now," Caroline said. "Now, for the last time, tell me why you jerked Cottrell and the other guys around? Why didn't you just give them an answer?"

Jimmy smiled. "Because of you."

"Me?"

"You showed me the error of my ways."

"What is that supposed to mean?" Caroline asked.

"You reminded me what I was and what I should be doing."

Caroline chewed on her lip, a nervous habit. She was looking like her old self lately, lustrous, Jimmy thought; her hair thick and glossy, her legs long, right up to her neck, and there was still something coltish about her; and even though she was out of her girlish twenties, there was something tentative and wise about her, an awkward, impossible mix that gave her a natural, wholesome sophistication. "You seemed to be going in all directions," she said, pulling away from him and sitting stiffly, her back pulled away from the knotted black leather upholstery. "Like you were just being thrown this way and that, experimenting with this group and that, with this ideology, and that—"

"Well, that shit's all over, and so is this." He leaned forward and said, "George, take us back to the hotel. We're out of this tank town in the morning."

"Fine by me, sir."

Jimmy pulled a bottle of Glendronach unblended Scotch whiskey out of the bar cabinet and poured himself a glass. He offered it to Caroline, who shook her head.

"So now tell me what all this was about tonight," he said. You were in bed with all those party lackeys, and I got to tell you, they weren't treating you with respect."

"I was there for you because"—she reached for Jimmy's glass and took a large, fortifying gulp—"because this is important . . . because I was fucking around with your head before. I guess I was fucking around with my own head. I was . . ."

Jimmy softened. Reflexively, he put his arm over the back of her seat. "Yeah?"

"It was about Pier. What she wanted. I was fighting Pier, but she was right about you. She knew what you needed."

"What Pier wanted for me was about Pier."

"Maybe, but she was right. So now I'm trying to make it right."

Jimmy giggled. "You want to make it right?" Caroline watched him warily, her eyes narrowed. "George, drive back to that building they call the capitol." Then to Caroline: "You want me to be governor? Okay, then we'll consecrate it right on the seat of power."

ANOTHER COOL BLUE NIGHT, MUSIC AND DRUMS SUBLIMINALLY pulsing, for tonight would be magic, serendipity itself—or so Caroline promised.

Midnight.

One of Elvis Presley's guards—not one of the Memphis Mafia boys—accompanied Jimmy and Caroline past the gates of the house on Perugia Way. The building was an oriental monstrosity, circular, with soundproof bedrooms, two-way mirrors, and white shag carpets. Former tenants included the shah of Iran and Prince Aly Kahn, who was married to Rita Hayworth.

Elvis had excused himself from his guests and had been waiting for them, skulking around the doorway like a child afraid of being found out. "The Colonel thought you might like to meet these guys," he said, grinning and looking embarrassed at the same time. He bowed to Caroline, then turned to Jimmy and said conspiratorially, "You know the Colonel, he always has to have everything set up like."

As they crossed the marble floor Elvis pulled Jimmy aside, saying, "Excuse me, ma'am, jus' for a second," to Caroline. Caroline sighed and occupied herself in the white-on-white living room.

Elvis looked down at his patent-leather boots and said, "The Colonel and me, we been fighting like cats and dogs. He threatened to walk, and I fired him, and everything you can imagine happened."

"Yeah?" Jimmy said, interested. "Jesus."

"It was never so bad with him before. I think we sort of both got nervous, you know what I mean?"

"I guess," Jimmy said.

"So we changed our contract. Colonel gets more money, and I get, you know, I get to do more of what I think best without the hassles."

"I thought you basically had everything you wanted. Your motion pictures are going well. Scuttlebutt is that Norman Jewison's trying to sign you to work opposite Sidney Poitier."

"Yeah, and there's other stuff, too, but, yeah, I'd play a nigger-hating cop in Mississippi. Poitier, he'd be a black cop, who—"

Jimmy started laughing, and Elvis, realizing what he just said, chuckled. "Man, they should just put me away."

"You going to take the gig?"

Elvis shrugged. "Colonel is really unhappy about it. Thinks it will hurt my reputation."

"I thought you just worked out a new deal with him."

"Yeah, he's always worried about the goddamn music, but the music's down the toilet," Elvis said, surprising Jimmy.

"Man, those people downstairs must be really getting you down," Jimmy said.

"Hell if they are. Hell, I didn't even want to meet those fucking sons of bitches. It's all Colonel's idea. He thinks it's good advertising, me showing kindness to the competition, you know? I think it's all bullshit, but he's probably right, huh? An' I should probably get back down there."

"Jimmy!" Caroline interrupted impatiently. "I really can't believe you guys. You've got the Beatles in here someplace, and you're just going to huddle in the corner like two little old ladies while I stand here with my thumb in my ear."

"I didn't know you were a Beatles fan," Elvis said, his voice a honey drawl. He liked Caroline.

"Big one."

"And you?" Elvis asked Jimmy.

Jimmy shrugged. "Not something I give a lot of thought to."

"But I'm a bigger fan of yours," Caroline said, her face bright with devilment.

"Yeah, honey, I'll bet you are," Elvis said, and just then Colonel Parker, who had been waiting—lying in wait—appeared. Elvis looked disconcerted, as if the Colonel had caught him out, as if he, the Colonel, had been standing there the whole while listening.

"I see my boy is giving you the lowdown on everything," the Colonel said, smiling and stinking of cigars. He wore dark slacks and a gray-peppered sport jacket over a striped shirt buttoned to the collar and closed with a western string tie. He shook hands with Jimmy, his hand large and powerful, belying his pudgy, fat-boy appearance. Then he bowed to Caroline. "Are these boys ignoring you, honey?" He winked at her.

"They sure as hell are, Colonel," Caroline said. "What do you propose we do to punish them?"

"Well, I'll tell you what. My boy Elvis deserves to be punished for leavin' all his guests down there all alone, don't you think?"

"They're all right," Elvis said. "They're shootin' pool with the guys. And I've only been up here for a few minutes, goddammit, anyway."

The Colonel ignored that and continued speaking to Caroline: "But I guess I just got a soft heart, so what about if Elvis takes you downstairs and introduces you to the band. Meanwhile, I'll have a little chat up here with Jimmy, if he doesn't mind." He chuckled. "So I s'pose it's your pal Jimmy who's getting punished, ain't that so, Elvis."

"I guess so, Colonel," Elvis mumbled.

Son of a bitch, the Colonel could still intimidate the hell out of him. I wonder what kind of deal Elvis cut. And what the hell has Caroline got me into here with the Colonel?

"Caroline"—the Colonel pronounced it "Kha-roh-line"—"we'll have a little talk later, before this boy takes you away, okay?" He squeezed Jimmy's arm to indicate whom he was referring to.

"Sure, Colonel, I'd like that," Caroline said, giving Jimmy a quick nod, as if to say, "Go do business."

"You know, Jimmy, Elvis never gives me any credit for understanding what he wants to do. Did Elvis tell you about the deal I'm putting together for him?" The Colonel gave Elvis a pointed look, then opened and closed his hand quickly, dismissing him, tantalizing him. Elvis dutifully escorted Caroline out of the room. "I've been talking with Hal Wallis about getting Elvis into a film with John Wayne," the Colonel continued, talking loudly so Elvis could hear, and then cutting his voice down almost to a whisper. "What do you think of that idea, Jimmy? Elvis would be a gunslinger or something who learns everything from John Wayne, who's like the teacher, you know what I mean? Except Elvis would be a faster shot than Wayne and end up having to kill him. What do you think?" Jimmy shrugged. "You see, Wayne is a has-been and on his way out, and Elvis is the big thing now."

"I don't know if John would see it that way."

"Elvis will be the lead," the Colonel insisted. "That's just the way it is. Now just follow me into my cubbyhole, and we'll have a little talk." Indeed, the Colonel did have his own office in Elvis's California mansion, a large room that was set up like a cafeteria, with a long table covered with an oilcloth set against the far wall, and a kitchenette and an open pantry opposite a polished, mahogany desk. He sat down behind the desk and motioned Jimmy to pull up a stool that was shaped like an elephant's foot. "I love elephants," he explained to Jimmy. "Elephant saved my life once. I was dead broke in some one-horse, shit-kicker town in Florida. Didn't even have enough money to buy a meal, much less pay my hotel bill. But would you believe it, I found an elephant in that hick town." He rolled his eyes upward, as if that town and that elephant were in heaven right above him, and he was staring right up at them. "It was left over from a circus or some damn thing, and so I borrowed that elephant and put on a promotion for the local grocery store, and that storekeeper—Mr. K. Cee Brannaugh was his name—made more money than he had ever seen before, and I made enough money to live pretty damn well for the next couple of days in that town. Ever since then, pachyderms have had a special place in my heart."

Jimmy just shook his head. He had just noticed a plastic sign affixed to the front of the Colonel's desk: ELVIS EXPLOITATIONS.

"Okay," the Colonel said, turning on a desk lamp with a covered-wagon base, "let's cut the bullshit and do business." He lit a cigar.

"Fine with me," Jimmy said, feeling awkward and angry, angry because this fat clown could actually intimidate him.

"Son, you ain't ever going to win no election if you can't look your opponent square in the eye."

"Well, if you were my opponent, I'd look you square in the eye."

The Colonel nodded. "I do believe you might." After a beat he said, "I wouldn't give you a chance in hell of beating Reagan. Reagan talks nice, he's got good presence, everybody likes him. Why would voters vote for you?"

"Well, if you can't get past that, maybe we've got nothing to say."

"No, son, I'm asking you a question." And so Jimmy answered; he explained the importance to ordinary working people of the free speech movement at Berkeley, black power, Watts, civil rights, and then he went on to Vietnam and free education and why he thought Reagan was dangerous. He explained what Brown had stood for, what he, Jimmy, stood for; and he watched the Colonel as he spoke, waiting for the Colonel's gaze to drift, watching for him to lose patience, watching for the right button, as Pat Brown would say, pushing the buttons; but the Colonel just watched him, expressionless.

"None of that means shit," the Colonel said flatly.

"So what does?" Jimmy asked.

"What I do for you, and whether we can come to an agreement."

Jimmy couldn't help himself. He burst out laughing.

The Colonel leaned back in his chair and puffed on his cigar. "You know how I made Elvis a star? I didn't let him appear too much in person or on television. It makes the fans clamor for a view of the product."

"I don't think that would work very well with an election," Jimmy said. *Jesus, his teeth are yellow.*

"If you know how to use the system, it works. Your opponent—is Reagan your opponent? Have you made the decision, or are you just testing the water?"

"I thought you and Caroline have this pipeline," Jimmy said sarcastically.

"She's a good girl, your Caroline. Well, answer the question, son." He grinned. "You know, if you become governor of the great state of California, I'll have to stop calling you son."

"I think you should stop calling me son right now."

"Are you in or out?"

"I'm announcing on Tuesday."

"You should have gotten me on board immediately."

"This is immediately," Jimmy said.

"Reagan is a whore," the Colonel said. "He's got all his little bitty bits of information that won't get anyone's back up, and he's trying to talk to everybody and be everywhere, and he's got this card system those professors set him up with." The Colonel took a last puff on what had become the stub of his cigar. "I talked to one of them."

"You what?"

"Oh, us show-business people do get around, don't we?" A good old boy's fake, pasted-on smile. "You want to know why the Beatles and their manager are downstairs? Because they're the opponents. I take them out, and Elvis won't have any trouble with all those other English faggots like the Rolling Stones and them others."

"How do you take them out?"

"With kindness. Elvis is the hero of them young boys downstairs. This is going to be the ultimate snow job. It's all about publicity."

"I didn't see any reporters. Caroline told me that everything was on the quiet."

The Colonel nodded. "That's right because *we're* goin' to control it. We got a boy here from a British magazine called *New Musical* something-or-other, and naturally, we got Caroline—"

Son of a bitch.

"—and a nice boy from *Rolling Stone* and one from *The New York Times,* but they got to keep everything a secret until it's all over with, and they weren't allowed to bring their cameras and tape recorders and all that, either. If you got a hundred reporters, it goes out of control. And I made the deal with the Beatles' manager, Brian Epstein, that his boys have to come here. They come here to me and Elvis because Elvis is the king, and maybe, if the Beatles are very good, we'll make them knights or something. But the real snow job has to be out there." He waved toward the window. "We snow the whole goddamn world. This new goddamn generation loves the Beatles, and if they love the Beatles, they damn well better love Elvis, too. Epstein and his boys get some. We get it all."

"Yeah, maybe, but I don't think any of this is relevant to an election, Colonel, with all due respect."

"Everybody says you're a nice boy," the Colonel said. "Are you going to marry that little girl of yours?"

"What?" Jimmy asked. "That's a hell of a rude question to ask."

"Are you?"

"I don't think that's anyone's business."

"I think it should be everyone's business. Do you love her?"

"My wife is barely cold in her grave. I really don't—"

"Look, I don't give a shit what you do—and, here, this is a freebie—I think you should announce on Tuesday, get married next month, and invite everyone in California to your wedding, especially your opponent."

"What will that accomplish?"

"Put him on *your* turf. The people will get it. They're not stupid."

"I think you're wrong about that," Jimmy said. "And it seems a pretty extreme way to send out an invitation."

"Good publicity, but you'll have to make sure you've got the right press and control it because otherwise he'll be in all the papers doing his hand thing."

"His what?"

"You don't know about that? How whenever he has his picture taken, he raises his hand, so it looks like everyone's deferring to him. If you're going to kick his butt, Jimmy, you got to know all about him. Maybe you can take away some of his voters, but some you ain't never going to convince, no matter what, all them people who are scared shitless of the students and the niggers and all that. Maybe you can pick up some of that vote, but what you really got to do is make new rules and pull out new voters, like the students and the nigger lovers and probably the niggers, and all them, and all your fans. The ones that'll kill for you, Jimmy, that's who you got to mobilize. You got to pick your fights and your opportunities, but I can tell you, you won't do none of that right without me. I'll bet you any bet you care to make on that."

Bullshit. Cowboy bullshit.

"Like I said, you got to make them feel like they just can't have you, that they got to work to have you."

"Yeah, and what do they have to do?"

The Colonel grinned at Jimmy. "They got to get off their fat asses and vote, and you got to give them lots of wedding cake and circuses."

"Colonel, you're—"

"Crazy like a fox," the Colonel said, lighting another cigar and puffing on it until he was wreathed with smoke. "You want to think I'm too uneducated and dumb to get you what you want, that's fine by me, son. But politics ain't one bit different from what I been doing for Elvis. Reagan's people know a little. He's doing good television. Notice he never does anything that's too long? Your boy Brown, may he rest in peace, he pissed everybody off with that long commercial that cut into regular television programming, remember that? Nah, you wouldn't. You weren't paying attention." The Colonel paused and examined his cigar.

"Jimmy, trust me, you ain't got a chance in hell without being married. You got to show all them you got through your grief and you're responsible. Come to think of it, it's time for Elvis to be getting married, too. Few years ago that would've killed his career dead. Now it'll help, like with you." He looked steadily at Jimmy. "Time's runnin' out. I got things to do."

"Did you work this all out with Caroline?"

"Not a word of it. Hell, maybe she won't want to marry you. I'd be trying like hell to marry her if I was you. But then again, maybe you don't care if you're associated with that shiftless generation of beatniks who don't believe in buyin' the cow if they can get the milk for free."

"What do you get out of all this?" Jimmy asked, ignoring the sarcasm.

"Tell you what, if you work with me and you lose, you don't owe me nothin' for all my work, except maybe some of my ordinary expenses."

Yeah, right.

"But if you win, then you do a film with Elvis. My choice. And I take the same percentage from you that I get from Elvis."

"If I win, I'm not going to have the time to be making motion pictures."

The Colonel shrugged. "I think you could manage one picture, but if that's a problem, then you just pay me the equivalent of what I'd be gettin'."

"And how much would that be?"

"Fifty percent of everything you would've earned on the picture," the Colonel said. "You want to win, you got to sup with the devil—or, in your case, you'd be suppin' with the angels. Just ask my wife." A wide yellow grin. "And if you get to be governor, maybe you could do me a little favor here or there." And then a segue into another story about how the Colonel bet Brian Epstein that Elvis was more popular than the Beatles.

A bass guitar twanged so loudly that Jimmy almost jumped off the stool. Drumrolls, guitars being tightened into tune; then microphone voices, pounding guitar rhythms, breaking glass, the first riffs of a hit song: "Can't Buy Me Love."

"Elvis is playing that bass," the Colonel said proudly. "I can tell. You want to go downstairs? Ain't going to be able to talk anymore up here."

THE MUSIC STOPPED WHEN JIMMY AND THE COLONEL ENTERED THE music room.

Elvis was sitting on the edge of a chair, still trying to get used to Paul McCartney's left-handed Hofner 500/1 bass. The band sat close to Elvis, except for Ringo Starr, who sat behind a set of drums on a raised platform in the middle of the room. Elvis's friends and bodyguards were all there, lounging on the carpet or on the white sofas. They were all dressed the same: black trousers and black short-sleeved shirts. Elvis, in contrast, was wearing tight gray pants, a red shirt, and a black silk jacket. He looked stoned, but the Beatles looked nervous and awkward in their gray suits with high button jackets. Their collars were open, ties loosened.

They were all in awe of Jimmy, just as they had been in awe of Elvis.

John Lennon was the first to speak. He walked up to Jimmy, extended his hand, and said, "Oh, you must be . . . James Dean."

Laughter, and Jimmy retorted, "Oh, I guess you guys must be friends of the Colonel." He wisecracked with Elvis and the others and then sat down on a couch with Caroline, Bit, and Elvis's shy, dark-haired girlfriend, Priscilla.

Priscilla nodded to Jimmy, and then, as if she had suddenly embarrassed herself, turned back to watch Elvis and his new best friends.

Caroline waited until everyone settled down, then she squeezed Jimmy's hand and whispered, "How'd it go?"

Jimmy shrugged, feeling uncomfortable.

But the Colonel, not to be outdone by any of the others, boomed, "This casino is now open for business." He was standing beside a distinguished-looking man—Brian Epstein—who was smooth, quiet, and boyishly handsome. The Colonel then flipped over the top of a large coffee table to reveal a roulette wheel. "I'm the pit boss. Who's playing?"

THE COLONEL DECLARED THE PARTY OVER AT 2:00 A.M.—AFTER HE had won three thousand dollars from Brian Epstein. "You boys got to come back soon," he said, "because I just about got Brian convinced to book you in for a benefit for my boy Jimmy, who's going to be the next governor of California. What do you think of that? And my boy Elvis will also have some news pretty soon, won't you, Elvis?"

Elvis had taken more downers than uppers; he looked at the Colonel and blinked twice.

"Ding, dong, the bells are goin' to ring," the Colonel said, nodding significantly to Priscilla—and Caroline.

He slapped Epstein on the back and smiled at Jimmy.

TWENTY-EIGHT

■

The Politics of Experience

It was a circus, but a very conservative circus.

There were no beards and longhairs. All the "kids," as they were called—the antiwar and civil-rights activists; the students and the hippies, the doe-eyed young women from Vassar and Smith; the boys from UNC and Yale and Cornell, who were top of their classes or hanging out at the fringes dropping acid and extolling the virtues of Timothy Leary and *The Politics of Experience;* the fat fans who just loved Jimmy and activism and politics and the communal friendship and sex; the blacks the whites the Hispanics who had participated in strikes and sit-ins and teach-ins and walk-outs, who had marched with Stokely Carmichael and Martin Luther King and joined acronymic organizations such as SCLC, NSA, NAACP, MFDP, and SNCC—had cleaned themselves up for Jimmy. "Get Clean for Dean"—another one of the Colonel's mottos.

There were young mothers and grandmothers and all the Committee to Elect James Dean people. There were celebrities—Elvis Presley, Jack Kerouac (ferociously sober), Eli Wallach, Lee and Paula Strasberg, Frank Sinatra, Eartha Kitt, Bobby and Ethel Kennedy, Edward Kennedy, Elia Kazan, Allen Ginsberg, Joan Baez, James Baldwin, Norman Mailer, Dustin Hoffman, Natalie Wood, Joanne Woodward and a rather sour Paul Newman, James Brown, Otis Redding, Adam Clayton Powell, Ursula Andress, Muhammad Ali, Rudolf Nureyev, Marty Wrightson, Sidney Poitier, Jean-Louis Trintignant, Nick Ray, Keenan Wynn, Joe DiMaggio, Andy Williams and Claudine Longet, Martin Luther King and his wife, Coretta, Hank Snow, and Brian Epstein and the Beatles, who were going to do a special benefit for Jimmy, along with Ray Charles and Harry Belafonte.

All the old guard of the state Democratic Party had been invited, including John Raymond Jones; Liam Laski; Paul Cottrell; Sam Yorty, mayor of San Francisco; Danny Cowles, who was now Jimmy's "official" campaign chairman; Robert Coate, the Democratic state chairman; and Eugene Wyman, California's Democratic National Committeeman chairman. There was a host of out-of-state politicos, including Bobby's advisors, who were also advising Jimmy. And, of course, Ron and Nancy Reagan were there.

How could they refuse a very public invitation to the wedding of the decade?

JIMMY AND CAROLINE WERE MARRIED IN THE WEE KIRK 'O THE Heather Chapel, the same chapel where Ronald Reagan and his first wife, Jane Wyman, were married.

The same chapel where the funeral for Pier was held.

The same cemetery—Forest Lawn in Glendale—where Pier was buried.

Caroline and Jimmy stood under a magnificent chandelier in a huge dining room. An army of silent waiters and waitresses fussed over the tables, making last-minute adjustments. Lights glittered and reflected from all the shiny surfaces, reflected from crystal and silver and fine china, from aluminum heating trays, musical instruments, and a menagerie of ice sculptures; soon the same transforming light would be reflected from the eyes of the beautiful people—and the powerful people. The guests would be called to dinner in a minute; right now, they were milling around outside in the great reception rooms. "Are you all right?" Caroline asked Jimmy.

They began to walk past the ranks of tables, rank upon rank that from a height would have looked like perfectly arranged linen-covered caskets.

"Yeah, I'm all right," Jimmy said, the fabric of his pale blue cummerbund rustling against his starched formal shirt. "I was just worried about you."

She looked small in her smart and simple white satin wedding gown. "Well, we knew what to expect," Caroline said.

"Yeah, and we should have told the Colonel to fuck off."

"I've got to give him credit—it's the best publicity stunt I've ever seen. How many people are there outside on the lawns, a few thousand?"

"But it's not a wedding," Jimmy insisted.

She laughed and took his hand, squeezing it. "Everyone's saying it's the most magnificent wedding ever."

"You deserve better than the Colonel's circus."

"We made a deal," Caroline said. "This is business, and it's good business. When you're elected, we'll take our honeymoon. That will be just for us."

"Yeah."

"James Dean, you surprise me. I do believe you're a romantic, under all that sleepy-eyed I-don't-give-a-shit stuff."

"I guess I am." They walked past an ice sculpture of an elephant balancing atop another elephant, and Jimmy said, "I guess the Colonel was right about it making a commotion with the news. I just don't know if it's the right kind of commotion. Bobby and the committee think it's just plain nuts."

"I think it may be nuts for us right now, too, but everyone's paying attention to you, Jimmy, and I can tell you that the spin for the headlines will be all right. The Colonel did it right. He might have been a little crass about it, but the idea that you couldn't ever marry again unless you had Pier's blessing is powerful stuff, Jimmy."

"The papers will twist it into looking like we're dancing on her grave."

"Some will. Most won't."

"Is the Colonel still outside distributing buttons?"

"No one could stop him. But the sideshow's outside, not in here."

"Did the Reagans leave?" Jimmy asked.

"Yes, mercifully."

"The Colonel sure as hell called that wrong, didn't he?"

"Are you talking about the debate?"

"I knew Reagan was going to do something like that."

"He's been challenging you to a debate for the past two weeks," Caroline said. She shrugged. "He just figured he had the cameras on him, so he'd try it on again. But did you see the look on Nancy's face when he asked you?" Jimmy shook his head. She grinned. "It was priceless. You'll see it on the news tonight. She looked like she swallowed a golf ball. I've already got someone working on a feature."

Jimmy stopped walking. He held both her hands and said, "Caroline, I love you."

"I love you, too, Jimmy."

"No, I mean it. I love you."

She looked at him quizzically, then said, "Sometimes I believe you."

"And right now?"

Caroline stepped close to him and said, "Right now . . . I believe you completely." She smiled at him, her tan face powdered, her tiara glittering in the wedding white light, and the maitre d' whispered over to them.

"Please excuse my intrusion, *monsieur, madame*." His accent was thick, probably fake. "May I open the doors so that you may greet your guests for dinner?"

Jimmy and Caroline followed him toward the high double doors. The Colonel was, of course, the first into the room.

"Jimmy, Caroline, congratulations!" He growled at the young men guarding the door, "Let me through or both your asses are gonna be fired." Wearing a white tuxedo, his blue cummerbund a tire around his waist, he pushed toward Jimmy and Caroline. Jimmy reflexively let go of Caroline's hand as the Colonel bore down on them. "Now we got to talk . . ."

THE LOS ANGELES JAMES DEAN FOR GOVERNOR HEADQUARTERS WAS a large storefront on Sunset, the windows covered with posters of Jimmy: Jimmy staring out at passersby, Jimmy wearing a work shirt with a tie loosened at the collar, Jimmy the citizen hero, the working-class hero, the proverbial common (millionaire) man, the movie star, the boy next-door, the next governor who can "make California work," the face on every button on every lapel.

But the most important activities were held at Jimmy's other L.A.

headquarters: the Colonel's James Dean for Governor office on the tenth floor of a glass-fronted building on Beverly Boulevard between Doheny and Robertson. There was nothing on the outside door or hall windows to suggest that this eight-room suite housed anything other than a company called Boxcar Enterprises. Inside, the offices were crowded with young people, "the kids" as everybody called them, the beautiful, golden, privileged young people attending to a multitude of tasks—filing, stuffing envelopes, scribbling on whiteboards, designating canvassing routes on maps with yellow markers, copying schedules, typing, manning the phones, and chatting when not looking busy. These were the Colonel's troops, the grunts; he prided himself in running this operation like a military campaign.

Jimmy, Caroline, Paul Cottrell (Jimmy's chief of staff), and the Colonel's team sat around a table in the conference room, drinking too-long-in-the-pot coffee and occasionally reaching into one of the Dunkin' Donuts boxes. There were boxes piled everywhere—boxes that contained James Dean T-shirts, buttons, bumper stickers, brochures, palm cards, magnets, stationery, postcards, and posters.

BE A REBEL WITH A CAUSE—VOTE FOR JAMES DEAN

DON'T DROP OUT, DROP IN WITH DEAN

Everyone but the Colonel looked dog tired. It was after midnight and late in the campaign; there was too much to do and not enough time to do it.

The Colonel stood beside a MAKE CALIFORNIA WORK lawn sign, happily puffing on an evil-smelling cigar and listening to Murray Goldfein, one of Bobby Kennedy's wunderkinds from Brooklyn. Goldfein was tall, over six feet. He had dark, curly hair and acne scars. Though his eyes were a beautiful, cold, intense blue, he wasn't handsome. Not ugly, but not handsome. He had been a croupier at the Sands in Las Vegas, had had both arms broken in the first Selma march, had organized freedom rides, marches, and sit-ins. He was an award-winning reporter, an ex-president of the National Students Organization, a full professor of economics and political science at Columbia University, and the director of the Louis Stadler Research Group, a political think tank funded by the John F. Kennedy Foundation.

The Colonel was most impressed that Goldie, as he called him, had been a croupier. He was even more impressed that Goldie had the skills and contacts to gather and mobilize an army of gung-ho, completely dedicated young people from all over the country.

Goldfein was directing himself to Paul Cottrell, Jimmy's chief of staff, goading him. "If Pat Brown were still alive, we wouldn't have a prayer. The state and the party have been steadily shifting to the right, yet nobody seemed to notice—until now."

"We noticed," Cottrell said. He was the only one of the old guard at the meeting.

"Oh, yeah?" asked Goldfein. "Is that why one of your boys told the *Chronicle* that a Republican can't win in November unless he gets the votes of Democrats, 'and Democrats won't go for Reagan'? That's a quote. Come to think of it, Paul, I do believe it was *you* who said that."

"That was six months ago," Cottrell said, "and it wasn't me, so why don't we just stick to business?"

"Because it's no fun unless I can stick it to you at least once at every meeting."

"I'm sorry, son, but I'm afraid I don't share your unnatural proclivities."

"Can we move on?" Jimmy said.

The Colonel stood over the party and grinned.

"We're making some small gains," Goldfein continued. "We ran another poll in the Norwalk community."

"Why there?" the Colonel asked.

"Because Paul's people polled there at the beginning of the Brown campaign. It's a Democratic, working-class suburb. Three out of four people are registered Democrats. We should kick ass there, but as Paul can probably tell you, the first poll showed that Reagan would have won by a landslide. Paul?"

Paul's ears turned red. "I think you're exaggerating the figures."

"Well, Paul might have forgotten, but the citizens of Norwalk are pissed off about everything—like why it would take a major battle with the Los Angeles board of supervisors just to get a street repaired. The residents don't trust government. They hate it. They want to be their own boss. That's why they incorporated Norwalk in 1957. They don't want big government telling them what to do, and they hate what they consider high taxes. They hate social services, welfare. They think it's all spiraled out of control. They believe that people should get a job and go to work. They hate the fair-housing law. I don't know if they hate blacks—there are only three black families living in the town—but they certainly fear them all out of proportion. They're scared shitless they're going to move in next-door, and there go the property values and in comes the crime. And they hate everything that's gone on at Berkeley. Makes sense that they love Ronnie. He's their man."

"Is he still their man?" Caroline asked in a soft voice.

Although Jimmy couldn't stand Goldfein, Caroline liked him. She thought he was funny—but then she also thought that Bobby Dylan was funny. Poor Bobby Dylan who just had that terrible motorcycle accident.

"Maybe not as much. They still like Reagan. They like what he stands for, and they like him because they think he's nice. But they also like Jimmy, especially the senior citizens." Speaking to Jimmy: "You play well with the oldies. Although the good citizens of Norwalk don't believe for a minute that they'll lose their jobs, they like what you say about safety nets for regular people. They perceive you as a rebel who will protect the old and needy but won't take shit from anyone. And thanks to your old man here"—he nodded to the Colonel—"who doesn't think what you do now can bite your ass later, they're perceiving you as taking some of the same stands as Reagan on important issues such as law and order. Colonel, I've seen the leaflets you've been letterboxing in those districts. They make Jimmy sound like a young Republican."

"It's about winning," the Colonel said. "Consistency don't mean shit. Right, Jimmy?"

Jimmy looked uncomfortable and mumbled something like, "Yeah, John Stuart Mill would certainly understand."

But the Colonel didn't quite understand any such business as the greatest good for the greatest number of people. For that matter, neither did Goldfein, who assumed that Jimmy was probably referring to some other philosopher, or being ironic.

"So it's boiling down to personalities," Goldfein continued. "But I think the blitz is working. Reagan doesn't have the kids on the ground knocking on doors, not to the extent we do, anyway, although we're thin outside the cities, real thin. Reagan's media is good, but so is ours. Anyway, gentlemen"—he bowed to Caroline and grinned—"and lady, we've come up twenty percentage points in Norwalk. We'd still get our ass kicked there, but at least they wouldn't leave their shoe in the crack."

Only the Colonel and Caroline laughed.

"Otherwise, all our polls pretty much confirm what we know. Nine out of ten people disapprove of the antiwar demonstrators. Crime, drugs, and juvenile delinquency combine to be the number-one issue. Number two is racial problems. The surprise is student unrest at Berkeley. That was down in sixth place. But we also tested reactions to various words, you know, "blacks," "Hispanics," "Watts," "Vietnam," "LSD," "DMZ," and you know what word topped off the scale? The highest-scoring reactive word was "Berkeley." It sort of hides, unless you go around it sideways; but that's the big emotional issue. Jimmy's absolutely identified with it, and Reagan is playing it up, which is what he should be doing."

"That's not helping me," Jimmy said.

"We've got a demonstration planned at Berkeley," said Leonard Washington, a quiet, reedy black youth who had seemed more interested in the paperwork he was examining than in anyone else around him. Washington was in charge of the Watts Mobilization Campaign, which was a statewide effort to get blacks and Hispanics registered to vote—for Jimmy.

"It's not a black demonstration," Goldfein said.

"They all know my involvement at Berkeley," Washington said dismissively. He was well spoken, with a surprisingly low, resonant voice. "We've got CORE and the SNCC on our side. We're going to stage a 'Clean for Dean' demonstration. Mario Savio has promised to do something for the cause, and if Robert Kennedy can make it, he's also promised to speak." Washington gave Goldfein a meaningful look; they each had their own agendas, but Goldfein was certainly Bobby's boy. He had come on board Jimmy's campaign as a favor to Bobby, in hopes that Bobby would take on Johnson in '68; Goldfein was one of the initiators of the "Dump Johnson" movement.

"Bobby can make it," Jimmy said.

"We'll poll after it's over," Goldfein said. "See if you guys can get your Patrick Henry thing through to the voters."

"You certainly know how to spend what money we don't have," Paul Cottrell said.

"Polls are important. It's the only way we know where we're going."

"And right there—that's what's wrong with the campaign," Paul said.

"Yeah? Then you can tell me how we're doing with the unions, right? You can tell me what percentage will vote for Jimmy, right?" Paul just shook his head, disgusted.

"How many will vote for me?" Jimmy asked.

"Right now you've got fifty-five percent."

"We should have a hundred percent."

"We're up from forty percent," Goldfein said.

"Yeah, in Norwalk," Paul said.

"No, across the state."

"What this campaign is about is getting Jimmy seen," the Colonel said, having had quite enough of listening.

A young, fresh-faced man with tortoiseshell-framed glasses and owl eyes said, "Well, we've been trying to get Jimmy out to Stockton for—"

The Colonel interrupted the operative and said, "I ain't allowing my boy to run around the state like a chicken with its head cut off. We got a benefit comin' up in Stockton, ain't that right?" The Colonel looked to his assistant, Tom Diskin, to confirm. Diskin nodded, and the Colonel continued, "You telling me we don't have enough radio and television time there?"

The operative shook his head.

"Television is what gets Jimmy seen. Did you get his posters on all the buses?"

"We're working on that."

"Call me tomorrow night and tell me that you done it," the Colonel said. Then he turned to Caroline. "You got all your television and newspaper people set up for that demonstration of Goldie's?"

"It's all taken care of, Colonel."

"What's going to get Jimmy elected is getting all them young people and nig— er, Negroes and 'spanics all over the state to vote," the Colonel said expansively. "Reagan don't got them, and he ain't going to. We're inventin' them, growin' them right out of the ground, so to speak." To Washington he said, "Everyone you and Goldie get narrows the margin."

"If you want to get Jimmy seen, we should let him debate Reagan," Paul said.

"No, it's much too dangerous," Goldfein said. "We can't control it, and Reagan has always shown best when he's doing Q and A or handling hostile journalists. He eats up press conferences. It's instinct. He never sweats. He loves it, and it's almost impossible to get around him on the issues. He's like . . . Teflon."

"That's good," the Colonel said. "We should use that. Teflon." He seemed to chew on the word, tasting it. "But you're full of shit, Goldie. Reagan ran off the stage and called Jimmy a son of a bitch when Jimmy said something to him. What did you say to him, Jimmy?"

"I attacked his integrity," Jimmy said, "and he said he would not stand silent and let anyone imply that. I wasn't implying it—"

"But he came back," Goldfein said. "He came back and apologized to the audience—and to you, Jimmy."

"Well, we won," the Colonel said. "We won in the press."

"Well, not to get Paul all upset over polling again, but the public perception is that Reagan is a nice guy who can lose his temper like anyone else, and that he did the right thing by apologizing. Jimmy was perceived as being the nasty."

"We won," the Colonel said flatly. "I don't give a shit what the polls say."

"Well, Reagan is certainly making hay now," Paul said. "Everyone believes that Jimmy's afraid to debate him."

"Let Reagan complain all he wants," the Colonel said. "We got bigger fish to fry."

"I'm going to debate him," Jimmy said quietly.

"That's not a good idea, son. If it goes wrong, you blow it in front of the entire state."

"I'm not Nixon," Jimmy said, fuming. "I can handle reporters or anyone else, as well as Reagan. It's my campaign, and I'd fucking appreciate it if one or two of you—besides my wife—would have a little faith in me." He looked to Caroline, but he had caught her out; she was frowning.

And the Colonel had opened the conference-room door to yell at the kids.

"YOU STILL WANT TO DEBATE REAGAN?" THE COLONEL ASKED.

"Yeah, of course I do."

"Well, pick me up right now. We got to talk and work up a strategy. Reagan is going to be at CBS in an hour."

"You want me to prepare for a debate in an hour?" Jimmy asked the Colonel.

"We got no choice, son. I found out that he bought an hour of airtime and plans to debate an empty chair with your name on it. I tried to buy the next segment, so you could follow him, you know, but they basically told me to pee up a pipe."

"Goddammit, I told you I wanted to debate him. This has hurt me, made me look like I'm afraid of him."

"You know how hard we tried, Jimmy, but his people put so many rules into the deal that you wouldn't've been able to say shit. He wouldn't agree to *any* kind of reasonable format. You got a brain. You need more than a buzzword to express yourself. You—"

"Okay, Colonel, cut the bullshit." Then, musing, castigating himself, "I should have just agreed to debate him in the first place, whatever the goddamn rules. Are you sure about this—this chair thing?"

"You just got to trust me, son. The Colonel's got his ear to the ground. You'll pick me up at my hotel, that right? You wouldn't leave the Colonel by himself."

"We're on our way."

"I have your word on that?"

"Yes, Colonel. You have my word."

The Colonel grinned at his reflection in the living room mirror. *This is going to be the greatest snow job ever.*

JIMMY, THE COLONEL, CAROLINE, AND JIMMY'S BODYGUARDS AR-rived at the studio three minutes before airtime, but the Colonel in-sisted that everyone stay in the car.

"I'm going up there and debate him," Jimmy said.

"Yeah, you are, but if you go up early, he'll get rid of his empty chair with your name on it, and we'll lose the advantage."

"The idea is for me to be there to debate him," Jimmy said, frus-trated.

"The Colonel's right, Jimmy," Caroline said. "Let the press get some photographs of Ron shaking his fist at your empty chair."

There was a knock on the window of the Rolls. The Colonel buzzed it down.

"Hi, Caroline. Hi, Mr. Parker. Hi, Jimmy." Sandy Kahn, reporter from the *L.A. Times,* was holding a Nikon X camera and had a canvas knapsack on his back. It looked heavy. "You ready to do the debate?"

"I've been ready," Jimmy said, and as they got out of the car, Sandy clicked one picture after another.

"Television crews all set?" Caroline asked Sandy.

"The wolves are all hungry," Sandy said, and Caroline nodded.

Once in the lobby, Jimmy was seen. A young man in a worn leather jacket called to his colleagues, and several television crews pushed toward him.

The elevator was crowded—his bodyguards, Jay and George, flanking him, pushing against him; the smell of aftershave, Vitalis hair oil, hair spray, lemon, sweat; cameras whirring; questions; commotion; Jimmy feeling sudden claustrophobia; answering questions, though, answering questions—

"Yes, I came for the debate. Mr. Reagan said he'd have an empty chair for me."

"How did you know about this debate, Mr. Dean?"

"Call me Jimmy."

The elevator lurched sickeningly, and the doors whispered open; then cameras were turning, lenses like curious, unblinking big black eyes; Jimmy noticed a bloody Band-Aid in the gray sand of the cylin-drical ashtray beside the elevator doors.

"So how did you know about the debate, Mr. Dean? Did Mr. Rea-gan notify you, did—"

"How'd *you* know about it, boy?" the Colonel asked (and under his breath, "Who the hell's side is he on, anyway?"), pushing forward, Jimmy and Caroline right behind, flanked by Jay and George.

Ahead stood a guard in a blue-black uniform with light-blue-braid epaulets; he was tall and husky, with crooked teeth, long, thin brown hair slicked back with pomade and tied with a red rubber band. He stood guard resolutely in front of a glass door, the door surrounded by more glass, a Plexiglas wall of great black lifting designs like wings.

"Mr. James Dean is here to debate Ronald Reagan," the Colonel explained to the guard.

"I'm here to debate Mr. Reagan," Jimmy said, cutting off the Colonel, speaking for the cameras going *click click click*.

"I'm sorry, sir, but I can't admit you, or anyone else."

"We were told that Ronald Reagan has an empty chair with Jimmy's name on it, and—"

Jimmy cutting off the Colonel again, playing for the press. "Maybe Ron would prefer to shake his fists at an empty chair, but I'm right here, ready and willing to sit right down in my namesake chair and debate Ron on whatever issues he chooses. But we're going to have a real debate. Ron can try on all the easy homilies that sound good at first but don't make any sense when you think about it later. I'm going to discuss the issues that concern the ordinary working people of California. Now, will you please notify him that I'm here? Or would he really prefer to debate an empty chair?"

"I'm sorry, sir, I can't do that. I can't admit you. Mr. Reagan has purchased the time, and I have orders not to let anyone enter."

"So you're telling me that Ron's alone in there with my chair?" Jimmy said, drawing a laugh from the reporters and television crew. "There are no reporters in there? Nobody but the technicians?"

"I don't know, sir, but I have orders not to let anyone enter."

Jimmy looked at his watch. "Well, Ron's already started debating the chair. Can you at least get one of the studio technicians to let him know that I'm here?"

"Sir, I'm under strict—"

"Can you just ask someone?"

The guard spoke to someone on his walkie-talkie, and a moment later a man in his thirties, in a dark suit, starched white shirt, and Harvard tie, came through and said to Jimmy, "I'm sorry, sir, but the program in question is a paid political broadcast, and no one is allowed to enter."

"Yeah, yeah," Jimmy said. "Well, can you just let him know I'm here."

"I'm sorry, sir, but the show is in progress."

"Okay, I understand. All I'm asking you to do is have one of the technicians stand in front of the window where he can see him and hold up a sign or something. All it needs to say is 'Jimmy's here.' That's not hard. That won't put anybody out. If Ron knows I'm here, he'll want to debate me—and he'll be furious at *you* and your network if you don't let him know."

The man squinted, as if thinking very hard about this, and said, "I'll see what I can do."

"I'm sure he'll want to debate me. That's what this whole goddamn charade he's putting on with the chair is all about."

"Jimmy," Caroline said, warning in her voice.

"I'll see what I can do, sir." And the man left.

"Ten bucks he's a lawyer," the Colonel said.

"Ten bucks you're right."

The man returned in less than five minutes. "I'm sorry, sir, but I'm afraid we won't be able to allow you into the studio."

"You didn't tell Ron I was here, did you," Jimmy said; it wasn't a question.

"Yes, sir, we did. I assure you."

"You held up a sign for him to see?"

"He was notified, sir."

"Well, if he doesn't want to debate me, will you kindly tell him to remove the chair with my name on it from the stage."

"As I reiterated, sir, Mr. Reagan is in the middle of a telecast."

"Telecast?" Jimmy asked, laughing. "Let me guess—you're a lawyer, right?"

"I'm sorry, Mr. Dean. I don't know what that has to do with anything."

Jimmy looked at the Colonel and smiled—more a frown. "Well, it does." Playing to his audience again: "I'm willing to bet that old Ronnie is kicking the bejesus out of my chair in there. He's probably giving it hell right now. And here I am, ready and willing, but locked out. But it ain't over yet, folks. Let me know who wins. My bet's on the chair." With that, Jimmy turned around, pulling Caroline with him toward the elevator, George keeping close, Jay ahead holding the elevator door, barring everyone else but the Colonel from entering, then down, down, down, the Colonel chuckling, Jimmy angry, frustrated . . . suspicious.

JIMMY SAT ON THE COUCH IN THE LIBRARY. CAROLINE HAD FILLED IN the shelves where Pier's dolls had been with leather-bound volumes and first editions; she enjoyed buying rare books at auctions. The room smelled of oiled wood, leather, and cigarettes. The only light came from a table lamp with a movable green glass shade. The shadows behind the green-tinged halo of foggy light were also green, and Jimmy remembered a poem from childhood, something his mother used to recite. *How green, green is my garden . . .*

Pier had loved the garden, loved to dig and plant.

"Do you like plants?" Jimmy asked Caroline.

"You mean houseplants?"

"I mean like working in the garden, that kind of stuff."

"Yeah, I guess."

"That sounds like a no to me."

Caroline laughed. "What made you ask?"

Jimmy shrugged.

"You want a drink?" Caroline asked.

"I'd prefer a joint."

"You're not doing that anymore, remember? That's all over."

Jimmy nodded. "We don't know each other very well, do we?"

She gave him a finger of Scotch in the heavy crystal glass he liked and sat down beside him. "We haven't had much of a chance yet. But we know each other better than you think, probably. We just haven't picked up on all the details. But we will, given time . . . providing that's what you want." She looked at him tentatively, and he laughed, took her hand.

"Of course that's what I want. We can play twenty questions when we're on our honeymoon. Fair enough?"

"Fair enough."

"The Colonel's got me scheduled all over the goddamn state," Jimmy said. "Have you seen the itinerary?"

She nodded. "I worked it out. I'll be with you about half the time, Bobby the other half."

"I thought we were doing all the gigs together."

"Well, I guess not. Colonel probably figures it's overkill. Anyway, I've got enough on my plate right here. Ron has finally gone quiet over all the debate business, though. We'll see."

"He still suing the network?"

"He'll drop it, I'm sure," Caroline said.

"I still wonder if he knew I was there."

"The network claims they told him."

"Then why didn't the reporters Ron let inside the studio see anything?" Jimmy asked.

"They weren't in the booth."

"They'd have seen it if a tech held up a sign."

Caroline laughed. "I don't think they needed to hold up a sign."

"I think the Colonel did something."

"Like what? Caroline asked.

"Something," Jimmy said.

"Well, if he did, it worked."

"If he did, I'll break his back."

TWENTY-NINE

■

Bitch Luck Boogie-Woogie

LOS ANGELES: NOVEMBER 8, 1966

Jimmy had fallen into a deep, snoring sleep; Caroline wouldn't wake him, not even for the Colonel, not even for Bobby.

After stumping around the state nonstop, Jimmy was exhausted and coming down with a cold. He was coughing and sniffling; that it was wet, foggy, and close—another filthy L.A. inversion—didn't help. Caroline had turned on the air-conditioning, but that only seemed to make him choke. Jimmy and Caroline weren't going to get to the Ambassador Hotel until after nine.

The polls had closed at seven.

"You should have woken me up earlier," Jimmy said.

"You needed to sleep."

"I can sleep for the rest of my life."

She shrugged. "You would've looked like death warmed over."

He grinned at her. "I do look like death warmed over." He leaned forward, grasping the backrest of the driver's seat, and said, "George, just drive around a little. I'm not ready to face the ravaging hordes yet."

"Okay, boss," George said. He was wearing his best suit. He and Jimmy had developed an easygoing relationship; Jay—who was sitting beside George—was too reticent and quiet, even for Jimmy. But that's what Jimmy had asked for—gray-flannel-suit bodyguards, shadow people.

"So much for the Colonel and his system."

"What do you mean?" Caroline asked, distracted. She was upset; her hands were trembling. But she looked beautiful tonight, Pier's big eyes, Jackie Kennedy's smooth, champagne charm and grace. She was wearing an Oleg Cassini evening gown made especially for her. It was conservatively off the shoulder but sexy, and the deep blue silk seemed to shimmer subtly and change hue whenever she moved.

"His system was to hold back public appearances," Jimmy said. "That was supposed to make the fans clamor for a view."

"Well, the fans are clamoring, I guess, and he felt it was time to give them a view. It's steam-engine time. Seems to be working."

"We'll see."

"Senior citizens, blacks and Hispanics, and most of the unions have all come out for you."

"We'll see."

"You sound like a broken record," Caroline said. "The networks are reporting that you're going to win."

"Not all—not ABC."

Caroline shook her head. "Okay, not ABC, but Roger Mudd from CBS and Sander Vanocur from NBC are at *your* suite in the Ambassador, waiting for you."

"They'll interview me and then go back and see Ron."

"Well, we'd probably better get over there, then. You shouldn't keep your fans waiting." She smiled at Jimmy, but he was gazing out the window into the drizzle-refracted lamplight; the world was wet and slippery, and Jimmy was unsure of everything, tense, frightened, and somehow angry. "I don't want to see the Colonel."

"Well, he's going to be there, Jimmy," Caroline said. "But this is your night—our night."

"I don't trust him," he said.

"It's a little late for that." She took his hand, and he felt her tremble.

"You know something you're not telling me, don't you?" he asked.

"No, Jimmy, for the thousandth time."

"The Colonel works for *me*."

"I know, Jimmy."

"I know *something's* bothering you because your hand's shaking. Are you okay?"

"Yes, Jimmy."

"Look, I'm sorry if I upset you. I'm just a little anxious."

"Yes, Jimmy, I know." She didn't want to go to the campaign suite either.

"If I win, if I beat Reagan, then I'm going to talk to your friend Budd."

"Budd Schaap?"

Caroline looked nervously ahead. George and Jay worked with Budd. "Little pitchers have big ears," she said in a low voice.

"I'm going to ask him . . . about what we talked about. She nodded, hoping he would drop the subject. "If I win, I'll get a straight answer. You know why?" When Caroline didn't respond, Jimmy said, "Because he won't know if I'm having *him* bugged."

"Are you stoned or what?" Caroline asked.

"Just stoned on love, darlin'." Jimmy giggled and nuzzled his face against hers. "I don't want to do this tonight," he whispered.

"Well, we've got to. This is going to be the most important night of your life. The best night."

He squeezed her breast, feeling the stiff wire bra. "That a promise?"

"George," she said loudly, "we'd better get over to the hotel. ASAP."

"Caroline, you're still trembling."

She laughed woodenly. "So are you."

EVEN WITH THE AIR CONDITIONERS TURNED ON FULL BLAST, THE Royal Suite on the fifth floor—the campaign suite—was hot and humid from the press of too many people. Six portable televisions blared out poll results; televisions were on desks, tables, and bookshelves, and one was on top of a huge, engraved armoire. There was the constant *chink-a-chink* of glasses, bottles, keys; the swish of silk and satin, organdy and organza; the chatter of beads and bracelets; conversation like high-volume television static; perfume mingling with sour breath, alcohol, and food decaying between teeth; the lemon scent of expensive cologne and aftershave; and faces, faces laughing, faces concentrating, faces nodding, faces bobbing, aberrant shades of pink, flesh-pink balloons bobbing in the bright light and heat, coruscating light, flickering, flickering, as Jimmy shook hands and kissed balloon faces, everyone directed toward him like filings to the magnet, the magnet of the moment; and George and Jay and Jimmy and Caroline pushed through the well-wishers and party faithful, toward the safety and relative privacy of the bedrooms.

They found Bobby and Ethel, Ethel four months pregnant. Jimmy had expected to see Bobby at the party but was surprised to see Ethel. "My, you look beautiful," Ethel said to Caroline, hugging her, then grinning at Jimmy; but even as he reached out to embrace her, the Colonel was practically on top of them, crowding them, taking up all the space, breathing all the air.

"Jimmy, I got to talk to you." The Colonel was wearing a dark brown suit, western tie with a brass clasp, and a large-brimmed, white cowboy hat. The edges of the lenses of his glasses were misted over; he was sweating profusely. Behind him, affixed to the wall, was a poster blowup of the front page of the October 29 *L.A. Times*: Below the headline PLEASE KEEP OUT were two photographs: one of Reagan gesticulating to an empty chair, the other of Jimmy trying to get past the studio guard. "Hello, Bobby, and hello, little lady." The Colonel bowed to Ethel, put his arm around Caroline, released her, and started to pull Jimmy away.

"Jesus, Colonel, give me a minute here. I haven't even—"

"Just a word, son."

"Excuse me," Jimmy said and followed the Colonel to a private corner.

"You look like shit," the Colonel said.

"That's what you wanted to tell me?"

"You're gonna need makeup or something before you go downstairs to make your victory speech."

"It's too close to call, that's what—"

"Whether you make a victory speech or a concession speech, you got to go down there."

"So what do you care what I look like?"

The Colonel smiled at him. "Because you're my boy. Now, you want to take that chip off your shoulder?"

"Tell me what you got to say."

"Here's your acceptance speech." The Colonel handed Jimmy a few sheets of lined yellow paper.

"I think I can do that on my own," Jimmy said.

" 'Course you can, son. This was cooked up by Goldie and the nigger."

"Leonard's his name," Jimmy said. "Leonard."

"Yeah, well, I just made a few suggestions for you," the Colonel said. "But you're the boss. It's your speech."

"That's right, I'm the boss."

"What are you so pissed off about? I just made you the most powerful person in California. Or you're just about to be, anyway. I think you—"

"I don't owe you. And I'm not your boy, Colonel."

The Colonel nodded. "I think you are, Jimmy. I think you are." And then the Colonel was smiling and backslapping, as well-wishers crowded around them, shaking their hands, as if both were celebrities of equal merit, and Caroline touched Jimmy's arm, guiding him out of harm's way. They spent a few minutes chatting with Marty, who seemed genuinely happy for Jimmy and Caroline and was earnestly playing the successful auteur all dressed in white. Jimmy owed Marty and was trying to pay up. There was a huge shout and clapping, everyone watching the televisions. Jimmy was ahead, but it was close. Jimmy had a drink but refused the next. He talked with Bobby, only then realizing that he finally felt calm. He might not be able to trust many people in this room, or the packed rooms adjoining it, but he was calm. He stared down at the thick, beige carpet and listened to Bobby, the nasal and drawn-out vowels of his Boston accent somehow comforting, and he thought of his cousin Markie, Bobby and Markie. One he loved, even though he hadn't seen him for years; the other he distrusted. Yet he owed Bobby. Perhaps Bobby had done so much for him out of guilt for Marilyn. They stood close together, shoulders hunched, as if unconsciously mirroring each other, then Jimmy was talking with Ethel. Ethel was comfort, sweet milk and kindness and children mixed incongruously with a wholesome, healthy wildness and eccentricity, but she looked drawn tonight, as drawn as Jimmy.

"The baby okay?" Jimmy asked.

"Baby's fine," Ethel said, patting her stomach. "They don't call me Old Moms for nothing."

"You okay?"

"Not so fine," Ethel said.

"Yeah, stupid thing to ask."

"No, it's not. I'm getting there, it's just—"

"Yeah?"

"The dream. The dream's all coming true. I told you about it, didn't I?"

Jimmy nodded. "At your brother's funeral."

"I really appreciated that you came," Ethel said. "You being so busy with the campaign and everything." She looked at her hands, examining them, as if she'd just touched something she shouldn't have, and said, "But I was happy to see you and Caroline. It really helped. A lot."

"We wanted to be there."

"You know what someone said who saw the plane crash?" Ethel said; she looked haunted, transported. "He said that he saw a man looking out the window and smiling, just before it hit. Whenever my brother George was in real trouble, he always smiled. It was a terrible smile, like a grimace. That man saw George in the plane. I know it was George smiling like that, and I can't imagine how he felt looking out that window while his plane circled, going down, going—"

"Ethel, don't," Jimmy said, putting his arms around her. "Let it go."

A woman with an expertly painted face and a sprayed helmet of dyed black hair gave Jimmy and Ethel a surprised look; she'd have something to gossip about—*Did you see James Dean and, would you believe it, with Robert Kennedy's wife, what's her name?*

"And Bobby told you about Kick, right?"

Kick was Ethel's niece. She had taken a little girl, a friend's daughter, for a ride in her convertible. Somehow, little eight-year-old Hope O'Brien fell out of the car and later died.

"Yeah. Caroline said she called you."

"Within the last three months, George dies, and then this business with Kick. Both times I had the same dream, the same dream I always have when something terrible is going to happen."

"Ethel, it's—"

"You got an explanation?" she snapped.

"No, I don't have an explanation."

"I'm sorry, Jimmy," she said. "God, I'm some friend. This is your big night, and here I am acting like an idiot."

"You're not acting like an idiot. This is difficult stuff."

But Ethel wasn't listening. She went on: "When I came into the lobby, just before, I remembered the dream, I felt it. It hit me, it really hit me. It's not over, Jimmy. Something terrible is going to happen again."

"No, it's not," Jimmy said, realizing how inane that sounded.

"I worry about Bobby, and you, and everybody. After Jack . . . I worry about Bobby all the time."

"That's only natural," Jimmy said.

"When I got pregnant again, I thought everything was going to change, that everything would be fine."

"It will be, Ethel."

"Promise?" She grinned at him.

"Promise."

"You remember that party, when Bobby was spending all his time with Marilyn Monroe?"

"Yeah," Jimmy said, suddenly wary.

"Somehow I feel the same way tonight."

"Bobby's just working the room," Jimmy said.

"Yeah, I just feel, I don't know. Empty, but I feel better seeing you. In two minutes I'm going to be so happy I'd jump into a swimming pool, if there was one here."

"There's one on the roof, I think," Jimmy said, smiling at her.

"Jimmy, are you happy?"

"Yeah . . . ?"

"I mean with Caroline."

"Where are you going with this, Ethel?"

"Sorry. God, I can't even keep my mouth shut. Look, I don't have any hard feelings toward Caroline. What she did with Bobby . . ." She laughed bitterly. "A lot of people did that with Bobby."

Jimmy squeezed her hand. "Who told you I wasn't happy?"

"No one. Honestly. I just . . . I just hope you love her. Do you?"

"Yes, Ethel. Very much."

She smiled. "I'm still in love with Bobby. Through it all." She smiled and said, "I guess I must be, with number ten in the oven." She patted her stomach. "Has Bobby talked to you about his . . . plans?"

"I'm not sure what you're getting at."

"About running against you-know-who," Ethel said. "I think he should do it. That's what he wants, but he's afraid."

"Afraid of what?"

"Past history."

"Because of Jack?"

"And Lyndon, too. I shouldn't be talking about this. He'd kill me, but he's afraid people would see him as . . . ruthless."

"So?"

"And he doesn't want to split the party," Ethel said.

"He wants it so bad he can taste it, doesn't he?" Jimmy asked. "But *you're* the one who's really afraid, aren't you?"

"Wouldn't you be?" She laughed at herself after she said that. "No, you wouldn't. Both of you think that you have to flirt with death to prove something."

Neither Jimmy nor Ethel realized that Bobby was standing nearby and had heard what they said. He put his arms around Jimmy and Ethel and said, "Naughty, naughty, this is Jimmy's night. She telling you about her dream again?" he asked Jimmy. "It's as cockeyed as that curse thing she dreamed up with my sister-in-law."

"Jackie?"

Bobby laughed. "No, Joan." He squinted at Ethel and said, "Birds of a feather."

"You're rotten through and through, Robert Francis Kennedy," Ethel said.

"Jimmy, you know when I decided I wanted to be president? It was when I was"—suddenly he changed his accent to mimic CBS news anchorman Walter Cronkite—"It was impossible to pinpoint the exact time and place where he decided to run for president, but the idea seemed to take hold as he was swimming in the Amazonian river of Nhamunda, keeping a sharp eye peeled for man-eating piranhas." Dramatic pause. "Piranhas have never been known to bite a U.S. senator." He patted Jimmy and said, "And I doubt they'd bite the new governor-to-be of California, either."

"How much have you had to drink?" Ethel asked.

Locking eyes with Jimmy, he said, "Not nearly enough." And then a shout went up, everyone clapping, pushing, rushing over to Jimmy and Bobby, congratulating.

"It ain't over till it's over," Jimmy said.

IT WAS ELEVEN-THIRTY.

The Embassy Ballroom was pandemonium, the crowd was shouting screaming chanting for Jimmy, and for Bobby, too, and Jimmy and Caroline, Bobby and Ethel came down a freight elevator with Jimmy's bodyguards. Bobby made it difficult for his ex-FBI security man Bill Barry; he wouldn't allow him to carry a gun. If Bobby had his way, he wouldn't have any security at all.

Neither would Jimmy.

Onto the speaker's platform, the rush, the wild singing in the ears, ahead like a writhing continent were Jimmy's supporters, adoring, loving; pennons and posters and balloons bobbed, two thousand people reaching out, this was the rush moment, this was all the marijuana rolled into a life-size joint, no wonder Kerouac, the silly asshole, was drunk, blasted, blasted out on the crowd.

Jimmy Jimmy Jimmy Jimmy

And Bobby was waving, smiling, bathing in it, for this would be his state . . . when he needed it, then Bobby at the mike, introducing Jimmy, but the crowd wouldn't stop applauding, and Ethel leaned over to him and said, "They're clapping for you, Bobby, not Jack—you," and

Bobby nodded and stretched out his arms, as if he were going to high-dive right into the crowd of campaign workers, party members, hangers-on, fans—all those who wanted needed had to be close to the sweaty charisma of power, as if by being close to Bobby and Jimmy, Jimmy and Bobby, they would live longer, freer, be richer, happier, immortality, this moment forever. There were young men wearing white T-shirts and red jackets, rebel accountants, rebel dockworkers, rebel cabdrivers; there were senior citizens wearing white boaters with photographs of Jimmy; and there were the ever-present kids, the hallmark of the campaign, the beautiful, idealistic, horny, energetic, enthusiastic loyal kids in suits and jeans, the kids who had worked their strong young hearts out for Jimmy, the kids who loved him wanted him. Wanted to *be* him . . . and for these thunderous, glorious, staccato moments, they were him.

"I don't know if any of you folks heard Ronald Reagan's concession speech," Bobby said, leaning in toward the microphone, "but to quote our opponent, 'From one actor to another, Jimmy; break a leg.' " Applause, cheering, but Bobby was in control, the crowd was listening, not screaming for him to turn blood into wine. Turning to Jimmy, "Now, I know you and Ronnie are old friends, that you go back to the old and early days of television"—laughter—"but I'm afraid that when he said break a leg, he was probably wishing you bodily harm."

The audience loved it, and Jimmy was laughing, laughing and remembering how he'd watched Bobby discover himself in front of crowds, how his voice had stopped cracking when he became excited over this issue or that, how Bobby had become an actor of sorts; and then Jimmy was in front with Caroline, Caroline trembling, now with stage fright, for this was different from anything she'd experienced; this was directed at her by dint of association and standing here and now on this charmed podium.

The crowds were tearing their throats screaming. It was a good ten minutes before Jimmy could speak.

He was the good boy, the good man, the regular guy.

BE A REBEL WITH A CAUSE—VOTE FOR JAMES DEAN
DON'T DROP OUT, DROP IN WITH DEAN
MAKE CALIFORNIA WORK

The smells in the air changed, subtly shifted into Hoosier summer, childhood summer. Jimmy smiled, as if he could see his mother in the audience, standing in the back, way back, standing on tiptoes to see him, straining to hear.

Jimmy thanked the workers, quickly ran through the litany of names, Goldie and Leonard's speech folded in his jacket pocket. "So I'm going to keep this short. After all, I don't want to interrupt the party." Shouting, clapping, Jimmy's image bobbing a thousand times on a thousand posters. "But you know who would have enjoyed this party? Pat Brown, may he rest in peace." Cheering.

"So maybe we should take a minute, moment of silence." And he bowed his head—*coon peering out of a henhouse*—watching, squinting into the crowd, the crowd shivering quivering with anxious energy, a few more seconds, one, two, three, and then "We did something wonderful today. We stopped dead in their tracks all those ideologues on the right who would foster fear and racism, who would take away our civil liberties under the guise of protecting them, who would pull out every societal safety net, who would . . ."

It felt like a second, being there onstage. Jimmy spoke for twenty minutes, made love to them with them for twenty minutes, twenty lifetimes as flashbulbs flashed blue-white, flashed like firecrackers, like blinking afterimages after looking into the sun on a perfect mirror sea, and then he was rushing through the kitchen, the back way, Caroline holding tight to him, thank-yous and congratulations from the cooks and kitchen staff, then through the pantry, down the back elevator to the cars waiting.

In the plush, cushioned backseat, and the blue-black flashing night, Jimmy held Caroline's hand and said, "It's the damndest thing, but I don't feel tired anymore. "You want to go dancing?"

THIRTY

■

Dancing in the Dark

SACRAMENTO: APRIL 10, 1967

"I thought you wanted to discuss the budget," said Carl

Lowenstein, the state finance director. He was a rabbit of a man, probably in his late thirties or early forties, but he looked sixty. He was balding, and he combed what hair he had from his right temple over to his left, covering his bald pate with a few smudgy strands, as if that would fool anyone.

"Yeah, well, let's start off by deciding if you're going to take the fall for all your creative accounting," Jimmy said, wanting to take a scissors and cut Lowenstein's long, carefully positioned and pomaded fringe. Lowenstein had been Pat Brown's finance director; Jimmy couldn't afford to jettison him just yet. "I really appreciate that you just forget to mention that I'd be inheriting a three-hundred-and-fifty-million-dollar shortfall."

"We had no choice but to delay any tax increases until after the election," Lowenstein said, "or Reagan would have eaten us alive. But we have a plan in place—"

"I have a plan," Jimmy said, tenting his hands on top of the walnut desk that was large enough to serve as a dining table for eight. He looked at the men and women sitting and standing before him, his team, his cabinet—or rather Pat Brown's team and cabinet, old Pat ruling from the grave—every one of them running a different agenda, everyone watching his or her respective ass, *no one watching my ass.* Jimmy smiled at them, hello and thank you and fuck you very much chief of staff, press secretary, cabinet secretary, finance director (but not for long), appointments secretary, legislative secretary, clemency secretary. Caroline sat on a folding chair to his right, perched on the edge like a bird, Caroline there for him, Caroline watching the others just as he was; but things were changing, changing quickly. He glanced at Goldie, who was now consultant to the governor, Goldie in a holding pattern until he could make his way back to Bobby, but in the meantime, in the meantime Goldie was part of Jimmy's unofficial cabinet, what Jimmy thought of as the true cabinet. Cameron Nicely, a deceptive name for a sharkskin lawyer, leaned against the doorpost of the paneled office, caught Jimmy watching him, and smiled. He was gazing at an engraved bronze plaque mounted on the front of Jimmy's desk, a gift from the Colonel: BREAK THE RULES OR GET OUT. Caroline had found Cameron; checkmark in the "tentatively trust him" category. Standing near the window to show herself off to best effect was Sheila Foster, his ersatz press secretary—that was Caroline's job.

Jimmy spoke now to Paul Cottrell, his new chief of staff. He didn't trust Paul, but Paul knew how to make everything go *clickety clickety clack* down the right tracks. Caroline hated him but agreed with Jimmy: perhaps he could be brought on side, eventually. "You know what I've discovered?" Jimmy said. "California is ranked as the sixth-largest economy in the world—or would be if we were a country instead of a state. And Carl is going to tell us that all we'll have to do is raise five billion dollars' worth of taxes to make up for his shortfall and balance the budget."

"It's not *my* shortfall, Governor," Lowenstein said.

"Yeah, it is," Jimmy said. Back to Paul. "I picked up one good idea at the governors' conference. We cut government spending by ten percent, right across the board, no exceptions. If we're going to ask the taxpayers for more money, we should show good faith."

Paul chuckled. "You can't do that. It will end up costing more money in the long run."

"Yeah, how?"

"Because various programs are funded to varying extents," Lowenstein said, interrupting. You take ten percent out of, say, mental health, and you're going to have those people out on the streets, and then there'll be a hue and cry, and you'll have to spend significantly more money to fix it."

"Carl's right," Paul said. "It will disadvantage some departments over others."

"Tough shit."

"Okay, let me put it another way. It will punish some departments and not others. Why not cherry pick?"

"Because it's not fair, it's discriminatory, it will piss everyone off."

"And this won't?"

"At least no one can claim that someone else received special privileges," Jimmy said. "That's been the problem in the past, hasn't it? Paul, I want every department to revise budgets. They have six weeks."

"They'll need more time than that."

"They don't have it," Jimmy said, "and I want you and Carl to go through every department and cut out every bit of pork, right down to the muscle."

"But not beyond ten percent," Paul said.

"Minimum ten percent. That's what I'm going to say I meant. Isn't that the way it works, Carl?"

"Why not just tell them straight out what you're going to do?" Carl asked.

"A novel idea," Jimmy said. "But I want to see what they consider can be cut, and I want to record who screams loudest about what."

"Sounds a bit sadistic to me," Paul said.

"Does it now?" Jimmy said, glancing at Caroline, who nodded. She knew the plan, knew, in fact, that Jimmy had no plans to cut mental health or education; the opposite, in fact.

Jimmy's phone rang, and Jimmy glanced at Caroline again: he had told Lorene, his personal assistant, not to put through any calls. He picked up the phone. "Yeah?"

"I'm sorry, Governor, but I have your cousin Marcus Winslow, Jr., on the line. He called the main switchboard, and they put it through to me. It's about your father, sir."

"Put him through. Hey, Markie, what's going on?" Jimmy said in a low, tentative voice as he turned away from everyone and gazed out the window behind his desk, gazed out at the gardens. His office suite was situated on the first floor of the East Wing, an ugly and uninspired addition to the Roman classical architecture of the state capitol. Above him were five floors of legislative offices. But at least the gardens were beautiful.

"Hey, Jimmy, I'm sorry to disturb you at your place of business, and, I guess, congratulations about the election and everything, but—"

"Yeah, Markie, just tell me."

"Your dad . . . passed away, Jimmy."

"When?" Jimmy looked at an oak tree, remembering building a tree house for Markie. He tried to resolve his father's face. He knew it—gaunt, long, tight, tight and loveless as the character Ray Massey played in *East of Eden*—he knew it, and he remembered how his father looked when Jimmy was a child, remembered how he parted his dark hair in the middle and greased it down "so it would stay put." But that was all. Right now, that was all he remembered.

"A few days ago. I just came back from the funeral."

Shocked, Jimmy asked, "You in L.A.?"

"No. He's been livin' at the farm with me, helpin' me out with the tractor business."

"Since when?"

"Over a year."

"Shit, someone could've told me."

"I was going to call you, but I promised him I wouldn't because of how you had words and all, and he felt like you'd think he was a failure for coming back home. But I should've called you anyway, Jimmy. I guess I failed you."

"You didn't fail anybody. I just . . . I don't know, I just would've liked to have seen him."

"You could've come down anytime."

"I didn't know he was there," Jimmy said.

"Yeah, well . . ."

You could've seen him in L.A. What did Lee Strasberg always say? "Woulda shoulda coulda."

"Aunt Ortense should've let me know. I just can't believe—"

"Nobody's heard from you for a long time, Jimmy, and Uncle Winton, he told us . . . well, you know . . . and my mom, well, she's pretty sick."

"I—"

"She's doing okay, it was nothin' to call you about."

"I should've been down to see you."

"Been a while, Jimmy."

"Yeah. How'd my father die?"

"Accident. One of them freak things. He drove into someone. They're all right, at least that's something."

"Yeah."

"Well, Jimmy . . . good-bye. I guess you're pretty busy. I'm sorry to have to bring you such news. I didn't think—"

"Didn't think what, Markie?"

"That it would bother you much. Uncle Winton said you were practically strangers, but he kept a scrapbook, all the times you was in the papers. I'll save it for you, in case you ever get back home."

"Thanks, Markie. I could come in, pay my respects. There must be something I can do."

"It's all over, Jimmy. Everything's been taken care of. Probably best to leave everything be for a while. You know."

"I'll call Aunt Ortense."

"She's not too good right now. Maybe wait just a little while."

Thinking hard about his father. *No tears, no feeling, why is that? Why is that?* "Remember when I taught you how to wrestle, and how you always used to want to play Captain Stormalong?"

"Yeah, Jimmy, I remember."

Then silence; he could hear faint static on the line, feet shuffling behind him; feel Caroline watching him, drilling through him with her gaze. "Well, thanks for calling," Jimmy said.

"You take care now," Marcus said. "And good luck with your new job. Everybody around here is real proud of you."

"Yeah, I can see that."

"You know what I mean."

"Yeah, I know what you mean." *Click.* And Jimmy waited for the upwelling of tears, for the rush of . . . something—memories, longing, regret—but felt only a quiet, poignant emptiness, and he turned on his cushioned leather swivel chair and told his cabinet that his father died.

Caroline leaned toward him, tense, concerned; Jimmy shrugged her off. He couldn't look at her. He didn't want any of that, didn't want empathy and sympathy and homilies; he just wanted to know why he didn't feel anything. He wasn't numb, though; thoughts filtered; he could feel himself, his aches and pains, all the small discomforts— shirt collar sweaty and sticky against his neck, tie too tight, underwear pulling; all of it, he could feel all of it, but his father was gone . . . but his father was never there, and his father didn't want him, didn't like him, *but he liked the scrapbook . . . he kept a scrapbook,* but the scrapbook was safe, it didn't ask for anything; and then it struck Jimmy: the emptiness was relief, freedom—all different aspects of the same thing.

Looking at Paul, then Goldie, back to Paul, he said, "Okay, what's next on the agenda?"

"Why don't we adjourn this meeting," Paul said. "You have personal things to take care of, Jimmy. This can all wait."

"No, it can't," Jimmy said, now glancing at Caroline.

"Jimmy, you need time—" Caroline said.

"Let's continue," Jimmy said.

"You can't do a meeting after finding out your father just died," Caroline said.

Jimmy knew she intended to take over for him, but he was focused; he wanted to continue the meeting. Looking at Paul, then Goldie, Carl, Sheila, and Cameron, he said, "It turns out that my father died some days ago. We weren't close." *Show them what you're made of. Wasn't that something my father used to say . . . or was it Reverend De Weerd?* "What's next on the agenda?"

Paul shrugged and said, "You need to decide what to do about Aaron Mitchell."

"Who?" Jimmy asked.

"He killed a cop," Cameron said, "and he's on death row in San Quentin. He's also black. Pat upheld the conviction, and it went up to the supreme court, which denied a stay of execution."

"And?"

"There's a mercy hearing scheduled this afternoon. It's up to you to decide whether to uphold the law or grant him a reprieve."

"That's pretty loaded," Jimmy said to Cameron. "I take it you're a death-penalty man."

"He killed a cop, Jimmy."

"Yeah, and he's a nigger to boot," Jimmy said.

Silence, then Paul said, "It's a hot political issue."

"It will be even hotter if you let the poor bastard fry," Goldie said.

"It's a law-and-order issue," Paul said, sighing, as if to show that he had infinite patience, but Goldie was a trial. "The law is the law. You can cover yourself. The people want this guy dead."

"I don't," Jimmy said.

Paul said, "I should tell you that the consequences—"

"We give him a reprieve," Jimmy said flatly. "Cancel the mercy hearing. What's next?"

"That's just about it," Paul said.

"For now," Goldie said.

"What's that supposed to mean?" Jimmy asked.

"Senator Beilenson is putting together a therapeutic-abortion bill,"

Goldie said. "He's proposing that women should be allowed to abort a fetus if their physical or mental health would be at risk."

"That's not news," Jimmy said.

"It goes farther than bills enacted in Colorado and North Carolina."

"So?"

"The act doesn't take into consideration the wishes of fathers, and if, say, a pregnant sixteen-year-old goes outside and smashes a few windows, she would be considered mentally unbalanced enough to qualify for an abortion. And Beilenson's got a cripple clause that is going to give further ammunition to the right-to-lifers."

"Are you a right-to-lifer?" Jimmy asked.

Goldie shook his head. "No, but I don't believe women should be given free rein—"

"You'd think differently if *you* were the one getting pregnant," Sheila said.

"That's neither here nor there," Goldie said.

"So what's your suggestion?" Jimmy asked.

"We should apply as much pressure as we can against Beilenson," Paul said. "He's a loose cannon." But Jimmy was looking at Goldie.

"Have a meeting with him," Goldie said. "Get him to drop the cripple clause." Then, after more discussion on administrative issues, they were gone, and Jimmy and Caroline were alone. "You want to take a walk?" Jimmy asked.

"Sure," Caroline said.

IT WAS LATE, ALMOST DARK.

The gardens were purple-green and leafy shadows, distant traffic noise, sudden humid smells, the cracking of twigs and gravel on footpaths, peeling benches, comforting boughs of sweeping trees, sprinklers splashing and making *pfutt pfutt pfutt* sounds; and then the street lamps came on, turning leaves bright green, creating a new shadow geography that was alternately frightening and comforting.

"I may change my mind about Sheila," Jimmy said. "Maybe there is someone in there, after all."

"Maybe. She does a good job."

"But I think you'd be better handling the press concerning my father."

"I'm just the person who should not be handling that," Caroline said. She was wearing a skirt and a thin blouse. It turned suddenly cool, and she shivered.

"Yeah. Okay."

"Jimmy, are you okay? You're acting really weird, considering . . ."

"Considering what?"

"That you just found out your father died."

He chuckled grimly. "Oh, that."

"Jesus, Jimmy."

"It's not like he was my father, like the relationship you have with your father. It's different."

"Still, I think you need to allow yourself to feel whatever . . ." She let her words trail off, then said, "Something's wrong, whatever you say." Jimmy didn't respond. "You know why I think that?"

"I'm probably about to find out."

"Because of the way you treated me at that meeting. You closed me out."

"I didn't close you out of anything. It was an open meeting."

"I didn't mean that. You brushed me away when you got off the phone. I think that if I would have reached out to you again, you would have slapped me."

"That's nonsense."

"Maybe, maybe not," Caroline said. They walked slowly along a dimly lit, winding path. Jimmy smelled herbs. "At the very least, we should postpone Elvis and Priscilla's wedding," Caroline said. "I'll call the Colonel and explain."

"We don't have to cancel anything."

"I didn't say cancel."

"It's only going to be a few guests—something like fifteen people," Jimmy said. "We'll have it at our place as planned. Sacramento will love to welcome Elvis, and you were all excited to hold a reception in the mansion."

"You're starting to sound like Paul," Caroline said, but Jimmy could see that she was pleased, that she wanted to have the small, private wedding in the Albert Gallatin mansion. She called it her "favorite house in the world," but Jimmy couldn't buy it for her—the governor's mansion wasn't for sale.

"It's too soon," she said, "and it's probably not a good political move."

"You said Sheila could handle the media."

"Yes, but—"

"Leave it, Caroline. It's a good thing to do."

"Okay, but we can't join them at the Aladdin Hotel in Vegas. That's out."

"Okay," Jimmy said. "Whatever you think."

"I think—"

"You want to dance?" Jimmy suddenly stopped and took her hand.

"What?" Caroline asked, giggling in spite of herself. Jimmy pulled her toward him and started dancing slowly with her.

They heard crickets, the scrunching of gravel, thunder—an impending storm.

"Jimmy, why are we dancing?"

Jimmy inhaled the fresh autumn smell of her hair, and as he held her close he tried to visualize his father's face, but instead he remembered playing Captain Stormalong.

The thin, shadowy ghost of Mildred stared through forests of darkness and death and distance at him, but his father was nowhere to be found.

"Caroline?"

"Yes?"

"I love you."

"I love you, too, Jimmy," said Caroline.

Pier.

Marilyn.

THIRTY-ONE

■

Promised Land

Bobby was still high from his encounter with the students

at Ball State University in Muncie, Indiana. He was stumping hard to be the Democratic candidate for president. Indiana wasn't Bobby's kind of state, but he had Jimmy with him.

Jimmy owed him, owed him for his gubernatorial election. But Jimmy paid his debts, you had to say that for him; and Jimmy was going to give him California on a plate—California was the prize: 174 delegates, and none of that proportional shit. *If I win*, Bobby thought, *174 delegates are mine. Payback time, everybody. Payback time.*

"So how d'you think I handled those students?" he asked Jimmy as they drove to the airport in a black

Lincoln Continental Town Car. George was driving; Bobby still didn't—wouldn't—keep his own bodyguards.

"You were hot, Bobby," Jimmy said.

"Next time we do a college together, we should switch. You do the speech and I'll follow up after they gasp."

"It's your election," Jimmy said. "You should do the schtick."

"You should have done it here. This is your home state. Christ, they wouldn't be stomping their asses off for me alone, I can tell you that."

"Yeah, they would've," Jimmy said.

"We'll have to plant someone at every college to ask us where we stand on educational draft deferments." Bobby gazed out the window now, drifting off, replaying this last interaction, the audience booing and hissing him when he told them that he was opposed to college deferments.

"I can afford to send my kids to college, but I don't think that the size of a parent's checkbook should determine whether a young man stays at home or serves his country. I believe that would be morally and ethically wrong."

Shouting, booing, fists waving.

"Okay, let me ask you a few questions. How many of you support continuing the deferments?"

All hands raised, shouting and chanting. A football crowd.

"And how many of you support an escalation of the war?"

More cheering.

"Okay, let me ask you one final question. How many of you who voted for the escalation of the war also voted for the exemption of students from the draft?"

Bobby smiled at them as it hit them, as they saw the contradiction in their logic. Gasp.

Checkmate.

And then they cheered, son of a bitch, they cheered.

Bobby felt a warm glow. If he could keep this up, if he could keep some of George Wallace's constituency without losing the black vote, if he could represent law and order here and civil rights there, if he could just be all things to all people long enough to win . . . He buzzed down the electric window. It was a warm day, a perfect day. "Hey, Jimmy."

"Yeah?" Jimmy looked tired, his face tight, strained. Too many people asking for too many favors.

"What did you think of Johnson's television broadcast?"

Jimmy shrugged. "I didn't think he'd quit, not so easily."

"Blew my mind, I can tell you that," Bobby said, "and it scared the shit out of me, too."

"Scared you? I thought it was what you wanted. You've been calling him a war criminal for escalating the war in Vietnam. I thought you hated him."

"I only compared him to Hitler once," Bobby said playfully.

"You've got a better chance of winning with him gone," Jimmy said.

"I'm not so sure. He took out my major issue." Bobby chuckled. "*Him*. And now he's making noises about a negotiated peace, which is what I've been calling for all along."

"McCarthy's got the same problem," Jimmy said.

"McCarthy's out. He tried to do what we did for you in California, but we're getting the kids now. He's losing. We're winning."

"Then what's your problem?"

Bobby laughed. "I guess I've got an issue or two left in me. You're right. I've got no problems. Not even with Lyndon. Did I tell you I had a meeting with him? He told me that our differences aren't that great. He said that Jack up in heaven would think he had tried his best to carry on the policies of our administration. You know, I think he meant it. So I told him . . ."

"What?" Jimmy asked.

"Believe it or not, I told him he was a good man. Even though he's a prick."

THEY BOARDED THE SIX-SEAT AERO COMMANDER PLANE FOR MIN-neapolis, where they were going to speak to blacks in the ghetto. This would be Bobby's meat and potatoes, Jimmy thought. It would be dangerous, and Jimmy could understand the joy, the rush of putting oneself in harm's way; but there was more to it for Bobby. He was the rich boy who had genuinely come to love the poor. He was passionate about the blacks, and civil rights, and ending the war.

Jimmy had to admit that Bobby had changed. But he still wasn't sure. There was still Marilyn.

And the son of a bitch had certainly called in the favors. But after this—no, after the California primary—Jimmy was done. All debts would be paid. Not even the Colonel could come back with his hand out, not after the son of a bitch had used Jimmy to inveigle his way into becoming Bobby's campaign chief. The Colonel was doing a good job; Jimmy had to give him that. But Jimmy wasn't going to act in the Colonel's motion picture, or pay him 50 percent of what he, Jimmy, would have earned if he did the picture.

"Is the Colonel meeting us in Minneapolis?" Jimmy asked after the plane took off. Jimmy didn't like flying in small planes, didn't like the sensation of being buffeted by the wind, didn't like the sudden stomach-wrenching drops and the constant droning of the engines.

Bobby grinned. "You know better than that. The Colonel's not going to associate himself with no niggers. I don't know what to make of him."

"Who does?"

"We did a background check on him," Bobby said. "Some funny stuff about his citizenship."

"Could that be a problem for you?"

"All fixed. Part of the deal, so to speak."

"I'd be careful of him," Jimmy said.

"Careful isn't the word. If he screws around with me, he goes down. And I explained to him exactly how that would be."

And what about Marilyn . . . after you explained exactly how that would be?

Jimmy looked around the plane. There was only Owen, one of Bobby's aides, who looked like he should still be in college or law school; an exhausted, rumpled Sheila Foster, who was "on loan" to the Colonel for the duration of the campaign; and a reporter from the *Minneapolis Star*. Bobby and Jimmy would give Sheila and the reporter time; but Sheila was a good flacker, and she seemed to care genuinely about Bobby. She protected him, gave him space; and no one, herself included, would bother him and Jimmy until they had a few minutes to relax. Jimmy had gained a lot of respect for her.

"I haven't seen your aide—what's his name? Ah, yeah, Frank Waters," Jimmy said, probing. "Don't you use him anymore? You know, the one who kidnapped me to have lunch with you and Peter Lawford?" *The one I saw at Marilyn's.*

Bobby seemed to flinch at that. "Yeah, Jimmy, he's still around. But I didn't think it would be wise—"

"I'll bet you didn't."

"I thought that was all behind us."

"No, Bobby—"

And then Sheila was leaning over them, looking daggers at Jimmy and looking meaningfully at Bobby, making small talk and introducing the reporter.

Bobby and Jimmy did the interview together. The reporter asked Jimmy a lot of questions about his hometown and whether he was planning a visit.

"I'm going to visit my aunt and uncle on this trip," Jimmy said. "They have a farm in Fairmont."

"I understand your father died recently, but you didn't attend the funeral," the reporter said. He was in his late forties, pudgy, baby-faced. Jimmy could see he was a hick wannabe and out of his depth—and he could see that question coming. But Sheila wasn't having any of it and said, with a charming smile, "Perhaps you should address yourself—your questions—to the next president of the United States. We'll be landing soon." She nodded, her waxen hair coiffed around her pretty face. Sheila the down-home local crinoline yokel, but it was all ruse and strategy: I'm a cute mommy, kiss me (and do what I say).

"Uh, excuse me, sir." The copilot stood in the aisle and addressed Bobby.

"Pierre Salinger just called and asked me to tell you that . . ."

"Yes, go on, Sam," Bobby said, looking up at him.

"Martin Luther King has just been shot."

"What?"

"In Memphis."

"Who? Why?" Bobby jerked backward, as if a bullet had just hit him, then he looked at Jimmy; and for that instant, it was as if they were staring at each other in a tunnel. Jimmy felt a familiar numbness and an awkward discomfort, as if he had been eavesdropping on a private conversation between lovers. The copilot stood where he was, as if he, too, had been eavesdropping and had been suddenly caught.

Bobby turned away from Jimmy, brought his hands over his eyes, pressing hard, as if to put them out, as if he had seen something he shouldn't, and he said, "Oh, God, when is this violence going to stop."

ACTIVISTS JOHN LEWIS AND WALTER SHERIDAN MET THEM AT THE airport. The police chief accompanied them. Onlookers and reporters shouted and tried to push through a police cordon to get to Jimmy and Bobby.

Jimmy and John embraced—they had paid their dues together on the Pettus Bridge in Selma, and had marched and spent time together subsequently. "You heard?" Jimmy asked. John nodded. He had been crying. His strong, handsome face had softened with grief. "You know Bobby?"

They shook hands, and John introduced Walter Sheridan and the police chief, a rather mild-looking man, an accountant all zipped up in blue.

"The word hasn't got out yet," John said. "When it does, all hell's going to break loose. Tonight's probably not going to be a good night for a gig in the ghetto."

Even now, John's sad, wry humor slipped through.

"He's right," the chief said. "You guys shouldn't be speaking tonight. It's too dangerous. I can give you a police escort, but I can't guarantee your safety. We're going to have our hands full, as it is. When the . . . when they hear the news, they'll riot. I'm right about that, aren't I, Mr. Lewis?"

"I can't say exactly what's going to happen," John said, "but I agree, it could be dangerous." He spoke to Jimmy and Bobby. "You guys might want to give it a pass this time."

"Jimmy, I'm going. You don't have to—"

"I'm going, too."

"We're going to speak," Bobby announced.

"Are you sure?" the chief asked.

"Yeah," Jimmy said, nodding to John. "We're sure."

"I'll go and take care of the reporters," Sheila said.

"You're not going," Bobby said.

"Fuck if I'm not."

WHEN THE LIMOUSINE REACHED THE GHETTO, THE POLICE ESCORT disappeared.

It was a cold, angry night, and there was iron in the air. The streets were mobbed with people, people who had not yet heard the news, people there for Bobby and Jimmy, and they were cheering and waving banners. Spotlights burned white and illuminated a flatbed truck where Bobby and Jimmy were to speak. Behind the truck was an oak tree, scarred and peeling in the brilliant light. John made an introductory speech, introduced Bobby and Jimmy, and then Jimmy was watching Bobby.

Bobby stretching out his arms, allowing the breakers of cheering and shouting to wash over him as he waved for silence—pray that the people remember that when he tells them the news.

Bobby in a black overcoat.

Bobby standing white and grim before two thousand people.

"I have bad news for you," he said, "bad news for all our fellow citizens and people who love peace all over the world . . . and that is that . . . Martin Luther King was shot and killed tonight."

Gasping, as if all the oxygen had just been sucked out of the world, then anguished screaming, crying, weeping, people shaking their fists, people standing motionless as if caught in freeze-frame, people dropping to their knees.

Finally, tentatively, temporarily . . . silence.

"In this difficult day, in this difficult time for the United States, it is perhaps well to ask what kind of a nation we are, and what direction we want to move in. For those of you who are black—considering the

evidence there evidently is that there were white people who were responsible—you can be filled with bitterness, with hatred, and a desire
for revenge. We can move in that direction as a country, in great po-
larization—black people among black, white people among white,
filled with hatred toward one another.

"Or we can make an effort, as Martin Luther King did, to understand and to comprehend, and to replace that violence, that stain of
bloodshed that has spread across our land, with an effort to understand
with compassion and love.

"For those of you who are black and are tempted to be filled with
hatred and distrust at the injustice of such an act, against all white
people, I can only say that I feel in my own heart the same kind of feeling. I had a member of my family killed, but he was killed by a white
man. But we have to make an effort in the United States, we have to
make an effort to understand, to go beyond these rather difficult times.

"My favorite poet was Aeschylus. He wrote: 'In our sleep, pain which
cannot forget falls drop by drop upon the heart until, in our own despair,
against our will, comes wisdom through the awful grace of God.' "

Amens. Rustling of clothes, shuffling of feet, the wind blowing
cold, smoke swirling, as if the riot fires had already been lit, dust coruscating in the beams of light, and Jimmy felt sudden fear as young
men on the shadow periphery shouted and chanted, "Black power!
black power! black power!" And the anger the rage the grief spread
like ink in clear water, and then Jimmy was on, Jimmy wearing a black
leather jacket, jeans, and a sweater, but there was no shouting for him
as he began to speak, to ride over the hecklers with his voice.

Breathing through the microphone, starting, saying: "What we need
in the United States is not division. What we need in the United States
is not hatred. What we need in the United States is not violence not law-
lessness, but love . . . and wisdom . . . and compassion and . . ." Then
Jimmy felt the choking, the gagging, the welling up of aching and pity in
his chest, in his throat, his mouth until he couldn't talk—pity for himself, for those around him, for Caroline and Pier and Marilyn and his
mother, for Nick Ray and Bobby, and pity for King, for King who hadn't
been a friend but an acquaintance, so why? he asked himself. So why?

He never cried, not out loud, certainly not in front of strangers, not
in front of all these strangers, shadows, dream shadows that would kill
him dead with knives and fists—crying for them? *Why?*

Jimmy stood in front of the microphone, the words choking in his
throat—"Oh, this is bullshit, I'm sorry, I'm . . ." And he shook his
head, and then looked at Bobby, who was staring hard at him, nodding
to him. Then Jimmy looked back at the crowd, back at the silent, silent

crowd, back at those who would kill him, those who would bring him home and welcome him, those who wouldn't give a thought to him; and later, later Bobby took his hand—Bobby who didn't usually touch or stroke—and said, "That was the moment, Jimmy."

BOBBY AND JIMMY FLEW TO WASHINGTON TO ATTEND THE MEMO-rial service. Caroline and Ethel would meet them there, as would Jackie and Ted and the ever-present Colonel.

Below, across the country, the cities burned. Washington was already under curfew; the troops were in the streets.

"You did good in that meeting," Jimmy said to Bobby, who was sitting beside him in the plane. No one had been talking. Sheila had tried to make a lame joke about their being in a flying coffin, but now, flying through the wispy flat whiteness of clouds, even the reporters were quiet, lost in their own white, wispy thoughts.

"Yeah?" Bobby asked, jolted out of his reverie. "What meeting?"

"The one with John Lewis."

"You two seem to have a strong bond," Bobby said. "Boy, was he pissed off, him and all his friends."

"Well, they couldn't find us," Jimmy said.

"We were in the goddamn hotel bar. They could have found us if they'd looked, all that 'Our leader is dead tonight, and when we need you, we can't find you.' "

"Well, they found us, and you've got their support. Telling them that they lost a friend and you lost a brother was good and how big business wants to defeat you because they think you're a friend to the Negro. Is that true? About big business?"

"Yeah, mostly. Jimmy?"

"Yeah."

"Would you consider being vice president?"

Jimmy laughed. "Not on your life. I got a state to run. I should have gone to school or something to learn how to do this shit."

"Seems to be working," Bobby said. "The press seems to love all your Creative Society business." He smiled, as he sometimes did when he was alone, thinking things through. "Is your cabinet really a lateral think tank?"

"Yeah, it is," Jimmy said, irritated. "For once in its life, the *L.A. Times* actually got it right."

Bobby stared hard at a spot on the chair. "I don't have anybody to do for me what I did for my brother."

"And you think I would do it?"

"If you wanted to."

"And why should I want to?"

"Because I need your help."

"And you're the king, is that it?"

"No, Elvis is the king," Bobby said. "I'm just the asshole trying to get through the primaries."

"You need to pick up the South," Jimmy said. "I can't help you with that, and, shit, I'm an actor, remember?"

"You mean you don't want to play second fiddle."

"Look what it did to Johnson."

"Yeah," Bobby said, looking away, "it made him president."

"You know what I mean. I don't want to be a yes man for anybody. Especially for you. You didn't consider being Johnson's vice president."

"I did consider it, but Johnson hated my guts then, just as he does now. But he was good for Jack."

"Just like you think I'd be good for you."

"It's the right path, Jimmy."

"This isn't a good time to talk about this."

"This is the perfect time to talk about this. Will you consider it?"

"Yeah, I'll do that. But—"

"You know," Bobby said, musing, lost. "King's death isn't the worst thing that ever happened."

"What?"

"You know that fellow Harvey Lee Oswald, whatever his name is, set something loose in this country."

"Yeah, I guess he did," Jimmy said, suddenly feeling exhausted, enervated, as he had when Marilyn died and later when he found out that Pier had committed suicide. He nodded off, and when he woke up, breaking out of scalding dreams just moments later, he found himself covered with a blanket. He looked over at Bobby and said, "You know, maybe you aren't so ruthless after all."

"Don't tell anybody."

And when he woke up again, Bobby was staring at him.

"Will you consider it?"

"SO EVERYTHING'S OKAY?" JIMMY ASKED.

"Yeah, clean."

Jimmy offered Budd Schaap a drink, a whiskey, which he accepted. "Where's your wife?" Budd asked.

"In Connecticut, visiting her folks." Budd nodded. "Why?"

"No reason." He finished his drink altogether too quickly and started to stand up.

"You don't like me very much, do you?" Jimmy said.

"I don't have feelings either way, Governor."

"I guess when you're bugging someone's house, you find out all those things that make for disrespect."

"Disrespect?"

"Sorry." Jimmy smiled. "Been hanging out in too many ghettos." Budd didn't get it. He shook his head. "Please, sit down. I know this is awkward. Did Caroline tell you that I wanted to talk to you?"

"Haven't talked to Caroline except when I swept your house for her," Budd said, lying; but he sat back down and accepted another drink.

"I need to know who was bugging me."

Jimmy didn't sit down; he stood by one of the high windows, and the light made a halo around him. Budd found it uncomfortable to look at him and glanced away.

"I can't—"

"I know you worked for Joe DiMaggio. Who else?"

"I did work for Joe. That's all. I don't know any more. I can't tell you any more."

"But you know who put the other stuff into my house, don't you?" Jimmy insisted.

"No."

"Look, I really need to know."

"Everybody needs to know."

"Okay, who *might* have had me under surveillance?"

"What did your wife tell you?"

"What you told her."

"Then that's all I have."

"I know Marilyn Monroe didn't commit suicide," Jimmy said.

"Yeah?"

"Goddammit, Budd. Please. Help me out."

"I can't."

"Why?"

"You know why, Governor. Put it down to business ethics. I can't help you. Even if I knew something, which I don't."

"Bobby Kennedy was having me bugged, wasn't he?"

"You need to let go of all this stuff, for your wife's sake."

"Is that a threat?"

"Jesus Christ, no," Budd said. "Look, I've got a plane to catch."

"Caroline tells me you read Proust," Jimmy said.

"I read lots of things."

"And you play dumb."

"I'm not willing to die to satisfy your morbid curiosity," Budd said, feeling frustrated and angry—and guilty.

"Well, at least now I know one thing."

"What's that?"

"That you're telling the truth. The house is clean. Otherwise, you wouldn't have said that."

"Look, Governor," Budd said, speaking in a softer voice, "I hear a lot of things, and most of it is bullshit, but you're fucking around with the Kennedys, and everybody's interested in the Kennedys. That's all it ever was. I don't think it was ever about you. Of course, now you're a politician in your own right."

"Cut the shit, and tell me what you're trying to say."

"You should let me sweep your premises regularly."

"Why, do you need the work?" Jimmy asked. Failed humor.

"Because I found something. It could have been just something left by the electricians or something. It's nothing you couldn't find any-where, nothing really out of the ordinary."

"But you think it's something," Jimmy said.

"I think somebody pulled the wires when they heard I was coming."

"Is it the phones?"

"As I said, it's just a gut feeling. The house is clean as a whistle."

"But you're not going to blow the whistle."

"If that's all, Governor . . ."

"Was it Bobby? Give me that much."

"Was it Bobby what?"

"In Marilyn's house. Did he—"

"I don't know nothin' about that."

"I need to know."

Budd stared down at the whorls in the blood-red Persian carpet. "Bobby had his own interests, but I don't think he was involved in her suicide."

Jimmy's face seemed to soften, but he said, "It wasn't a suicide. Was it?"

"Bobby was there, before . . . and he was there after, cleaning up, sort of," Budd said. "That's all, and to answer your question, or your joke, no, I don't need the work. Get yourself someone else to do your house cleaning, Governor. I got to catch up on my Proust."

"I don't trust anyone else," Jimmy said.

TUESDAY, JUNE 4, 1968.

It felt like a replay of Jimmy's election night: the same hotel, the same suite, the same humid, crowded rooms, drinks spilling, hail-fellow-well-met slaps on shoulders, hushed insiders' conversations, eye contact leading to illicit liaisons, evening gowns, jeans and T-shirts, favors exchanged, flashbulbs incandescing, burning purple retinal afterimages in seeking eyes, and noise, the hum of voices punctuated with laughter, a hundred cocktail parties compressed into one, and five floors below, in the Embassy Ballroom, three thousand of the party faithful were talking shouting shoving screeching buzzing laughing, eating, drinking, looking up at televisions for election results, looking down at wristwatches, drinking schmoozing reminiscing waving placards balloons posters pennons and getting ready . . . getting ready for their candidate to embrace them, to electrify them, to prove and justify to everyone in the great, high-ceilinged, chandeliered room that hope was indeed alive and well.

By 9:30 P.M. the ballroom was so overcrowded that Los Angeles fire marshals had to cordon off the main entrance; well-wishers and supporters were allowed in only when someone else had squeezed out of the room.

In the suite, Jimmy and Caroline played host, even though it was Bobby's victory night; and they chatted with Bobby and Ethel's friends and relatives, with George Plimpton, Jimmy Breslin, Teddy White, Ted Sorensen, and Steve Smith; they talked with Carl Reiner, Paul Schrade of the United Auto Workers, and Bobby's de facto "unofficial" bodyguards for the night—Los Angeles Rams defensive tackle Rosey Grier and Olympic Gold Medalist Rafer Johnson. The room was filled with luminaries, with directors and producers and actors, with singers—notably Elvis and his bride, Priscilla, dressed like a virgin queen in white sequins—with politicians, friends, and enemies. Jack Kerouac was on the wagon, dressed in a wrinkled suit, standing close to Nick Ray, as if for protection; and Jimmy—with one arm around Caroline and the other around a pregnant Ethel (her eleventh)—tried valiantly to do a passable Jewish shtick with Milton Berle.

It was a glorious night, and Caroline looked beautiful, beautiful and pregnant; that was her gift for Jimmy, and the swirling of guests, the crystal noise, muted light, and cosseting human warmth seemed singular and perfect to Jimmy, as if he were seeing everything and everyone for the first time.

Handing out cigars. Hugging Ethel and whispering, "We're going to the Factory for the real victory party." Showing off Caroline as if she were a new discovery while Bobby polished his speech in a locked bedroom.

Elvis: "Hey, Jimmy," nodding, bowing to Caroline, "we goin' to make that record together or not?"

"Maybe we should wait until I'm done with politics."

The Colonel: "Jimmy, Caroline . . . Jimmy, I need to speak to you."

Walter Cronkite: "Jimmy, we've got an interview scheduled after the press conference."

What press conference?

Frank Mankiewicz, one of Bobby's aides: "Jimmy, Bobby asked me to let you know you're doing a press conference together after his victory speech. It'll be in the Colonial Room."

"Where the hell is that?"

"Don't worry, we'll all be going together. Paul Schrade and Jesse Unruh will be involved, too." Unruh was the speaker of the California State Assembly.

"The Colonel, too?" Jimmy asked.

Mankiewicz laughed. "No, we're not letting him near Bobby, or anyone else tonight."

And then Kenny O'Donnell, one of Bobby and Jack's oldest friends, announced: "Here it is, everyone, final results are forty-six-point-three percent for Bobby—"

Shouting, hallooing, clapping.

"Forty-one-point-eight percent for McCarthy, and eleven-point-nine percent unpledged."

Booing, and then Bobby appeared, grinning and relaxed, shaking hands with everyone, pushing his way through the large suite toward Jimmy and Caroline and Ethel, and aides and friends pressed after him, as if they needed to be close, to be attached. He hugged Ethel, then kissed her wetly and loudly on the nose.

"Ugh," Ethel said, laughing and wiping her face. "I'm going to have to wear a veil to protect myself when you win the presidential election."

Bobby kissed Caroline and grinned at Jimmy boyishly. "I feel now for the first time that I've shaken off the shadow of my brother. I feel I made it on my own."

"You did, Bobby," Ethel said. "You did."

Jimmy shook Bobby's hand, and they squeezed hard, one trying to roll the knuckles of the other. They laughed, let go, and Jimmy said, "You sure the Colonel didn't orchestrate this?"

"What?"

"Kenny reading the numbers and you suddenly appearing."

"Why, of course," Bobby said, laughing, and on cue the Colonel appeared.

"You boys takin' my name in vain?"

"That's exactly what we're doing, Colonel," Bobby said, and then they were all out the door—Jimmy's bodyguards in front of them, Bobby's behind; and Jimmy, Bobby, Caroline and Ethel, aides, and a favored reporter broke away from everyone and took the freight elevator down to the kitchen. Walked briskly past wheeled tray stackers and stainless-steel steam tables, walked toward pantry doors that swung open; but before Bobby pushed through the doors, he stopped and asked, "Well, Jimmy, what did you decide?"

"What do you mean?"

"You know goddamn well what I mean. You said you'd give me an answer today. Well, it's today."

Jimmy grinned mischievously. "You're right. I'll tell you—after your victory speech."

"You fucker," Bobby said, and pushed through the doors.

Caroline looked at Jimmy quizzically; he had told her that he would turn Bobby down. "Have you changed your mind?"

"Maybe," Jimmy said, smiling and patting her stomach.

Outside, in the ballroom, people were singing "This Land Is Your Land," shouting "Bobby power! Kennedy power!" chanting, "We want Bobby! We want Jimmy! We want Bobby! We want Jimmy!" George and Jay were scowling at them.

"Come on, no time," said one of Bobby's aides.

People pushed into the pantry ahead.

"We'd better get out there," Jimmy said. "I'm supposed to be doing the introduction." But in those few seconds, Bobby had been swept up onto the podium. As Jimmy pushed through the shouting crowd, his arm protectively around Caroline, Bobby was at the lectern, saying, "Hello, everyone. You know, I had this great opening line planned, which is 'I want to express my high regard to Don Drysdale, who pitched his sixth straight shutout tonight, and I hope that we have as good fortune in our campaign.'" The room seemed to shake—earthquake shouting, screaming, feet pounding, streamers waving, as if the podium were a ship and the crowd waving bon voyage to loved ones. "And you know, that's all very fine, but I need to be talking about the high regard I have for the people right here in this room who have made our victory—our victory—possible, and you know who just happens to come to mind?" Bobby glanced around the podium. "Well, what do you know, he's finally decided to grace us with his presence."

The crowd clapped and shouted for Jimmy. "I'm just a shy person," Jimmy said, leaning in front of Bobby to get to the microphone.

"Well, when he's done upstaging me"—

Laughter, hysteria—"I would like to thank the governor of this great state, Jimmy Dean—you know, that, uh, actor."

More laughter, and "Jimmy Jimmy Jimmy Jimmy."

"I've asked the governor a very important question, but you know how shy he is?"

You son-of-a-bitch bastard . . . you know the answer. And he did, Bobby knew that Jimmy would say no and mean yes. He knew. *You've certainly got brass balls.*

"So maybe we'll get an answer tonight."

Cheering, and then Bobby was in full form, thanking Steve Smith, Cesar Chavez, Jesse Unruh, Paul Schrade, Rafer Johnson, Rosey Grier, his dog, Freckles, on and on, then into the meat, glancing at Jimmy, and Jimmy knew that Bobby was flying, *this is the moment, Bobby, right now, this is your fucking moment . . .*

until you become president . . .

if then . . .

Jimmy was holding Caroline's hand and smiling. Reflected glory.

"I think we can end the divisions within the United States," Bobby continued. "What I think is quite clear is that we can work together in the last analysis. And that despite what has been going on with the United States over the period of the last three years—the violence, the disenchantment with our society, the divisions, whether it's between blacks and whites, between the poor and the more affluent, or between age groups, or over the war in Vietnam—we can start to work together again. We are a great country, an unselfish country, and a compassionate country, and I intend to make that my basis for running over the period of the next few months. So, my thanks to all of you, and it's on to Chicago, and let's win there."

The crowd was wild, and people were pressing around the podium as Bobby gave the V-for-victory sign and smiled. "Hey, Jimmy," Bobby said, "come on, we're taking a shortcut through the kitchen to the press conference. Otherwise we're never going to get through all this. Hurry!" He jumped off the three-foot-high podium, and Jimmy followed.

"Bobby, I can't get down!" Ethel called. Caroline rushed over to help her.

"Jay, take care of Ethel and Caroline!" Jimmy shouted, and Jay was beside him and Bobby was holding his wrist and Kenny O'Donnell was holding Bobby's wrist, pushing, pushing through the crowds, then through the swinging doors into the pantry, but the crowd followed, trying to get to Bobby, trying to get to Jimmy, and the maitre d', a chunky Viking of a man in a tuxedo, cleared a path for Bobby.

"This way, Senator . . . this way, Governor."

Two busboys rushed toward Bobby and Jimmy, who stopped and shook hands with them, and Jimmy saw it first, saw a glint of metal against the metal of the steam tables, saw the young man in an open white shirt and jacket—dark, handsome, chiseled face, curly hair— saw him raise the .22-caliber Iver Johnson Cadet revolver as he shouted, "Kennedy, you son of a bitch!"—and in that instant there were two things becoming one, the noise of the pistol, the first *pop*, and Jimmy in motion, reflexive motion, unthinking motion, and Jimmy pulling Bobby out of the way, saving him, pushing himself, like pulling an oar, one second, one thought, one *pop* out of *pop-pop-pop*, a slow-motion instant, as the bullet struck Jimmy in the forehead, tearing through the brain, releasing light . . . and Jimmy could see only light, blinding blond light.

Bobby?

No sensation of falling.

Caroline?

Nor pain.

Pier?

Only light and warmth, as if he were baking in the sun, burning in its yellow, consuming warmth, burning out all events, memories, and dreams.

Marilyn? Momma . . .

Momma?